KNIGHT VISION

KNIGHT VISION

ALICE BIENIA

Issued in print and electronic formats.
ISBN 978-1-990193-10-1 (Paperback)
ISBN 978-1-990193-07-1 (EPUP)
ISBN 978-1-990193-08-8 (MOBI)

Editing by: T. Morgan Editing Services
Cover and Interior Design by: Damonza.com
Published by: Cairn Press | Calgary, Alberta, Canada

ALSO BY ALICE BIENIA

Jorja Knight Mystery Series

Knight Blind

Knight Trials

Three Dog Knight

Knight Shift

Anthologies

Last Shot

To Leanne and Tyler, with love

ONE

N O ONE HAD tried to kill me in over two months, my leased vehicle was still in one piece, and I had beat my previous Candy Crush score three consecutive times this week. Which might explain why I felt antsy. Life isn't all sunshine and kittens, and given my history I'd give better than even odds that my luck was about to change.

I watched the clock count down on the infinity-shaped loop displayed in the heart on my screen and groaned. I wouldn't be beating my previous Candy Crush score this time.

"Holy jeez." I jumped up, hand on my chest. A woman stood in the doorway.

The hairs on my neck prickled as dark eyes assessed me from behind emerald-green framed glasses.

"Sorry. I didn't hear you come in."

"I'm looking for Ms. Knight."

"You found her." I held out my hand. "I'm Jorja Knight."

Her grip sent a tingling sensation up my arm. My heart settled into a nice steady pound.

"My name is Misty Lane. I read about you in the paper. You solved that murder a few months back. The Houdini Killer."

Shaun Allen, a young reporter, had been sent by Postmedia

News to do a story on me and my part in capturing the Houdini Killer, a *nom de plume* given to the killer for his vanishing act after murdering a prominent businessman in his highly secured home.

"So, you read Shaun's article. I'm still trying to smooth over some ruffled police feathers." I waved my hand at the beat-up wooden chair in front of my equally beat-up wooden desk. "What can I do for you?"

She sat, crossed her legs, and gazed around the room. My eyes followed hers. The place was a rat hole, but the rent was right, and the décor and musty odour discouraged my innate desire to use it as a hideout from the world. She was taking her time, and I started to wonder if she was some sort of voyeur, interested in the morbid details of Stephen Bradford's death, the case she referred to.

Her eyes drifted back to mine. "I need your help to prevent a murder."

"Prevent a murder? Whose murder are we talking about?"

"I'm afraid it might be mine."

Her eyes were like frozen ponds, reflecting back nothing. A tiny muscle jumped below her right eye. I admired her ability to deliver the line with so little emotion.

"Why do you think you might be murdered?"

"Someone is watching me, leaving me messages." She pulled her cell phone from her purse and swiped the screen several times. "Here." She held it out to me.

Die bitch die was scrawled in red block letters across the windshield of a white Subaru Forester.

"This is your car?"

"Yes. I phoned the district police office. As far as they're concerned it's just another act of senseless vandalism."

"But you're convinced otherwise."

"There have been other incidents. I'm getting phone calls, several a day, just dead air but I can tell someone is on the line.

Yesterday, I found a bird on the back step of my shop—one of those magpies. Its head was missing…sliced right off."

I winced.

"There's more." She took a deep breath. "I'm a psychic medium and clairvoyant. I can see the past and the future."

I managed not to recoil in disbelief. As a former forensic lab analyst, I had spent most of my life putting my faith into science, that which was measurable, observable, repeatable. Then again, when it comes to death, consciousness, and quantum physics, I'll be the first to admit there is a shitload of stuff I don't understand.

"Interesting. Go on."

She exhaled and gave me one of those nods that said she was impressed I even entertained having this conversation.

"I first sensed something wrong about a month ago, at a group reading. At first, the feeling was fleeting, vague. Over the weeks the vision has become clearer, stronger."

"What do you see?"

"A dark-haired woman, about my age and height. She's walking down a dark path. She's in danger." Her hands painted a story only her mind saw. "I feel cold, very cold. The woman falls, tumbles into a dark void. The ground comes up to meet her. It's a dark, desolate place, filled with broken things, all rusted—decayed. Suddenly, I can't breathe—in or out. In that second, I know I'm going to die." She lowered her hands, now clasped below her neck, and sat back. "Now, this vision, this premonition, occurs almost daily."

The woman she described did look like her. On the other hand, she could be anyone. I was forty-one, five feet eight and had dark hair.

"In your vision, you describe a dark-haired woman falling and someone observing. Are you the observer, the one who feels cold, or are you the woman who is falling?"

She pursed her lips thoughtfully for a minute. "Impossible to say if we are one and the same."

"What about the place this woman dies. Some sort of junkyard?"

She looked at me steadily. "The images are in my mind's eye. You have to understand that *seeing* can be literal or steeped in symbolism and somewhat open to interpretation."

"Okay. What do you think your vision is telling you?"

"Falling can signify abandonment, by a caregiver, like a parent. Junk often means rejection, being tossed aside, like junk in real life."

"I see. Are you saying the woman in your vision was abandoned? That she's been rejected? If so, does that apply to you?"

A flicker of something crossed her face.

"I suppose it could apply to any number of people. Me, the woman in my vision, possibly the killer. Even you."

Her green eyes pierced mine, and a cold chill ran down my arms. I tore my eyes away from hers and cleared my throat.

"You said this premonition started about a month ago. Anything happen back then to trigger this vision or cause someone to want to harm you?"

"Nothing I can recall."

"And the dark-haired woman you see. You think it's you?"

Her brow furrowed as she gave it a moment of consideration. "I'm certain I'm foretelling a woman's death. I, or a woman who resembles me, will be strangled to death. Given the disturbing messages and phone calls I'm receiving, I believe that woman is likely me."

"Okay, so tell me, who wants you dead?"

"I don't know. Otherwise, I'd be telling my story to the police." She smiled, a small, apologetic smile that didn't linger.

I sat back, taking note of her worried eyes, yet confident

demeanour. This woman was asking me to prevent a murder, based largely on a psychic forewarning. Of course, the dead-air calls and a guillotined bird meant something. Still, it was an unusual request. My fingers see-sawed the pen they held nervously. Were premonitions really that different than a strong hunch or gut feeling? Could something logical, reasonable, be driving her belief that she would be killed? Or could there be something to her belief in spirits, the afterworld?

Curiosity overrode trepidation. I took the case.

TWO

MISTY STOOD IN the middle of the circle, her arms raised shoulder height, her palms facing upward. A soft breeze materialized from nowhere, gently blew back her hair and played with the edges of her bell-sleeved tunic. The soft background music stopped. The room fell silent, save for the occasional muffled sniff of a young woman standing across from me.

I surveyed the circle. A mishmash of paying hopefuls, their rapt faces turned expectedly toward Misty. The demeanour of the older couple to my left made me think they were here for a thrill, a new experience to share with their bridge friends, rather than a desire to connect with the dearly departed. Next to them stood a middle-aged woman who occasionally patted the arm of the young, emotional woman standing to her left. Rounding out the circle, an older man of Mediterranean heritage, a twitchy young man who repeatedly pushed up the frames of his glasses, and two middle-aged men who held hands.

"I'm sensing a woman. A mother figure. Has anyone lost their mother unexpectedly? Perhaps at a young age?"

Misty turned toward me, her eyes on mine. My gut clenched.

The young woman across from me let out a sob. "Oh my god. I did."

Misty tilted her head ever so slightly in my direction, gave me a knowing look, then turned to the woman who spoke.

Somehow, Misty knew the young woman's mother died of cancer two years earlier. That the mother's favourite colour was yellow, that she had collected ornaments—penguins.

Misty addressed the sobbing woman. "She wants you to know she's at peace. She says thank you for always thinking of me, for being a wonderful daughter. She knows you bought her a penguin when you were in Cabo. You did, didn't you?"

The woman looked up through tears and nodded.

Misty laughed. "Not an easy feat. A burro from Mexico, yes, but a penguin! She knows she's in your thoughts every day. She's so proud of you. She wants you to live your life, live it fully, and know that she's always with you."

I blinked rapidly. Several people dabbed their eyes. Next Misty had a message for the Mediterranean-looking man, from his recently departed wife. The reading ended shortly afterward. Misty's face was pale. A thin layer of moisture shone on her forehead.

While waiting for the last of Misty's clients to depart, I wandered around the shop. The front was devoted to healing stones, incense, sage. I stopped at a poster offering her Past-Life Healing service. For a mere two-hundred and eight-five dollars, her guided meditation, with help from spirit, would help one overcome the emotional obstacles from past lives, obstacles hindering present success. And to think I'd spent thousands on my therapist trying to clear the emotional blocks from this lifetime alone and still hadn't moved past them.

"I want you to know your mother's spirit started to come forward before the young woman's mother made herself known."

I startled. Engrossed in reading, I hadn't heard Misty approach.

"Your mother's spirit is like her, timid, somewhat reserved. When the other, brasher spirit rushed forward, she stepped aside."

I swallowed the familiar lump forming in my throat and told myself she could have researched me on the internet. It would have taken some digging but a few articles about my mother's death twenty years ago still lingered in various archives.

"Was today's reading typical?"

"Pretty much. Sometimes spirit comes forth so vividly I can see the expression on their face. Today, I felt the first woman's spirit tap at my chest—that signals they died of something like cancer, or a heart condition." She pushed a strand of hair off her forehead. Her upper lip glistened with moisture.

"You look exhausted. Is everything okay?"

"After the second spirit showed herself to me, I felt a darkness. It's hard to explain. I felt panicky."

"A darkness? Related to that poor man's wife?"

"No, no. It was someone or something else."

"The feeling's gone now?"

"Yes, although I'm still a bit shaky."

"The people at the reading, have you met any of them before today?"

"The older couple have been in the store before. Oh, and that man, the fidgety one with the thick-rimmed glasses. I've seen him at one of my other readings but haven't had a chance to talk to him. He must really want to connect with a loved one but unfortunately no one's stepped forward yet."

"So, spirits don't always come forward to connect with their loved ones?"

"No. I'm merely a conduit for them to speak to their loved ones. I never know who will come forward or when."

"Thanks for inviting me to sit in. It was fascinating. Do you have time for some questions now?"

"Of course."

I had googled Misty after she left my office yesterday. She

was starting to garner attention. She was a frequent speaker at a national wellness conference and had even worked with law enforcement agencies on occasion.

"You said you don't know anyone who'd want to kill you. Can you think of anyone who might have an issue with you or you with them?"

Misty bit her lower lip and shook her head. "No, not really."

"I need to start somewhere—even if it's to eliminate people in your life as possibilities."

Misty's forehead crinkled in thought. "Well, there's Peoria Benson. She owns Healing Waters, at the end of the block. She's got a real hate on for me."

"Why is that?"

"I don't know. I dropped by her store to introduce myself the day I opened shop. She crossed her arms and glared at me the whole time. Wouldn't shake my hand. It was so uncomfortable. I said hello, wished her well and left."

"When was that?"

"A little over a year ago. Before this, I had a smaller shop in Marda Loop."

"Is it possible you met this woman, Peoria, before? Any chance you have a mutual friend or acquaintance?"

"No—never laid eyes on her until the day I moved in. I've barely spoken to her since. I go out of my way to avoid running into her. I've heard she bad-mouths me to her customers."

"What about other tenants in the building?"

"There's just me and Healing Waters now. We're not tenants, we're owners. We pay a maintenance fee, like a condo fee, to keep the common areas of the building in good repair. Or we used to. The building's been sold recently. I don't know what the new owners have planned."

"Only two shops in this whole building?"

"Mr. Sherbaz owned the space between us, but the new build-ing owners bought him out. The second floor used to hold small apartments. They've been empty for years."

"Anyone else? Boyfriend? Ex-boyfriend?"

"I haven't dated anyone in almost a year."

"What about your last boyfriend? What was he like?"

"Doug? He was a total ass. It wasn't obvious at first, but as time went on, I noticed whenever he didn't get his way, he'd make me pay for it with his bad mood. So, I ended it."

"How did he take it?"

"Not well." She snorted. "I kept running into him for months afterwards. At one point, I thought he might be stalking me. I haven't seen him in four or five months now. I heard he's dating someone else. Frankly, I'm relieved to hear he's moved on."

"What's Doug's last name?"

"Liederbach. Please don't go there. I don't need any more drama with that guy."

"Don't worry. I go to great lengths to avoid putting my cli-ents in harm's way. Anyone else? Disgruntled suppliers, business partners, customers?"

"No."

"What about friends, family?"

She turned away, hugging crossed arms against her chest. She took a few steps then turned back. "I don't have much in the way of family. My father died when I was a child, my mother's in a nursing home—dementia. I've moved around a lot, lost track of friends." She shrugged. "Other than the occasional guy I let into my life, there's no one. I'm focused on building my business, my career."

"Is it possible you revealed something in one of your readings, something someone wanted to remain a secret?"

"I suppose it's possible. If I did, it obviously didn't mean anything to me, because I didn't pick up on it."

"You didn't notice anyone becoming upset or agitated?"

"No. I don't recall anything like that. Most people are grateful to receive a message from loved ones who have passed."

"Mind if I go out back? I want to see where you park, maybe have a chat with this Peoria Benson."

Misty led me through the back of the shop, which contained a storage area, a small office, and a tiny kitchenette. She unlatched and pushed open the back door.

"This is where I found the bird." She nodded at the lone crumbling concrete step leading to the parking area.

Once outside I surveyed the building, one block-long, red-brick structure, punctuated by several doors and a few windows. The brick walls were covered in graffiti, or perhaps in this neighbourhood it was called street art.

I walked the length of the alley. Each store had several reserved parking spaces, for the owner and customers. Across the alley was a row of smaller brick buildings, and two wooden houses converted into stores. Overhead, power lines sagged between wooden poles. Plenty of places to install a surveillance camera if I needed to later.

I stopped at the end of the alley and looked back. Misty's fear and growing panic during the reading had been clear. The million-dollar question was, who or what was threatening her?

"Hey, you!"

I turned and almost passed out. A shirtless man, hair matted and unkept, lunged at me.

"Are you threaten' me? Dopin' up my coffee?" He grabbled hold of my sleeve, his face now inches from mine, his eyes black, his breath hot and noxious. "You can't shut me up. They tried. Shot me full of drugs. Burned holes in my brain. It didn't work. Know why?"

I wrenched my arm free and staggered back, heart pounding. Keeping eyes on him, I stepped past.

He took a step after me. His voice rose to a crescendo. "I've been saved by the Lord Jesus seven times. Seven times."

His bark followed me as I made my way to the front of the building.

"For true and righteous are his judgments. For he has judged the great whore, which did corrupt the earth with her fornication."

I reached the corner and turned. *Please don't let this be who we're dealing with.*

THREE

I PUSHED OPEN THE door to Healing Waters and stepped inside. The sound of gurgling water filled the room, punctuated by a bird's *chickadee-dee-dee* call. Grateful for the peaceful ambience after being accosted by the crazed zealot in the alley, I took a deep breath. A large glass-topped counter to my left displayed an array of creams, powders and herbs. A woman stood behind it. A cloud of Givenchy perfume reached me before her voice did.

"Welcome," she sang out. "Have you been in our healing and wellness centre before?"

"No, I haven't. I was just passing by—the name intrigued me."

"Let me get you a brochure." She reached under the counter and handed me a glossy folder with her beaming face on the front. A quick glance told me it had been airbrushed, photo-shopped, or taken ten years earlier.

"We're a full-service spa and rejuvenation centre. You'll see in the brochure we offer everything from mani-pedis and facials, to injectables and phototherapy. I highly recommend cryotherapy. It will leave you feeling refreshed and rejuvenated, inside and out. We have a state-of-the-art cryogenic chamber, the first of its kind in Calgary."

"Cryogenic? Isn't that where people deep-freeze their bodies after death, in the hope that scientific advances will allow them to be revived later?"

She threw back her head and laughed, a forced, brittle sound.

"My dear, you're too funny. Cryotherapy is truly amazing with solid science behind it. It slows the aging process by improving circulation, increases metabolism for faster turnover of cells and releases the body's natural endorphins. The result is more energy, smooth glowing skin, reduced wrinkles. Each procedure burns up to eight-hundred calories, so it can help with weight loss too." She added the last bit brightly, her eyes roving over my untucked shirt and the way my jeans stretched across my thighs.

Yeah right. Next, she'd tell me she was a hundred and four. I glanced at the four empty pink-leather chairs in the small reception area.

"You do all that here?"

"Of course. Our private treatment rooms and cryogenic chamber ensure our clients' comfort and keep them away from prying eyes." She nodded toward the front glass door, but her tone pointed at me.

"I'm pleasantly surprised. The building looks a bit…how should I say? Sketchy."

Her face pinched. "The new owner is expanding commercial space into the second floor. Healing Waters will occupy the entire top floor when it's finished. It will become a destination spot for those seeking rejuvenation and aging well."

"Business must be good if you're expanding."

"There's a need for services like ours in Calgary. This was once a very vibrant shopping district. Then the likes of that psychic down the street moved into the building."

"I did notice the shop." I added a level of disdain to my voice. "Do people actually believe in that stuff?"

She moved swiftly to my end of the counter and lowered her voice, although she and I were the only ones here.

"A friend of mine went into her store to check it out. She said it's full of cheap stuff, made in China. Incense and scented candles, beads hanging over the doorway." Her nose wrinkled. "When my friend told her she suffered from anxiety, that woman actually suggested a spiritual cleansing. She said her anxiety was probably an unresolved relationship with someone who passed, or blocked energy from a past life. Can you imagine?"

I shook my head in sympathy. "Sad to think people are so desperate they fall for these quick-fix solutions. I mean, really."

"I'm hoping she moves on after the renovation. Or sooner. Sharon, who owns Ivy and Lace across the street, says the level of merchandise thefts has gone through the roof since she set up shop here. She used to get a lot of businesspeople from downtown. Now the place is crawling with all these hippy-dippy types."

"I can see that you cater to a completely different clientele."

"She encourages all the riffraff in the neighbourhood. Like that crazy preacher out there." She nodded out the window. I turned. The shirtless man now stood across the street, waving a cardboard sign. He shouted at a passerby, clearly agitated.

"Encourages him?"

"She brings him coffee and sandwiches. At that rate he'll never move on." She tossed a strand of wavy blond hair back over her shoulder. "I'm on the neighbourhood revitalization committee. We intend to clean up this neighbourhood if it's the last thing we do."

The door opened behind me, and Peoria stepped back, her face wiped of the annoyance creasing her face. "Welcome," she sang out melodically.

I nodded my thanks and slipped out the door. Peoria Benson had the personality of a viper and the sincerity of a street grifter.

The speed at which she switched off the spit and vinegar and put on her tranquil face told me she had a lot of practice. I had met her type before. She fed off drama, creating it if none existed. Peoria clearly disliked Misty, but death?

I stepped out onto the sidewalk and pulled out my phone, noticing two voice messages, both from my friend Mike Saunders. I met Mike at Global Analytix, where I had toiled as a forensic analyst, before moving on to private investigation. Mike was a former Toronto Police Services detective. His retirement didn't last long. Hard to grow orchids and loll around the house, after thirty adrenaline-filled years chasing bad guys. He embarked on his second career shortly after moving to Calgary, providing consulting services to Global Analytix, as well as to Calgary Police Services. His message asked that I call back. The urgency in his tone worried me. I tapped his name in the phone log. He answered, out of breath.

"Hi, Mike, how's it going?"

"Jorja. I'm in a bit of a bind. I just got a call from the Toronto General Hospital. Julie—she's been in an accident."

"Oh no. Is she okay?"

"Not sure. She's in ICU. I'm on my way to the airport now."

The edge in his voice stopped me in my tracks. I'd never heard Mike this rattled. He was trained to remain calm and contained in a crisis. Julie was Mike's oldest daughter, the only child from his first marriage. I had met her once, a friendly woman with Mike's dark eyes and sarcastic sense of humour.

"Is there any way you could look after Smitty and Wess for me? Mrs. Niedswiki is away visiting her sister."

"Of course, I can, Mike. Don't worry about your cats or anything else on the home front."

"You know the key code. Oh, and I told Mrs. Niedswiki I'd keep an eye on her place till she gets back."

"Don't worry, Mike, I'll look after Smitty and Wess, and keep an eye on her place too. Have a safe flight. I'll be thinking of you. Hope Julie is going to be okay." The fact that Julie was in ICU was scary, but all I could do is hope she'd be all right.

"Yeah. Me too."

I hated these reminders that we really had no control over our destiny. Everything was fine until, in a blinding second, it wasn't.

FOUR

THE ONLY MODERN thing about Mike's place was the keyless entry lock he installed when he bought the place. I punched in the code, the one I used whenever Mike needed me to drop in on the place to check his plants and cats. Mike's cats were beautiful grey-haired Persians, but finicky eaters who needed to be fed twice a day and freaked out when taken out of their home environment. The few times I had looked after them, I found it easier to stay at Mike's rather than run between his and my place. As soon as I opened the door, Smitty came running and wound himself through my legs.

"Hey, little buddy." I reached down and petted him, while he mewed his greeting. "Where's Wess?" Wesson was the shy one. I would likely spot him later, under a bed or crouched next to a stack of books in Mike's office, pretending to be invisible. I set down my overnight bag and flopped on the couch, groaning with exhaustion. Smitty immediately jumped on my chest and began kneading me. "Oh no you don't, you're not going to make me your cozy little nest, not yet anyway."

Groaning, I got up and headed for the kitchen. After preparing the cats' food and putting down fresh water, I entered the little sunroom someone had added to the back of the house decades earlier. If you met Mike, you'd never guess the big man with the gruff demeanour and gravely voice brushed his cats' teeth, ground pure organic food for their dinner, and grew orchids on the side. He adored Smith and Wesson, AKA Smitty and Wess, almost as much as his grandchildren. I teased him about it by calling him grand-paw.

I checked Mike's plants and plucked off a spent bloom on one of the orchids. I peered through the plexiglass panes at the garage Mike had converted to a workshop last year when he decided to take up metal sculpting. A quick glance to the right told me nothing was amiss in Mrs. Niedswiki's backyard.

Mrs. Niedswiki, a tiny Polish woman and one of the neighbourhood's original inhabitants, usually looked after Mike's cats when he was away. I was relieved to hear I wouldn't be seeing her. She worshipped Mike and even though Mike's and my relationship was strictly platonic, she always gave me the fisheye, muttered in Polish and made what sounded like spitting noises at me.

Walking back through the kitchen, I spotted Wesson, playing statue on top of the fridge. I ignored him, as any acknowledgement would send him scurrying into hiding again. I knew he was waiting for me to go away so he could jump down from the fridge to eat. I loved cats and planned to get one of my own—as soon as my lifestyle allowed. I picked up my bag and headed for Mike's office-turned-spare-bedroom.

I opened the futon, got ready for bed, and climbed in. I opened my laptop. Nothing from Mike. I debated whether to send him an email. A quick glance at my watch told me it was almost eleven in Toronto; Mike would likely be landing now or maybe on his way to the hospital. He probably didn't know any more than when he had called me. I'd have to wait until morning for an update.

Now that I had a moment to think, my thoughts returned to

my new client. Misty really hadn't provided me much of anything to go on. And I knew that when I took the case. Had Misty's self-proclaimed gifts raised some unmet desire in me to connect with the netherworld? Then why the gut clench and cold sweat when Misty mentioned my mother's spirit stepping forward?

I shook my head, pulled my laptop closer. This time I moved past the obvious marketing information on Misty and searched deeper. She worked with law enforcement agencies from time to time and several cases she worked on were profiled in back issues of Real-Life Crime magazine. Once such article described the hunt for a killer, the drama starting in Billings, Montana.

Riley Tanner had a history of petty thefts and minor assaults when he went big time. For some unknown reason, Tanner decided to rob a gas bar, armed with a .308. His initial success likely emboldened him and in the following weeks several gas bars and liquor stores were hit. Tanner took great care to arrive hooded, wore gloves and a Darth Vader mask, which not only hid his features but altered his voice.

His confidence and level of aggression grew hand in hand until finally he shot a woman who refused to let him take her car at the state liquor store he had just robbed. She survived the attack, but a couple living on a rural farm did not. Both were shot, their place ransacked, their vehicle stolen. Ballistics tied their deaths to the weapon used to wound the woman at the liquor store.

Misty approached the state troopers, claiming she had a strong sense of who the killer was. She said the man they were looking for had a scar on his face, possibly from a fire or explosion. Misty said the colour tan kept coming up, that the man they were looking for had a tattoo on his chest. That he would be found near a rock tower. She told the police they should look for a dark-green truck. The police, at that time, were looking for the older murdered couple's grey Chevy Silverado. Two days later, a used car dealer, two towns over, reported a dark-green Ford F-150 had been stolen off his car lot. Suddenly, Misty had a lot more credibility.

The police found Tanner several weeks later, living in an abandoned hunter's cabin. The man they arrested had brown hair, and although he did not have a tattoo on his chest, he did have multiple scars including one on his face, shrapnel from an explosion while serving a stint in Iraq.

The chief of police praised Misty for her help in getting Tanner off the streets. The reporter covering the story gave Misty a lot of exposure, including a full-column interview with her after Tanner's arrest. The story was carried by several newspapers, including the Bozeman Daily Chronicle. However, an editor at the Bozeman Daily Chronicle thought Misty's involvement was overplayed. He pointed out that the large rock found sitting next to the hunter's cabin was only about two and half feet in diameter, a far cry from the rock tower Misty had described. Although the word tan and the perp's name, Tanner, could be construed as interesting, he claimed accepting scars on his body as tattoos was ridiculous. He attributed the scar on his face as pure bloody luck and even hinted that she may have had some way of knowing that the green truck had been stolen since the car lot owner was a friend of a friend. Regardless of who you believed, Misty's involvement in a high-profile homicide raised her repute.

Tanner was given two consecutive life sentences. I doubted he had anything to do with Misty's current vision. Of course, Tanner could arrange for a hit from prison, so I couldn't rule it out a hundred percent. But why wait three years? On the other hand, waiting three years might be exactly the length of time needed for Tanner to rebuff any allegations that might arise after Misty's death. In any case, Tanner was still behind bars.

Misty's fear seemed real. Her gut or premonition told her she was in trouble. I needed to apply logic and reason to the situation. She believed she was going to be murdered. Who would want her dead? And why?

I stared at my computer screen. All motives are driven from either the past, present or future. Future motives are usually driven by something the killer wants from the victim that is only attainable once they're dead. Could be money, other assets or fame. It could even be love, and the faulty belief that with the victim out of the way, the loved one would be theirs to have. Misty wasn't wealthy, at least not yet. Although her reputation was growing, it's not like she was in a race with anyone specific for international attention. Or national attention, for that matter. There was no current boyfriend or lover.

If not driven by a future motive, then the motive must come from the past or present. Misty didn't seem to have many people in her life, past or present. According to her, there were no spurned business partners, angry clients. She didn't seem to have many friends and little in the way of family, but then again, I didn't know much of her past. Perhaps someone was seeking revenge, righting a wrong, planning payback.

Too tired to tackle the social media sites, I yawned and closed the laptop. Smitty was already lying on the foot of my bed, his paws folded under his chest.

Someone was spraying the walls with graffiti, near Misty's shop, but that happened every day in pretty much any part of the city. The message on her car, the dead bird and the feeling someone was watching her made Misty's concerns real. She called it a premonition, a forewarning. Something was going on, something real.

My phone, already muted for the night, vibrated on the bed beside me. I didn't recognize the number. Worried it might be Mike, I picked up.

"Jorja! It's Misty. He's been here! Please come."

FIVE

TRAFFIC WAS LIGHT this time of night. As soon as I turned off Memorial Drive, I saw the flashing red and blue lights. My hands tightened on the steering wheel. Flashing lights meant trouble, at least in my book.

Two police cars blocked off the entrance to the street. I pulled over, parked and started walking. Further down, a large area was cordoned off by crime-scene tape. Several investigators wearing purple gloves were busy combing the ground. A police photographer was documenting the scene, her camera flashing at regular intervals. I joined a group of bystanders at the corner.

I spotted Misty on the other side of the parked police cars. She wore a ripped denim jacket over plaid pyjama pants, her feet stuffed into green Doc Martins. She turned as I arrived, as if sensing my presence. She rushed toward me.

"Jorja. You're here." She grabbed my arm, pulling me over.

A young, uniformed officer strode toward us. "Please step back, miss. No one's allowed beyond this point."

Misty clung to my arm. "She's with me. I called her. I need her here."

The officer looked at Misty, then me. He nodded and stepped back. "Stay right there. Do not move further."

"What happened? What's going on?"

Misty clung to my arm. "I found a woman. She was there, just by my patio." Misty nodded toward one of the main-floor condo units.

"Is she going to be all right?"

"No." Misty shuddered. "She's dead." Her eyes, black orbs in her pale face, turned to me. "I saw him."

"You saw who killed her?"

She shook her head, confused, perturbed. "I saw a man crossing the street. I thought I recognized him. He got into a parked car and drove off in a big hurry. Didn't even turn on his headlights. I checked my patio door to make sure it was locked and started to pull the blinds shut. That's when I noticed something—noticed her…at the edge of the patio. I flicked on the outside light. She was right there. Right on my patio."

Misty's condo was on the main floor of a six-storey condo building across from a construction site. The construction site was enclosed by eight-foot-high plywood walls plastered with signs advertising a new condo complex. The concrete walls for the first few levels had been poured and rebar spikes poked out from the foundation, waiting for the next layer to be added. There were no streetlights along this section of road. Could this be the dark path Misty saw in her vision?

"You thought you recognized him?"

We turned as a man approached. He held up ID, impossible to read from this distance in the dark. "Detective Brighton. Ms. Lane?" He looked from Misty to me and back again.

Misty nodded. "That's me."

"A few more questions, if you don't mind. Can you go over again what you saw and heard?

Misty nodded and pulled her denim jacket tighter around her. "I got home around 9:20. I let myself in and went into the bedroom to change."

"Did you enter through the patio?"

"No, no. The patio doors don't have a lock on the outside, they only lock from the inside. I entered through that entrance, there." She pointed to an opening midway down the front of the building. "I got ready for bed and went to check that my doors were locked and to close the blinds. Like I do every night."

"Do you remember the time?"

"Yes. It was a few minutes before ten. I planned to watch *Mary Kills People* on the TV in my bedroom." Her voice broke. "It comes on at ten."

"Okay. Take your time. You're doing good."

"The blinds on the patio doors were partially closed. I reached up to pull them shut, and I…I noticed a man, getting into his car across the street. He took off in a big hurry. He drove straight east, and out of sight. Didn't even turn his headlights on."

"Did you happen to notice the make of car?"

"It was a Chevy Impala. Grey."

"Can you describe him? Height, weight, what he was wearing?"

"I didn't really get a good look at him. He was average height, maybe light-brown hair."

"Average height? Like my height?" asked the officer. "What about build?"

Misty seemed to notice him for the first time. "Maybe, a bit shorter. Not much shorter. I'd say medium build, but he was wearing a coat and it was sort of billowing behind him so not sure."

"What kind of coat? What else was he wearing?"

"Umm. Like maybe a ski jacket, navy or black, I think. And jeans. He wore boots. Not dress shoes or runners—some kind of boot."

"Did you see his face? Profile?"

"No."

"Long hair, short hair? Balding?"

"I don't remember. Short, I think. But not like a buzz cut."

"Anything familiar about him? What about the car? Have you seen it in the neighbourhood?"

Misty paused just long enough for the officer and I to exchange glances.

"I don't think so. One of my ex-boyfriends drove a Chevy Impala. That's how I recognized what kind of vehicle it was. I didn't see a plate number or notice anything about the car itself. Just that it was grey."

"Light grey or dark grey?"

"Kind of medium grey."

"But it wasn't your ex-boyfriend?"

"No. I just mentioned him because, you know, it's why I recognized the kind of car it was, not that I saw him."

"Can't hurt to have the boyfriend's name. We won't contact him unless someone or something else gives us reason to."

Misty folded her arms and kicked at the edge of the curb with one of her boots. The detective watched her carefully.

"Ex-boyfriend. You can't honestly think he showed up and killed some girl right in front of my condo? Why would he do that?"

Detective Brighton waited.

Misty kicked the curb harder. "His name is Doug Liederbach. He owns the Hogshead Cellar over on Eighth Avenue. I haven't seen him in months. I want it to stay that way. I had enough drama with that man. Besides, the man I saw is heavier than Doug. Doug's a slender guy. He runs."

"Don't worry. We don't go around accusing people, nor do we reveal how they might have come to our attention if we find any reason to talk to him. Now, after the man drove off. What did you do?"

"I checked that the door was locked and then started to pull the blinds the rest of the way across. At first, I thought there was a garbage bag or something out there. There's always garbage blowing in from the construction site. I flicked on the outdoor light." Misty shook her head. "That's when I saw her. She was lying there—so still. I…I should have checked if she was alive… but I couldn't. I ran and called 911. I was so scared." She looked up at Brighton. "What if she was still alive?"

"You did the right thing, Ms. Lane. One last question. Did you hear anything, a noise, see anyone else or anything that didn't seem right or was out of the ordinary before you found her?"

"No, nothing."

"No one lurking about earlier in the day, or sitting watching the building?"

"I was at work."

"Right. And where's that?"

Misty rattled off the address and Detective Brighton checked it against the contact information she had provided earlier. He handed her his card. "We'd like you to come down to the station tomorrow morning and give the man's description to one of our sketch artists." Misty took the card he offered and nodded. We watched as Detective Brighton moved on to talk to another bystander. A car from the Medical Examiner's Office arrived.

The front entrance to the building was still cordoned off and several investigators combed the street. I followed Misty around to the side entrance and we went inside. Her hand shook as she unlocked the door to her unit. Once inside, Misty shivered and rubbed her hands up and down her arms.

"I can't get the image of that poor woman out of my head. I don't think I'm going to be able to sleep anytime soon. Come on in." I followed her down a short hallway, which led to the open living room and kitchen. Misty opened the cupboard over the fridge and pulled out several bottles. "Do you want a drink?" She asked over her shoulder, "Vodka, Gin, Anisette?"

I usually refrained from drinking with clients, especially new clients, but I was tempted.

"No thanks, but please don't change your mind on my account. Pretty gruesome discovery. You don't know who the woman is, do you?"

"No. I didn't see her face." Misty shuddered. "A plastic bag was wrapped over her head…a grey plastic bag. She had dark hair though."

"You think it's the woman in your vision? The one walking down a dark path or lane before being attacked, before falling?"

Misty poured herself a shot of vodka, threw it back. I noticed she wasn't wearing her glasses tonight. Maybe she had contacts.

"I don't know what to think. I can't even think straight. It can't be a coincidence."

"It would be a hell of a coincidence if it was." I watched her pour another shot. "You seemed nervous when the detective asked you for your ex's name."

"Did I?" She shook her head. "My god, I'm cold right through." She grabbed the bottle and waved it in my direction. "You sure you don't want one?"

"Thanks, I'll pass. I know you said you don't think your ex has any reason to harm you, but I get the impression you're afraid of him. Did he ever hurt or threaten you?"

"He never hit me, if that's what you mean."

"Someone doesn't have to hit you to be menacing."

"I should have never gotten involved with him—don't know what I was thinking. Doug's very into himself. It took me longer than it should have to realize it. He doesn't believe in my gift, my abilities. This is who I am. What was I doing with a guy like that?" She sank down on the couch. "The night we broke up, he was so angry. He said no one broke up with him—he was dumping me. That it better be what I told everyone and if I said different, he'd kill me."

"Whoa. Sounds like he has a temper."

"Doug wants what Doug wants and he's not exactly open to compromise. Maybe I'm not either. I think he was jealous of the attention I was getting. He'd say the most outrageous things when we were out with friends. I think he did it to bring the attention back to him. That's why we fought."

"What kind of things?"

"Stupid things. Let me see. Oh, one time we were having dinner with friends and he said that being psychic usually ran in families. Like in my case—since my grandmother was also psychic. He went on to say it was like mental illness. No guarantee you'd inherit it but people with mental illness in their family tree were more disposed to developing it themselves. He just wouldn't shut up. We had a big fight that night on the way home. I asked him if he thought I was mentally ill. He said something like, based on my inability to take a joke, yes."

"Nice guy."

"I know. I don't think he meant that comment about killing me. It's the stupid kind of thing people say in the heat of the moment. I haven't noticed him hanging around for a good while now. When that detective asked for his name, I was afraid it would lead to another angry confrontation and what with everything else, I can't face the thought of having to deal with him."

"So, you don't think it was him getting into the car? But you thought there was something familiar about the guy."

"It was just a brief flash that went through my mind. Like I should recognize him, but I didn't. Then it was gone. I'm pretty sure it wasn't Doug though."

"Well, stay vigilant. If you think you see him hanging around again, you might want to mention it to the police. They may not be able to do anything, but it can't hurt to alert them to this guy's behaviour. Even if he hasn't physically threatened you, fixations play out in many ways, not all of them healthy."

Misty shuddered and poured herself another shot.

"You feel okay about staying here? I could drive you to a friend's place or a hotel?"

"No, I'll be fine. From the looks of things, the cops are going to be out there for a while."

"I guess I'll head home if you're okay on your own now. You've given the police everything you know, it's in their hands."

Misty walked with me down the short hall toward the front door and stopped by the front closet. "That poor woman." Her voice was flat, cold.

I turned as Misty pulled out a navy knee-length wool coat from the closet.

"She was wearing a dark-blue wool coat. Like this one."

"Is that what you were wearing tonight when you got home?"

"Yes." Her pupils were black, all but obliterating the colour of her eyes. "It goes well with tan pants. She must have thought so too."

We both stared at the coat silently. "You mentioned this to the police, didn't you?"

"God no. It's bad enough that I think I'm going insane, without everyone else thinking so too."

"What do you mean, going insane?"

Misty shook her head. "It's nothing. It's just I haven't worn this coat in almost a year. I spent over half an hour looking for it this morning. It's like I *had* to wear it and when I couldn't find it, I became obsessed with it."

"Misty, you need to tell the police about this."

Misty stood still, her eyes large, unblinking.

"Are you okay?"

"The woman I found. She was laid out in a cross."

"A cross? What do you mean?"

"She was on her back. Her arms straight out to each side. Her legs were together, tight, perfectly straight. No one dies like that."

I met her eyes. The worry there reflected my own.

"The police will have definitely made note of that. What do you make of it?"

"I don't know. Part of me wants her to be the woman in my vison, but mostly I don't want it to be her. Does that make sense?"

"Absolutely. You sure you're going to be okay?"

Misty nodded and turned to hang up her coat. Her fingers fumbled with the hanger. She turned, pushing a wisp of hair off her face. "He's going to kill again. I just know it."

"Let's hope they find him, before he has a chance. Don't forget to lock up after I leave."

"Oh, no chance of that."

I stepped out into the hallway and waited until I heard the safety chain slide into place. Whoever killed that poor woman had staged her. Laid her out like a cross. The killer was sending a message. But what? And to whom?

SIX

I PAUSED AT THE entrance to the Hogshead Cellar long enough to read the small article pinned to the corkboard, next to the menu. The article was yellowed, clipped from a newspaper, announcing their opening two years earlier. According to the reviewer, the place boasted tasty Tapas-style sharing plates, sexy wine, and an upbeat vibe. It predicted its owner, Doug Liederbach, a former chef who once competed on MasterChef Canada, would edge Hogshead into Calgary's top ten restaurants. The current downturn in the economy was slowing its progress.

I stepped through the door, and spotted the hostess stand at the top of a short flight of stairs. A young woman in a short, tight-fitting black dress greeted me enthusiastically and led me to a small table by the window.

The wine bar was small, maybe twenty tables in total, half of which were tables for two. Wedged in between high-rises, smack in the middle of downtown, it was the kind of place that did well over the noon hour and again for a few hours in early evening, providing those who wanted to unwind after a busy day with a glass of wine or early moviegoers a bite to eat. Today, the place was nearly empty. Maybe because it was a Saturday.

I ordered a pinot noir, braised chorizo and roasted cauliflower.

The guy behind the bar brought over the wine and a bread tray. I recognized him from the photo in the article I just read, and from his Facebook page I checked out earlier. He placed a glass on the table in front of me and asked if I'd like to try it before he poured.

"Pour away."

"Also, we have here, some toasted crostini rounds finished with crushed walnut and olive oil, fig spread and whipped goat cheese, compliments of the house."

"Thank you. You're Doug Liederbach, aren't you?"

"I am." He looked pleased, probably thinking I recognized him for one of his not-too-shabby achievements.

"My name is Jorja Knight," I said, offering him my hand. I looked around the room, the remaining foursome was getting ready to leave. "Would you have a minute to chat? I'm doing a story on Misty Lane for *Swerve*. I'd like to ask you a few questions about her, if I may?"

His smile faded. He took a step back stiffly and looked over his shoulder at the empty bar. Hard to claim he was too busy.

"Let me get rid of this carafe," he said.

I watched him carry the wine carafe to the bar, then busied myself spreading cheese and fig jam on a round of crostini. I scrolled through the messages on my phone until I found the one Mike had sent me earlier. *Julie in medically induced coma, on breathing tube—vitals stabilizing slowly.* The last message in the thread was me telling him to stay strong, that he and Julie were in my thoughts.

Doug returned a few minutes later, and I waved at the empty chair across from me.

"I understand you and Ms. Lane dated for a while."

"We had a very on-and-off relationship. Mostly off. I really don't have much to say about her. What's your angle, anyway?"

"Combined human interest story and the role of mysticism

in modern society. I've heard good things about Misty, read some accounts of her involvement in helping law enforcement agencies. Of course, some think she's just smoke and mirrors. Everyone is entitled to their opinion." I laughed.

He relaxed, but only slightly.

"I'm less interested in her abilities as a psychic. I'm more interested in Misty the person. You know, what's she like when she's not doing a reading? Is she caring? Funny? What does she do in her downtime? That sort of thing."

I watched him weighing out what to say. Finally, he said, "This gift of hers runs her life. There is no downtime. She's very ambitious. I thought I knew who she was, but after I broke up with her, I questioned if I really ever did."

"I suppose it would be hard to separate the two. I gather it's not the sort of thing you can switch off and leave at the office. Is that what you meant when you said it runs her life?"

"Pretty much."

"Did you ever attend any of her readings?"

"Formal readings? No. I'm not into that sort of thing." He shifted in his chair, crossed his arms and looked out the window.

"What about her background? I mean, I know the public stuff. She went to college, worked for a communication firm after graduation and packed in her career to practice her gift full time seven or eight years ago. But what about her childhood, family, close friends?"

"I never met any of her friends."

"Did she talk about them or her family?"

"No."

"Why is that?"

"Look, I really don't want to do this. You should be talking to her publicist."

"She's next on my list." I waited.

"You're not going to quote me, are you?"

"Of course not. I should have mentioned that. I'm just doing background research on her. It helps me formulate the type of questions I'll be asking her later."

"I really don't have much more to say." He sighed and shook his head. "Misty can turn a fun dinner party into a macabre evening just like that." He snapped two fingers, a scowl creasing his face.

"How so?"

"Have you ever been out with friends, just laughing, having a good time, when someone brings up something depressing? Or something no one cares about? I can't tell you how many times she'd suddenly start telling someone their dead grandmother had a message for them. Or that they shouldn't blame themselves for their brother's suicide. Bit of a downer, wouldn't you say? Not to mention most of my friends don't believe in an afterlife."

I nodded. "Never thought of that. I guess it's one thing if you sign up for a reading, but I can see how people might not appreciate being forced into that kind of conversation without permission. Her grandmother was psychic too, wasn't she?"

"According to Misty, yes."

"What can you tell me about her childhood?"

"All I know is she grew up somewhere on the west coast. I told you, she never talked about her past or family."

"Do you know why?"

"You'll have to ask her. Whenever I pressed, she said she didn't want her personal information out there. For safety reasons."

"Safety reasons? Was she receiving threats, or anything that might have led her to fear for her safety?"

"Not as far as I know. She plans on being world famous. She doesn't want her fame to interfere with her family's desire to live a quiet private life."

"Makes sense. Do you mind telling me who ended the relationship, you or her?"

"Technically she did, but only because she beat me to the punch. Apparently, I wasn't being supportive enough."

"Have you seen her since?"

"I ran into her a few times after we broke up. Chance run-ins." His eyes met mine steadily. "I haven't seen her in at least five or six months."

"She invited me to a reading the other day. I must admit I was impressed."

"Like I said, I've never been."

"Odd question, but do you drive a grey Impala?"

"I do, why?"

"As we've been talking, I got a sense I've seen you somewhere. I thought you might be the guy I saw jump out of a grey Impala to help a lady whose groceries had spilled. In Bridgeland—yesterday evening?"

"No, not me."

"Maybe I'm remembering you from MasterChef Canada. I don't watch a lot of TV but occasionally, I find myself bingeing."

He grunted and put his hands on the table, ready to push off. "We done here? I know I haven't been much help but it's pretty much all I got."

"That's okay. Thanks for chatting with me. Love your wine bar, by the way—I'll have to come back and try out more of the menu when I have time."

"Come say hello whenever you're back. I'm usually manning the bar. Good luck with your story."

I didn't know what to think. At first, I wasn't sure he'd even entertain my questions but on the other hand, he didn't provide anything of much use. His answers were curt. He wasn't eager to provide examples or elaborate on his views and opinions. His body language confirmed his reluctance to talk about Misty. I could see why she had been hesitant to cough up his name. Did I think Liederbach hated Misty enough to kill her? Didn't appear so from our brief conversation. He seemed to answer my questions truthfully enough, but he was definitely holding something back. And in my book, being evasive was the same as being deceptive.

SEVEN

"TALK TO THE pope. He knows everything. It's in the bible." His voice rose over the noise of the traffic.

I stepped around him, avoiding eye contact. Today, he wore a shirt, and over it a cardboard sign, like one of those sandwich boards. It was covered in tight, green crayon scrawling, too small to read without divine intervention.

"The good book is written in English. All the famous writers and philosophers write in English. Benjamin Franklin, Jon Edwards, Bob Dylan. You ever listen to Dylan? Dylan's a prophet, man." He punched the air to emphasize his point. "He knows the answer. You need to listen to his songs A.S.A.P.—A fuckin' SAP."

Misty looked up as I opened the door, letting in the steady rumble of engines idling on Kensington, traffic already building for the afternoon crush. I closed the door, muffling the traffic noise and the dishevelled guy's proclamations. I waited while she finished up with a customer. I didn't need psychic powers to see she was emotionally exhausted and dragging ass.

"Jorja. How are you?"

"I thought I'd drop in and see how you're doing."

"I'm still shook up. I didn't sleep at all last night."

"I can see you're exhausted."

She shuddered and hugged herself. "I may close up shop early today."

"Might not hurt. Sounds like the police know who that poor woman was. It was on the news this morning. They aren't releasing her name though, until next of kin are notified."

She nodded. "Did they say anything else?"

"No. Just that a forty-two-year-old woman had been found dead last night in Bridgeland and homicide is investigating."

"I couldn't even bear to look out my window this morning. When I drove out of the garage, I could see the yellow tape around the front." Misty walked to the front window and peered outside. Someone passed by and she quickly stepped back.

"Have you given more thought about sharing your vision with the police?"

She turned, pulled the edges of her knee-length sweater across her chest and stared out the window.

"Misty?"

"Sorry?" She turned back toward me. "I'm walking around in a fog today."

"Your vision. Maybe you should mention it to that detective you were talking to last night. Detective Brighton, wasn't it? I think he'd be interested to know that you and the victim were similarly dressed last night."

"I'm not sure how it'll help. I mean, if it's the woman in my vision…she's dead. I didn't have a chance to stop it. And if the killer made a mistake and thought it was me, then what? I can't tell police much more than I've told you. Which isn't much."

"I see your point, but they may see it differently. I've talked to Peoria Benson and your ex. Peoria strikes me like the type that could stir up drama in a monastery. Hard to imagine her risking ruining her nails or scuffing her Jimmy Choo shoes to skulk around in the alley let alone guillotining a bird. She seemed pretty certain you'd be moving out of the building once the renos were complete, leaving her the entire space in the building."

Misty stopped pacing. "Ha. In her dreams. The new landlord did offer to buy back my space. I told him no. I'm not going anywhere."

"Was the offer not lucrative enough?"

"He offered me ten percent over what I paid for it. Not nearly enough to compensate for the hassle of moving and all the cost and effort associated with changing contact information on all the brochures, business cards, social media and internet sites. Besides, it's worth staying just knowing I'll be an irritant in Peoria's side."

"I talked to Doug Liederbach earlier today."

"Oh god. What did he have to say?"

"That you and he didn't always see eye to eye, but that you are smart and ambitious."

Misty raised an eyebrow. "You're kidding."

"If he's holding any resentment, he's keeping it hidden."

"I'm relieved. Maybe the next time I think I see him in my neighbourhood I won't freak out."

"I also checked into one of the cases you worked on with the police. Tanner, the guy you helped police catch, down in Montana, is still behind bars."

She turned surprised eyes toward me. "Oh, I didn't even think about that."

"Do you still believe you're in danger? Or do you think your premonition was about the woman who was murdered?"

She frowned, thought for a minute and resumed pacing. "Something's not right. The murdered woman did have dark hair and is my age. My first thought was that the woman was supposed to be me." Her fingers tapped at her lips while she paced the shop slowly, deep in thought. "Now I'm not so sure." She stopped, mumbled something, shaking her head. "Why the human cross? Sacrifice? Redemption?"

Misty started pacing again, occasionally muttering something to herself.

She stopped and looked back at me. "I just don't know."

"If your vision is foretelling your own death, what or who from your past would want to harm you? Who from your past might feel ill treated, whether real or perceived?"

"That would make this too easy wouldn't it? I honestly can't think of anyone."

"High school or university frenemies? Family?"

"No. I told you. I didn't even go to high school. I mean, not physically. We lived off the grid—before living off the grid became popular. I did my high school through correspondence."

"Okay. Family?"

"No." She waved a hand at me. "I told you. My father died when I was eight, my grandmother a few years later. My mother wasn't well. She pretty much gave up after their deaths. Her health isn't good. She's in a nursing home. I don't need people harassing her."

"Okay, what about more recently? Someone you worked with. Someone who maybe thought a reading revealed something they wanted kept secret."

She thought hard. "Nothing like that comes to mind. Sometimes people leave disappointed because they didn't make connections with their loved one. But I always tell them at the beginning of the reading, it's not my choice. I don't determine who reveals themselves to me or when."

"Can you think of anyone who might have had a bad reaction to what they were hearing?"

"You know how many people I meet in a year? I've had people break down and weep with joy and others go numb. Most are happy, grateful. I've had letters from people who tell me they were finally able to let go of sadness or anger or guilt and feel at peace." She stopped, her face flushed. "Why does it have to be someone I knew or know? Maybe it's some wacko who has it in for dark-haired women or thinks psychics work for the devil."

"It's crossed my mind. Look, you have a gift for discerning details so subtle the rest of us may not notice. I want you to focus on the premonition, anything you can discern about who the attacker might be or why they would want to kill you, or anyone else for that matter. I'm going to focus on the mundane details of the here and now."

I wanted to remain open to the idea that our beliefs about time, space, matter and how our own minds worked might be different than we supposed. But it was a lot easier for me to assume something earthlier was in play.

"Is it fair to say you may be picking up on subtle signs, tiny details, feelings in the here and now that others don't see? The vision is a prediction as to what's likely coming before your mind can even articulate it?"

"Oh god, that's exactly it!" She nodded gratefully. "When I was a child and first noticed these things, my grandmother explained it to me by saying some people were just born knowing more than others. I believe everyone has this ability, but only a few have bothered to develop it. Have you ever read *The Secret Life of Bees*? Lily, the girl in the story says, 'The body knows things a long time before the mind catches up to them.' I love that."

"That's a great quote. So, until this killer shows his hand further, I want you to write down every detail from these visions or premonitions you're experiencing. When they happen, who is there with you."

"I can do that."

"I'll see what more I can find out about the poor woman who

was murdered in front of your condo. Maybe there is a connection to you or maybe not, either way it'll be good to know."

I wasn't convinced Misty's past didn't come into play here. Her reluctance to talk about it made me even more curious. I knew from personal experience that people who didn't want to talk about their past did so for a reason. The reference to being abandoned or discarded like junk intrigued me. But discarded how? Physically, professionally, emotionally? And when was the past? A few months ago, a year, a decade?

"In the meantime, keep vigilant, watch your back and let me know if you notice or see anything, physically or from your vision."

"Don't worry. After last night I'm on high alert. I have one more meeting today and I'll close up shop afterward and head home. This evening I'm meeting with the board members of DIVERSE. They're finalizing plans for their spring gala, and I offered to help them raise funds needed to support new immigrants. It's a really good cause. Which reminds me. I'd like you to be there." She picked up her phone and started typing. "I just sent you my publicist's contact info. Give her a call, she'll give you the details."

My phone pinged as her message arrived. Misty resumed wandering around the shop, tapping her lips with her right forefinger.

"Anything wrong?"

She massaged her temples, eyes closed. "I'm getting a sense of something. A bright light…it's hot."

I waited.

"Sorry, it's gone."

The door to the shop swung open. A woman breezed in.

I stepped out onto the sidewalk; the traffic noise filled my ears immediately. I walked to the corner, noticing the guy with the cardboard sign had relocated to the other side of the street. Foot traffic broke into two paths, skirting around him. My eye was drawn to a man standing still on the sidewalk behind him. As soon as he saw that I had noticed him, he dropped to one knee and made it look like he was tying a shoelace, then quickly stood. He glanced nervously in my direction. The light turned red and I started across the street. He broke into a full run, pushed past some people exiting the four-storey building behind him and disappeared inside. He was long gone by the time I reached the building entrance. I noticed he wore work boots.

EIGHT

SMITTY CAME RUNNING as soon as I opened the door. I reached down and scratched the side of his face and in front of his ears as he rubbed up against my leg. He followed me to the kitchen, giving me friendly *murrrps* along the way. Wesson perched on a shelf in the living room, eyeing me unblinkingly. I walked into the kitchen and picked up their food dishes, both empty. Either Wesson was coming down from his lofty perch to eat while I was away, or Smitty was going to be one hefty kitty by the time Mike got back.

I fed the cats, then went back outside to check on Mrs. Niedswiki's place. The gate of her three-foot-high picket fence opened without a squeak, the sidewalk leading up to her front steps free of weeds or dirt. I pulled out the few advertisements sticking out of her mailbox and picked up the bundle of flyers lying on her front steps. I made a circuit around her house, making sure nothing was out of order. The neighbour on her other side peered at me from behind kitchen curtains but disappeared the second I waved.

On the way back, I plucked out the mail in Mike's mailbox, retrieved his bundle of flyers from the front flower bed, and headed inside. I was glad I'd stopped at Giovanni's, my favourite deli, on the way home and eaten a sandwich, as suddenly I was too exhausted to do anything.

I picked up the remote, turned on the TV and muted the sound. Smitty meandered over and jumped up on my lap, turning circles until he found a spot he liked. I scrolled through the messages on my phone and saw a text from Mike.

Give me a shout when you get home.

I glanced at my watch. The message was sent forty-two minutes ago. I sent a text back. *Just got home. Would love to talk. Call me if you're free.*

I jerked awake when the phone vibrated twenty minutes later, sending Smitty tumbling off my lap.

"Hi, Mike. How are you doing?"

"Okay. Tired. Gemma arrived today."

Gemma was Julie's mother, Mike's first wife. Mike said they parted amicably. Gemma wanted a husband and Mike had been pretty much married to his job at that point, but they both worked hard to do what they thought was best for Julie.

"Gemma stayed with Julie, while I drove Billy to Hamilton this afternoon. He's going to stay with his dad until we know what's going on with Julie."

"You've had an exhausting day. You probably didn't get much sleep last night either."

"I spent the night at the hospital. I've been up for over forty hours. I just got to my hotel room and am about to crash for a few hours. Gemma and I are going to stay with Julie in shifts."

"That's good. Your text said they put her in an induced coma. That's the good kind of coma, isn't it? Better than when someone dives into a coma all on their own."

"I just hope they know what they are doing."

"I'm sure they do. What happened? Have they said what's wrong?"

"No. She collapsed at work. Her co-workers called an ambulance. By the time they got to her she was already in shock. The blood work shows she has a massive infection, so they put her into a coma and are administering antibiotics. They still don't know what's causing the infection. Her vital signs have stabilized."

"I know there's nothing I can do for Julie, but I wish I was there to keep you company."

"Trust me, you're an enormous help. How're my furry munchkins?"

"Smitty was lying on my lap until a second ago. Wess is treating me like I'm some sort of alien that's invaded his space. Everything's fine here. Picked up Mrs. Niedswiki's mail, which was duly noted by her other neighbour. I'm keeping busy with a new case."

"That's great to hear." The exhaustion in his voice was clear.

"I won't keep you. Hope you get some sleep tonight. I'm thinking of you and sending Julie wishes for a speedy recovery. You'll keep in touch, won't you?"

"You bet. And…uh…thanks, Jojo. I can't tell you how much I appreciate you being there for me."

"That's what friends are for. Night, Mike."

I was glad to hear that Mike's grandson would be taken care of by his father, Julie's ex. At six he was a rambunctious little fellow. Mike swore he had ADHD but having met him once I thought he was just a modern-day kid, too used to getting his own way.

I sat up and unmuted the TV. The newswoman was talking about the murder.

"Police have released the name of the woman found dead Friday evening. Lori Watson was found in the late evening hours on a quiet street in Bridgeland. Lori Watson was forty-two, single and worked as a nurse at a nearby senior care facility. No further details are being released, but police are treating it as a homicide."

There was no mention that Watson's face had been covered with a plastic bag, her body laid out in a cross. Details the police would likely prefer the media not know. Pulling my feet up under me, I opened my laptop. As soon as the browser came up, I typed in Lori Watson.

Lori's social media presence was typical—LinkedIn profile, Facebook page, Pinterest account. Her Facebook page told me she graduated in 1998 with a nursing degree. Her work section listed various clinics, her last position—wellness coordinator at the Evergreen Continuing Care facility.

At first glance it looked like Lori Watson had led a low-risk lifestyle. She worked in an area of town that was low risk for violent crimes Although Lori was a low-risk victim, killed in low-risk neighbourhood, it was high risk for the offender. Given the body's proximity to the entrance of Misty's condo building, the killer took a big chance of being seen. Of course, the construction site across the street would have provided some degree of cover but the possibility that someone would see him was still strong.

Suddenly exhausted, I closed my laptop. I made a stop in the kitchen to set up the coffee maker for morning and got ready for bed. Smitty jumped up on the foot of the bed as I turned out the light. Misty said she didn't know if her premonition about a dark-haired woman being killed related to this woman—Watson—or herself. If it wasn't about Watson, it was a hell of a coincidence. She kept insisting no one in her life would want to harm her. So why hire me?

I pounded the pillow into a more comfortable shape. The last thing I remembered as my head hit the pillow was thinking that I'd have rely on my own special powers on this case—the ability to doubt and question everything I saw and heard.

NINE

I WAS UP EARLY and on my second cup of coffee when I heard the paper hit the front door. Smitty spun out on the floor and headed for the bedroom. I made my way through the front room and opened the door. The paper lay in the flowerbed. I had it unfolded by the time I got it inside. A picture caught my eye, an eerie nighttime scene of the street in front of Misty's condo building, emergency vehicles standing nearby. The headline announced: *Parents Grieve Loss of Daughter.*

The story didn't tell me a whole lot more than I already knew about how she had died. The coroner had officially ruled Lori Watson's death a homicide. The cause of death determined to be compressional asphyxia caused by significant trauma to the neck. The rest of the story focused on her life, heart-wrenching comments from her two brothers, friends, and parents.

Smitty circled, looking for the best place to lie down, then lowered himself onto the section of paper I was reading. I learned that Lori was a widow. Her husband was killed in a backcountry avalanche eight years ago, while snowmobiling with friends. Her parents were devastated, as were her brothers and various other family members. The article ended with a plea from her brother asking the public to come forward with any information that might help police find his sister's killer.

Smitty stood up and pawed at the paper.

"Okay, okay, I know." I got up, fixed food for the cats then got ready for my meeting with Misty's publicist. There had been no change in Julie's condition yesterday. I had used the day to pick up some groceries and drop by my condo to grab a few things. Thoughts about Misty and Lori Watson had intruded all day.

My musings returned as I drove to Tara's office. Did the killer mistake Watson for Misty? He had taken a big risk, killing Watson right out in the open. Perhaps it had provided him a perverse degree of excitement. I kept thinking of the killer as a he, although it's possible it was a woman. Some killers liked to spend time with their victims after killing them. Particularly those who had sexual motives or for whom killing satisfied some bizarre belief or mistaken ideology. Perhaps the killer had intended to take her away somewhere where these rituals could be performed. Maybe Misty had interrupted the killer when she flipped on her interior lights.

Tara Boyd's office was located on the main floor of a townhouse several blocks from Misty's condo. She was waiting for me.

"Come in, come in." She shook my hand as I entered and ushered me to a table which was set up in the middle of what would have been the living area in the townhouse. Tara Boyd looked just like her website photo, young, blonde, and polished. She exuded the type of energy I imagined personified a publicist.

"Can I get you a coffee?"

"That would be great." I slid a chair out from behind the sleek, honey-oak table and sat. Other than the table, the room held a glossy white cabinet, a white leather armchair and two large portable dome lights, which I assumed were used to create the right lighting when recording videos. My eyes travelled to the staircase that ran up the far wall and I wondered if Tara lived upstairs. "Have you been working with Misty long?"

"Almost two years now." Tara poured two coffees and brought them back to the table, her high-heeled shoes clicking across the gleaming hardwood floor. She set one in front of me and sat down across from me, closing the laptop in front of her.

"How did you and Misty meet?"

"I did my internship at McGraw Digital while Misty was there. She watched out for me, like a big sister. Then a few years ago she contacted me. Her reputation as a medium clairvoyant was growing, I had just gone freelance, and she needed help developing her new career. The rest, as they say, is history."

"Misty told me she's been working to establish herself for seven or eight years now."

Tara leaned back in her chair and crossed one knee over the other. "Misty is extremely talented. She works hard at her craft. People talk about overnight successes, but it usually doesn't happen that way. Of course, talent, opportunity and luck help but it's mostly about persistence. I have no doubt she'll soon be on the international stage."

"Did she tell you about her premonition? And what happened two nights ago?"

"I couldn't believe it when I heard. She predicted a dark-haired woman, roughly her age and build, would be killed, and a woman fitting that description *was* killed. Right in front of her condo. It's amazing."

"Do you believe she's no longer in danger?"

"Misty believes she's still in danger. Maybe, the woman who was murdered is only one of several the killer has murdered or intends to kill."

"Any thoughts on who might want to harm Misty?"

"Anytime you put yourself out there, you open up the risk

of attracting unwanted attention. It's frightening. Has to be a psychopath."

"We'd all like to believe that the people in our lives won't hurt us. But the stats show that most people are killed by someone they know, not crazed strangers. If I'm to believe her premonition has some validity, and I do, I need to consider possible motives behind the threat."

"Despite her public appearances, Misty is a very private person. She doesn't have a lot of people in her life."

"Let's start with the ones we know." Lori Watson's death changed things. I was no longer chasing a dark shadowy figure visible only in Misty's mind. There was a bona fide, living, breathing killer out there. "She's mentioned a woman who owns a shop in her building, giving her grief. Peoria Benson."

Tara winced, picked up her coffee and took a sip. "They clearly have a mutual dislike of each other. I know she'd like to see Misty move out of the building, but I can't imagine someone resorting to murder over retail space."

"I had a quick chat with Benson, and I agree. What about Misty's private life. Her friends."

"Did she tell you about her ex-boyfriend. Doug Liederbach?"

"She did. What do you know about him?"

Tara uncrossed her legs, set her coffee on the table, and leaned forward. "He has a hard time with rejection."

"Really? Tell me more."

"After Misty broke up with him, she saw him watching her place, usually late at night."

"But she hasn't seen him lately."

"True. However, Misty's not the only one he fixated on. His previous girlfriend filed a restraining order against him."

"Misty never mentioned that."

"I didn't hear it from Misty. An acquaintance of mine happens to know the woman he dated before Misty."

"Do you know the woman's name, the one who filed a restraining order?"

"I never met her. But I know she owns a little jazz bar in Inglewood. Let me think." She tapped one long crimson nail against her cup and stared at a spot on the table. "It has a cute name…something cat, like kitty cat…no that's it, Jazzy Katz."

"I'll look into it. Anyone else?"

"I can't think of anyone." Tara leaned back. "Like I said, Misty likes her privacy. I find that's the case with quite a few people in the public eye. Extroverts thrive on that kind of attention, but for introverts like Misty, it drains them. They need alone time to recharge."

As a card-carrying member of the introvert club myself, I got it. "What about her past? Friends from university days or the company where you both worked?"

"She never talks about her past. I know she grew up on the coast. I know her mother still lives out there somewhere. She might be in a nursing home."

I scanned the room. There was nothing here that gave me any hints about Tara's past either, except for two framed university degrees hanging on the wall below the staircase. I turned back to Tara.

"She mentioned her father died when she was quite young. Do you know why or how?"

"A highway accident. Misty once said something about the Coquihalla Highway being a graveyard for truckers."

"Can you think of anything that might have happened to trigger these feelings of dread she's been experiencing? She said they started about a month ago."

"No. Wait. Strike that. I remember about a month or so ago

she showed up for a meeting and seemed rather down. When I asked her about it, she said she just found out an old friend of hers had died. Someone she grew up with."

"Do you know where or how?"

"No. Sorry. You'll have to ask her."

Why hadn't Misty mentioned it to me? Perhaps she thought it irrelevant, but the timing interested me. I wondered what, if anything else, she had filtered out.

"Tell me about this event she has coming up."

Tara leaned forward, her voice quickening. "The DIVERSE gala. It's a great opportunity. Not just from the perspective of raising her profile but to use her talent to help newly arrived immigrants re-establish their lives. It's this Thursday at the Royal Canadian Legion—the downtown location. I have an interview set up for Misty right after this meeting with a reporter. It's going to get a lot of media attention. I'll have a ticket waiting for you at the entrance."

"Okay, thanks." I pulled my phone out from my jacket pocket and entered the date, then tucked it away. "I'm assuming there is a list of attendees for these types of events."

"Yes, of course. We send out thank yous after the event to everyone who attends and ask if they want to be added to Misty's monthly newsletter."

"Misty told me that lately she's become anxious, fearful, during some of her readings. Makes me wonder if someone in the audience is triggering these feelings, subconsciously or otherwise."

"I never thought of that."

"Is there any way I can get information on who attends the gala as well as who attended her previous readings? Say, in the last month or two?"

"I'm obligated not to share personal information like phone

numbers or addresses, but I'd be happy to send you a list of attendee names."

"Thanks. Will there be any security at this event?"

"I'm afraid you're it." She laughed, then stopped short. "You don't think someone will attempt something at the event, do you?"

I thought back to the woman who had been killed in front of Misty's condo. Misty said her face was covered with a plastic bag, her body laid out in a cross. But one murder didn't exactly establish a pattern nor predict a second one.

"Not likely."

"We'll also have a videographer at the DIVERSE gala. We'll be using recorded snippets from the evening for Misty's social media."

"Sounds like you've thought of everything. Anything else I should know about or watch for during the event?"

She smiled brightly. "I'll keep an eye out for you but if you can't find me after you've picked up your name badge, head back to the stage and let one of the stage crew know you've arrived. One of them will take you to the back. Misty will arrive about thirty minutes before the event starts. She doesn't like to engage in conversation before her readings. She needs time to relax, open herself up to spirit."

"Right."

"The best place for you during the event is backstage. You'll have a good view of the stage as well as the audience. The front row is reserved for the media, dignitaries, and Misty's special guests. There's a meet and greet planned with them after the event."

"Got it."

I heard steps outside and the door opened. Misty stepped in, followed by a man.

"Oh, sorry. Didn't realize you had someone here. Oh, Jorja. Hi."

"No worries. We just wrapped up," said Tara as we both stood.

The man with Misty stepped back in surprise. "Well, well, if it isn't Jorja Knight. Fancy meeting you here."

I reached over and shook his hand. "Shaun. Nice to see you again."

He looked from me to Misty, then Tara, and back again. "This can't be a coincidence. You ladies working on something?"

I glanced over at Misty. When we first met, she had mentioned that it had been Shaun's article on how I helped nab the Houdini Killer, that had led her to me. Now I wondered if that was the only reason.

"Shaun is doing a piece on me," Misty hurriedly supplied. "You know, about the DIVERSE gala on Thursday."

"Sounds like it'll be quite the event. Well, I'll leave you to it. Nice seeing you again, Shaun."

I left slightly miffed that Misty hadn't mentioned the death of an old friend to me when I asked her if anything happened around the time her premonition evolved. Hard to believe that she hadn't been aware of the restraining order filed against her ex-boyfriend by a former girlfriend. Now, I was curious. And following up on my curiosity was what she was paying me for.

TEN

JAZZY KATZ WASN'T very busy when I got there. Half a dozen tables were occupied, at best. I walked over to the bar and sat where I could keep an eye on who came and went. The bartender sauntered over.

"What can I get you?"

"Bourbon. Booker's, if you have it. No ice."

He drew out his forefinger and thumb, made to look like an imaginary pistol, and pointed it at me. He was either going to bring me a bourbon or shoot me in the alley later. While he was gone, I looked the place over. A small stage stood in one corner, the sign announced Lady and the Tramp, a jazz duo, was live at 8:00 p.m.

The canned music filtering into the bar was slow, low and sultry, something Diana Krall would sing. Tables were crammed in close to the stage and to each other. When full, the place would be crowded, hot and noisy.

The bartender brought my bourbon and placed it on a paper coaster. Classy. And totally unnecessary, the profusion of nicks and gashes in the wooden bar top reminiscent of a Jackson Pollock painting.

"I'm looking for Becca Katz."

"She usually comes in around four."

I nodded my thanks and he slipped away to cash out a customer.

I watched a table of four getting ready to leave, three guys and a gal with hair the colour of Orange Crush. Goodbyes were said. One man remained. I averted my eyes, but it was too late. He sauntered over and slid onto the stool next to me.

"Hi there, gorgeous."

"Hi."

"Whatcha doing?"

"Having a drink."

"All by your little self?"

"I usually manage quite nicely on my own."

He glanced at my barely touched glass. "Looks like you could use some company."

"Look, I'll be blunt. I'm not here to drink or to make friends. I'm waiting to talk to the owner."

"I don't mind waiting. I'll buy you a drink after," he said and winked.

"Thanks, but no thanks. Have a good day." I pulled out my cell phone and turned back to my drink. He slid off the stool and stepped away. I didn't bother watching his departure. Perhaps a bit gruff, but there was no room in my life for a new man.

As it was, I was still trying to figure out how Azagora fit in. Or even if I wanted him to fit in. No denying I had a thing for the head of the city's Special Crimes unit, Inspector Luis Azagora, and we had occasionally scratched each other's itch. The physical attraction between us was insane. Last year we tried to address it with a non-committed relationship that ended at sex and no investment of emotion. Perhaps not the smartest move on my part. But beyond that? Hard to see how my PI life could mesh with Azagora's political aspirations.

Besides, I was avoiding him. Ever since I saw his picture in the social pages of the Herald, with the woman he took to the Inspirer Community Development charity gala last month. Someone he clearly deemed to be more socially flattering to his image than me. The caption below the picture identified her as a board member of the Elizabeth Fry Society. Azagora's hand clearly on her waist, a half smile on his lips. Or maybe I was just bitter because he outdid me at the whole non-committed relationship thing.

I took another sip of bourbon and savoured its warmth as it slid down my throat. A woman stepped out of the back and walked up to the cash register. She wore jeans, strategically torn to disguise how expensive they were, and a faux-fur vest over a camel-coloured, long-sleeve sweater. She turned to ask the bartender something, laying a hand on his arm. He bent his head toward her and a second later she glanced my way. I took a sip of bourbon and watched her mosey out from behind the bar. She stopped at a table to chat and laugh with the couple sitting there, then slid onto the stool next to me.

"Danny says you're looking for me. I'm Becca Katz."

"Hi. Jorja Knight. I'm a private investigator." I reached into my purse, pulled out one of my cards and handed it to her. "If you have a minute, I'd like to ask you some questions about Doug Liederbach."

"I don't want to have anything to do with that creep."

I nodded sympathetically. "My client thinks he might be stalking her."

She nodded for me to follow and led me to a small table in the back corner. "So, he's back at it. Why am I not surprised?"

"I understand you two dated for a while."

"Biggest mistake of my life."

"What can you tell me about him?"

"He's a creep. Very controlling. He's passive aggressive in his approach. At least at first. Maybe that's why I didn't notice it right off the bat. He makes you think you're being overly sensitive or misinterpreting what's being said, until it becomes blatantly obvious that it's not your imagination. Even then I found it hard to accept that he could treat me that way. He's got a temper—but he hides it until he's got you under his thumb. So, some other poor gal fell for his good looks and fake charm. Sorry to hear that."

"When and how did you meet him?"

"I guess it was about three years ago. He moved into my brother's condo. My brother took a transfer to Puerto Rico for work and wanted me to rent out his condo for him. Doug answered the ad I posted."

"You checked him out?"

"I did. He grew up on a farm in Saskatchewan, then moved to Alberta. He took culinary classes at SAIT, then started working. He told me he met a guy, a retired geologist, who had just bought into a winery in BC and he offered him a job out there. He got his vintners certificate and ended up managing this winery. But there was some sort of disagreement between the partners of the winery and they ended up selling it. I don't know the details. Doug moved back to Calgary. After he signed the contract and moved into my brother's place, we stayed in touch. He seemed to know a lot of people and he was fun to be around. I went to a bunch of his parties and we started dating. But as I got to know him, I realized his friends weren't really friends, most only knew him a few weeks or months. No one stayed friends with him long, and I know why. He's an ass, a hot-tempered one at that. Everything about him is offensive."

"So, you broke up with him."

"Yes. After we broke up, I cancelled his lease—told him my brother was coming back and needed his condo."

"I take it he didn't react well."

"I expected him to be angry, but I never imagined he'd go to such lengths to make my life miserable."

"You filed a restraining order against him. You must have been afraid he'd hurt you."

"Hell, yeah, I was afraid."

"He was physically abusive?"

"He came close to hitting me once, but I told him if he did—the police would get a call and I wasn't afraid to lay charges. It was his fascination with guns that freaked me out."

"He owned guns?"

"After he moved out of my brother's place, I had to have the bedroom walls re-plastered. He had maybe thirty guns, all mounted on the bedroom wall."

"Did he ever take them down?"

She laughed embarrassedly. "Oh yeah. It was part of his fore-play, his little fantasy to help him get it up. He liked to wave a gun around and pretend like he was going to shoot me unless I did…uh…what he demanded."

"I see. Did he ever take the guns and his fantasy out of the condo?"

"That's the thing—as time went on, he started picking me up from work—with a gun. I'd walk outside, and he'd pull a gun on me, make me drive somewhere to have sex. It was hard to tell what was real and what was his twisted fantasy. But he had trouble getting aroused unless he had a gun at my head. He didn't want me. He just wanted someone to play out this sick game with him. And as time went on it just got sicker. I ended it."

"Was it always threats with guns?"

"No. A few times he pretended to abduct me at work. I say pretend because we'd decide to meet after work. Once he drove me out of town—started to choke me. I almost passed out. We had a big fight. I told him if he ever tried something like that again

I'd leave for good. He didn't try choking me again but after that I noticed his eyes when he played the game—and didn't like the way he looked at me—like a hungry animal. I ended it shortly after that."

"He stalked you?"

"My god yes. He'd be standing across the street, just staring, when I got off work. I noticed him outside my condo. Once I came out of my mother's house, and he was there, watching me. He aimed a gun at me that day. I have no idea if it was loaded or not, but I didn't care one way or the other. At my mother's place, if you can believe it. I started reporting these incidents to the police, mostly because I wanted it on record. Then my house was broken into. I'm positive it was him. I hired a private detective. He managed to film Doug stalking me and documented the dates and time. The detective told me Doug was getting off by making me afraid. After we had about twenty of these incidents documented, I filed harassment charges."

"And after the court order?"

"I didn't see him around my place or work after that. I did run into him a few months later, at the mall, but I figured it was a chance run-in. He didn't pay any attention to me. Even though it's been almost two years, whenever I hear something late at night, or see the kind of car he drives, or someone who looks like him from the back, I freak out."

"You think he'd carry a grudge this long?"

"Grudge, fantasy, delusion. Oh yeah. I feel for your client. She needs to do whatever it takes to make sure this creep is off her back."

"If he's stalking her, I'll be able to provide evidence."

Becca leaned in toward me. "You know, part of me is relieved at the idea that I may no longer be at the centre of his obsession.

On the other hand, it makes me crazy to think this creep just gets to move on to terrorize some other woman. I hope you nail him."

After my chat with Becca, I had another drink, left cash on the bar and stepped back outside into the sunlight. I pulled my sunglasses down over my eyes. Misty didn't believe Doug Liederbach to be capable of murder. After talking with him, I had been tempted to dismiss the possibility. After hearing about his fantasy, I changed my mind. Maybe Liederbach was escalating his sick fantasy from mere playacting to real life. Perhaps he *had* planned to abduct the woman found dead at Misty's condo, take her somewhere, where he could have gotten his sick fix by watching her fight for her life, plead with him in fear.

Maybe he killed her in front of Misty's condo in order to see Misty's fear, whether real or in his mind's eye. A fear that fed his desire.

I took several steps and whipped my head around. A grey Impala disappeared around the corner.

ELEVEN

I SPENT THE EVENING on my laptop and by midnight I was still wide awake. Not just awake, but totally revved up. The level of energy that isn't conducive to falling asleep. I packed up the laptop, turned my phone over on the nightstand and tried reading. After checking my watch every ten minutes for the next hour or so I must have dozed off. It was pitch black when my eyes snapped open, my senses pinging on all cylinders. My ears strained for what had woken me. Nothing moved, no noise. The clock next to the bed clicked. The numbers 3:15 glowed comfortingly in the dark. My muscles slowly relaxed.

Smitty jumped on the bed, landing on my chest. He meowed then crouched and let out a soft growl. I threw back the covers and bolted upright. Smoke.

I ran into the kitchen, Smitty at my heels. Everything seemed fine. Rushing to the back window, I peered outside. Flames licked at the side of Mike's garage.

I grabbed my phone, calling 911 while struggling into my jeans. I ran through the sunroom and out the back door, praying Mike had already turned his outside taps back on after the winter freeze. Cranking the water tap left, I felt the hose jump in my hand as bits of air and water exploded from the nozzle.

I pulled the hose with me as I ran to the garage. The back fence was ablaze and thick black smoke billowed from the garage. Choking, I aimed the water blindly at the flames while the sound of fire engines grew louder.

Three firefighters jumped from the firetruck before it was even fully stopped in the alley behind Mike's garage. A minute later the back gate crashed open and two firemen entered the yard, spraying what looked like foam against the side of the garage. I ran back and turned off the water as a second truck arrived. One of firefighters entered the garage through the side door and I heard the main garage door opening. Ten minutes later all was under control. A police car arrived, and one of the firetrucks left. Mike's neighbours were watching the show from their back porches.

Suddenly racked with shivers, I ducked inside to grab my jacket. I had run outside without shoes and my feet were freezing. Properly dressed, I went back outside to survey the damage. The fire had been set in one of Mike's garbage bins, which stood in an alcove built into the back fence. An accelerant had been used to get a good blaze going quickly. Next the fence caught fire and then spread until it reached the garage. The vinyl siding on the garage hung in great gobs and was the source of the acrid smell and black smoke. The door frame to the garage door was heavily singed, but the door and structure itself escaped damage. The back section of fence would need to be replaced.

I filled out a report providing all the details of who owned the house and what my relationship was to the owner and all those little nitpicky things needed in a police report. Finally, the last emergency vehicle left. The fire was being attributed to vandalism. One of the police officers had questioned neighbours, but like me, most had been asleep and saw and heard nothing.

Back in the house, I had a quick look for Smitty and Wess. Smitty was lying in the middle of my bed, Wess nowhere to be seen. Still cold, I crawled into bed, careful not to disturb Smitty, and lay there until the grey light of morning.

I got up when the coffee maker beeped. I stumbled into the kitchen. Smitty had relocated himself somewhere as dawn approached but wandered into the kitchen as I poured my coffee. I fixed food for the cats and put down fresh water. I called for Wess, not really expecting him to come running.

I reached out to pet Smitty. "Hi, buddy. Quite the night. Are you okay? How's your brother?" Smitty gave me wide berth and headed to his food. *Great, now they're both annoyed with me.* I took my coffee back into the bedroom then headed for the shower. By the time I returned to the kitchen, freshly showered, dressed, and ready for the day, Smitty's food was half eaten. Wess' bowl looked untouched.

I poured another cup of coffee and walked from room to room. No Wess. I checked closets and under the furniture. The churn in my stomach deepened. He couldn't have gotten out of the house last night—could he? Shaking, I walked through the sunroom, pulled on my jacket and stepped outside.

"Come on, Wessie, where are you? Come on, baby." I peered under the porch, checked the flowerbeds and then the garage. I opened the garage door and peered up and down the alley. "Oh god, where are you, Wess?" Closing the garage, my mind replayed what I remembered of the night. I didn't see Wess as I ran outside, but was I even paying attention?

Back inside, I searched the entire house one more time. I couldn't just leave for the day, could I? Was he really missing? What was I supposed to do? Maybe I should check with the neighbours. I felt sick.

I picked up Smitty's food and water dish and carried them into the bedroom, then moved one of the litter boxes into the room. Smitty followed me in and out, curious as to what was going on. I picked him up and gave him a snuggle. "Just for a few hours, buddy." I put Smitty down on the bed and closed the door. I hoped that when I got back this afternoon, I'd see evidence that Wess was around and eating or at least using the remaining litter box in the sunroom.

I peered out into the backyard, unable to focus on anything but Wess. He had to be hiding. It was the most logical explanation and the only one I could accept. And if he was, he wasn't likely going to come out while I was still here. I pulled on my coat, stepped out onto the front steps, and pulled the door shut behind me.

Mike's paper lay halfway down the sidewalk. I picked it up, carried it with me to the car and tossed it on the front seat. Something caught my eye. I unfolded the paper. Misty's face beamed up at me. Her interview with Shaun Allen and a plug for her 'spiritual healing' event at the DIVERSE gala Thursday night. I started to read.

"You're freaking kidding." Shaun Allen had not only plugged Misty's event, he made Misty out to sound like she ran circles around law enforcement and routinely solved murders cases that baffled police. She had obviously told him about her prediction that a dark-haired woman was going to be killed—and that she was the one who found Lori Watson, dead on her patio. Worse yet, the article went on to say Misty and I were working together to solve the murder. I swore under my breath. Shaun Allen was the one who wrote up the piece on my role in the capture of the Houdini Killer. The article that brought me to Misty's attention. I knew he'd think something was up when he saw me at Tara's yesterday. He closed the article with a prediction that the pairing of sleuth and soothsayer would soon run the killer to ground.

I tossed the paper aside, cursing silently. The cops were already unhappy with Shaun Allen's account of how I solved a murder that had baffled police for months. What the hell was Misty thinking?

As the morning wore on, my annoyance turned to fear. Shaun Allen's article was like a red flag being waved in front of a bull. If Misty was the intended victim, she might as well have poked the killer with a sharp stick.

TWELVE

THE MAN WITH a cardboard sign was back, this time across the street from Misty's shop. He was agitated, shouting at pedestrians and drivers alike. The sidewalk in front of Misty's was cordoned off, as well as the curb lane where several service trucks were parked. I drove around the corner and pulled into the alley. I called Misty to let her know I was coming in through the back.

"Quite the commotion outside," I said, stepping inside. "It's crazy out there. What's happening?"

"They're taking out the gas lines to the vacant apartments upstairs so renovations can start."

"But they've blocked access to the front door of your shop."

"Am I lucky or what." Misty shrugged. Her energy was subdued. She seemed defeated. "I only have one reading today, hopefully they will be gone by then."

"Tara gave me the scoop on the gala. I asked her to get me a list of names of those who attended your readings in the last month or two as well as who attends the gala. Maybe we can spot a pattern, someone who is showing an obsessive degree of interest in attending group readings and events. Someone in the audience may be triggering your sense of dread."

"That's a good idea. I never thought of that."

"Speaking of obsessive, what do you know about the preacher—the guy out there, shouting fire-and-brimstone messages."

Misty glanced out the window and shrugged. "Not much. He's homeless. Sometimes he sleeps in the alley behind the store. I've occasionally brought him food. He says his name is JC. He doesn't rant and yell all the time. Why? You don't think he has anything to do with the messages someone's been sending me."

"No, I'm more interested in him as a witness. He seems to spend a lot of time on your street, maybe he's seen something. Too bad he talks in riddles."

"Sometimes he makes sense." She turned to me and tapped her lips with her finger. "Are you okay?"

"Yes, of course. Why?"

"Oh. I just had a sense of something. Was there a fire?"

Every nerve in my body tingled. *Seriously?* "Yeah. It's nothing. Some vandals lit a fire in the alley where I am staying. You see the article on the dead woman, Lori Watson?"

"Yes." She turned to me, hand at her neck. The sunlight streaming through the window caught the rings on her fingers and made her amber earrings flash like wolves' eyes in winter. "I want to find whoever killed her. Whether he meant to kill her or thought she was me, doesn't matter."

"Is that why you told Shaun Allen we're working on the Lori Watson murder? Because we're really not."

Misty walked to the window and peered out. She turned and stared at me for a second, her eyes uncertain. Then something flickered in them.

"Tara thought it was a good idea since Lori's death had just been in the news."

"So, you're willing to let people think you and I are working on solving her murder, just for the publicity it will stir up?"

"I am going to help find her killer. I got a call from Lori's brother yesterday. He asked me if I would help. I said yes. I just didn't get a chance to tell you."

"If the killer mistakenly killed Lori Watson thinking it was you, then he's still a threat to you. I'm not sure letting him know you're specifically seeking him is a good idea."

"But if he did mean to kill me, then you and I *are* hunting him down."

"I just wish you'd kept my name out of it."

"I tried, but Shaun said he knew we were working together. He kept pressing me. He insisted I tell him. Said if I didn't— someone else would."

I nodded. I knew how persistent reporters could be. And I knew the minute he saw me leaving Tara's office he'd suspect that I wasn't there to hire a publicist for myself.

"By the way, I had a chat with one of Doug's previous exes. The one who obtained a restraining order. Did you know about that?"

Misty stopped pacing. She clasped her hands together and brought them in front of her lips.

"Yes, I did."

"Why didn't you tell me about Doug's gun collection. Or the bondage and choking games he likes to play."

Misty shook her head. "It's not Doug."

"I'd still like an answer."

"I don't know. I guess I was embarrassed."

"Embarrassed? Embarrassed that he's a sick fuck? Embarrassed that he harasses women to the point they fear for their lives?"

"Yes," she choked out. "All of it. He's a total perv. I knew it and went out with him anyway. I feel so stupid. Why the hell did I do that?"

"Sorry. It's not your fault. I'm just frustrated. I've met men like him. I shouldn't let it get to me."

"I finally had the guts to walk away and I wish he'd just disappear." She flicked her hand like she was shooing away a wasp. "I'm sorry, Jorja. I was embarrassed and now I'm mortified that I didn't tell you. It's just that if he's the evil presence in my premonition, I feel like I would know somehow. Why wouldn't I have felt it earlier? Why now, after so many months of not seeing him?"

"That's a good point, but I think you should tell Detective Brighton about Doug, and you should also tell him that Lori Watson was dressed similarly to you the night she was killed. Let the police determine if both are relevant or not."

I watched her chin tilt up ever so slightly as she looked away. Introversion wasn't all we had in common.

"Listen, if I'm to be any use to you, you're going to have to be open with me. One woman is already dead. You were pretty convinced your life was in danger the day you came to my office. Other than your vision, you haven't given me much to work with."

"I know."

"You're discounting things before giving me a chance to rule them out. I'm getting the sense you might prefer to handle this yourself."

"No, not true. I am sorry. I'm scared—my brain's all muddled. I need you to work with me on this."

I hated to push her like this, but right now I was feeling as impotent as Doug Liederbach.

"Who is this friend who passed away? Tara mentioned a friend of yours died right around the time the premonition or visions started."

Misty looked startled. "You mean Carla Princeton?"

"I guess. Unless you've had several childhood friends who passed away recently."

"No. Of course not. What's Carla's death have to do with anything?"

"What happened to her?"

Misty's face grew rigid. "I don't know. I hadn't spoken to her in over ten years. I got a letter from a friend of my mother's. She occasionally writes to let me know how my mother is doing, since she's no longer capable of doing so herself. She mentioned that Carla had died. An accident, she thought."

I know I was being bitchy, letting my frustration with this case get to me. But given my short time as a PI, the ratio of wackos to honest people hiring me to do honest work was shockingly high. Misty was clearly guarding her past. Then again, we all have our secrets. I don't talk about my past except to one or two of my closest friends. When asked about family I usually say my parents have both passed. I don't mention it was a murder-suicide. My brother and I are estranged. We haven't spoken in over ten years. Which is why I figured if Misty wasn't talking about her past there might be a skeleton or two in her closet as well.

"Okay, look. My turn to apologize." I blew out a long breath. "I'm frustrated and shouldn't be taking it out on you. The reality is, we don't have much to go on and one woman is already dead."

"I'm sorry. I really am. I really didn't think the news about Carla mattered to what is happening to me."

I walked out of Misty's shop slightly appeased. I could understand why she didn't want anything more to do with Doug Liederbach. Who knew how far he'd go to get his kicks? Still, Misty claimed she didn't think he was capable of murder, or maybe she was afraid to be the one to call attention to him. Even if he didn't kill Lori Watson, Liederbach deserved the attention of Detective Brighton just for being an arrogant misogynistic fuck.

Peoria Benson exited her shop, sashayed toward the vintage Porsche convertible parked behind the store and climbed in. I watched her scooch over until she was almost on top of the grey-haired man behind the wheel. Peoria wrapped her arm around his neck and nuzzled his ear. The Porsche backed out; the man seemed oblivious to the woman at his side. I watched them drive off.

After leaving Misty's shop, I drove around for a while hoping to get some insight, some clarity, some damn idea about what to do next, until I realized I was being a danger to myself and everyone on the road with me. I turned my car toward home. Then realizing my mistake, U-turned and headed to Mike's.

Lori Watson's killer deserved to be caught, punished. I had no issues with Misty trying to help the Watsons find whoever did this but now it wasn't just a newspaper article. She was inserting herself fully into the case. She was going to get herself killed. That wasn't a premonition—it was my prediction.

THIRTEEN

ESS' FOOD LOOKED untouched. I peeled off my coat and headed to the sunroom. Picking up the kitty litter scoop I shifted through his litter box. *Damn.* Walking back into the main house, I opened the bedroom door. Smitty shot out and ran to Wess' bowl.

"Oh no you don't." I picked up Wess' food bowl and placed it on the kitchen counter. Smitty wound his way through my legs, reached up and dug his claws into my leg.

"Ouch. Hey—use your scratching post. Or is that payback for losing your brother," I muttered under my breath. I bent to pet Smitty, who continued to weave himself through my legs. He couldn't have eaten all his food yet. I peered into the bedroom. He had plenty of water left, but his food bowl was empty.

"Sorry, buddy, you'll have to wait until dinner." Mike liked to keep his cats on a regular schedule, whenever possible. He said it made them less anxious, since they knew what to expect. I grabbed a flashlight off the top of Mike's fridge. "Come on, let's go find your brother."

An hour later I was seriously worried. I even closed all the closet and bedroom doors behind me, once I'd searched the space, to prevent a sneak runaround on me. Wesson was gone. I fought off the urge to pour myself a huge shot of bourbon and pulled on my coat. I entered the sunroom, closing the door behind me. I checked the Plexiglas panes for any broken ones or cracks and crevices that would allow a cat to escape. The place was airtight. The thought of Wess wandering lost in the neighbourhood made my legs weak. Shaking, I opened the exterior door and stepped outside.

"Wesson!" I crouched and shone the flashlight under the deck. Getting up, I brushed the dirt off my knees and wandered through the small garden. I stopped every few steps and called his name. There was no responding *mew*. The garage door was stuck. I shouldered it open and gasped. Heart pounding, it took me a second to realize the ominous shape was Mike's welding helmet and fire-resistant apron hanging on a hook on the opposite wall. A welding machine and various sculpting tools lay on a large table in the middle of the garage, various twisted metal shapes and objects lay against the walls. I called for Wess and felt ill when I didn't get a reply. I left the garage door open a crack in case he was hiding inside and backed out.

The fence was a mess, several boards broken. The back gate was closed but the gap between it and the ground and the now broken boards provided a clear path for a kitty to wander through. I opened the latch and entered the alley. The smell of burnt vinyl still hung in the air, the vinyl siding next to it buckled and sagging.

Gravel crunched under my feet as I made my way down the alley, calling Wess' name. I stopped every few feet and listened, peering into nooks and crannies, hoping he'd emerge from some pile of lumber stacked against a garage or crawl out of a wheel well. At the end of the alley I turned and circled back along the front street. I felt lightheaded, jittery. How could I have lost Mike's cat? Images of Wess—frightened, hungry—tore at me. What was I going to tell Mike?

I detoured up Mrs. Niedswiki's front sidewalk and picked up the bundle of flyers on her step. At Mike's, I opened the small side gate and walked into the backyard. I stood, chilled, shaking, overwhelmed with self-pity. I climbed the back step, took one last look around and entered the sunroom. Smitty greeted me at the door.

"Hey, precious, how'd you get back here?" I knew I closed the door from the kitchen on my way out. It was still closed. "How the hell," I muttered. As soon as I was back in the kitchen, I noticed some of Wess' food gone. A glimmer of hope pushed through the heaviness that had wrapped itself around me. Maybe Wess was still inside, somewhere. More than likely Smitty helped himself to a nibble before transporting himself to the sunroom. How had he done that?

I poured myself a stiff shot of Glenrothes, sat on the couch and pulled out my phone. It was only five o'clock in Toronto. Mike was never going to forgive me. He'd say he did, but it would always be there, a scar in our friendship, like the one on my right side—compliments of a co-worker who lost his shit and stabbed me in my own lab at Global Analytix, two years ago.

I pulled open my laptop and googled how to find a lost cat. The website outlined ten things to do and six things to not do. I felt better after reading. I had managed to avoid doing anything on the list of things not to do, which included leaving food outside for the missing cat. I had already executed the first few steps of the ten recommended steps. The website urged me to remain calm. It reminded me that lost cats are frightened cats. They will tend to hide even if their owners are calling them. The site recommended I repeat my search for five days, going back out after dark, and checking as many nooks and crannies as possible for a five-or six-house radius. Sometimes cats are more willing to come out at night rather than during daylight. They can hide effectively in pipes, vents, hedges, toolsheds, or even on roofs. Or he could be trapped. It urged pet owners to check recliner chairs, box mattresses, chimneys, dresser drawers, behind books in a bookcase, behind access panels, and appliances.

I looked around Mike's living room. I had searched thoroughly but not as thoroughly as the website suggested. I felt better. I'd call Mike, then follow the steps on the website. I pulled out my phone, checked the time and brought up Mike's number. He answered on the third ring.

"Hi, Mike, how are you doing? How's Julie?"

"I'm okay. Julie's doing better today. Her vitals are looking good. If they don't get any worse over the next forty-eight hours, they're going to bring her out of the coma."

"Thank goodness. That'll be a relief."

"I'll say. She's not out of the woods yet, but we're feeling hopeful."

"I'll keep my fingers crossed."

"Me too. How are things on the home front?"

"Oh, okay." I didn't know if I should tell Mike about the fire and Wess. Didn't he have enough to worry about? On the other hand, he deserved to know. It was his house, his cat.

"You sure? You sound kind of down."

"Uh, well, there have been some unfortunate developments here."

"Like what?" Mike's voice sharpened. No going back now.

"I was debating whether to tell you or wait, seeing as you have bigger issues to deal with right now, but someone set a fire in the alley, behind your fence. The firefighters got here quickly and put it out right away. Unfortunately, some of your fence got broken in the process and the vinyl siding on your garage kind of melted because of the heat."

"Is everyone okay?"

"Well, yeah. I'm sorry, Mike."

"Don't apologize. You didn't start the fire, did you?" He laughed, and I could hear the relief in his voice.

"Of course not. I woke in the middle of the night and smelled smoke. I called 911, right away. Thank god the firetrucks arrived within minutes. The garage itself doesn't look damaged, but the garage door and frame are singed. I have a copy of the police report for your insurance."

"Good thing you were there and woke up when you did. Any damage to any of the neighbours?"

"No. Just your place. It looked like someone started a fire in one of your garbage cans, then the fence caught on fire."

"Happy to hear it was contained."

"Very funny."

"Come on, it's okay. Could happen to anyone."

"Yeah, well, that's not the worst of it. When I went back inside after it was all over, I couldn't find Wess. He still hasn't shown up. I'm positive he didn't run out of the house when I ran outside. Or at least ninety-nine percent sure. I'm just sick about it, but I can't think of any other explanation for why I can't find him. God, Mike, I'm so sorry. I don't know what to do."

"Jojo, listen. It's going to be fine."

I wiped the tears off my face. Great. Mike was relying on me for one small favour and now I was the one needing consolation. "I called the Calgary Humane Society to let them know he's missing, in case someone brings him in. I've searched the house and through the neighbourhood, but there's no sign of him."

"Knowing Wess, he wouldn't have run outside. Wess is the proverbial scaredy cat. He wouldn't have run toward the commotion, he's hiding somewhere."

"I've looked everywhere, Mike. I'm just sick with worry. I don't mean to dump this on you, but I can't just go about my business with him gone."

"Have you checked in the cellar?"

"The cellar? No. How would he have gotten down there?"

"There's an air intake vent below the bookshelf in the spare bedroom. It's loose—the screws have worn a hole in the plaster. I've been meaning to fix it."

"You think he might be in the vent?"

"One time I came home and couldn't find him anywhere. This was about six months after I got him. That night I woke to this god-awful caterwauling reverberating through the house. I almost had a heart attack. The little goofball crawled into the heating ducts. I ended up taking the covers off all the bloody air vents in the house, afraid he was stuck in there. He popped up in the sunroom two days later."

I laughed shakily. "Okay, as soon as we're off the phone I'm going to look."

"I'm sure he's fine."

"Thanks, Mike. Sometimes I wonder why you put up with me."

"We're friends, right?"

"Right."

As soon as Mike and I disconnected, I grabbed the flashlight and ran into the spare bedroom. I lay down and peered under the bookcase. The space was only four or five inches high. I had looked under the bookcase earlier but hadn't noticed anything. I offloaded two shelves of books and slowly pulled one side of the bookshelf away from the wall. There was the air intake vent, just like Mike described. One edge stood a few inches from the wall. Could Wess really have crawled in there? I reminded myself that all that fluffy grey hair made him look much bigger than he was.

The cellar door was built into the living room floor, near the kitchen doorway. A metal ring lay in a small recess at one end. I pulled; the door flipped open. I stared into the gaping blackness.

Crap. The door stood open, leaning just beyond a ninety-degree angle. There didn't seem to be any additional gizmo to hold it propped open. I shone my flashlight down the ladder. *You've got to be kidding me.* I placed one foot on the upper rung and applied weight. I turned and descended three rungs, my head still above floor level. I turned, ducked and peered into the space.

Three walls appeared to be made of cinder blocks, the other wall dirt. I shone the impotent beam around the room. The air was cold, stale. Some sort of contraption stood at the far end, a primitive furnace or heater. I recognized a newer water tank next to it. Crudely built wooden shelves stood on the other side, and an assortment of neatly stacked items. I picked out a cooler, golf clubs, several cardboard boxes, including a long one with picture of a Christmas tree on its side. Wess could be hiding behind any one of them.

"Wess," I called softly. "Here kitty, kitty. Come on, fellow, dinner time." I straightened and peered around the living room. Smitty was sitting near the couch washing a paw and ignoring the whole escapade. I turned and descended the ladder until my foot found the floor. I took several steps toward the shelves. I shone the flashlight around but saw no reflecting green eyes. I looked upward. Several rectangular heating ducts crisscrossed the ceiling. I reached up and tapped my flashlight on one of them. Nothing. The floor creaked above me.

I scurried up the ladder, breathing hard, expecting something to grab my ankle on the way up or slam the cellar door shut before I got out. Misty's voice percolated in my head. *"A dark-haired woman, about my age and height...descends into a dark, cold space."* I had dark hair and was about Misty's age and height.

I scrambled out, turned, and shuddered at the gaping black hole. I lowered the cellar door with a thud. Smitty watched me unblinkingly. I looked around. Some people found these older houses charming. I didn't. Their worn shabbiness fed my melancholic and overactive imagination.

"Come on, Smitty, let's go to bed."

Smitty followed me into the bedroom and settled on the pillow. I closed the door, got ready for bed and climbed in. The bedroom was pitch black, disorienting. My eyes searched for signs of light. A shiver ran down my back as I recalled Misty asking about a fire.

I grabbed my cell phone and, using its faint light, stumbled across the room and propped Mike's desk chair up against the door handle.

FOURTEEN

THE LOBBY OF the Legion was abuzz with excitement, a frenetic energy fuelled by appetizers, wine and beer. Two women sat at a table at the entrance. I picked up my name tag, headed to the cash bar, and grabbed a soda with lime. I turned to survey the crowd. A mix of business folks, media types and ordinary citizens. Everyone seemed happy to be here.

Tara Boyd emerged from the main room. She stopped to chat with a woman with huge hoop earrings and a stunning floral embroidered jacket that caught my eye, even though I'm usually immune to such things. Tara moved through the room, deftly stopping for a quick word with everyone in her path as she wove her way toward me.

"Jorja. Glad you're here. I'll take you back if you're ready."

I placed my half-drunk soda on a small table already containing a few empty glasses. "Ready right now."

"Did you see the article in the paper? Look at this crowd! Twenty minutes until showtime and we've sold out."

I nodded and bit back a remark about how I couldn't help but notice the article, since my name had been dragged into it along with Misty's.

The main room was darker than the lobby, dark-green velvet

curtains cordoned off the stage. Tara led me to a set of stairs, right of the stage, swept aside the heavy drapery and motioned me to enter. Misty was already there, pacing. She rubbed her temples, muttering to herself, oblivious to our presence. I glanced at Tara. Out of public view, she dropped her smile. Her eyes looked worried.

"I thought this might be a good spot for you to observe the evening's performance. When the curtains are open you can stand as far as this green tape on the floor, without being seen by the audience."

I glanced down at the strip of painter's tape someone had applied to the parquet floor. "Perfect. Where does that door go?" I nodded toward a single steel door with a push bar below a dimly lit exit sign.

"There's a small area back there for coats and personal belongings of the event participants, an office and another door leading out to a small parking lot for staff. The outside door is locked. You need a card key to come in that way."

"Mind if I have a look?"

"Go right ahead. I'm sure it's fine. I'll leave you to it." With another worried glance at Misty, she hurried back through the curtains and down the stairs. I could now hear people laughing and talking as they filtered into the main room.

I tiptoed past Misty and out the side exit door. The space back here was clean, but the linoleum floors and plaster walls showed the building's age. I poked my head into a small room that held a couch, some easy chairs, a coat rack and a small kitchenette area. I continued down the hall, past what was obviously the office, then a washroom and to the back exit. A small window, the glass grid with wires built into the pane, looked out onto a dark alley. A few cars were parked to the left of the door, the brick of the adjacent building forming an impregnable wall to the right. The door opened with a push bar but appeared firmly shut.

I walked back and stepped out onto the stage. A young man was fiddling with spotlights. Misty's deep breathing wasn't working. Her level of nervousness was noticeably higher than mere minutes ago.

"Are you okay, Misty?"

She startled, as if she hadn't noticed my arrival with Tara, minutes earlier.

"Oh, Jorja. Yes, yes, I'm fine. Everything okay?"

"Everything's fine. I'm going to park myself here, while you're on stage. Do you need anything?"

"No, no. I'm just doing some deep breathing to calm myself."

The curtain swayed, and Tara reappeared, this time with the woman in the floral embroidered jacket. She introduced her to Misty and the three of them stood chatting. A few minutes later the young man finished with the lights, crossed the stage and stood awkwardly waiting for a break in conversation. Finally, he interjected. Time to get microphones set up. Tara and the woman with her would use a wireless handheld microphone. Misty was equipped with a wireless headset.

The curtains opened ten minutes after the announced start time. The lights dimmed in the auditorium and soft ethereal music filled the room. A minute later Tara stepped on stage and waved to the cheering, clapping audience. She introduced the woman she brought to the stage with her, who headed up DIVERSE. Once the welcome address was delivered, Tara returned to the stage to introduce Misty. She flashed Misty a huge smile and slipped off to the right as Misty entered from the left.

The place was packed. I spotted Shaun Allen, several members of the Stampeder football team, and the mayor in the front row. Misty sounded breathy, her nerves showing. After her opening remarks, the faint music playing in the background ended. Misty called for volunteers from the audience. A woman joined her from the second row. Misty stood for a nerve-wracking minute in the hushed silence, waiting for spirit to make its presence known. She visibly relaxed after the first reading. After several readings she seemed more herself, laughing with her audience participants. She moved into group readings with multiple audience members joining her on stage. I noticed she favoured the left side of the room, rarely venturing past mid-stage and never selecting participants from the right side.

Misty was impressive. She was on point most of the time, either that or the people she read were extremely suggestive. The audience gasped, and vigorous clapping erupted after she told a man who lost his wife due to cancer that her spirt was grateful he donated his own bone marrow to help her nephew survive his fight with leukemia, after she passed away. The nerves returned though when the lights lifted for the portion of the event where she answered questions from the audience.

She often stopped to clear her throat, her hand resting at its base. A few wanted to know when she discovered her gift, did other family members have the same ability. A man from the far side of the audience asked her about being a clairvoyant. Her nervousness increased. After she finished her explanation, he jokingly asked her what the numbers would be for the upcoming lottery.

I noticed a man get up from the far side. He walked to the back doors but didn't exit. The stage lights kept him in the shadows. Misty swayed and took a few staggering steps. A murmur ran through the audience. I saw Tara from the corner of my eye, heading back on stage. Misty stared at me, but I was certain she didn't see me at all.

"Let's hear it for Misty, everyone." Tara had her microphone and was addressing the audience. Misty closed the gap between us, her face unnaturally pale. I rushed forward and caught her as she collapsed.

The curtains closed and the stagehand, previously working the lights, ran to help me get Misty off the stage. We half carried her into the small reception room at the back of the stage. Misty was shaking uncontrollably.

"We should call for an ambulance," I said.

"No. No ambulance. She'll be fine." I looked up as Tara rushed in.

"She doesn't look fine to me, Tara. She's having some sort of seizure."

Misty's eyes lifted to mine, beseechingly. "I felt the darkness…it was so cold."

"You're okay. You're safe now." But I knew I couldn't protect her from her own mind. No one could.

She struggled to sit up. The stagehand rushed to the kitchenette area and poured a glass of water. Tara sat down next to her and pulled her up against her shoulder, making soothing noises while stroking her hair.

A knock sounded at the door.

"Everything okay back here?"

Tara stood up. Her smile materialized as she saw Shaun at the door.

"Shaun. Yes. She's just exhausted. It was a very intense night for her, wouldn't you say." Tara deftly manoeuvred him away from the door and I could hear her babbling as she ushered him away.

Misty struggled to sit up. I slid a hand behind her back as she reached for the glass of water, the water sloshing down the front of her blouse, her hand shaking as she took a sip.

"Should I call someone?" the stagehand asked as he took the glass from her.

Misty shook her head. "I'll be fine."

He placed the glass of water down on the side table next to the couch, nodded at me and headed off to do whatever he needed to do.

"Now really, are you okay, Misty?"

Misty clutched at my arm. "He was here, Jorja. I felt him. A dark energy. It felt like my soul was being sucked out of my body." Her eyes were round, her pupils dark with fear. "I saw the devil, Jorja. He's real."

Many of the living had glimpsed the devil. He came in different disguises. Sometimes he lived in a bottle or a syringe.

"I noticed you stayed on this side of the stage. Was there someone or something in the audience that made you reluctant to cross centre stage?"

"That's where he was. I felt him."

"Did you see someone you recognized?"

"No. The stage lights were so bright; I could only make out people in the first few rows. Even when they raised the lights later, I couldn't see much past the first five or six rows."

"Right at the end, did you notice a man get up and head to the back of the room?"

"No," she shook her head vehemently. "I didn't see anyone."

Tara breezed back in. "Misty. How are you doing? People are waiting out there. Are you up for your meet and greet?"

"I can't." Her breathing quickened. Her upper lip was damp. "I need to go home."

Tara's smile tightened. "The mayor is out there. And newspaper reporters."

Misty continued to shake her head; her hands fluttered as she tried to wave Tara off. I could see Tara weighing the options—force her into a meet and greet with the public and watch Misty deteriorate into some sort of blithering mess or face Misty's fans alone.

"Maybe best I take her home," I offered.

Tara looked relieved. I helped Misty gather up her things and Tara hustled back to the night's patrons.

"My car is parked out front, but that means going through the crowd. Or there's the back door?"

Misty chose the back-door route. We let ourselves out and I waited until I heard the door click shut behind us. Misty paused, took a deep breath, her shoulders relaxed. She held her hand over her heart and stared up at the night sky. "I'm so glad to be out of there. I can finally breathe."

Now I was the one growing anxious. The alley, dark and narrow, and overlooked by brick walls, closed in on every side. I pulled my purse off my shoulder, comforted by the weight of the ten-inch metal bar inside. Holding my purse ready in one hand, I linked my arm with Misty's and turned down the alley, toward the street.

"Come on, let's go."

I pulled Misty along. The dark brick walls on both sides of the alley loomed above us, cutting off light from the street. My nerves jangled with each step. A noise rustled to my right. My eyes darted to a dark shape, barely noticeable, huddled in a back-entrance recess. Eyes followed us fearfully as we made our way past a dumpster. Ignoring the conflicting urge to dig money out from my purse to hand him or pull out the metal bar, I urged Misty to hurry. *Coward.*

Finally, the alley lightened. The streetlights cast a mellow glow on the path in front of us. I let out my breath. I jumped as something swooshed past my head and landed with a thud in front of us. Misty screamed. Dust rose from the ground and blurred my vision. I tightened my hold on Misty's arm and ran, dragging her, screaming, behind me.

FIFTEEN

MISTY'S HANDS SHOOK as she tried to unlock the entrance door. I took the key from her and a minute later we were inside her condo.

"What happened? Where are we?"

"You're okay, Misty. You're home. Someone knocked a bag of sand off the roof of the Legion Hall when we were leaving. Don't you remember?" She looked ashen. I led her to the couch. Her skin felt cool, clammy.

"Here, lie down." I grabbed one of the throw cushions and stuffed it under her feet, elevating them slightly. Her pupils filled her eyes. Their lacklustre blackness frightened me. She was in shock.

I ran down the short hall and found a bedroom. Misty wasn't fine. I should call 911. I pulled a blanket off the foot of the bed and hurried back. I stopped. My eyes roved around the room. "Misty?"

I turned back down the hall. I checked the bathroom and then poked my head into the bedroom where I had been a minute ago. Empty. I crossed the hall and checked the second bedroom. My heart pounded against my chest and I reached out a hand to steady myself against the wall.

"Misty?" I moved cautiously back down the hall to the living room. My purse lay on the coffee table, the metal bar inside. "Misty? Where are you?"

I peered around the end of the wall. She wasn't in the kitchen. I slid softly into the living room. A faint breeze swirled at my feet. I looked up; the patio door was open. Blood rushed through my head. I blew out through pursed lips, took a huge breath, and crept to the coffee table. I unzipped my bag and pulled out my cell phone and ten-inch metal bar. The bar was a present from Mike the day we celebrated the arrival of my PI license. He said it would last longer than flowers. I looked down at the hand gripping it, the blue artery in my wrist pulsing. The frailty of life suddenly as thin as the skin stretching over it.

I keyed 911 into the keypad, gripped the metal bar tighter and inched my way to the patio doors. At the door, I paused, took a deep breath and flicked on the outdoor light.

Misty stood in the spot where Lori Watson had been found. Her lips moved silently.

I peered into the shadows, then stepped outside. "Misty. Come inside. Now." The sharpness of my tone seemed to cut through to her.

"Jorja. He was here. I feel his presence. He was here."

I took her arm and pulled her back inside, sliding and locking the patio door behind us.

"I know he was here. It's where you found the murdered woman. Lori Watson."

"No. From the gala."

"From the gala? What are you talking about?"

I led her back to the couch and tucked the blanket around her shoulders as she sat back down.

"The same dark energy I felt tonight, at the gala. The same presence was here. Just now."

I shivered in spite of myself. For one split second I wondered if she could be mentally unbalanced.

"Tell me what you remember from the gala about this dark energy you're talking about."

"I was nervous tonight. More so than usual. But once I was on stage and engaging with people, I loosened up. I felt fine."

"I noticed the same thing. You seemed to be having a good time. The audience loved you. So, what happened?"

"About halfway through I felt this dark energy coming from the right side of the room. To my right. I ignored it best I could. Once the lights came on it got a hundred times worse. Irrational thoughts filled my head. I couldn't see the audience—just the first few rows, really. But I could feel him." She started to shake.

"It's okay. You're fine now. Then you opened up your event to answer questions from the audience."

"Right."

"Tell me about what you felt like then."

"I felt claustrophobic. The lights were so bright. Their beams pinned me to the spot. I couldn't move. I heard voices asking questions and I did my best to answer. I couldn't even tell where in the room they were coming from. Or which voices were real and which ones were in my head. I was a sitting duck for anyone out there who wanted to kill me. I think I started hallucinating. The lights became beams from his eyes, evil eyes, pinning me to the stage. Like some bug."

"I noticed you became more agitated, after the lights were raised. You were standing just to the left of centre stage. You looked to your left several times but never to your right."

"That's where it was worse. To my right."

"What did you see or feel? What was worse?"

"Dark energy. The killer was there tonight. I know it." Misty's breaths came quicker now. She looked furtively over her shoulder.

"He was here tonight too. Out there. On the patio."

A string of fear rippled down my spine. I suddenly realized how easy it would be for someone to be watching us. I got up and crossed to the patio doors. My eyes dropped to the latch, confirming it was closed. I flipped a bird at the darkness, angry at the thought that the killer might be standing out there, and pulled the blinds closed.

"I'll get the list of attendees from Tara tomorrow. Maybe you'll spot a familiar name."

Misty nodded, but I didn't think she was listening.

"I don't think you should stay here tonight. I could take you to a hotel. Or you could stay at my place. I'm overnighting at a friend's place and my condo is free for the night, if you want it."

"Thanks, but I'm too exhausted to go anywhere. I'm going to sleep on the couch. With the lights on."

"If you're sure?"

"I'll be okay." She looked up and nodded gratefully, wiping her face with a corner of the blanket.

We were both exhausted. The adrenaline had been pounding through my veins ever since someone threw the fifty-pound bag of sand off the legion roof when were leaving. "You sure you're okay?"

Misty nodded mutely.

"I'll come by tomorrow to check on you. Okay?"

Misty got up and drew a shaky breath. She followed me to the front door. I waited until she locked up behind me. I had a dozen questions for her, but we'd both been through enough tonight.

I walked down the corridor, stepped outside, reached back, and gave the entrance door a last pull to make sure it was locked. A movement on the staircase inside caught my eye. I craned my neck but saw no one there. I waited. Nothing moved. Probably just someone heading upstairs to their unit. I hurried down the lit sidewalk and stepped out into the darkness of the street.

SIXTEEN

I PRESSED THE BUZZER for the umpteenth time. Misty wasn't answering. *She could be in the shower.* Ten minutes later I tailgated two young men into the building.

Misty didn't answer my repeated knocks on her door, each progressively louder. I called her cell. No answer. Her lack of response to my earlier texts worried me—especially after what happened last night.

I banged on the door with my palm. "Misty, it's Jorja. Open up." I thought about going around to knock on her patio door but if she was home, it would likely scare the bejeezus out of her.

"Misty." I knocked louder. I heard the worry in my voice. "If you don't open the door, I'm calling the police."

Several tense minutes slid by. I heard the chain being lifted. The door opened a crack. Misty's hair stood on end, her mascara smudged under puffy eyes. A deep pillow crease dented one cheek.

"Sorry," she mumbled. "I didn't sleep a wink last night. I finally took some sleeping pills around seven this morning. What time is it?"

"Four o'clock."

"Friday?"

"Yes, Friday." I followed her back to the living room. "If you show me where you keep your coffee, I'll make you some while you go freshen up."

Misty pointed to the fridge and stumbled down the hall to the washroom. A blanket and scrunched pillow lay on the couch. The silk tunic she wore last night lay crumpled on the floor. I did a quick calculation in my head. The sleeping pills should be wearing off soon, assuming she only took one or two.

Coffee was made and my laptop open on her kitchen table by the time she reappeared, her hair wet from the shower.

"Thanks. My head still feels fuzzy, but I needed that."

"Tara sent me a list of the attendees and the dates of the events and group readings you held in the last six weeks."

I looked over at Misty sitting next to me. She cradled her coffee cup to her chest with both hands, and her eyes stared unblinking at the open computer screen.

"I entered all the dates of the events at the top of the spreadsheet, attendee names underneath."

She nodded and I thought I saw a flicker of interest cross her face.

"You told me that you've been overcome with dread at several of your readings. That you felt a dark energy or presence in the room. I know it happened at the gala last night, the large reading you did at the Plaza theatre last month and this reading here." I pointed to the column containing the names and date of the reading I attended at Misty's shop the day after she hired me. Misty sat up. Maybe the coffee kicked in.

"Do you remember which other readings left you with similar feelings?"

"Yes, this one two weeks ago and…ummm, this one here." She pointed at the screen. "It was the very next one after my first group session at the Plaza."

I scanned the list of names who attended events on the dates

Misty flagged. Only five names overlapped two or more of the sessions. None of the overlapping names attended all five sessions, but two of them had attended three of the sessions during which Misty sensed a dark presence. I sat back, disappointed. If this were a test I'd been running in my lab back in the day I would have declared the results inconclusive.

"I guess I shouldn't have expected it to be this easy." I placed an asterisk behind the names of the individuals who had been present at two or more readings. "Do you know or remember any of these people?"

Misty peered closer. "I recognize some of the names in these lists, but none of the ones marked with an asterisk."

"Okay. What about the reading I attended?" I pointed at the screen. "There were only seven people at that reading, besides myself. Do you know any of the others?" I pointed to a D. Rieckhoff. "Do you know this person? The name shows up on the reading you flagged at the Plaza a month ago."

"Ummm, let me think. The young woman, the one whose mother came forward, her first name was Chelsie. The man who I read that day was Mr. Stavros. He stayed after the reading to introduce himself and to thank me. That leaves the older couple, the young man with the dark glasses, the two cute middle-aged gays and the other woman, remember, dark hair, fiftyish?"

"Right. Well that didn't get us as far as I'd like but it's a start. Tara said she'd send me the gala list tomorrow. The photographer will have the raw video she took at the gala to her by Monday. Maybe you'll spot someone or something from the gala list or the video."

Misty nodded, stood up and headed to the kitchen for a refill. As soon as she was back, I asked her the question that had been preying on my mind.

"Why don't you want to talk about anyone from your past?"

"I…I just don't."

"Look, you insist it's not your ex Doug. You hold back some pretty significant information about his behaviour, you think Peoria has it in for you—your words, not mine—but claim you don't know why."

"But I don't."

"Okay, I can buy that. You keep saying it's no one from your past. You say you're too busy to have any friends, so that leaves us with Tara, her assistant Natalie, and what? A psycho?"

Misty stared into her coffee cup; her lips puckered then drooped.

It could be a psycho or a serial killer but whoever it was, they were watching, waiting, sending her clear messages of harm. "I'm going to run these five names down, to see what I can find out about them. It's not much of a lead. None of them attended all of the sessions where you experienced distress, but maybe they noticed something." I wasn't going to hold my breath.

She nodded but I could tell her mind was elsewhere. She rested her elbows on the table and rubbed her temples. "I was afraid of this."

I looked over at her. "Afraid of what?"

"I couldn't prevent her death. I may have even caused it."

"What do you mean? Whose death? Lori Watson's?"

"I'm not always successful, you know. I saw my father's death when I was eight. A fiery crash. Several weeks later he was killed on the Coquihalla Highway. A semi lost control, jackknifed, and swept my father's car off the highway and down a ravine. The trucker was fine, my father's burnt body, charred remains. There have been other incidents over the years. A little boy died, choked to death on the playground by the lanyard he wore around his neck—his school ID. I saw it before it happened, but I couldn't tell which school in time to warn them. Why am I sent these visions only to fail at preventing the horrible outcomes? I've even started to believe that I'm somehow to blame."

"Blame how?"

She looked up with angst. "What if I am not predicting these deaths but invoking them?"

I hadn't expected the conversation to go here—this was so fucked up. I could maybe stay open to the idea of extrasensory perception, to the idea some people could see auras, other people's individual energy fields. But not this.

"Misty, look at me."

Her eyes lifted to mine. The fear was gone, replaced by an emptiness that frightened me more than anything she said.

"You came to me for help. You need to trust me. You see things, notice things others can't. Put enough of these together and suddenly something clear emerges. We all make thousands of tiny predictions every day. Contemplating when a light will turn red, who is at the door, or if a child running fast will fall. Scientists know the brain can accurately foretell what is going to happen when it comes to mundane events in our lives, and now they're beginning to look at the brain's ability to use the same process for making predictions about events further out. You have the ability to do that. But I refuse to believe you have the power to control what happens. That only happens in Stephen King novels."

A glimmer of something in her eyes told me I had broken through the despair that registered there.

"Stay positive, focus on something else, and stay vigilant. Don't go walking down any dark, deserted alleys. Most of all, don't put someone else's behaviour or their actions on your shoulders. We all have free will. Everyone gets to make their own choices. God, listen to me. And that's the end of my sermon." I laughed.

"Thanks, Jorja."

"I'll send you a copy of the spreadsheet I made. Have a look at the sessions where you felt negative energy and enter anything you know about any of the attendees in the column next to their names. Or make a note if you remember something that happened at one of these events. Something you didn't expect or found odd. If any of the names from the gala show up on the sessions you flagged, I'll add them to the spreadsheet and send you the update. We can go over it when we meet at Tara's office on Monday."

Misty's phone rang as I closed my laptop. She turned to answer it. A guttural noise erupted behind me. Misty's phone hit the floor.

Misty bent over, clutching her stomach. Her mouth was open but there was no sound. I rushed over to her.

"What's wrong? What is it?"

Misty moaned and started shaking. I looked at the phone and picked it up.

"Hello?"

At first, I heard nothing. I thought it might be a wrong number, but then I heard it. Someone was on the line.

"Hello? Who is this?"

A few seconds passed and whoever it was disconnected.

"Who was it?"

Misty's face was white. She was gulping in air.

"Slow down, slow down. You're going to hyperventilate." I sat next to her as she perched on the edge of the couch. "Now breathe in—one...two...three." After a few minutes Misty had her breathing under control.

"It was him." A great shudder rippled through her.

"Him? Who?"

"The killer." Misty gulped in a shaky breath.

"Slow down. How do you know?"

"He said so."

"Tell me exactly what you heard."

"I picked up and said hello. At first, I thought there was no one there. Like all the other times. Then I heard a man's voice. It sounded strange. Like a robot. The voice said, 'I killed her.'"

"That's it? He didn't mention Lori by name?"

Misty shook her head.

I opened her phone log, copied the most recent number into my phone, then opened the information on the number. It was a local number but gave no other hints as to who the caller was. I held Misty's phone for a second then hit redial.

The phone rang ten times before I disconnected.

"No answer, no voice mail." I sat back and thought for a second. "It's probably a crank call. Your name is in the paper, that story Shaun Allen wrote. The one about you predicting a woman's death. The article claims Lori Watson was that woman and that you and I are working together to solve her murder. This is exactly what I was afraid of."

"What do I do?"

"You need to let Detective Brighton know. It's probably a crank call, but we can't chance that it's not."

We both sat silently for a minute.

"My help isn't always welcomed in these situations, especially by the police," Misty said.

"I get it. Calgary Police Services might not be as keen to work with a psychic as the Bozeman Police were when you helped out on the Tanner case." It was an understatement. I knew the head of Special Crimes, Luis Azagora. He didn't tolerate visions, premonitions—or feelings. On the other hand, his hard-nosed logical, unemotional approach was the very thing that attracted me to him. That and the fact that he was smokin' hot.

"Look, I'm not saying you need to go into detail about your premonition but telling them Lori Watson was dressed similarly

to you the day she was murdered outside *your* condo might interest them. That sack of sand dropped from the top of the legion
was real. One or the other of us could have easily been killed, or
badly injured. Now you've had a phone call from someone claiming to have killed Watson. These are not premonitions. They are
real. Promise me you'll think about it."

"I will."

The way she averted her eyes told me that thinking about it
was all she was going to do.

SEVENTEEN

A SLIGHT MOVEMENT IN Mike's neighbour's living room curtains told me my arrival was being monitored. I picked up the bundle of flyers off Mike's front step, let myself in and pulled off my boots. I tossed the flyers into the recycle bin and made my way to the kitchen. Smitty meandered in from the back hall and greeted me in his usual fashion. His food dish still held a bit of food. Wess' dish was licked clean.

Smitty's lack of urgency to get me to refill his bowl told me what I already knew. Smitty rubbed himself against my legs, then walked off. *Just as I thought.* I sighed, ground up some chicken, cleaned the cat bowls and loaded up fresh food and water. The internet article I had read said it was important to keep up with the cat's routine, in the event Wess was hiding.

Smitty was sitting on a stool looking out the front room window. I took a photo of him and printed it off using Mike's printer. He and Wess were almost identical in appearance, Smitty's hair only slightly lighter in colour than Wess'. The test copy I printed convinced me the likeness was good enough and copy quality poor enough that the real difference wouldn't be noticeable. If I didn't get Wess back, I'd never forgive myself.

As dusk descended, I grabbed my flashlight, pulled on my

boots and coat, and headed outside. I knelt and shone the light under Mike's deck. No bright eyes shone back at me. I got up, dusted off my knees and explored the garage. Slowly, I crept down the alley to the end of the block, calling Wess' name every so often. There were so many places for him to hide—the space between the garage and fence next door, the hedges two doors down, a pile of bricks and lumber standing ready, across the alley, for some summer project.

Back at Mike's I shrugged off my coat and breathed on my hands trying to get some warmth back into them. The posters were now spread for blocks across the neighbourhood. Suddenly hungry, I opened the fridge and eyed the remaining chicken breast on the top shelf. I closed the door, disgusted that I momentarily considered eating Smitty and Wess' food. I opened the cupboard and poked through the flour, sugar, cooking oil and spices. The urge to eat my body weight in pastries grew stronger. I pulled open the remaining cupboard doors, hoping I had somehow over-looked an entire chocolate cake, or at least a bag of Oreo cookies.

I grabbed Mike's scotch and poured myself several fingers, splashing some on my hand as an image of Wess' body lying dead in a gutter flashed through my mind. *Stop it.* I wanted the day to end, but my wired state wasn't conducive to sleep. I checked all the cupboards, drawers and even opened the oven door although I hadn't cooked a thing since arriving at Mike's. Cradling my drink, I stepped into the living room and sank into the couch. I needed to focus on something else. I lay my head back and closed my eyes.

The house was eerily silent. Something creaked and I heard a metallic thump from the basement. I sat up. Likely the ancient furnace, or one of the pipes. I looked at the glass in my hand. Empty. My eyes fell on the bottle of scotch sitting on the kitchen counter. At this rate, I'd have to get Mike another bottle before he got back.

I unfolded myself and put one foot on the floor, bending to stand up. That's when I saw it. I walked toward it and bent down for a closer look. A rather large black button. I looked back at the couch, which sat three feet away. Smitty now lay on the middle cushion, his front feet tucked in under him, his blue-grey eyes observing. I looked over at the cellar door. The button hadn't been on the floor when I descended the cellar stairs yesterday. I would have seen it. No way it had been there this morning when I left.

I put my glass down and crept through the house. My mind questioned everything. The slightly open closet door, the way the window blinds were positioned. I opened Mike's bedroom door and flicked on the light. Everything looked okay. I walked over to the closet and pulled it open. Inside, the small safe where Mike kept his gun stood locked. I let out a sigh of relief.

I crept back into the living room and stood listening. Nothing. I picked up the flashlight from the kitchen table and slid silently to the cellar door. *What if I open it and he's right there?*

The button wasn't mine. It hadn't been there this morning. I shook out the tension in my shoulders. Maybe Smitty dug the button out from somewhere, from between couch cushions or from under a bed, and paw-handled it into the middle of the living room. I was making too much of this. I walked over to the cellar door and paused.

Don't do it.

I pulled open the cellar door and jumped back. Nothing. I crouched and shone the flashlight at the floor and in an arc around the ladder.

I stepped down three rungs and stopped. Bending over, I peered into the darkness. The air was cool, dank. Every horror story I'd ever watched came flooding back. A woman, alone and scared, ignores common sense and descends into a dark unlit basement. I scurried up the ladder and lowered the cellar door, breathing hard. I dragged the couch over until it sat over the cellar door. Smitty jumped up and ran into the bedroom.

I checked all the doors and windows to make sure they were locked, and pulled the blinds closed. I contemplated removing some of the air vents, in case Wess was hiding in the cellar, then worried that Smitty would pull a disappearing act on me. At least that's what I told myself. I grabbed my laptop, phone and flashlight, closed the bedroom door and propped up the pillows. I climbed in and opened my laptop. The bookcase was still pulled a foot from the wall. Maybe Wess would come up for a visit once the lights were out. *Or something else.*

I shook off the images crowding my head and looked down at my laptop. I stared mindlessly at a newsfeed headline about some tabloid that paid a great deal of money for a salacious tip about Trump. I closed my laptop, shaking my head. Fifteen minutes of my life I wasn't prepared to give up.

Smitty was already curled up on the spare pillow next to me. A loud thump wiped thoughts of sleep out of my head. Someone had set fire to Mike's fence. Someone had been in the house. Was someone targeting Mike? Or were they targeting me? I slid out of bed and pulled the chair out from behind the desk and wedged the back up against the door handle. Shivering, I climbed back into bed, reached up and turned off the light. A minute later my fingers fumbled across the top of the nightstand. The cool, smooth surface and weight of the flashlight were reassuring as I slid it under my pillow.

I lay there for what seemed like hours, my mind a jumble of thoughts. What if the whole purpose of Misty's vision was to find me? What if I was the dark-haired woman?

EIGHTEEN

A FLICKER SHOWED UP at five a.m. and started its insistent pounding on Mike's house. Hard to believe a bird that small could be so annoying. I was ready for Mike to come back. The week had flown by, but I wasn't sleeping well at night. Every creak, groan and thump sent my imagination racing. Maybe the fence fire wasn't an act of vandalism. Had someone wanted to draw me out of the house? I shuddered. Had they hidden in the house until I left? Were they still in the cellar? The whole idea creeped me out. Then what? As far as I could tell, nothing was missing. Why enter the house and take nothing? *Maybe they left more than a button.*

I threw back the covers and pulled the chair away from the door. Smitty shot out of the room as soon as I stepped into the hall. After fixing his breakfast, I crept through the house, looking into every nook and cranny, lifted lamps to check underneath, felt along the top of each shelf and cupboard. My search revealed nothing, no listening devices, no hidden camera. I stared at the cellar door. I had warned Misty not to walk alone on deserted lanes or descend into creepy dark cellars. I needed to heed my own advice.

The coffee machine beeped. I poured myself a cup, pushed

aside the folded newspaper I had retrieved from Mike's front step and sank into the couch. Hugging the coffee cup to my chest, I lay back and closed my eyes. I was a mess. I had spent the better part of last year training myself to be positive, to not let crappy little things get me down. But it had all disappeared in a minute, replaced by my seven-step program to making myself miserable. A process I had down pat. First—imagine the worst, no, even worse than that. Revisit the past, remember every horrible little thing that's ever happened. Tell yourself things will never get better, take every little thing personally, remind yourself that you're all alone and the people in your life really don't care. Exhausted from wallowing in my misery, I tried to lift my spirits by reminding myself that pessimism is a critical aspect of survival.

I startled at the sound of my phone. Keeping one eye on the cellar door, I hustled back to the kitchen, picked it up off the counter and hit accept.

"Tara. Hi. What's up?"

"Just checking to see if we're still on for tomorrow?"

"Yup. I'm good if you are."

"All set. I just got the video and checked it to make sure I could open the file. Have you heard from Misty? I'm really worried about her."

"Not today. Why?"

"She texted me last night. Actually, 3:00 a.m. this morning. She's closing her shop. Wants me to cancel all her readings, interviews and public events."

"For good?"

"I hope not. She has an interview on Breakfast Television coming up and I'm trying to get her on the CTV Morning Show."

"Did she say why?"

"She says she feels responsible for what happened to that

woman. The one who was killed in front of her condo. She wants to focus on helping the Watson family find her killer."

"Did she mention the phone call she got?"

"No, what phone call?"

"Someone called her claiming to have killed Lori Watson. I advised her to talk to Detective Brighton about it. You know, in case it's not a crank call."

"You mean someone is threatening her?"

"In a manner of speaking, yes. I'm not happy about Shaun Allen's article. Telling the world she's working on the Watson murder opens her up to all kinds of potential harassment."

"That may be, but this won't be the first time she's gone after criminals."

I had read Tara right. She seemed more concerned about Misty missing her public appearance than her state of mind.

"Well, someone might be trying to cancel her performances permanently. Let's hope we get a clue or two from the video as to who or what she sees at her readings that might be triggering her fear."

"The sooner we can get this over with the better."

"By the way, thanks for sending me the list of attendees. I've whittled the previous lists down to five names I'm interested in. Only one of those names was on the gala list. Maybe there's something there, maybe not."

"Glad to be of help."

"Right. See you tomorrow."

Detective Brighton wasn't going to be thrilled to hear that Misty planned to put her full focus on finding Lori's killer. If the killer had intended to kill Misty, and killed Lori by mistake, she would be putting herself right in the killer's path. It was a gutsy move on her part, or pure stupidity.

I glanced at my watch. A thought had entered my head

sometime during the night. Misty's premonition, the vandalism, and frightening messages she received, and Lori Watson's death, may be separate, unrelated events. Since Misty was hell-bent on finding Lori Watson's killer, my best bet would be to focus on who was harassing her. Maybe it would lead us to the same place or maybe not. A metallic thump sounded from below. I hurried to pack up.

The street in front of my office building was blessedly empty, a rarity considering its proximity to downtown and numerous furniture stores and art galleries. Then again, it was Sunday. I parked just feet from the front door and let myself in. The light in the entry was off, the doors to the small café locked, the café dark. I headed to the staircase and took the stairs two at a time. The corridor was dim, none of the light from the lobby making its way to the second floor. The landlord was one cheap bastard, who reminded tenants when they complained about the state of the building that you get what you pay for.

Technically, my best friend, Gab Rizzo, was the lease holder of our office space. One of her exes stiffed her with the lease and took off for greener pastures. The lease had no early-release clause and locked her in until November of this year. Gab and I started sharing the space and the rent right after I got my PI licence and she set up her personal chef catering business. Neither of us got many visitors to the office, but it was close to downtown and provided a convenient place to hang one's hat for a few hours. We still hadn't figured out what we would do come November. But for now, with Gab off attending a cousin's wedding in Mexico, I had the whole decrepit place to myself.

I looked over my shoulder at the empty hall, unlocked the

door and flipped on the lights. They buzzed and flickered, slowly emitting a sickly bluish-white glow. I plunked my laptop on the desk in the reception area and poked my head into the back office, then checked behind the door. I felt relieved when I found no one crouched there with a long-bladed knife in hand.

The events of the last few days left me unnerved. I was worried about Mike's daughter, Julie, and heartsick about losing Wess. The idea that someone torched Mike's garage on purpose and might have gained access to Mike's house had me spooked, and I was annoyed that Shaun Allen and Misty had dragged my name into a story meant to sensationalize Misty's powers and Thursday night's event. A trifecta of emotions—worry, fear, and anger. I sat at the front desk, opened my laptop and logged on.

Misty was insistent that her ex couldn't be behind these attempts to frighten—if not harm—her. She claimed she never felt the dark energy she felt now when she had been with Doug. Had she never been wrong? She's the one who cautioned me that premonitions were open to interpretation.

Why did she feel this dark energy during some readings but not others? She claimed she also felt it on her patio where Lori was killed. Wouldn't that suggest a physical presence? Doug told me he had never attended one of Misty's formal readings. But that had been back then, not now. My eye ran down the lists again, but I already knew his name wasn't there. Logic told me someone was triggering her feelings of dread.

I sat back and rubbed my eyes. Maybe I was going about this all wrong. What if I was trying to make connections where there were none. I knew someone was harassing Misty. The message on her car window, the dead-air phone calls, the dead bird were all good indicators. Until yesterday all I had was Misty's accounts of these incidents. But two nights ago, someone had dropped a sandbag off the roof where Misty was holding an event. Of course, anyone could have made their way up the metal ladder running up the back side of the legion to the flat roof, even earlier in the day. Except someone had known we were leaving by the back door.

At first glance it did look like Lori Watson's death and Misty's premonitions were related. Lori had been killed, strangled, just like in Misty's vision. But I had nothing concrete tying the killer or Lori Watson to any of the earlier threats to Misty. What if whoever was harassing Misty and whoever killed Watson were two different people, for two different reasons.

I got up and paced the small room. Who, what, and why? Those, of course, were the proverbial questions. Unfortunately, who and why were intricately linked. Who could be doing this? Last night someone tried to kill or seriously injure Misty. The one thing I knew for certain was that it wasn't some netherworld creature who had lifted that bag over the ledge. It was human. That probably narrowed it down to a dozen people at best. I needed to find out who of that dozen might have a motive.

I pulled up the City of Calgary website and searched recent development permits. Urban Works, on behalf of Lehman Group, had filed and been granted a permit for the redevelopment of the building Misty and Peoria Benson occupied. The initial open house and online public engagement phase, outlining the plan to convert the residential units on the second floor into commercial storefront space, had met no resistance from the community. Most of the feedback was concerned about the lack of parking in an already congested neighbourhood.

Could the attacks on Misty—the dead bird, the dead-air calls, the message on her car windshield—be attempts to sway Misty to close shop? Sell her piece of the property to Lehman Group? I sat back and rubbed my eyes. Why would Misty's tiny space be of such importance to them?

I remembered Peoria's face when she talked about Misty's shop. Like she had just opened the refrigerator and discovered a month-old zucchini, oozing under the fresh tomatoes. Interestingly, Misty's shop was now closed until further notice. Of course, a woman's death had led to that and I was working on the premise that the two weren't connected.

I called Misty. It went to voice mail. I'd barely hung up when I heard footsteps thundering down the hallway. Someone on a mission. The door burst open. Doug Liederbach stood in the doorway, fists clenched.

"What did you say to the cops? And that bitch you're protecting."

"I have no idea what you're talking about."

He took a step toward me. His face taut, his lips pinched tight.

I stood up. "Hey, calm down. What happened?"

"The cops came to see me. Said someone saw me in front of Misty's place the night they found that dead girl."

"So?"

"So? They think I killed her. I didn't even know her. Why would I kill her?"

I shrugged. "The cops must have reason to think you did if they're hassling you. Didn't they tell you why?"

"They gave me some bullshit about me stalking Misty after we broke up."

"Did you?"

"She's lying. I didn't touch her. I never even talked to her. That bitch is always lying."

"Why are you telling *me* this? What is it that you think I can do for you?"

"If you're not in on it, then you're a lot dumber than you look."

"In on what?"

"Misty's little publicity stunt. How convenient that she *sees* a dark-haired woman who will be killed. How convenient that a dark-haired woman is killed in front of her condo. How convenient that a reporter just happens to be interviewing her and gets to hear about Misty's self-proclaimed premonition."

"What are you saying? That Misty had that poor woman killed so it would appear her predictions were true?"

"You think I'm kidding? For your information, that psycho bitch you're protecting has killed before."

"What do you mean?"

"Just like I thought. She didn't tell you, did she?" His chest heaved. I looked at his face, red with the effort of restraining himself.

"You tell that bitch I was nowhere near her condo that night or any other night for that matter. If she thinks she saw me, she's delusional. She better let the cops know too. Otherwise, I might just have to share my little story with them. Or that reporter. I'm sure he'll find it interesting. *I'm* the one who should be afraid of her—and you should be too." He turned and stormed off.

What the hell was that? Were Misty and Tara creating the most outrageous publicity stunt ever? Is that why I was so bothered about the whole newspaper article mentioning me. That at some level I had considered the possibility myself. But how would she have known a dark-haired woman, like the one in her vision, would be killed? It couldn't be a coincidence.

I sank back down into my chair. Now that Liederbach was gone, I realized I was shaking. Had I just seen a sample of the anger that drove Doug's previous girlfriend to file a restraining order and made Misty uneasy whenever his name came up. Misty had been adamant she didn't want to draw attention to him. So why had the police paid him a visit? They must have checked his background, looked up the restraining order filed against him, confirmed that he still drove a grey Impala and decided it was prudent to pay him a visit.

Or maybe they talked to Becca Katz and she told them about the games he liked to play before sex, that he had anger management issues and owned a shitload of guns. Was Liederbach every bit as dangerous as Becca Katz thought? At least he was on their radar now.

Was his comment about Misty having killed someone just angry rhetoric? Or is that why Misty refused to talk about her past?

NINETEEN

A CREW WAS HARD at work removing the windows from the second floor of Misty's building. Scaffolding had been erected over the sidewalk to protect pedestrians from falling debris. The closed sign was prominently displayed in Misty's store window. Healing Waters was advertising a Spring Tone-Up. Today the ranting street preacher had some kind of metal contraption strapped to his back. Closer scrutiny revealed it was an old ironing board frame. The narrow end towered two feet over his head and had a cardboard star attached to the top. He noticed me peering at him. *Shit.*

I looked away, rolled up the window and double-checked the door locks.

"Hey, you!" He stepped off the sidewalk and walked to my car. "I'm not afraid of you. You know why? God made me. He protects me." He held his arms out, his body forming a cross, the top of the ironing board now dangerously close to an overhanging street sign.

Why couldn't the damn light turn green?

"Judge not and you shall not be judged. Beware of Satan. He has fornicated with our women, with our animals. You will know those that have the blood of Satan in them. They salute the world with the sign of the dead."

The light turned green and the cars in front of me inched forward. He walked alongside my car until I sped up. His words followed me as I drove off.

"For true and righteous are his judgments. For he has judged the great whore, which did corrupt the earth with her fornication."

What was with him and whores? Damn, that was one messed-up guy.

I parked in a strip mall and arrived at Tara's at the same time as Misty. Her hair hung in greasy strands below a black fedora she had jammed low on her forehead. The faux leopard-fur coat and wool pashmina wound around her neck looked out of kilter for the warmth of the day. Her hands shook as she reached for the door handle.

Tara already had her computer set up. She urged us to sit and offered us water or coffee. Misty removed her coat, leaving her hat and scarf in place. Her eyes reflected far more fear than I knew were in mine. This was real. But real what? Was she being tortured by her premonition, which now seemed to have reached obsessive levels, or mental illness? Or could this be an Oscar-worthy performance?

I sat down as Tara returned with two cups of coffee.

"Here you go, ladies. Ready to see the video?" She looked from me to Misty then back again and raised her eyebrows. Misty picked up her coffee cup and stared into its depths.

I nodded. "Okay. Let's roll this thing."

The video was short, thirty minutes at most. The intent was to cut it down to several ten-second shots that would end up as less than a minute-long trailer to add to Misty's website and social media.

The photographer didn't capture the whole audience—most

of the video focused on Misty and the first two rows, where the special guests had been seated. We watched it twice. It was obvious Misty became fixated on avoiding the right side of the room halfway through the event.

The second time through, I noticed her interaction with the audience and how the questions she asked were formulated to solicit information. "How does the colour yellow resonate with you? Do the numbers five or twelve mean anything to you?" Questions the audience participants were eager to answer. *Brilliant.*

"Notice anything?" I asked after we finished watching it for the second time.

Misty shook her head. "I remember feeling very uncomfortable with the right side of the room. Now that I see the video, I'm shocked at how obvious it was."

"You don't seem upset watching the video, now."

"I'm not surprised that the presence I felt isn't here, now. It never is when technology is involved. I know there are people out there trying to deduce spirit energy fields with special heat-sensing equipment and such but that's not how it works with me."

"What did you see that made you avoid the right side of the stage?"

"I don't know. If I saw something or someone it's not registering at the level of consciousness."

"Did you notice the man who got up and walked to the back of the room right before the event ended?"

"No. The lights were so blinding I couldn't see past the first few rows."

"How did you make out with the list of names I left you?"

Misty pulled out some crumpled pages from her purse and spread them out in front of me. "I recognized thirty names from the gala, but only one of them attended any of the other events where I felt this dark energy. Someone named Les Bagoda. I don't know him. A lot of the names I do recognize are of the special guests sitting in the front rows."

"Yeah, I double-checked. Other than Bagoda, I don't see any of the gala attendee names showing up on the events you flagged where you remember feeling disturbed. You sure none of these names mean anything to you?"

"No. They don't. I told you."

I turned to Tara. "Is there any possibility one of these other five people we've flagged could have been at the gala on Thursday night? Somehow got in without registering?"

"We do take walk-ins at the bigger events—assuming there are seats available."

"Was that the case on Thursday night?"

"Yes. I think we had about fifteen spots left when the doors opened. But those were snapped up well before the event started. We would have taken their names when they paid at the door and made up a name tag. Their names were added to the list I sent you."

"Could they have paid with cash?"

"Yes."

"So, it's possible someone could have given a fake name and slapped on a name tag and entered the auditorium that way."

"I suppose."

I groaned silently. So much for my semi-logical approach. If I intended to harass, stalk, or kill someone, I'd probably use a fake name as well. I stood up and walked over to the window. Every lead I had was leading nowhere. And who is to say the person or presence Misty was feeling couldn't have been a server or one of the maintenance crew. I looked back at Tara and Misty. Their conversation had shifted to Misty's upcoming events. I snapped to full alertness at hearing my name. Misty was telling Tara about the phone call she received from someone claiming to have killed Lori Watson.

"Did you let Detective Brighton know?" I asked.

"No. I meant to call him but forgot."

My eyes met hers and she looked away. "There isn't much I can tell him. You tried the number from the caller. It went nowhere. He probably used one of those cheap throw-away phones, or perhaps a stolen one."

"Still. The police may be able to find information I can't." I pushed away my growing annoyance, returned to the table and sat. "An interesting visitor showed up at my office yesterday. Doug Liederbach."

Tara groaned; Misty sat up. "What did he want?"

"Seems the police paid him a visit. He wasn't happy about it."

"See. This is what I was afraid of."

"Misty, the man may actually be a danger."

"I wish you hadn't gone to interview him. It's bad enough one of us is in danger."

"Now you're telling me you think Liederbach is dangerous? And that he might harm me?"

Misty remained silent. Tara excused herself and headed to the washroom.

"I want to approach this as scientifically as possible. I'm looking at things we can see and touch or hear. You add another source of information to the situation—a level of detail I can't hear or see."

Misty nodded.

"We have five names. Harris, Bagoda, Rieckhoff, Palmer and Lee. Each of them were at two or more of the readings during which you sensed a dark energy. You saw the video. There is someone or something in the audience that is making you afraid. Maybe it's not one of these five but it's somebody."

Misty nodded reluctantly. "It appears that way, doesn't it?"

"I want to find these individuals. Once I find them, I'd like you to see them in person, see if they illicit any reaction from you. Assuming these names are real, of course."

"And if they don't?"

"Well, then we're no worse off than we are now. And if one of them used a fake name, I'll certainly be interested in finding out why. You're obviously still sensing danger. You were receiving threats before Lori Watson was murdered and still are. Maybe she was the woman in your vision or maybe not. Either way, someone threw a sandbag at you leaving the gala a few days ago. Someone called you claiming to be Lori Watson's killer. Maybe the killer phoned to taunt you, your psychic abilities. Or maybe it was a prank call. At this point, I have no bloody idea what is connected and what is not. I can accept that a spirit may be trying to send you a message, but whoever killed Lori Watson is real. The phone call was real, the threats are real. Whoever is doing these things knows you, either from the present or the past."

"Why do you think the killer knows me?"

"I'm using the term lightly. Let's just say whoever is harassing you—threatening you—knows who you are, what you do, where you work, where you live, your phone number, what kind of car you drive, not to mention the public information out there about events and where you will be on certain days or evenings, and now of course who you are working with."

Misty took a shaky breath.

"Why are you working so hard to hide your past?"

"I'm not. There's nothing in my past but old hurt and pain. I have no desire to resurrect any of it."

"Someone might be working hard to make sure your past

doesn't stay hidden. Any sins in your past someone may want you to atone for?"

"I don't know what you're talking about."

"Really? What about a murder?"

"Who told you about that?"

"Totally irrelevant. Are you going to tell me about it or are you going to make me dig out the information on my own?"

"It was Doug, wasn't it? Bastard! He has no business bringing up my past. With you or anyone else."

"That may be, but he threatened to go to the papers with whatever story he's got."

"Damn him." Misty grabbed her coat and stormed out onto the street.

TWENTY

I CAUGHT UP TO Misty near the Starbucks, at the end of the street.

"Misty. Talk to me."

"Okay. Okay." She swiped away a tear. "You might as well hear it from me."

Why was I pushing her this hard? Did I really believe her past had anything to do with this? But if I harboured doubts that her past had anything to do with her prediction that she would be killed, her reaction to Doug's comment had me convinced there was something there.

The Starbucks was full, buzzing with conversation and laughter. We ordered coffees and waited, finally snagging a table in the far corner. I waited while Misty made two trips to the bar to add more sugar and cream. She settled into her chair, took off her coat, rearranging it several times on the back of her chair, and took a sip.

"Promise you'll keep what I tell you to yourself." She looked at the tables nearest to us and glanced over her shoulder. No one was paying us any attention.

"Who or why would I tell?"

"Okay," she sighed. "It happened a million years ago. I was

seventeen at the time. A friend of mine killed her husband in self-defence and eventually pleaded guilty to a charge of manslaughter. I was initially charged as an accessory, but the charges were dismissed. And rightly so. I had nothing to do with his death."

"See, not so bad. You're innocent."

"The community passed judgment on us way before the final verdict was read. My family didn't exactly fit the average island resident profile to begin with. My grandmother could read people's auras, their life energy. She could see illness or death before any medical prognosis. People were afraid of her, of us." Misty laughed bitterly. "The thin veil of social acceptance we lived under dropped faster than a canary in a gassy coal mine, once I was charged."

I felt the old familiar churn in my gut. I knew firsthand what it was like to be the focus of a small community's lies and gossip. Misty stared at a spot on the floor somewhere to my left. Emoting sympathy wasn't one of my strengths, but I needed to let her know I felt her pain.

"Believe me, I know how something like that can destroy families. And mess with your mind for a long time."

She nodded gratefully.

"What about your friend? What was her story?"

"She was pregnant at the time. Her husband, Cash, was older than her. He was abusive, especially when drinking. She wanted to leave him but didn't know where to go. We didn't even have a proper high school on the island, let alone somewhere for her to get help. One day he came home, angrier, and drunker than usual and started hitting her. She thought he was going to kill her, and the baby. She grabbed a kitchen knife and fought back."

"I take it he died."

"He died on the way to the hospital. My friend was hurt

pretty bad. It's a miracle she didn't lose the baby. I couldn't believe it when they filed charges against her."

"Why were you charged?"

"I had nothing to do with it."

"So, what happened?

"My friend had been over earlier in the day. We spent a couple of hours dreaming up baby names, laughing, you know, just hanging out. After lunch she wanted to go down to the beach. I wanted to go but my mother wasn't doing well, and I remember she was all in a knot because the place was a mess and we had no food in the house. So, I stayed home to clean. My sister didn't have any problems leaving me to deal with the mess and our mother though. She went to the beach with Carla."

"Your sister! You've never mentioned a sister."

"Yeah—well. I used to have a sister—in another life. Ivy. I haven't seen her in an awfully long time." Misty fiddled with the scarf at her neck. Her eyes swept across the room, the tables filled with people, sharing, talking, laughing.

I could relate. It's hard to tell someone that you have a sibling who doesn't want you in their life.

"Well, you're not alone in that department. As I've gotten older, I've come to realize it's more common than we think. Does your estrangement have something to do with what happened to you and your friend?"

Misty picked up her coffee and held it against her chest. She shook her head as if she still didn't believe it, then nodded. "It had everything to do with it." She took a sip of coffee, sat up and leaned toward me.

"I knew something bad happened the minute Ivy came back from the beach. She said Cash, Carla's husband, was there with two of his buddies. They had been drinking. Cash was angry about something. He started calling Carla names, told her to go home, clean the house, maybe make supper for a change. Carla argued with him. Threatened to leave him. After a while, she left, and Ivy left too. Not long after Ivy got home, Cash showed up looking for Carla. He was totally wasted and furious. He forced his way into the house and was screaming, started pushing me around. I couldn't make sense of half of what he was saying. I was worried for Carla. She'd told me that he shoved her around when he got like that and she was scared of him."

"Couldn't you call the police?"

"Cash's family had money. They owned most of the business on the island. His uncle was police chief. Everyone knew it was pointless to lodge a complaint against a member of the Irving family. They could make life miserable for anyone who did."

"Sounds like a stellar bunch. What did you do?"

"I told Ivy to go—warn Carla. Tell her to leave, to go to her mom's place until Cash cooled down. Ivy went. I finally convinced Cash that Carla wasn't at our place. I told him I thought she had taken the ferry over to Powell River. I wanted to send him off on a goose chase, anything to give Carla time to get out of her house, get somewhere safe."

"What about your mother? Wasn't she home?"

"She was upstairs. Most days she couldn't look after herself, let alone us."

"Must have been frightening."

"It was. I finally convinced him to leave. I knew he shouldn't be driving, but there was no way I could stop him. I was worried that he would get to Carla before Ivy had a chance to warn her."

"You couldn't phone her?"

"Carla didn't have a phone at the house. Cash had a radio phone in his truck but nothing at the house. We had a phone, but it was on a party line. None of us liked to use it. There was always someone listening in."

"So Ivy ran down to warn Carla that her husband was on the war path."

"Yeah. She came crashing through the back door about a half hour later. She was really shaken up, sobbing and not making a lot of sense. I remember being annoyed because she was wearing one of my shirts. The stuff from her closet was strewn all over our room upstairs, but she felt like she could take my stuff whenever she wanted."

Funny how small childhood hurts had a way of lingering.

"Are you and Ivy twins?"

"No. I'm a year older. Eleven months, actually."

"So, what happened?"

"Ivy took the shortcut to Carla's, a path through the woods. Carla didn't answer when Ivy called out to her. She ran up to the house calling Carla's name and opened the back door. She said she saw Carla lying on the floor. And all the blood. She heard someone moan and that's when she noticed Cash lying on the floor by the table. She thought he might get up and attack her. She called for Carla, but Carla wasn't moving. She didn't know how badly either of them were hurt. As soon as I got the gist of what happened, we called the police."

"So how did you get implicated?"

"A witness said he saw me running frantically through the woods. Running away from Carla's house with blood on my shirt, my hands. Well, he got that part right—Ivy had been wearing my shirt. And she had gotten blood all over it."

"Ivy didn't admit it was her? Why?"

"Ivy was always in trouble. She was headstrong, never listened, didn't seem to care if she got into trouble. My mother threatened to send her away if she got into any more trouble. I think I told you, she had health issues and couldn't deal with Ivy. With both our father and grandmother gone, Ivy was pretty much all the family I had. She was a mess. We decided to say I was the one who ran down there to warn Carla, that I found her unconscious and bleeding on the floor. That I had nothing to do with it—which, of course, I didn't."

"Pretty skimpy reason to lay charges. There must have been something else."

I watched the colour come back into Misty's cheeks. She looked away for a moment then took a shaky breath.

"A witness came forward. He helped to cement our version of things by claiming he saw me running back from Carla's." She swallowed hard. "Cash was stabbed with one of our kitchen knives. They found it by the back door."

"Did your sister pick it up? Is that how she got blood on her—I mean, *your*—shirt?"

"She said she couldn't remember, so that's what I said too. Then a friend of ours came forward and said that they heard Carla and I talking about how Cash's family wouldn't let anything happen to her and their precious grandchild if something happened to Cash." She took another breath and let it out with a sigh. "That part, unfortunately, was true. We had talked about it, but we were just kids. I did want Carla to leave Cash. I'd been vocal about it. I didn't like him; he was a bully. People said I had been trying to break them up, that I was spreading rumours about Cash, about Carla. That I had told Cash the baby Carla was carrying wasn't his. That I was the one who caused him to fly into a rage."

"Did you say those things?"

"I never said the baby wasn't his. Carla had a big crush on Cash since she was fifteen. She was seventeen when she married him and was pregnant six months later. But she wasn't happy about his drinking, and he was a mean drunk. There had been rumours that he had been cheating on her."

"Was your sister called to tell her side of the story?"

Misty picked up her coffee with both hands and stared out the window. When she turned back to me her eyes were distant. Her lip trembled.

"I convinced her to keep quiet. The path to Carla's house is treed. I really didn't think anyone could have seen her clearly."

"Your sister happily let you take the brunt of the attention."

"It wasn't like that. She was terrified that she'd be sent to juvie. She drank and stole things; she'd already been caught with drugs. When she turned sixteen, she borrowed her friend's car without asking and rolled it. I spent hours, days, reassuring her everything would be all right. I told her even if something went wrong, they wouldn't do much to me. I was under eighteen when this all happened. In the end, Carla pleaded guilty, said I had nothing to do with it."

"Your friend pleaded guilty? Sounds like self-defence to me."

"It was self-defence. At first, Carla said she didn't remember stabbing Cash, but later she admitted to remembering that she picked up a knife from the kitchen counter. She remembered trying to defend herself with it after he got home and accused her of cheating on him. He started hitting her. She blacked out. The prosecution argued that she had ample time to get away. That she knew drinking caused Cash to become violent, but she encouraged it that afternoon and further enraged him by arguing with him and threatening him."

"Bastards. It's always the same story isn't it—poor little rich boy—trailer-trash girl with her get-pregnant, get-rich scheme."

"Like I said, there was a lot of pressure on the investigating officers to charge someone. Cash's family was wealthy, well known. They wanted to see someone take the blame for their son's death, someone other than Carla, who had been beaten by Cash. They wanted it to be a planned murder, making Cash the victim, not

Carla. They tried to make it sound like Carla and I set the whole thing up to get rid of Cash. Anyway, there was enough confusion and doubt about the time, whether it had been me or Ivy that was seen, the reliability of some of the witness statements, that the charges against me were dismissed at the preliminary hearing."

"And your friend went to prison?"

"Cash was stabbed nine times, five knife wounds to his chest, four to his back. They claimed the level of damage Carla inflicted went beyond defence. Carla's lawyer claimed it was justifiable homicide. The prosecutor thought otherwise. Given the circumstances, she eventually pleaded guilty to manslaughter. She was sentenced to ten years in prison but was eligible for parole after seven."

"What happened to the baby?"

"She put it up for adoption."

I nodded. "The grandparents didn't object?"

"After what happened, they chose to believe the baby wasn't Cash's, that Carla planned all of this to get at their money. The trial was so ugly. Afterwards, they wanted nothing to do with her."

"And you perjured yourself to protect your sister."

"You have to understand. Ivy was all I had left. I didn't want to think about what would happen if anything happened to her." Her hand trembled on the table next to her coffee cup. She shook her head and her voice cracked. "Maybe it was a mistake. I've always protected Ivy. I don't know why. Maybe guilt." She gave a half-hearted shrug. "In retrospect…I may have done her more harm than good."

I let Misty sit in silence. Her blank stare told me she was somewhere else. I glanced at the faces around me, their happy smiles and animated voices jarred with the story unfolding at our table.

"So why the rift between you and your sister?"

"Afterwards, my sister withdrew into herself. The rumours about my involvement in Cash's death continued to circulate. She did nothing to defend me, although I couldn't really expect her to come clean after the trial and all. A vote of confidence in my innocence would have been appreciated. Despite what I did, I ended up losing her anyway. After the trial, we drifted apart."

"Where is she now?"

"I don't know. I know that's hard to believe. She lived on Vancouver Island for a while. Then I heard she moved to Mexico. She turned into a bit of a recluse. Some grand plan to live cheaply, teach yoga and become the next Margaret Atwood. That's Ivy for you, footloose and fancy free. She has a knack for ignoring reality and avoiding responsibility."

"She writes?"

Misty grimaced and shrugged her shoulders.

I got it. My brother and I were estranged. At first incomprehensible, now a mere fact of life. I too had no idea where he was at this moment, but I could locate him if I tried. Something about Misty's story clicked in my mind.

"Carla is the childhood friend your mother wrote you about. The friend who recently died."

"Yes. Sad isn't it? We had such dreams for our future. Seems like a lifetime ago." Misty's eyes flitted around the room. The silence stretched.

"Did the letter you got say how Carla died?"

"She thought it might have been a boating or swimming accident, she wasn't sure."

"Where was this?"

"She didn't say. I assume it was on Vancouver Island."

"What was Carla's last name?"

"Princeton. Why?"

"Let's just say that I've learned from personal experience that things you think are long gone and buried have a way of cropping up again when you least expect it. Sorry for prying, but it's hard to know if something is related or not without knowing the details."

"And now that you know the whole sordid story?"

I thought for a minute. I understood her reluctance to talk about her past. It would take a whole lot for me to drag my skeletons out of the closet to dangle in front of someone. Something about the story didn't sit right. She had covered for her sister. Then they just drifted apart? Something told me I still didn't have the full story. She protected her sister because she didn't want to lose her. She did it out of guilt. What did that mean?

Misty was watching me carefully.

A witness, someone in the community, had been unable to distinguish the Lane sisters. Was it merely poor eyesight or did the sisters resemble each other? My eyes met Misty's and for a split second it felt like she could read what was going through my mind.

"Could your premonition be about your sister, not you?" *Or me?*

"I won't lie, the thought crossed my mind. But you keep reminding me that I'm the one getting threatening messages."

I nodded. Maybe I was overthinking things—looking for connections, motives where there were none. Or maybe I wasn't digging deep enough.

TWENTY-ONE

SHE WAS LATE. Then again, good help is hard to find. I paid for my much-needed coffee and selected a table near the back. Just when I thought she was going to be a no-show, the door opened. A gust of wind blew in leaves, and Sal. She lifted the dark sunglasses off her face, peered around the room, dropped the glasses back over her eyes and hobbled over.

"Sorry I'm late. Hip's killing me this morning. Arthritis. I'll be fine once I get going." She leaned her gnarled walking stick against the small table and lowered herself gingerly into the chair across from me. Several people watched us under the guise of using their smart phones.

"Hi, Sal. Can I get you a coffee?"

"Double mocha latte, shot of vanilla."

I got up.

"While you're up, see if they have banana bread, would ya?"

I ordered her drink, a slice of banana loaf and got a refill for myself. Arthritis my ass. She'd been on a bender and the dark sunglasses weren't my only clue. The tattered knee-length trench coat she wore was buttoned incorrectly, one side hanging lower than the other. It and the tan twill pant she wore underneath were smudged with dirt. My guess from retrieving bottles from garbage bins. Her skin was an unhealthy grey and her hands had that all-too-familiar tremble.

"Here you go." I set her latte down in front of her.

"You're a peach, Jorja. A real peach. Whatcha got for me?"

"I need you to hunt down some names. If your hip can handle it."

"Don't worry about me, doll. I'll manage."

Sal had attended one of my four-day PI courses last year. I'd held it on two consecutive weekends and repeated the course three times over the next twelve months. I didn't necessarily want to teach, but it generated some much-needed income during slow spells. The side benefit was meeting people like Sal. She was determined to get her PI licence. Her gruff demeanour and lack of attention to grooming provided her a perpetual, unintended bag lady disguise. Not a bad thing if you were doing surveillance. I had hired her twice before, situations where a pair of eyes or boots on the ground were needed and technology wasn't an option. Payment was usually cash and, best of all, Sal was never interested in the details.

I pulled out my list of names. "I've got five names here. I want to know more about them. Who are they, where they live or work, either will do. Find out what kind of car they drive, get a phone number if you can. A photo would be a nice touch. But don't sweat it if you can't get it all. Whatever you can get on them, easily. Legally."

"No need to mince words with me, doll. You mean cheaply." She pulled the list over and turned it around. "Last names only for some of them. And a PO box number, eh? At least you got the postal station location."

I had already googled each of the names. The search engine either brought up nothing or dozens of hits—the problem with only having a name and no other information. I had narrowed down a few of the names to one of two or three likely possibilities and was leaving the rest to Sal.

"I don't have a lot of time or a huge budget. Hope you can run these down for me in a couple of days."

"Gotcha, doll." She crumpled up the list and stuffed it into her pocket. She brought her latte up to her mouth with both hands and smacked her lips after a quick sip.

"You still got my number, Sal? You know how to reach me, right?"

Sal was old school, relying on a cell phone the size of a brick, something she might want to remedy if she ever did become a PI.

She tapped the side of her head. "The bod's gone to shit, but the mind's like a steel trap."

"Okay. Do you need anything?"

"Wanna spot me a twenty? In case I need to grab a cab or some damn thing."

I pulled out three twenties and slid them over to her. Sal grunted her thanks.

"You payin' for breakfast today?"

Sal was as subtle as a carnie at the annual fair. I sighed and pulled out my wallet.

TWENTY-TWO

ITT WAS MID-AFTERNOON when I pulled into Giovanni's parking lot. Two men in coveralls were erecting a large sign in the mall parking lot next door. A couple of other guys were pulling wire fence panels out from the back of a five-ton cube truck. I pulled open the front door to Giovanni's. The warm air was scented with meatloaf, spicy spinach penne with Italian sausage and Giovanni's spicy all-day breakfast scramble. The front glass counter held a smattering of pastries, cinnamon-raisin rolls, lemon loaf, and raspberry scones.

I picked up a coffee and a panini. Detective Brighton was already at one of the small tables near the back. I slid into the chair across from him.

"Thanks for meeting with me."

He finished chewing, swallowed and waved a half-eaten burrito at me.

"Gotta grab a bite when the opportunity presents itself. This burrito is outta this world."

"You've never been here?"

"No. Might have to add the joint to my list." He took another bite and said around the bulge in his cheek, "You said you had something for me. On the Lori Watson murder?"

"Yeah. You know I'm working for Misty Lane, the woman who found Watson's body."

"She's a psychic, right? Communicates with the dead." He shook his head and popped the rest of the burrito in his mouth. "Don't tell me she's had a message from the dead woman."

"It would make things easier if Watson could tell us who strangled her, wouldn't it?"

He picked up his coke and downed half the bottle. "So, what do you got?"

"Misty isn't just a psychic, she's also a clairvoyant. She can foresee the future."

He was already shaking his head.

"Hear me out. She's had this premonition. That a dark-haired woman, about her height and build, would be killed, choked to death. She actually believed or believes that the woman in her premonition is her, that she is foreseeing her own death."

"Looks like she's wrong."

"Maybe."

"What do you mean, maybe. We have a body that says she's wrong."

"Last Thursday someone dropped a fifty-pound sack of sand off the building where she was holding an event—missed her by inches." I could tell I had his attention. "It so happens that the night Watson was murdered on Misty's patio, Misty arrived home wearing tan pants and a dark-blue, car-length wool coat, with a black cross-body bag—the strap worn across her chest. Check the photos you have of the crime scene. Both women have shoulder-length, dark-brown hair and are five-seven, give or take an inch and Watson was dressed similarly to Misty that night."

I watched the gears churning as Brighton leaned back. He let out a low whistle. "Now that *is* interesting. Suspects?"

"No one specifically. I know you need to keep certain details of the Watson murder out of the public eye, but the way she was killed, the way the body was found, seems personal. Not what you'd expect from a random attack."

He nodded slowly.

"An obvious candidate is Misty's ex-boyfriend, Doug Liederbach. I believe one of your guys had a talk with him. Liederbach gets his kicks by frightening women. He came to see me the other day, seemed upset that you or one of your cop friends paid him a visit. I guess he doesn't want word of his sexual fantasy thing involving guns, abductions and choking to get out."

"He threaten you?"

"Indirectly. But the way Lori Watson was found…staged. It doesn't exactly fit, does it?"

Brighton rubbed his chin for a second, then leaned forward. "Not that you heard this from me, but I agree—this murder wasn't a random attack. It *was* planned. It was personal."

"Even though the two women were dressed similarly, I can't believe Liederbach would have made such a mistake."

Brighton shrugged. "Who knows how these guys think. What better way to frighten his ex than to have someone murdered right outside her door?"

"If it's Liederbach, he's one sick puppy. But I don't think it's him. Neither does my client." I finished my panini and crumpled the wrapper. "Two days ago, someone called Misty claiming to be Watson's killer. Or I assume the statement, 'I killed her,' was referring to Watson."

"What? Shit! Why am I just hearing about this now?"

"It could be a crank call. There was an article in the paper, claiming she was working on solving the case. Nevertheless, I advised Misty to call you."

"Well, she didn't." His eyes bore into mine, accusingly.

"That's why I'm following up with you. I was there when she

got the call. I checked for information on the number, but it was blocked. I did a call back from Misty's phone. It went unanswered. I have the number here." I pulled out my cell phone and read him the number I had jotted down in my notes. "It's probably a throw-away, but maybe you'll be able to pin down where the call was made."

"Yeah, days after the fact. Either one of you hear the term obstruction of justice?"

"I'm here, aren't I?" This wasn't a good time to tell him Misty had decided to devote herself to finding Watson's killer.

Detective Brighton grunted.

"Look, don't make me out to be the bad guy. Regardless of what you may read or have read in the paper, I'm not trying to solve the Watson murder. I'll leave finding Lori Watson's killer up to the police. I'm trying to find who has been harassing and threatening Misty. They may be one and the same or not. I just thought I'd let you know."

I got a coffee refill on my way out. Detective Brighton thanked me grudgingly when he left. Misty wouldn't be happy when she found out I met with Detective Brighton, but I had no regrets. She was frightened enough to hire me to find out who might be planning to kill her, but not frightened enough to mention she might have been the intended victim to the investigating detectives when a woman was found murdered steps from her door?

I pushed aside a thought that I might be playing some other sort of role here, other than mere investigator. A thought that crossed my mind more than once since I had taken this case. Was it her and Tara's intent to bring me in to lend credibility or some sort of validity to her part in solving Lori Watson's murder? I shook my head. That made no sense, since she hired me before Lori was murdered. It would imply a certain level of certainty in her prediction. A level of certainty I didn't want to think about.

As I pulled out of the parking lot, a sign being erected in the mall next door caught my eye. I turned in to the mall parking lot for a closer look. The sign notified customers that the mall would be shut down July first. Below the notice was a drawing of the planned eight-storey building which was to be completed by spring. Giovanni's deli would be one of only a handful of original buildings left in the area.

The logo at the top was nondescript, blue letters LBI superimposed on a triangle, the sides made up of a hammer, nail and ruler. I had seen that logo before. I was almost certain it was the same logo I had seen displayed in front of Misty's building. I decided to swing by and confirm.

I was still a block away from Misty's shop, waiting for the light to turn, when someone banged on my passenger window. I jumped and craned my neck to get a better look.

"Are you looking for God? Or the devil?" he yelled.

Crap. The preacher.

"Well, here he is!" He threw out his arms wide and stepped back.

Passersby were now staring.

"And you," he pointed at me through the glass and shouted. "Do you not know that you are here to judge? Judge the false prophets, the fornicators, the miscreants and the executioners. The Lord Jesus is calling on you to avenge the fallen angel of mercy."

I inched the car forward and he stepped back. The light turned green. Had he misspoken? Had I misheard? My grandfather, who had been injured and nursed back to health during the war, always referred to nurses as angels of mercy. Was I making too much of his ramblings? Or had he heard about Lori Watson's death, knew she was a nurse and knew that I was somehow connected?

TWENTY-THREE

SMITTY YAWNED AND stretched when I let myself in but didn't come to greet me. My welcome was growing thin. I walked over to where he lay on the couch and gave him a scratch behind his ear. A quick glance at Smitty's food dish confirmed my worry. He wasn't eating much. He hadn't eaten much of his food yesterday either. Today both bowls of food remained largely untouched. *What if he's sick?*

I googled 'cat not eating,' and read. Not eating was a serious issue and more dangerous for cats than dogs. The article recommended getting a veterinarian's assessment as soon as possible. If they could rule out physical issues, then anxiety or depression might be the reason Smitty wasn't eating. I felt sick. The website went on to say that changes in routine, how the household furniture is arranged, or new food or new people can affect a cat's emotional well-being, especially sensitive cats.

I picked Smitty up for a cuddle. He didn't feel thinner, or did he? I looked at his bowl again. He had eaten a bit of food and the water in his water dish was lower than when I filled it.

"Please don't be sick, little buddy." I gave him one last hug and set him down as he started to scramble out of my arms. He seemed perky enough. I pushed the couch back to where it belonged and filled Wess' water dish and put it back on the floor in its usual place. Smitty ran over to have a sniff then turned away. I dumped the old food out of both dishes, prepared Smitty's supper and put some of it in each dish and set them down on the floor. Smitty ignored both.

I was clearly messing things up. Smitty probably wasn't eating because he missed Wess. *What if he starves to death?* I blinked away tears and pulled on my boots and coat. I locked the back door and after checking the backyard, made my way around to the front street and started knocking on doors. I had been calling the Humane Society and Animal Services regularly, but no one brought in a cat that looked like Wess. I headed south, then after a few blocks, crossed the street and made my way back. No one had seen Wess.

Mrs. Niedswiki's neighbour opened his main door, leaving the screen door firmly shut. I held up one of the missing cat posters I had made. He waved me away—the kind of wave a despot uses to send away the minions.

Mrs. Niedswiki's place remained dark. Her newspaper lay on her step. I opened the gate, climbed the stairs, and picked up the bundle.

"Holy jeez!" I staggered back, almost falling off the step.

Mrs. Niedswiki's withered face glared at me through the small window in the door. Hand to chest, I held up the paper.

She opened the door. One hand clutched the front of her sweater, the material bunched in her bony hand.

"Mrs. Niedswiki, you're back."

She continued to glare.

"I was just picking up your paper and mail. Mike had to fly to Toronto. His daughter, Julie, is in the hospital."

Her unblinking beady eyes bore into me. No sign she comprehended or even heard what I said. I fought back an overwhelming urge to make the sign of the cross. I held out the paper and bent my head, a little peace offering.

She grabbed it from me. "*Ppfft, ppfft ppfft.*"

I turned and ran, tears blurring my retreat. What the hell was wrong with her. Why did she hate me? I punched the code into the door lock and let out a weak laugh. What the hell was wrong with *me*?

Back inside, I poured a drink and composed myself. I checked my watch. Mike would be starting his night shift at Julie's side. I punched in Mike's number.

"Hey, Mike. How are you doing?"

"Good. Gemma just left to go get some sleep. I'm keeping Julie entertained."

"She's awake!"

Mike laughed. "She came out of her coma this afternoon. Hard to tell exactly when—she kept drifting in and out. But she's wide awake now."

"Thank goodness. I'm so happy to hear that. Please say hi and tell that I'm thinking of her and sending wishes for a speeding recovery."

"I'll do that. How about you? How are you doing?"

"Wess still hasn't shown up. I checked in the cellar yesterday but didn't see him. I put up posters and canvassed the neighbours. I'm just sick about it."

Mike's silence cut through me. "Mike?"

"Try to not worry. It's only been a few days."

Now, I knew he was worried too. Finding a lost cat was like finding a lost child. The first forty-eight hours were critical. Chances diminished with each passing day.

"Mrs. Niedswiki is back."

"She is? Hope her sister is doing okay. Did you get a chance to talk to her?"

"No. Just picked up her paper tonight and handed it through the door to her. She never says much to me." I swallowed hard. "She spit at me."

Mike laughed. "I think it's some superstitious thing she does to keep evil spirits at bay. It's a good thing."

"Yeah, sure. Any idea when you might be back?" I hated myself for sounding whiny.

"Planning to fly back tomorrow night. I'm teaching the forensic evidence course to Azagora's new recruits Thursday and Friday. I'll fly back here on the weekend. Maybe Julie will be home by then. Either way, I want to make sure my girl is all right."

This was Mike's third year teaching the forensic evidence course to new members rotating through Calgary's homicide unit. He and Azagora worked well together and not just because Azagora was his client. Mike had a lot of respect for Azagora, which made complaining to him about my relationship with Azagora a tad awkward. They were at different stages of their lives. Mike had already retired once, he had mellowed, he'd seen a lot of shit in his day and not much rattled him anymore. Azagora was still feeding the fire in his belly.

"I can't tell you how happy I am to hear Julie is doing well. I won't keep you."

I was relieved to hear the good news. Finally, something positive. Smitty jumped up on the couch next to me and pushed his head against my thigh.

"Your grand-paw is coming home soon." Smitty mewed and rubbed his head against my hand, then jumped down and headed for the bedroom. "And then, he's going to kill me."

I stood up, contemplating another drink. I shook my head, returned my empty glass to the kitchen and headed for the bedroom.

The bedroom closet door stood open. I froze, my heart

pounding against my chest, my hands cold and clammy. Was I going insane? I had definitely closed the closet door before I left the house. I don't care how clever and ingenious Mike's cats were, there was no bloody way they could open that door. I looked around, my fear growing. Someone had been in the house.

TWENTY-FOUR

I ROLLED DOWN THE car windows as I drove to Kensington. Fresh air cooled my car and brought some colour to my face. I turned onto Tenth Street and slowed as I passed Misty's shop. Today the logo, prominently displayed on the fencing separating the sidewalk from traffic, jumped out at me. An eye-shaped oval in the centre of a triangle with the letters LPI at the apex. Lines radiated from the top of the triangle. Were they supposed to represent light? Energy? The logo reminded me of something the Illuminati would have used.

Misty's shop was still closed. The bricks on the front of the building looked like they had been power washed to their original reddish colour. I turned at the corner and took a right into the alley. A dark-green Oldsmobile was parked behind Healing Waters.

All three parking spots behind Misty's store stood empty. I pulled into one of the spots, got out and tried the back door. It was locked. I knocked and waited. Nothing. I pulled out my cell and phoned the store number. A recording came on telling me the hours of operation but didn't mention that the store was temporarily closed. I called Misty but she didn't answer her private number either.

I slid back into my car and glanced over at the Olds. Two long-haired men sat in the front seat. I took a more scrutinizing glance, pretending to be engrossed with my phone. They definitely weren't clients—more likely construction workers on a break. I checked my watch, put the phone down and started my car. I turned to make sure nothing was behind me as I started to back out and yelped.

The preacher stood next to my car. Today he wore a shirt, stained with sweat and heavy with its odour.

"I'm not afraid of noooo…body. You know why?" His voice rose. "Because I do this." He crossed his two forefingers, leaned forward, and held them inches from my face. His pupils were huge. His eyes darted nervously.

I nodded and leaned away from the window.

He took a step forward then straightened and held his arms out to his side. "When you do this—it's a cross—it protects you. Even nobodies like me. Are you a nobody?" He leaned forward again. His voice reached preacher pitch. "I'm a nobody. Can't kill a person with NO body, and a person with NO body can't kill you. Well, the devil can kill a NO body but not if the Lord Jesus Christ is in your life."

I rolled up the window, engaged the locks and put the car into reverse.

He bent until his eyes were level with mine. His voice, slightly muffled, penetrated the glass. "I have witnessed Satan's dark cloak of evil. He has made his presence known. I have been saved by the Lord Jesus Christ seven times. Do not forsake the Lord."

The guys in the green Olds were staring and laughing. I slowly backed out, praying that my car wouldn't hit him, requiring the good Lord to save him an eighth time.

I debated going back to Mike's place but couldn't face Wess' absence. Then I felt guilty about leaving Smitty alone. I picked up a coffee and headed back to my place. It would feel good to sleep in my own bed tonight.

I let myself into my condo. The place had that clean, empty smell, like no one lived there. I tried Misty again and when she didn't answer called Tara.

"Hey, Tara, it's Jorja. I've been trying to get a hold of Misty, but she's not answering. Have you heard from her?"

"No. I know she's closed her shop for a few days. She's not at home?"

"Well, if she is, she's not answering her phone. Maybe I'll swing by her condo later and make sure she's okay. She didn't look that great when I last saw her."

"I've never seen her looking so exhausted. It's like something has drained all the energy from her body."

After the call, I sat back and thought about my last conversation with Misty. Maybe rehashing old memories, all those horrible days surrounding her friend's trial had left her emotionally spent. It hadn't been my intention to open that black hole. What did bother me was that two women with connections to Misty had died within the last month. Okay, Lori Watson's connection was dubious at best—still, what are the chances that a childhood friend dies and then a few weeks later a woman is murdered on your doorstep.

I set my coffee on the coffee table, plunked myself down on the couch and pulled my laptop out of my bag. As soon as I had it booted up, I typed in Carla Princeton. A bunch of references to various Carlas came up and dozens of links to websites about Princeton. I sighed. Why couldn't I get lucky—just once.

Did Misty really not know where her sister was? I thought about my brother. We hadn't spoken in years. He blamed me for our parents' deaths, and even though I tried to reconcile when I got older, too much time had passed. He had his own life and it didn't include me. The last address I had for him was Boston. For all I knew, he could be living in South America or New Zealand studying the kookaburra.

The conversation I had with Misty replayed in my head. Misty had lied to protect her sister. From what? Police questioning? Further social condemnation? Why couldn't she have simply told the truth? Had she really been afraid that her mother would send Ivy away? And if she thought her sister might be the one in her premonition, the one in danger, why not try to locate her, warn her. Why not have me track her down? Cause that's what I do. I track people down.

Four hours later I hadn't tracked anyone down. But I did find two short sentences, in the Sooke local paper, dated roughly six weeks ago. A hiker had found a woman, presumed drowned on a nearby beach near Albert Head Lagoon. I called the Sooke RCMP, told them who I was and that I was trying to track down a woman named Carla Princeton for a client of mine regarding a personal matter and had, in the course of my search, learned a young woman had been found dead who matched the description given to me by my client. The woman who answered the phone didn't question how I knew what the dead woman looked like and put me through to Corporal Reed.

I gave an even vaguer story to Corporal Reed, hinting that perhaps Carla Princeton had been left some money by my client. Corporal Reed was very accommodating but told me she wasn't the lead investigator on the case. She did however confirm that Carla Princeton's death was a homicide, and that Carla was known in the community as Carla Prince. Corporal Reed had taken the initial call when a hiker found Carla's body on a small beach, near Sooke. At first glance it looked like a drowning, maybe a suicide. The coroner had a different opinion and homicide detectives were called in.

"She'd been in the water a few days, likely killed elsewhere and washed up where she was found. She had some small bruises at the base of her neck, seawater in her lungs. The coroner thought she was strangled or choked until unconscious, then dumped into the water."

"That's dreadful. Are there any leads at this time?"

"Not to my knowledge. Several local people saw Carla Saturday morning. Looked like she might be heading off for a day of hiking and birding. She was carrying a backpack and often went looking for birds along the various trails around here. Her friend actually reported her missing when she failed to show for a planned dinner date the following day."

"Who was that?"

"Billie Thomson. She owns Billie's Café in Sooke. She and Carla were good friends."

I sat back stunned. I wonder what Misty would think when she learned that Carla had been murdered. I shook my head. I'm sure she wouldn't be pleased at my digging into her death.

I glanced at my watch. I'd have to head over to Mike's soon, feed Smitty and pack up my stuff. I checked my email, but Misty hadn't replied to either of the emails I had sent her earlier. Nothing from Sal. No surprise there, I didn't expect to hear from her this soon, and certainly not by email. I picked up the remote control and turned on the TV. Realizing I hadn't eaten all day, I got up, combed through my kitchen cupboards, and returned with a handful of stale crackers.

Something on the TV caught my eye. I turned up the volume. Lori Watson's brother was making a brief statement on behalf of the family. A memorial service had been held for Lori Watson this afternoon. Her ashes were interred at a private family ceremony afterwards.

Lori's brother thanked the community for their outpouring of support. He spoke eloquently, emotionally about his sister's death, the impact it had on him, her friends, the family. Near the end of his speech, he asked the public to contact police if they knew anything about the crime.

The camera panned to the small group gathered behind him—Lori's parents, family members and close friends. Misty stood at the edge of the group. Lori's brother's voice strengthened as he announced that the family was working with a clairvoyant medium and that she had received a strong message about the killer. He turned and quickly glanced at Misty as he delivered this statement, then turned back to the camera. He ended with, "Our family is confident that the information we have will lead to the killer's arrest. Justice for Lori's senseless death."

I cursed silently. What the hell was wrong with Misty? Did she have a death wish? Misty looked ashen, gaunt. Normally I don't notice these things, but her appearance was so altered from that first day in my office that it made me sit up. Dark circles framed her eyes, but it was their lack of expression that disturbed me the most. Her hair was pulled back into a messy knot, wisps stuck out like quills from the back of her head. She wore a long, loosely woven cowl-neck sweater over a floor-length floral skirt and as the TV camera panned toward her again, I noticed she had entangled several fingers into the wool of her sleeve.

I sat back and stared at the TV screen, the news anchor already introducing the next story. What was Misty trying to do? What if the killer was watching this? The sound of my heartbeat all but blocked out the TV. Suddenly I knew. Misty was no longer resisting. She was ushering the dark energy into her life.

TWENTY-FIVE

MISTY MUST HAVE been waiting for me. She buzzed me in as soon as I hit the call button. By the time I reached her condo door, she had it open, waiting for me.

"Come on in, Jorja. Sorry it took me so long to get back to you. Are you okay?"

Her eyes flashed, brief indication that she wasn't totally consumed by whatever tormented her.

"I'm okay. Why?"

"Oh. Nothing."

"Nothing? You sure? You don't look well."

Her fingers clasped something, hung at the end of the silver chain around her neck. "It's nothing. Just an odd feeling. Like maybe you've lost someone or something." She turned pained eyes toward me.

Was she talking about my mother or Wess? Or maybe my faltering relationship with Azagora. *Creepy.* "No. I mean, not really. One of the cats I've been looking after is missing. I'm sure he'll turn up."

She closed her other hand over the one that held her necklace, shook her head and turned. I followed her into the living room, which was strewn with clothes, books, papers. She motioned me to the couch. Several crystals and minerals were arranged in a circle on the coffee table. A jar of what looked like weed sat next to them.

"I'm getting a clearer…" The kettle's whistle cut her comment short. I watched her shuffle into the kitchen and unplug the kettle. She stood, staring at the kettle, as if she expected something more from it.

"Misty? Are you okay?"

"It's beginning to rain."

I looked out the patio door, the sun bright on the flagstones outside. The hairs on the back of my neck tingled.

"Nines and sevens, maybe ninety-nine or ninety-seven," she whispered.

I got up. "Misty?"

"Four steps down, he lost his crown."

Misty still stared at the kettle. I touched her arm. "Misty?"

She turned her head and smiled. "Jorja! Would you like some tea?"

Whatever she was having, I wanted none of it. "Thanks, Misty, but I've already drank a gallon of coffee today. Why don't you let me help you fix it?"

"You know, I think I'll pass too. I have no idea why I put the kettle on."

"Well, let's go sit down then." The suggestion was more for my benefit than hers—the last few minutes had unnerved me.

She followed me back to the couch and we sat. Her eyes seemed unfocused, she stared past me, but she sounded more like herself. I looked at the crystals on the table and the jar of what? Leaves? Has she partaken of some magical elixir meant to heighten her connection with spirit? Or just a handful of valiums.

Misty noticed me eyeing the display laid out on the coffee table.

"Many of earth's minerals and gems have healing and

metaphysical properties. This one"—her finger hovered over a cluster of pale-green and white rectangular crystals—"is Apophyllite. It helps to create a conscious connection between the spiritual and physical realms. It enhances recall of past-life experiences and communication with the spirit world."

The lines around her mouth loosened, and her voice became stronger.

"This one is Black Kyanite," she said, pointing to a dark-grey specimen. "See how it's made up of these little blades. That's why some people refer to it as witches' broom. It's a very powerful mineral and aids in the manifestation of vision and clairvoyance. It has a calming effect and retains no negative energy."

"And the one around your neck?"

Her hand clasped the pendant hanging from her neck, two white spheres embedded in a glossy black material.

"Cristobalite. It belonged to my grandmother. It stimulates the Third Eye, the ability for advanced sight in the psychic realm. It is said to help the wearer merge the intuitive self with the willingness to acknowledge signs from otherworldly beings."

Her face softened; some light returned to her eyes.

"It's been a tough day. I saw you on the early evening news. They played a clip of Lori Watson's brother speaking to the media after the funeral. So, you're officially working with the family to find Lori's killer?"

"It's the least I can do. I feel so bad for Lori and her family."

"You're acting like it's your fault. It isn't."

She swallowed hard and looked at her hands lying deadly still in her lap. "I don't have all the answers, but I feel like I'm the reason."

I realized that pitching a logical response would do nothing to change the feeling she held. "I heard Gregg Watson say you've received some information that might lead to the killer's arrest. Have you had any more phone calls?"

"No phone calls. But yesterday, someone wrote the word 'liar' across my door. It was written in block letters, this time with red lipstick."

"Liar? Here at your condo?"

Misty nodded; her face tightened. I watched her fingers twisting the Cristobalite over and over until the chain around her neck shortened.

"Any idea why someone might write liar? And lying about what?"

"If only I knew."

"I still think you should be sharing all of this with Detective Brighton."

Misty unwound her necklace. "Did I ever tell you about the Hasting case?"

"No. That name sounds familiar though." The Hastings had direct lineage to one of Calgary's early families. "Wasn't their daughter kidnapped?"

"The Hastings' daughter was abducted. Virginia Hasting was the one who called me. She wanted me to help the police find their nine-year-old daughter, Marissa. Marissa had been taken from the house during the night, three days earlier."

"I remember now. The Hastings had been doing renos at their house. There had been a number of contractors and service people at the house, right before their daughter was taken."

"That's right. The Hastings gave police the names of all the contractors who had been at the house in the last four months. Security cameras in the neighbourhood showed a white van driving past the house several times at around three in the morning the day Marissa was taken. They initially focused on the gardener, but he was cleared."

"Everyone must have been pretty rattled. The amber alert ran for days. But she was found, wasn't she?"

Misty nodded. "The minute I met with Virginia, I felt a strong male presence. Nothing specific, mind you, other than it was of an older man. I felt he was meant to help us. Virginia told me her father had died the year before and at first, I thought it was the girl's departed grandfather. And it may well have been part of it, but I kept seeing animals, dogs, cats, rabbits, goats. I saw fire, felt its warmth. Sometimes fire is a symbol for home. So, I started to think maybe the girl was being held on a farm or somewhere where there were a lot of animals."

"I remember now. They found her in an abandoned granary, didn't they?"

"That's right. The neighbour next door, an older gentleman, ran a local animal shelter. People took animals they found or could no longer keep themselves there. He tried to find these poor creatures another home. Anyway, the feelings I first felt when I met Virginia were strong but vague. It wasn't until she gave me her daughter's favourite sweater that I started to see things more clearly. I told the police that besides the animals, I kept seeing round shapes, and the number 52. The police finally found her in this round steel granary, just off Range Road 52."

Shivers ran up my arms. "Impressive."

"Well, a lot of people didn't think so. The amber alert went out quickly after Marissa was taken. A couple of street cameras caught a white van on Deerfoot, heading north. We both know once you leave the city, there's not much out there except farms."

"Yeah, but Range Road 52?"

"Again, some people said it was just a matter of good police detection. And I won't take that away from them. Once the amber alert went out, they figured whoever had her would want to get off the main road quickly. That gave police a certain area to search in, at least to begin with. They started canvassing the rural communities. The man who ran the animal shelter remembered seeing a white van. They focused in around his area, and then noticed one of the main roads running past his place was Range Road 52. The rest is history."

"That was one lucky little girl. Most abductions don't end up that well." I waited a minute. "I heard Gregg Watson say you've received some information about the killer."

"Gregg gave me one of Lori's sweaters." Misty took a shaky breath. "I took it with me and forced myself to step out onto the patio. The fear came back. Boy, did it come back. I saw a fire, a raging fire, but it gave off no heat. Instead, I felt cold. I saw a woman descending into a dark cold space. A male presence was very prevalent. A darkness, evil. The numbers one, nine and seven kept repeating in my mind."

"One, nine and seven, huh? Any idea why they'd be relevant?"

"No, only that they're important. Especially the sevens and nines."

"Are you going to share this with the police?"

"Not yet. I wasn't exactly welcomed the last time. Virginia Hasting was the one who hired me and insisted that the police listen to me. But I've told the Watson family I'll gladly share anything I find with the police that might be of use to them." She leaned over and clutched my hand. "Remember the nines and sevens. If anything happens to me, follow the numbers. This is how you'll find him, it's the numbers."

"Follow them? To where?"

"I don't know yet. I just know they are important."

I waited, hoping there would be more. She started to say something then shook her head.

"I've got someone hunting down the five names we came up with, the individuals who were at the readings where you felt a dark presence. If we can locate them, I'd like you to meet with them. Maybe you can confirm or dispel that these individuals have anything to do with what you are sensing."

She nodded vaguely. She got up and began pacing, lost in her own world.

I cleared my throat. "I also made some inquires about your friend, Carla Princeton. She changed or shortened her name to Prince. Her death wasn't an accident. She was murdered."

Misty turned, her mouth open in silent shock. "My god, no. Are you sure? You don't think…let me see." She rubbed her temples as she resumed pacing.

"Did Carla have dark hair? Could she be the woman in your vision?"

Misty sank to the edge of the couch and clutched the stone at her neck. "This changes everything. This must be stopped."

"What's changed? What has to stop?"

"I'm sorry." She reached out a hand unsteadily. "I don't feel well. Please. Can you let yourself out? I need to lie down."

"Okay. Can I do anything, get anything for you?" I stood up at the shake of her head. "Hope you feel better soon. I'll give you a call once we've tracked down those five people."

"Be careful, Jorja. It's all unravelling."

"What's unravelling?"

᪣

I pulled my sunglasses down over my eyes as I walked out into the sunshine. Carla Prince had been murdered, as had Lori Watson. It wasn't fair. None of it was. Not their deaths, the toll it was taking on their families, on Misty personally, her business; nor that the killer could be out here enjoying this glorious day. Sevens and nines. Maybe the numbers would mean something to the police.

Could they be the last digits on a licence plate? Numbers on the licence plate of the grey Impala Misty saw drive away.

I got into my car and surveyed the street. A couple walked by, hand in hand, a man played with his dog. Hard to believe a woman lost her life here. Misty was starting to come undone. Not sure all the crystals were helping her. The way she reacted to news of Carla's murder spoke louder than words. Why did she insist on talking in riddles? *It's unravelling.* If she knew something, why not say so? And what, exactly, changed?

TWENTY-SIX

THE TENSION IN my shoulders built as I made my way up Mike's sidewalk and punched in the key code. Smitty came running as usual. *See, he's not sick.* I bent down and rubbed the side of his cute furry face, while my eyes scanned the room for Wess, or reassurance that no one else had been here while I was out.

It didn't take long to pack up. After I had everything stuffed back in my carryall, I checked my watch. Mike's plane wasn't due to land until almost midnight. Should I wait for him and apologize face to face? I pulled the sheets off the futon, stuffed them into the washer and turned it on. I called the Humane Society. No one had brought in Wesson. I gathered up my coat and stepped outside. My legs felt heavy, my energy drained. Images of Wess filled my brain. Ugly, horrible images. "Stop it," I hissed out loud, pushing the images out of my head.

The wind whipped up the dirt in the alley and threw my hair across my eyes. I swallowed the ache in my throat and called out Wess' name. At the end of the alley, I turned back. My pulse quickened as a cat darted out from underneath a fence and froze. I took a step forward and he took off, ducking under a car parked across the lane. Not Wess.

By nine o'clock the sheets were washed, dried and back in the closet, the dishes all done and put away, the place spotless. Nothing looked out of place. No lone buttons lying on the floor, no open doors. Maybe I had let my imagination get to me. I gave Smitty a pat on the head, sent Mike an email to say I had fed him, turned on the outside porch light and pulled the door shut. *Wuss.* I threw my bag into the back seat and climbed in.

For some reason, I couldn't bear the thought of going home. I checked my watch. Everything in Glenmore Landing would be closed. Except McDonalds. But I wasn't craving a McFlurry. A few minutes later I was parked down the street from Jazzy Katz. A man staggered out onto the sidewalk as I reached the entrance. A long meeting with Jim Beam.

The place was busier than I expected for a weeknight. Tonight, a woman stood behind the bar, looking frazzled. The band, Soul Mates, was pumping out a bluesy tune with a strong beat. I found a table tucked in at the back, near the short hallway to the washrooms. I wasn't feeling like the strong capable woman I imagined myself to be. I had lost Mike's cat, folded like a cheap TV tray in front of Mrs. Niedswiki, and had taken my frustration out on Misty, blaming her for my lack of traction on her case.

The waitress came by and I ordered a double scotch, no ice. I pulled open my laptop. I typed in Carla Prince. Finding nothing, I tried the name Princeton on various sites, with various spellings, but nothing else came up.

I tried Cash Irving. Nothing on Cash Irving. Lots on Irving Oil and dozens of other Irvings—but none mentioning a dead brother, or a sister-in-law who went to prison. I snorted. Not that anyone would include that in an interview or a bio.

I picked up my glass and noticed it was nearly empty. I stared at the remaining drops of amber. I liked the taste, the warm feeling that immediately loosened the tightness in my neck and shoulders and calmed the critical little voice in my head. The weight of the glass felt good in my hand. The only thing that kept me from falling down that rabbit hole was the image of my father, staggering home, raging drunk, lashing out at my mother while she tried cleaning him up. The resigned look on her face, the sadness in her eyes. Maybe Carla Princeton would have ended up like my mother. Then I realized she had. They were both dead.

The waitress caught my eye. I shook my head, set the glass down and mouthed *coffee*.

I still didn't know which west coast island had been Misty's home but from the sounds of it and the lack of schools and such infrastructure, the trial wouldn't have been held there. I checked the BC provincial and supreme court websites. There I found several documents of interest but closed to the public due to a publication ban. I checked the codes on the documents listed— one was for the preliminary hearing and referenced a M. Lane, a second for a bail hearing, later that same year. The ban also covered the trial documents from the following year, likely due to the age of certain witnesses, the accused, or her co-conspirators. Or maybe the publication ban was meant to protect the baby's privacy. Carla would have given birth sometime along the way.

My coffee came, and I leaned back and took a sip and pushed it away. I should have saved my three bucks—late-night bar coffee was only brewed for those who couldn't taste it.

The band resumed playing, laughter and conversation rising to a new pitch. Suddenly I was impossibly tired. I closed my laptop and signalled the waitress for my bill.

I stepped out onto the sidewalk. The cool air felt good against my face. I glanced at my watch. Mike should be home or almost. I tilted my head back and took a deep breath. A few stars were visible despite the soft glow of city lights. The street was quiet now, all the rational people already in bed. A lone figure stood in a doorway across the street, made known to me only by the red tip of a cigarette. My pulse quickened, as did my step. I shifted my laptop under my arm and pulled out my car keys. I listened for echoing footsteps but heard none. Safely in my car, I realized I had been holding my breath. I turned on the engine and pulled out onto the nearly empty street.

TWENTY-SEVEN

I THOUGHT I'D SLEEP like the dead, back in my cozy bed with no creepy cellar or weird creaking noises to wake me, but that wasn't the case. By four in the morning I knew it wasn't going to happen. My mind raced from one thought to another. Maybe I had written Peoria Benson off too quickly. After confirming that Lehman Group was redeveloping the building Misty and Peoria Benson occupied I had dug further and discovered they had filed for and obtained redevelopment permits for fourteen different properties in and around the downtown area, including the strip mall behind Giovanni's. These guys weren't messing around.

The building that housed Peoria's and Misty's businesses sat in a prime location, but instead of tearing the building down to build a more lucrative commercial space it was being renovated. Did the building have some special meaning to Benjamin Lehman? I got out of bed, retrieved my laptop, and googled Lehman Group.

John Lehman started the company in the post-war phase, when service men were returning from war and looking to settle down, find work, raise a family. Timing is everything. By the seventies, Lehman had moved beyond residential development and into the lucrative high-rise business. By the time John Lehman officially turned the reins of the company over to his oldest son,

Benjamin, in 1997, the company had expanded across Alberta and into BC. Benjamin Lehman expanded further and added a commercial renovation and redevelopment arm.

Ben Lehman had been in the news several times in the past year. He was very litigious, and I suspect it was how he funded his operations, evening out the highs and lows in the real-estate market. He had sued pretty much everyone—construction firms, marketing companies, realtors, investors and even a politician or two. Most settled by giving Benjamin a wad of cash rather than watching their fortunes drain away through bad publicity. Although he was well known for the real-estate deals he negotiated, rumours abounded that he might be involved in less legal activities.

A photo caught my eye. Ben being interviewed outside the courthouse, where he had just successfully appealed a fraud conviction. He won his appeal because the confession of the lead witness in the case was deemed to have been illegally obtained. There behind him on the sidewalk stood his wife, his daughter and son-in-law, and his partner and close friend, Mathew Tucci.

An image popped into my mind. A black vintage Porsche convertible. Peoria Benson snuggled up against a grey-haired man, her hand caressing the back of his neck. Benjamin Lehman. Would Ben Lehman force Misty from her space just to make his mistress happy? Did Peoria Benson have some sort of hold over Benjamin Lehman? More than just the fact that he was cheating on wifey number three. It wouldn't be the first time I underestimated the level of depravity some people engaged in to get what they wanted.

By the time the soft grey light of morning crept into the living room, my head was filled with all sorts of wild premises, none of which held water. I gave up, pulled my yoga mat out from behind the couch and began my somewhat regular routine. Then I showered, dressed, checked my email and delved into the dozens of un-newsworthy items in my newsfeed. An hour later I sat back and rubbed my eyes. Why had I just scrolled through the top thirty Tacky Décor Don'ts.

Before I had a chance to decide what I was going to do with the rest of the day, my phone buzzed. An unknown caller.

"Hello?"

"Found 'em, doll. Piece a cake."

❧

I watched Sal inhale her steak and eggs. She had spread several photos and unfolded the paper I had given her, now crumpled and covered in scribbles, on the table between us. She swallowed loudly and pointed her knife at a photo of a woman. "C. Palmer. Christina. She's a realtor in Okotoks. I didn't even have to wait for her to show up. Went to the post office out there and asked about her. Took me less than an hour to find her."

I peered at a photo while she sawed off another piece of steak and chewed. "Got to chattin' with one of the other realtors in her office. Seems Christina's been checking out your client for a potential gig. She's thinking of hiring a psychic for one of her charity events." She turned one of the scraps of paper around and read. "The Palmer Real Estate Road to End Homelessness Expo."

"Good to know."

"Next"—she stabbed at another photo—"Mark Harris. There're twenty-three Harrises in the phone book. This one owns a little coffee shop in the East Village. Cosmos Café."

"Interesting."

"Tats up one arm, down the other. Stars, angels, moonbeams, all that shit. Might explain why he's so interested in what a psychic has to say. You never know though what's going on upstairs, if you get my drift."

She turned her fork sideways and scraped up the last bit of hash browns, using a finger to help the last few pieces onto her fork.

"That leaves the two names who were at three events and one who attended all four of the events my client flagged for me."

"Okay. Guy with the PO box you found. D. Rieckhoff. Daniel. I got chattin' with one of the clerks at the post office where he picks up mail. Nobody treats those dames right. You notice they're always women? They can pay 'em less and get away with it. She said a young man usually picked up the mail in Box 107. Sure enough, he came by the next day. I only had to wait five hours. I trailed him home. Bungalow in Bankview. One of those cutesy outdated dollhouses. Checked the garage in back. There's an old white Toyota Camry parked back there."

"Good job, Sal. You're brilliant at this."

I thought I saw a momentary flash of appreciation crack the don't-fuck-with-me look she usually wore on her face.

"Talked to several neighbours. Daniel lives there with his mother. She's maybe in her late seventies, early eighties. They keep to themselves. No wild parties, no noise. If there was a Mr. Rieckhoff, he's been gone for years. The son takes care of the place, runs errands, gets groceries, maybe works part time—construction. One of the neighbours said they hadn't seen the old lady in a while. Might already be in a nursing home, or dead."

"Sounds like her son's a big help to her. Don't see enough of that these days. Did you get a photo?"

"Yeah, but it's not going to do you any good. Guy walks around in a hoodie." I looked at the photo she slid over to me, using her fork as the prod. He was white, medium height, medium build, face obscured by the hood of his grey hoodie.

"Maybe my client, will recognize something familiar about him," I said.

Sal grunted. "Number four on the list. Les Bagoda. He works at one of them tech companies. Integrated Solutions. Their office is in the northeast. Industrial park, off Deerfoot."

Sal shoved a coffee-stained post-it note in my direction and stabbed at another photo, this one of a guy getting into a Dodge Charger.

"Last but not least. Angie Lee. Took me a little longer to find her. Finally had to call in a favour from a pal of mine who has access to addresses." Sal loaded the last bit of egg and steak onto her fork and winked at me as she lifted it to her mouth. "Gave an address in Forest Lawn. Angelina Bertolli. Used to live in apartment unit 267, at that address."

"Used to?"

"Moved out two weeks ago. No forwarding address. Neighbours didn't know her. Had only lived there maybe three months."

"She attended four of my client's readings in the last six weeks."

"Readings? Your client a palm reader?"

"No. Her skills go way beyond palm reading. She's a psychic-clairvoyant."

"Yet, you need me." She cackled.

"Ironic, isn't it?"

"Lee's mail is still going to her old address. The new tenant leaves it in the lobby for the mail delivery person to pick up. Several pieces from the Marda Healing Clinic in Mexico. One of those scammy places where they charge an arm and leg for organic fruit juices they claim trigger your body's own healing power. Healing power my sorry ass."

"Sometimes people are desperate. The money buys them hope, at least for a while."

Sal rolled her eyes. "If I only had a few months to live I wouldn't be drinkin' any damn fruit juice." She pushed back her plate, patted her stomach, and belched. "Don't have much else on her. I can run her down for you, but it's going to cost. Up to you."

"Wow. Five for five. I can't believe your luck."

"Luck ain't got nothing to do with it, sweetheart."

Suddenly I could see her picking PO box locks late at night or breaking into apartment buildings. I didn't confirm.

"Sal, Sal, this is what I love about you. So, what do I owe you?"

She reached into her pocket and pulled out a couple of crumpled receipts. "A hundred and forty bucks to Uber it to Okotoks and back. Used some of the sixty you spotted me to jog that little lady's memory, the one who works at Postal Station M. Didn't get a receipt for that. Two lunches and a dinner," she pointed at a few balled-up pieces of paper.

She looked up at me and waited. I nodded.

"Fifteen hours, boots on the ground, comes to six hundred dollars—seven hundred sixty, with the expenses." She sucked in her cheeks and squinted at me. She was charging me forty bucks an hour but less than the going rate for surveillance.

I reached into my purse and rummaged for my cheque book. "A cheque okay with you?"

"Sure. I know where you live, doll."

I had no doubt she'd look me up if the cheque bounced. I wrote out the cheque for eight-hundred dollars and passed it over. "I added a small bonus for being quick and efficient."

She took the cheque and stuffed it into her coat pocket without looking at it. "Muchas gracias, amiga. Let me know if you want help running this Lee chick down. I'm not opposed to checking out that clinic in Mexico."

I was still smiling as I drove home. Despite Sal's outward appearance, and her somewhat dubious investigation methods, she possessed qualities that gave her a high likability score. I mentally reviewed the information Sal brought me. Nothing about the five people who attended the readings I was interested in seemed out of the ordinary. Now that I had full names, addresses, a few photos and even a workplace for a few of them, I'd be able to dig a little further. Misty might have a connection to one of these people that wasn't immediately obvious. Regardless, I wanted Misty to meet with each of them face to face, to see if any of them evoked the dark energy Misty described. If the face-to-face meetings didn't reveal anything, I'd be back to square one. No, that wasn't right. I would have made some progress. I'd know I was barking up the wrong tree.

I let my thoughts drift.

I could understand why Misty didn't want anyone digging around in her past. As her fame grew, reporters would be hassling her and her family, desperate for any tidbit of information to attract readers. But this aversion to talking about anyone or anything in her past made me think there was more to the story she told me about her troubled teen years than she shared. Someone had scrawled the word *liar* on her shop window, and now on her condo door. Doug's twisted face came to view. *"She's used to lying."* What had he meant? Was it only in reference to Misty's desire to hide her past?

The news that Carla Prince's death was a murder had thrown Misty off equilibrium. She claimed it changed everything. I recalled the look in her eyes as she cried *"It has to stop."* Of course, the threats, the murders, had to stop. Something danced at the edge of my mind, flitting elusively, annoyingly.

I pulled into my parking stall and cut the engine. I leaned back, closed my eyes as my head fell back, then snapped forward. I had momentarily forgotten my current rental was missing headrests. The sudden jarring shook a thought into place. Misty had lied to protect her sister. Was Misty keeping more secrets? Could Ivy have been the one who killed Carla's abusive husband?

TWENTY-EIGHT

I GLANCED AT MY watch. The longer I waited, the more difficult this was going to become. This was as good a time as any. I stared at my phone for several minutes before scrolling through to Mike's name. I took a deep breath and tapped his number.

"Mike. How are you? How's Julie?"

"Good. Gemma is staying with Julie until Saturday and I'm heading back there this weekend for a few days. We're hoping Julie might be out by the weekend, but I want to make sure she has everything she needs. Her ex is going to keep the kid another week to make sure she's up to looking after him."

"That's a relief. Do they know what happened to her?"

"Yeah. A viral infection that resulted in encephalitis. She may have gotten infected through a mosquito bite, while on holiday."

"Wow! Scary how something like that can become life threatening. Is she going to be okay?"

"They're still monitoring her, running tests, but expect a full recovery."

"Thank goodness. And how are you doing? How was the flight home?"

"Good, long. Slight delay leaving. Got home just after two

this morning. Felt great to sleep in my own bed—even though Smitty and Wess insisted on sleeping on top of me."

"I'm so sorry, Mike, I don't know what to say. Wait a minute. Did you say Smitty *and* Wess?"

"Yeah."

"He's home? Is he okay? I couldn't find Wess anywhere! I thought I lost him for good. I've just been sick about it."

"He's fine. Mrs. Niedswiki had him."

The silence stretched as I counted to ten. "What do you mean she had him?"

"I guess when she got home from her sister's, one of the neighbours told her about the fire in the alley and that you were canvassing the neighbourhood for Wess. She knew he wouldn't have run outside. He's terrified of the outdoors. I've taken him out in the garden a couple of times, and he slinks down and runs full tilt back to the house. When he gets inside, he's actually panting. Poor little guy leaves sweaty pawprints on the floor. Takes him hours to calm down."

"Oh. I didn't know he'd be that scared."

"Mrs. Niedswiki knew he'd be terrified, so she went over, found the little guy hiding and took him home with her."

"Thank god he's safe." *The bitch!* "I wish she would have said something to me, left a note maybe." I hadn't realized Mike gave her and I the same key code for his house when he was away, but then again, why wouldn't he.

"She isn't exactly the communicative type, is she? Maybe because her English isn't that great."

"If she tried using it more, she might have mastered it by now." I remembered her tight little grin. That bitch had enjoyed watching me crawl under the deck and march around the neighbourhood putting up posters. I shook my head. *Gratitude, Jorja. Gratitude.*

"I'm just happy he's okay. More than happy. You know, at one point I thought someone had been in the house. Never mind. I'm just thankful she's keeping an eye out for you and the cats and that Wess is safe."

Mike and I chatted a bit about his upcoming course. He mentioned the article on Misty and me in the paper.

"I wasn't happy about that. I wanted to call the paper and give them a blast, but Misty told the reporter during her interview with him that she had hired me, and he has every right to quote her."

"You know reporters. They're always looking for some juicy tidbit or twist to a story, regardless of the danger they may be putting people in. Watch your back."

"Don't worry, I will." I knew Mike only cautioned me because he cared, not that he thought I was incompetent. I found myself growing annoyed, nevertheless. Maybe left-over annoyance at the Polish hag's cat-napping.

"Why don't you come for supper next Tuesday night. You can tell me all about it. Unless you have plans?"

"I should be making you dinner after the worry I put you through about Wess. Then again, I never turn down a free meal."

I felt better after the call. Wess was okay, Julie was recovering, Mike was back, and my client was still alive. Speaking of which, I was starting to feel guilty. She was paying me good money and I really hadn't made much progress other than holding her hand. But as soon as you start thinking like that, the universe corrects and sends a double whammy. Which is why when my phone buzzed, I knew it would be bad news.

TWENTY-NINE

"JORJA. IT'S TARA. Have you seen the news?"

Heart in my throat, I strode across the room and picked up the remote. "No, what happened?"

"There's a fire. At Misty's shop."

I flipped to the news channel and turned up the volume.

"We're bringing you news from a situation unfolding now in Kensington. The historic McLaren block is engulfed in flames. Fire crews are battling the blaze, and crews on scene are working to prevent the fire from spreading to surrounding buildings. No news of any injuries at this time. The building was currently undergoing a renovation and only two tenants remained in the building. We are hoping everyone got out okay and that there are no injuries. We'll keep you updated throughout the evening. Back to you, Lisa."

I was in my car and out on Fourteenth Street before realizing I had no recall of leaving the condo or saying goodbye to Tara. Misty's building was on fire. I glanced over my shoulder and spotted my purse and phone on the back seat and breathed a sigh of relief. I turned onto Glenmore, a plume of black smoke now visible over the downtown area. The knot in my gut grew bigger.

Traffic was impossible as I got closer to the downtown core.

A combination of road closures in and out of downtown, due to construction, and several lanes now closed around the burning building brought traffic to a standstill. I pulled off Macleod Trail on Twenty-Fifth Avenue and found street parking. I tried Misty's number while I hustled over to the Erlton C-Train station and jostled my way out onto the train platform with the other commuters.

I tried calling Misty once on the train. Again, no answer. I got off at the Eighth Street station and made my way north. Traffic was gridlocked in all directions. A helicopter buzzed overhead. The stench of smoke was thick now.

A news update said Tenth Street was cordoned off to traffic in both directions and police were starting to route drivers away from the Tenth Street bridge. My brain chatter grew louder. Did Misty know about this? She must. I called Tara, hoping I hadn't rudely hung up on her. She didn't answer her phone either. The adrenaline kicked in, leaving me feeling jittery, like I had consumed way too much coffee.

I joined the foot traffic making its way out of the downtown and hit a bottleneck at Memorial Drive. Despite the Traffic Police urging pedestrians to continue moving forward, a crowd had gathered. Flames still licked the side of the building and an occasional tongue of orange shot out from the roof. Black smoke billowed out of the upstairs windows and seeped from between the cracks in the brick. Misty's shop windows were already cracked and blackened with soot. The building wasn't going to survive. I rushed down the block and joined the onlookers at the barricade that had been set up on Tenth Street. At least five firetrucks were on the scene, perhaps more around back.

"Is it as bad as it looks?"

A woman next to me replied, "One of the firemen came around from the back a few minutes ago and said the blaze was contained to this building. They evacuated the apartment building at the corner and all the buildings behind this one as a precaution."

"Any word on what happened yet?"

"No. Someone said they thought it might have started on the roof. The building was being renovated."

We waited silently, mesmerized by the scene in front of us. The air was acrid, and it was hard to breathe. A few people next to me started to cough, then moved on. I looked around. The small lane leading to the back of the building was barricaded, the flashing red lights of the emergency vehicles visible against the smoke-filled sky. I stepped back from the barricade and moved down the street. Where was the preacher?

I kept moving north. I could see the news vehicle at the northern barrier to Tenth Street. I headed that way. I heard the crowd shift and murmur behind me. I turned. Several members of the emergency response team were moving the crowd back. Someone ran past me saying they were worried the roof might collapse.

I reached the news trucks. A small crowd was gathered here, waiting for any news that might be shared.

A news reporter was speaking into a mike. "As far as we know, there was no one inside. We have with us the owner of Healing Waters, Ms. Peoria Benson. Ms. Benson, this must be devastating for you. We understand the upper floor of the building was being renovated as part of your plans to expand your business."

Peoria stood next to the reporter. When the reporter mentioned her name, she took one hand off the other, still clutched over her heart, and brushed back a strand of hair off her face.

"I can't believe this is happening. My dream…my entire life's work going up in smoke. I had plans to expand all the space on the second floor into a world-class spa. I don't know how I will ever recover from this."

Was Peoria funding the renovation herself? I hadn't considered the possibility.

"Ms. Benson, this is pretty devastating, especially for someone like yourself and the owner of the other shop in the building, Mystic Miracles. Any idea what started the blaze?"

Peoria stiffened at the mention of Misty's shop. "The building was once a landmark in the city. Unfortunately, the last few years have taken its toll. We've had a number of squatters move in upstairs, there have been break-ins, acts of vandalism. It was my intention to use my business, Healing Waters, to bring back the grace and beauty of this building and help to revitalize this once vibrant neighbourhood. Unfortunately, certain people weren't happy that the building was being renovated, the area being gentrified."

"Are you saying the fire might have been set on purpose?"

"I'm not saying this was set on purpose, but when you have people living in sleeping bags in spaces that have been shuttered for good reason, lighting open fires in metal barrels, this is what happens. It's careless disregard for the property of others. These people need to be arrested. Now hard-working small business owners, like myself, are out on the street."

Whoops. Her lack of empathy for the homeless is going to ruin her chances at a go-fund-me page.

"Do you have insurance?"

"Of course, I have insurance," she snapped. Peoria brushed back a strand of hair and smiled her most pious smile, as if suddenly remembering she was on television. "Forgive me, you can see how stressful this is." Her lip quivered. "I do have insurance, but my business will be shut down for months, if not longer. No insurance policy will cover that. All my equipment is gone. If I were to try and set up elsewhere, I need to find appropriate space, accessible to my clientele. I had the only cryogenic chamber in the city. It took eight months to get it here from Sweden. I have no other income."

Now tears coursed down her face. A woman stepped out from the crowd and led her gently away from the cameras.

I had seen enough. I turned to walk away. That's when I saw him. A dark-haired guy, thick-rimmed glasses, mid-twenties. I had seen him before, watching Misty's shop. The man turned, spotted me, and bolted. I broke into a run.

I raced down the street, dodging people as I tried to keep him in sight.

"Hey, wait up. Stop."

People were staring. The man turned, then sped up. A woman with a stroller stepped out in front of me. I dodged her and slammed into a barrier which had been set up to funnel pedestrians the right way along the street, and hit the ground. The searing pain in my knee sent a jolt of fear through me and made me queasy. I sat up, clutching my knee. My eyes searched the crowd, but the dark-haired man had melted from sight. I glanced down at my jeans. No blood.

Limping back toward Memorial Drive, I found myself staring unseeing at the people walking past me. A buzzing sound brought me back from my detached introspection. Misty's number was on the screen.

"Hello, Misty?" I stepped out of the main traffic and held a finger against my other ear.

"Misty? Are you there? Can you hear me?"

A crackling noise came over the phone. I thought I heard something, then the phone went dead. I redialled Misty's number. No answer. I hung up, more worried than before. Was that Misty on the line? Why didn't she answer?

I limped back to the C-Train station. Had I heard someone speak or was it just the combination of noise on the street and static on the line? By the time I reached my car I had convinced myself that no one had been on the line.

THIRTY

SUNLIGHT FILTERED INTO the bedroom. I pulled my cell phone off the nightstand. Ten to seven. I had clocked all of about two hours of sleep, tossing and turning between recurrent snippets of a nightmare. I dreamt I was lost in a dark network of tunnels. I took a stairwell down into a shadowy storage area, a dark, evil place. I hurried past twisted metal, burnt-out car shells, keeping a fearful eye on the claw-armed, human-like creatures with torn, blood-spattered clothing, watching me with vacant eyes. I rushed headlong around the corner looking for a way back, a way out. He stood at the end of the dim corridor, waiting for me. The preacher.

Fully awake, I groaned and checked my messages. Nothing from Misty, nothing from Tara. I climbed out of bed and limped to the washroom. It was going be a long day. I ran through my yoga routine, one ear on the morning news, the other listening to the voices in my head arguing about what to do next.

I stared at the TV screen. The great gaping holes on the second floor of the once red brick building, were framed by swaths of blackened brick above each opening. Broken glass and rubble lay strewn on the sidewalk in front of the building. The morning news hosts were speculating as to what might have caused the fire.

My phone dinged, alerting me to a new message. I reached for the phone, expecting it to be Misty or Tara. It was neither. My best friend Gab had sent me a short video clip of her in Los Cabos getting ready for her day-long camel outback adventure to an Eco-Farm. The message read *Don't let the smile on my face fool you. My camel hates me. Already stepped on my foot and spit in my face…not a fan.* I had to laugh. Gab was a bit of a fashionista and liked the finer things in life. I wondered which of her cousins had roped her into this.

I texted back, *Never a dull moment with the Giovanni-Rizzo clan. Hope there's tequila with lunch. Watch your back, girl.* I attached a GIF of a camel nipping the rider in front of it on the butt. Momentarily cheered, I got dressed and headed to the little outdoor mall at the east end of Glenmore Reservoir.

Coffee helped. I sat upstairs in the little café and read about yesterday's fire on my newsfeed. "The fire started at the McLaren building on Tenth Street NW some time in the early afternoon. Forty firefighters were called to the scene and managed to contain the fire to the building. Construction at the site started several weeks ago, as a massive renovation was planned for the building. Chief Fire-Prevention Officer Kamar Lapoor said the fire started on the roof of the building. Roofers were seen working on the roof the morning of the fire, but no further information has been released as to the cause. Lapoor said the division will be working with Urban Works, the general contractor for Lehman Group, to determine damage and create a plan for the site once the extent of damage has been determined. Investigation into the cause is continuing."

A second article about the fire included an interview with Peoria Benson. The article also mentioned Mystic Miracles as the second business destroyed in the blaze, but that the owner could not be reached for comment. Tara must be ripping her hair out.

I sent Misty another text and considered other options. I decided to track down Lori Watson's brother. Misty was working with the Watson family to try and find Lori's killer. Maybe they knew where she was. Half an hour later, I managed to find Gregg Watson's Facebook page. I sent him a message asking him to contact me as it was urgent that I locate Misty.

I sat back, looking around the small alcove. The cushy chairs, tastefully dim lighting and distance from the boisterous coffee drinkers downstairs made it one of my favourite spots. A woman quietly cleaned the few tables that had emptied. She moved toward me wordlessly and raised an eyebrow at my stacked bowl and plate. I nodded and she whisked them away. Moments later she returned with a coffee carafe and refilled my mug. I loved this place.

At nine o'clock I called Tara's office. She answered promptly.

"Jorja. Sorry I didn't get back to you last night. The phone has been ringing off the hook. Have you seen or talked to Misty? I'm really worried."

"As am I. I called and texted her several times yesterday and this morning. She's not answering." I thought about the peculiar phone call from Misty's number yesterday and the garbled word I thought I heard—but decided it would only confuse the situation.

"I mean, her shop just burned down. How can she just disappear like this—without a word."

"There's been nothing on the news about anyone being injured in the fire," I said. "I'm going to go to her condo, check around. There's no way she hasn't heard about the fire. I've tried contacting Gregg Watson. Maybe he's heard from Misty or knows where she is."

"Good thinking. Misty needs to get on this right away. I mean, there are appointments to rebook, insurance to deal with."

Half an hour later I was in front of Misty's condo. I called her again and when she didn't answer I got out and made my way to the entrance. I pressed the intercom button to her unit. Nothing came back at me. Her sudden disappearance troubled me. I was starting to think a wellness check by the police might be in order.

I don't know what I expected to find but I decided to drive down to her now burnt-out shop. Surely the firefighters would have checked the building for injured people…or bodies. What had Misty said about fire? Didn't she say she saw flames but felt no heat? I shook my head. At the time I thought she might be referencing the fire started behind Mike's fence. I was no longer sure.

Traffic was still somewhat snarled on Tenth Street. Barricades remained on Memorial Drive, closing off the northbound lanes on Tenth Street. Southbound traffic on Tenth Street was reduced to one lane. I detoured over to Eighth Street and doubled back. Tired of fighting the traffic congestion, I veered into a small parking lot on Second Avenue and parked. As soon as I got out of the car, I could taste the acrid odour that lingered in the air.

I reached Tenth Street and crossed to the west side. Several passersby had stopped to gawk at the McLaren building, or what was left of it. The devastation was far worse close up than on a television screen. Crews were already pulling out the contents of the building, including material from Healing Waters and Misty's shop. I hope Misty had insurance and backed up her files. I walked around to the side street. Barricades and police tape cordoned off access. I stood across the street and stared down the alley. Looked like the preacher lost his home too. Where was he? I circled the block, then headed to the south side of the building.

I found the preacher standing on the corner near Memorial Drive—subdued today. Proclamations covered every inch of the cardboard sign he wore, from his neck to below his knees. The tightly scrawled scribbles were impossible to read with a causal glance.

As I got closer, I noticed he looked juiced.

"Hey, preacher."

It took him a second to realize someone might be talking to him. A real person, not one of the voices in his head.

He turned toward me, a huge black smudge on his forehead. It took me a minute to realize it was a cross. A flashback sent me back to my childhood, going to early-morning mass with my grandmother and having the priest smudge a cross onto our foreheads. Ash Wednesday. I always wiped mine off on the way to school; my grandmother still had hers at nightfall. I thought back to those years. I don't even remember when Ash Wednesday occurs. Sometime around Easter. Shows what a good Catholic I am. But Easter was long gone, we were coming up on June now.

"Hey. I know you. Is today the Sabbath?"

"No. It's Thursday."

Something woke within him. "And on the fourth day there was evening and there was morning."

"Excuse me. I'm looking for a friend of mine." Why was I talking to this man? "She owns Mystic Miracles. That little shop at the end of the building that burned down." I turned and pointed at the cracked and charred wall of the building.

"I know her. She's the blessed daughter of Mary Magdalene, from whom seven demons were driven out."

I sighed. "I can't find her. I've looked everywhere. Have you seen her?"

His eyes widened; he made the sign of the cross. "They who place themselves in opposition to the truth expose themselves to the just and terrible judgment of God."

"Did you see what happened to her?" What the hell was he talking about? This guy was seriously screwed. And so was I.

His face twitched. "Satan is among us," he shouted. "Satan, Devil, Beelzebub, Lucifer, King of Babylon, Abaddon, son of

Evil." He took a step forward, his face scrunched, and hissed, "He took her."

"The devil took her? How do you know him to be the devil?"

"Revelation Chapter 9 Verse 11 - 2. When he opened the Abyss, smoke rose from it like from a gigantic furnace, obscuring the sun and sky. Out of the smoke came locusts, given the power of scorpions. They were instructed not to harm any plant or tree, but only those who do not have the sign of God on their foreheads. They were told not to kill them but only to torture them. During those days those captured will long to die, but death will elude them." He suddenly stepped toward me, his face inches from mine, his breath foul. "He defies the Lord. He hurts animals. Birds."

I heard blood rushing through my head. "When did you see him?"

"He's here among us. I see him often." He straightened and turned as two young men in suits rushed by. "Repent," he yelled after them. "For you are of your father, the fornicator, and the lusts of your father are yours."

I glanced back at the preacher as I crossed the street. I hated to think what lulled him to sleep at night. The guy was a ranting lunatic, putting a religious spin to everything he said and saw. But I had no doubt he had seen someone at Misty's shop. A man who hurt animals. Hurt birds.

THIRTY-ONE

W E CIRCLED LOW over the water, the dark ripples below breaking white near the shore. I let out a sigh of relief as the tires touched the tarmac, the engines whining as the plane raced to the end of the pavement. Thirty minutes later, I exited the Victoria airport, in my rented Chevrolet Spark. The overhanging clouds turned to mist, which settled on the windshield like maple tree sap in the spring, but a lot easier for the wipers to clear. Car tires hissed and sent up their own mist, shrouding the greenery along the highway, a stark contrast to the still brown landscape I left just hours ago.

Tara and I finally contacted the police yesterday to report Misty missing. Gregg Watson messaged me in the morning to say he hadn't heard from Misty either. The police had taken Misty's disappearance seriously, especially after we mentioned that in addition to having her business destroyed by fire, Lori Watson had been killed at her condo, and Misty had been receiving threats. As a courtesy, I called Detective Brighton and let him know Misty was missing. Maybe he'd get wind of Misty's disappearance through official channels, but I felt compelled to let him know, even though it meant listening to him chastise me about interfering in police business. I didn't offer any of my half-baked theories about who or why someone might mean her harm, especially as half-baked might be overstating my thinking on the situation.

Ironic that Sal had tracked down the five people we were interested in so quickly, only to have nowhere to go with the information now that Misty had disappeared. So much for being able to prove or disprove my theory that one of them might be linked to the disturbing thoughts and feelings she had been experiencing at certain of her events.

I could only hope that Misty had checked herself into some obscure bed and breakfast with no Wi-Fi or external distractions so that she could focus on the messages her spirit friends were sending her. After reporting her missing, I had gone home and explored several crazy thoughts that had been circling my mind the last few days.

I needed to talk to someone from Misty's past. Someone who knew Misty, knew her sister, knew Carla. Maybe it would turn out to be nothing, but *my* gut told me the connection to what was happening to Misty started there.

I had followed up on the meagre information Corporal Reed, the RCMP officer stationed in Sooke, had shared with me. She had mentioned Carla Prince had been reported missing by a friend who apparently owned or ran Billie's Café. It hadn't taken me any time to find the café's location and information on its owner, Billie Thomson, on the internet.

I crossed the bridge, pulled over and checked the Sooke map for directions into town and Billie's Café. I slowly made my way through Sooke's quaint downtown and turned toward the harbour. The mist had lifted, and several low clouds hung over the water, white streaks against the lush green of the surrounding hills. It was mid-afternoon and sunny by the time I pulled up to Billie's Café.

Billie's had a rustic vibe to it, starting with the cedar plank siding on the outside. I opened a wooden screen door and stepped into a small bright space. The black-and-white tiled floors stretched from the door to the wooden counter near the back of the café, where one could place an order. Red-vinyl-covered stools stood in front of the counter and three booths on each side of the room completed the seating arrangement.

A woman, her grey-streaked hair pulled back in a ponytail, stood rinsing a pot behind the counter. She turned as I approached.

"Gorgeous day out there, isn't it?"

I nodded. "It certainly is. I can't get over the scenery."

"Is it your first time here?"

"It is. I lived in Vancouver for a while, back in the day. I've been to Vancouver Island a number of times, but never to the southern tip."

"Hope you get a chance to explore the area. So, what finally brings you down here?"

"Unfortunately, business, not pleasure. I'm looking for Billie Thomson."

"Oh. That's me." She looked slightly puzzled; the smile narrowed a smidge.

"Jorja Knight," I said, reaching out my hand. "I'm a private investigator. I'm trying to find out more about Carla Prince's death for a client of mine."

Billie wiped her hands on the apron she wore over her jeans and a blue plaid shirt and came around the counter. "Jared," she called over her shoulder. "Can you look after the front counter for me, please?" A young man, still in his teens, came out of the kitchen. A lot of men were starting to look like they were in their teens to me.

"Coffee?" she asked.

Once we had coffees in hand, Billie led me out the side door to a small covered patio. "Hope you don't mind sitting outside, I thought you might appreciate the privacy and my customers won't be interrupting us with their hellos. Conversation can get pretty boisterous, like at a big family dinner."

"Not at all."

"You said you're looking into Carla's death for a client?"

"My client and Carla grew up together, childhood friends. They lost track of each other over the years. Then about a month ago she got news of Carla's death, through a mutual friend. She only just found out that Carla's death is a being investigated as a homicide. I tracked down Corporal Reed, and she's the one who mention you alerted them to Carla's disappearance."

"I was so shocked. Not that there was a murder—our small community has had its unfortunate share over the years. But Carla? I can't imagine anyone wanting to cause her harm."

"Had she lived here long?"

"She moved here about fifteen years ago," she said warily. "I don't understand. What is your client's interest in Carla's death?"

"This may sound a bit…strange, but my client is a clairvoyant medium. She had a premonition that a dark-haired woman would be killed, strangled. She had this premonition right around the time Carla was killed. At the time, she didn't know Carla had been killed. The premonition did not go away. Two weeks ago, another dark-haired woman was killed, strangled, right in front of her condo. Her vision of a dark-haired woman's death persists. She feels she might be the next victim. She hired me to help her find and stop whoever is doing this. I'm looking for any sort of connection between these women."

"Oh my gosh." Her eyes widened. "I never imagined it could be…what…a serial killer? Of course, I'll help. What can I tell you?"

"What was Carla like?"

"She was quiet, but easy to get to know. She was well-liked.

She did a lot for the community. She was such a positive person, always giving people a hand, wherever it was needed. A real joy to be around. I miss her so much." Billie looked away, and wiped the corner of her eye, then turned back. "She loved nature and she loved to paint. It wasn't unusual for her to go off hiking for the day, sketchbook and charcoal pencils in hand."

"Is that what she was doing the day she went missing?"

Billie nodded, her voice flat. "A hiker found her and called police. They found her backpack with all her sketching material just down the beach."

"Corporal Reed said she had been attacked before going into the water."

"Yes. At first, they thought it might be suicide. But I knew she'd never kill herself."

"When did you report her missing?"

"Carla and I were supposed to have dinner together on Sunday. I usually close the café at 4:00 p.m. on Sunday and we had planned to meet here. When she didn't show I went to her place. I had tried calling her several times during the day and got no answer. When I saw she wasn't at her place, I alerted the RCMP. They started searching right away.

"Several people said they saw Carla walking along a trail, toward Albert Head Lagoon. No one saw her after that. Two days later her body was found washed up on a rocky beach. Corporal Reed said they had checked with a nearby penitentiary, but everyone was accounted for. Just as likely a complete stranger killed her rather than a low-risk offender out on a day pass, but they had to check."

"I was told that although she was found on the beach, the coroner determined she'd been in the water for at least twenty hours, at some point."

"It was awful. They called me to identify her body." She

swallowed hard, her hand resting at the base of her throat, her eyes tormented. "The trail weaves in and out. There are several places that provide a good, but steep, vantage point. She may have been attacked there and pushed into the water. Her hands and face were so badly scraped and cut I barely recognized her. The coroner said it probably happened as her body came to shore and washed up on the rocks."

"I'm so sorry. Sorry you lost your good friend, sorry that she died. My client was shocked when she heard Carla had been strangled. The friend who wrote her thought Carla's death had been an accident. We only found out a few days ago that it's a homicide."

We sat quietly, each lost in our own thoughts, the sun warm on my face. The sound of children laughing at the small playground next door to the café seemed a cruel contrast to Carla's death.

"She was happy here?"

"She was content, at peace." After a pause, Billie said, "Did you know she wrote a weekly column for The Beacon, our local paper? She thought she might try her hand at a children's book someday. Illustrate it herself. She did love to paint—watercolours. She tried to capture all the beauty she saw in nature. I have a few in the café, if you want a look later. I have permission to sell the rest at our summer fine arts show. We'll donate the proceeds to the Sooke Creative Common. Carla helped establish the creative, sat on the board of directors."

"I'd love to see her paintings. Did Carla ever talk about her past? The time before she moved here."

Billie grew pensive, sipped her coffee, stole glances over her shoulder at the children playing next door.

"My client grew up on the west coast. She and Carla were good friends right through high school, although I believe Carla may have never finished. The plan was to get married, have kids, live somewhere their kids could play together. Carefree, teenage dreams. But things didn't go that way."

"You know Carla's history then?"

"I know she spent some time in prison. Sounds like she may have gotten a bad rap. From the little my client told me, the victim—her husband—was a real piece of work."

Billie nodded. "She didn't tell many people. I mean, would you? Sometimes it's best to leave the past where it belongs."

I nodded. "Did she tell you she was pregnant at the time?"

Billie nodded. "She rarely talked about her past. But on one of those rare nights when she became melancholic and let herself have one too many glasses of wine—which, by the way, was two for her—she told me about him."

"So, it was a boy. My client wasn't a hundred percent sure."

"Yes. A big, healthy baby boy." Billie put her coffee down and rubbed her arms as if a sudden cool breeze cut through the calm humid air.

"She never even had a chance to hold him. Not even once. I don't know why they did that back then. Barbaric, really, ripping a newborn baby out of its mother's arms. What harm could it have done to let her hold him?" Billie shook her head. "I can't believe how they treated her. Carla said her baby was the true victim. She wasn't a religious person, more spiritual than that, but she told me she said a prayer for him every night since the day he was born. She prayed he had a better life than the one she would have subjected him to."

"She never knew what happened to him?"

"No. She told me that on the day he turned sixteen, she registered her name with Adoptions Canada as someone who wanted to meet her child and was open to being contacted. I don't know if you know, but Adoptions Canada looks to the adopted child to be the one who has final say over whether they want to reconnect with a birth parent or not. They have to be at least sixteen though."

"No one contacted her?"

"No."

"That's a shame." Life was like that, missed opportunities and broken dreams. I gave myself a shake. It was times like this that made it hard to see life through a half-full-glass lens. Becoming a private investigator was limiting my success at seeing every event as an opportunity for some good.

"The RCMP probably asked you all these questions, but did you notice anything in the days and weeks leading up to her death? Anything unusual happen, or did she seem worried or bothered in any way?"

"No. That's why the idea that she may have killed herself was totally ludicrous."

"No one new in her life? Anyone in the picture who wasn't there months ago?"

"No. She rented an apartment when she first moved to Sooke, but about five years ago she bought a little place on the west edge of town. She was finally getting around to fixing it up, making it her own."

"What about contractors? Anyone working with her?"

"Carla?" Billie laughed. "Nope. She was a DIY gal, all the way. Claimed it was half the fun."

"You wouldn't have a picture of her, would you?"

Billie pulled out her cell phone. "Actually, I do. This one is from our Christmas Fair." She handed me her phone. Billie stood with her arm around another woman with short dark hair, streaked with grey. Carla was laughing and looking up at Billie, who was a good three or four inches taller than her.

I handed the phone back. "She looks happy. My client will be glad to hear she found herself a new life and a good friend."

"Thank you. That's what makes this so hard. Why would someone do this?"

"That's what we're all trying to find out. The only commonality I've been able to find so far is both women who were strangled had dark hair. They were both happy, kind, willing to lend a helping hand. Maybe that's what killed them…the willingness to stop and talk to or help a stranger. A stranger who's psychotic or evil."

"Let's hope your client isn't the next target and that you and the police find whoever did this. If you give me your email address, I'll send you the photo," she said, taking her phone back. "You can forward it to your client. It's too bad she and Carla never got a chance to reconnect."

Billie invited me back into the café to look at Carla's watercolours. These weren't for sale, she said, just some she was keeping as a memento. I had noticed the pictures when I first walked in. Billie excused herself as I made my way around the room. The watercolours were done in soft muted blues and greys, mostly landscapes and a few of the boat marina. Billie returned with an eight-by-six-inch watercolour.

"I want your client to have this. Carla would want her to have it. See that small island in the background? That's Texada Island the way it looks from Powell River. That's where they grew up. I believe Carla painted it from memory."

"I can't thank you enough. Misty will love this. It's very kind of you."

I left Billie my card, and she promised to keep me apprised should there be any new developments. I glanced over at the painting, now sitting wrapped in brown paper on the seat next to me. The one thing I noticed about Carla's paintings is the sky was always painted a pinkish-purply hue. Very pretty, but for me it invoked feelings of a storm brewing.

THIRTY-TWO

T HE SUN, ALREADY low on the horizon, peeked out as I neared Comox. Traffic had been steady, and I felt like I had been driving all day, and in a sense I had. I glanced at my watch, looked for a break in traffic and passed a cube truck. The driver probably thought I was an idiot, risking a pass on this stretch of highway to shear off mere seconds in my race to the Little Lane Ferry Terminal. Trees and farmland flashed past me. I pulled back into my lane, eyes scanning the time on the dash for the umpteenth time. I rounded the curve and blew out my breath. The Salish Orca was still docked, cars still coming off the ferry. People stood in the sunshine next to their vehicles, chatting, having a smoke, soaking up the sunshine as they waited for the last ferry of the day. I purchased my ticket, followed instructions to pull into the second lane. The cube truck rolled past me along with ten other vehicles, as they were waved into the far lane. *Karma, Jorja.*

I rolled down my window and leaned back. The sound of gulls and the clank of cars rolling off the ferry onto the loading ramp barely registered. As the day wore on my mood had deepened. Nostalgia—with perhaps a touch of regret. Regret for what, I don't know. Vancouver had been home for seven years, four to attend university and three at my first job at a BC government lab. My first year at university had been rough. I hadn't known anyone, and it had been a bit of a shock coming from the small mining town in northern Ontario where I grew up. I handled it by drinking…a lot. It was also the year my parents died. I left the spring semester early to deal with it but, in reality, I had been dealing with it most of my adult life.

I met my best friend, Gab, in my second year of university and life took a definite swing upward. We roomed together the last two years of university and became friends. Lifers. After university, Gab took a job in Toronto and I stayed behind. It hadn't been the best of times nor the worst. Today, something had unsettled me. I felt the need to finish what I came out here to do and go back. Maybe the island was too zen for me. Maybe it brought up too many memories. Sooke had that touristy, retirement community vibe to it, as least what I had seen of it. Maybe that was it. I was being reminded of my own march forward into a future of growing my own vegetables, dabbling in arts and crafts and…what?

The drivers started climbing back into their cars. A few minutes later, loudspeakers announced boarding instructions. I turned on the engine, adding to the humming throb of engines around me. I waited in trepidation as vehicle after vehicle headed up the ramp. Just as I was certain I'd be left waiting in the parking lot for the morning ferry, a woman in coveralls removed the orange cone at the front of our line and waved us through. Once parked, I locked up the car and headed to the upper deck.

The ferry was full. People lined up at the small kiosk to grab a sandwich or something to eat, a chore to be taken care of before disembarking in Powell River. I stared out the window. Snow still capped the mountains framing the blue water and bright fresh green of the surrounding trees. I sat, exhausted, refusing to think. There weren't many nursing homes in the northern gulf islands. I had searched for nursing homes and senior residences on Texada Island, then widened my search to include all of the sunshine coast as well as Bowen and Denman Island. I finally found a Mrs. Lane in Powell River. With any luck she'd turn out to be Misty's mother.

The ferry bobbed up and down, sending a thick white spray into the air, a smooth crossing by west coast standards. I shifted one seat over to accommodate a family of five. A young couple stood braced against the wind on the outer deck, their arms wrapped around each other. I closed my eyes to the chatter, the children racing around under the watchful eyes of parents.

It was almost dark when I checked into my motel, which was a stone's throw from the Westview ferry terminal. The room was cold, clean and very retro but not a result of planned decorating. The combination added to my lacklustre mood. The tiny kitchenette reminded me that the burger I picked up on my way out of Sooke was the only food I had eaten all day. I walked over to the window and looked out over the water, the sun leaving pink streaks in the darkening sky. A fragment from some childhood ditty came to mind. *Red sky at night, sailors' delight.*

I pulled the drapes and turned up the dial on the hot water radiator. Grabbing a sweater from my overnight bag, I locked up and took the stairs to the main level. The small café off the lobby was closed. I bought a bag of Doritos and a diet coke from the machines next to the registration desk and returned to my room.

I woke in the dark, fumbled for my phone and discovered it was already after seven in the morning. With any luck I would be on my way back to Calgary by evening. The thought cheered me. A quick shower, a stop in the lobby to pay my bill and I was on my way to Sunset Terrace. The morning was cool and cloudy, the waves out in the harbour choppy and grey against the deep green of the rolling hills.

Sunset Terrace was everything I expected. A low curved building, with good views of the Bay or the parking lot, depending on which side you found yourself. Maybe the rooms were assigned by age. Or would the rooms with good views be saved for those who still had the wherewithal to enjoy them? More than likely it was strictly a function of price.

I parked, got out, and my car door *thunked* closed. The air lacked warmth and smelled faintly of fish, seaweed, and water-soaked pebbles and sand. A ferry boat whistle broke the stillness. I made my way to the double front doors and stepped inside the small enclave. I searched the directory listing, found and buzzed the manager.

Inside, a thin man wrestled his walker off the elevator. He stood uncertain for a few minutes then made a beeline for the door. He buzzed me in and gave me a vacant grin, his eyes scrunched into two thin slits. I thanked him, stepped inside but remained by the door. So much for security. Or maybe he figured if you became a resident at Sunset Terrace, there was a good chance you'd outlived all your enemies.

A woman rounded the corner, stopped, then stepped toward me. "Were you the one who rang me?"

"Yes. I'm Jorja Knight." I extended my handed and nodded toward the stooped man who had managed to wedge his walker in between two armchairs in the small sitting room off the entry. "That kind gentleman buzzed me in."

"Oh." She smiled then held up a finger. "Just a sec." She turned. "Walter, are you stuck?" She walked over to him. "Do you remember what I told you?" He tilted his head toward her. "If you can't go forward, what should you do? Walter? Do you remember what you should do?" I heard him mumble something. "That's right, back up. Back up, there you go."

I must have misheard. I thought he said bugger-off not back up. Maybe my hearing was going to pot.

"You're here to visit with Mrs. Lane? Are you a friend of the family?"

"I know her daughter, Misty. When she heard I was coming to Powell River she asked me to drop in on her mother if I had the time."

"I must warn you; Mrs. Lane's medication keeps her sedated and she is experiencing a moderate level of dementia."

"I understand."

She led me to a table in a small sitting room which was an extension of the larger dining room. A man and a woman sat at one of the tables playing cards. Another gentleman snoozed in his wheelchair next to the fireplace, which remained unlit.

A woman wearing nurse scrubs pushed a small frail woman in a wheelchair into the room. She angled the chair in next to the table and bent over to speak to the woman.

"Doreen. You've got a visitor this morning. This nice lady has come to visit you."

Doreen craned her neck upward to look at the nurse, a puzzled smile on her face. The nurse turned to me. "She's a bit hard of hearing. I'm Corrine. I'll be back in a bit to see how you're doing."

I nodded my thanks, pulled out a chair and moved it closer to her wheelchair.

"Hi, Doreen. My name is Jorja. I'm a friend of your daughter's. Misty."

She turned her head toward me.

"Misty wanted me to stop by, see how you're doing."

"Misty?"

"You remember your daughter, Misty?"

The smile faded. "Is she here?" She looked around fearfully, her fingers tugging at the bottom of her sweater.

"No, no, she's not here."

"I tried to stop it."

"Stop what, Doreen?"

Her jaw worked but nothing came out. Her gnarled fingers gripped the arms of her wheelchair. She started rocking, a guttural sound escaping slack lips.

"It's okay, Doreen. It's okay." I patted her hand. "It's a beautiful day. Have you seen how pretty the water looks this morning in the sunlight?" I got up and pushed her wheelchair over to the window and crouched next to it. She stopped rocking; her face remained dark, troubled. "I'm sorry, Doreen, I didn't mean to upset you. Oh, look at all the gulls."

Suddenly a flock of gulls swooped by, their calls heard through the single-pane window. Doreen looked up and clapped her hands together. Her fingers, barely meeting, emitted no sound.

Nurse Corrine returned. "There you are. Enjoying the view, Doreen?" She tilted her head at me and gave her head a small shake.

"I'm afraid mentioning her daughter only seemed to upset her. Can I ask you something?"

"Sure, hon, what is it?"

"Doreen's daughter got a letter in the mail five or six weeks ago. About a childhood friend who passed away. She said it was from her mother, but that someone helped her write it. Is Mrs. Lane more lucid at times?"

"No, dear, I'm afraid this is one of her better days. I don't think that letter was from Doreen."

I nodded. "Does anyone come to see her regularly? Perhaps her other daughter, Ivy, or a friend?"

"The Sisters of Mercy set up a senior buddy support group. It's made up largely of seniors themselves, who are still living independently. They are paired up with residents at Sunset Terrace or individuals who may be having a long stay at the hospital and are alone or with no family nearby. Mrs. Kennedy is Doreen's buddy. She was the librarian here in Powell River for years but is retired now. She comes and reads to Doreen every Thursday."

I said my goodbyes, paused at the doorway to look back. Nurse Corrine had turned Doreen's wheelchair around and was pushing her out of the room. Doreen's head lay tilted against her shoulder. She turned her head, the tendons in her neck sinewy cords. Her eyes stretched wide, the pupils black holes against the bulging whites of her eyes.

THIRTY-THREE

THE FEAR IN Doreen Lane's face stayed with me as I drove through town looking for a place to eat. Life was meant to be lived. Hard to accept that the remnants of what had been Doreen were left trapped inside that brittle shell. A shell that no longer served her well.

Feeling more human after eggs, toast, sausage, and a good start on my daily requirement for caffeine, I pulled up to a bright-blue, two-storey wooden clapboard house. Betty Kennedy hadn't been hard to find. As the former long-term librarian of the only library in town, she remained an active member of the community and still taught the Memoir for Seniors writing program at the library. A woman stood on the front porch, watering can in hand.

I got out, walked up the sidewalk.

"Good afternoon, I'm Jorja Knight." I climbed the steps; the wood weathered a pleasant grey. "Are you Betty Kennedy?"

"I am. It's nice to meet you. I was just giving my flower pots their daily shower. Please come in." She led me inside. "Might I offer you something? Coffee? Iced tea? I just made some."

I accepted her offer of iced tea. She gestured to the two arm-chairs arranged by the front window, facing each other across a small round marble-topped table. "Let's sit by the window."

I sank into the nearest chair and awaited her return. I could see my car parked out front through the branches of a massive Hemlock. A squirrel darted from around the trunk, froze, then shot up the bark and disappeared into the greenery above.

Betty returned with two iced teas, placed them on the table between us and sat down. "Now how can I help you? You said you are working with one of Doreen's girls?"

"Yes, Misty. You know her?"

"Oh yes. I've known Doreen and her family since the girls were little. Not sure if they would remember much about me." She leaned forward. "I hope she's well?"

"In one sense, yes. Someone has, however, been leaving her threatening messages, vandalizing her property. She hired me to find out who and why. Then, a woman was murdered, right in front of the building where Misty lives. A woman who resembled Misty."

"Murdered? Oh my. Do you think Misty might be in danger?"

"I'm afraid so. I don't know if you know, but Misty is a psychic-clairvoyant. She had a premonition, a strong sense that a woman, fitting her description, would be murdered. Choked or strangled to death. She didn't know who. It was only after the murder of Lori Watson, the woman killed in front of her condo, that we started to think Misty may have been the intended victim. Then recently, Misty told me about a letter she received from someone who visits her mother and writes occasionally to update her on her condition. A letter in which she learned that Carla Prince, a childhood friend of hers, also died."

"Why yes, I sent her that letter. There's a group of us who volunteer our time to visit with the sick or infirm. Sometimes we're the only visitors they get. The world is so different today, families spread all over. We spend time reading or playing cards or sometimes we just sit with them to watch TV. I occasionally write to Misty to let her know how her mother is doing. We always sign the letter on their behalf or sometimes leave it unsigned, as I do in Doreen's case as she's not lucid enough to dictate a letter."

"Misty told me her mother has dementia. I know she appreciates the updates she gets. She was saddened to learn of Carla Prince's death."

"Carla didn't have an easy life, and when I read she died…at such a young age. Well. Heartbreaking, really."

I nodded. "I became rather curious when I learned that Carla's death occurred right around the time Misty first started getting this premonition that a dark-haired woman would be killed, strangled to death. Recently, we found out that Carla's death is being treated as a homicide. Like Lori Watson, the woman found in front of Misty's condo, Carla was also strangled to death."

"Strangled to death? Oh my! I never heard. I came across her obituary notice and it said that she died suddenly. I just assumed it was an accident of some sort."

"We realized Misty's premonition could have been about either of the murdered women, or both. Someone is still leaving Misty threatening messages. Misty believes she may be the killer's next victim."

"How astonishing." Betty sank back against the cushions and covered her mouth with her fist, then leaned forward. "Are you sure? This is like a story right off the pages of a murder mystery or thriller. She has gone to the police, hasn't she?"

"Yes, of course. The police have made note of her premonitions, but as you can well imagine, the premise lacks details. All we have are the threats Misty has been receiving and the fact that two dark-haired women were both murdered, strangled. Misty hired me to help her follow up on the physical clues. Possibly prevent a third murder."

"Oh dear. Prevent a murder, you say. Did she sense these women were in danger? Do you think their murders are related?"

"It's hard to say. There's certainly no current evidence to suggest they are related," I added hurriedly. "But that's why I'm here. I'm trying to find out if there could be a link between the three women."

"My goodness. I didn't know Carla had been strangled. I saw her obituary in a copy of the Island Echo. It comes out twice a month. The obituary had a picture next to the write up and I immediately recognized Carla. I thought Misty would want to know since they had been such good friends. Such a tragedy."

"Had you known she had shortened her name from Carla Princeton?"

"No, not at all. It was the picture, you know. Otherwise, I'm not sure I would have noticed the obituary."

"What can you tell me about the Lane family? How did you come to know Misty? Do you keep in touch with her sister too?"

"I knew both the Lane girls. I met them when they were quite little, still in grade-school."

"I thought Misty was homeschooled?"

"No, both attended elementary school on Texada. There's no high school on the island so most of the kids take the ferry over to Powell River, but some choose to finish their schooling online. Of course, Misty would have already told you that." She took a sip of lemonade and resettled herself against the cushion. "Back then, when the girls were little, I used to make a trip over to Texada twice a month. I had a van filled with books." She laughed heartily. "I guess it was my version of a mobile library. Texada didn't have a library of their own, and the school library was pathetically small, if you could even call it that."

"So, you would go over with a supply of books, kids would sign them out and exchange them for others on your next visit?"

"That's right. Ivy was the first to catch my attention. She'd take out the maximum—five books per child back then, and my goodness did that child read. She'd leave with her stack and be first in line waiting to get more when I returned. I noticed that after she had her books picked out, she'd go and help her sister pick out books to read, five books as well."

"Let me guess."

She laughed. "You got it. Took me a few trips but I quickly figured it out. I would ask Misty what she liked or didn't like about a particular book she had signed out and noticed the answers she gave me were always vague."

"Clever."

"She was a clever little thing. She just wasn't into books that much."

"What else do you remember about them?"

"They were close in age and similar in appearance, but they were as different as night and day. Misty was the wild one. She was very outspoken, almost defiant in nature. Her grandmother had psychic abilities, or that's what everyone said. When Misty was about eight or nine her father was killed in a car crash. After that Misty started telling everyone that he still talked to her, that she could talk to the dead."

"Did people believe her?"

"Some did, but most thought the death of her father had, well, affected her mind. Her mother, Doreen, who I'd met through church a few years earlier, seemed to take her husband's death particularly hard. The grandmother stepped in to help take care of the girls. She may have encouraged Misty's fanciful proclamations and predictions."

"You don't believe her psychic abilities are real?"

"I didn't back then. Not that I didn't believe some people have the ability to notice minute details the rest of us gloss over. I just thought it was Misty's way of dealing with her father's death. That her insistence that she talked to him, that dead people told her things, was her way of convincing herself she still had some control in her life. That she and others could be safe. That death didn't just randomly strike people down, that there was some forewarning, some predictability to what was unfolding."

I nodded. "You said *back then*. What about now?"

"I hear she's making a living at being a medium. I've read about her on the internet. She's becoming a celebrity. I may never understand it, but she does have the ability to notice things others don't. I think she's become very skilled at reading people, their body language, the subtle verbal cues they provide. She has an amazing memory, I'm glad to see that she's bundled these skills to do something positive with her life. She uses her abilities to help people feel at peace with the loss of their loved ones. To assure them their loved ones are okay and bear no regrets or hard feelings."

"Just like she tried to deal with her own father's death, although not in perhaps so refined a manner."

"Exactly. No harm in that, is there?"

"What about Ivy. You said they were different, but were they close?"

"Oh yes. Being older, Misty was taller, the stronger of the two, of course, but otherwise you'd have thought they were twins. But they had different temperaments. Ivy was the quiet one, more sensitive. She loved to read and write. She was highly creative, constantly wrote little stories."

The hairs on the back of my neck prickled. Misty had said her sister was the wild one, the troublemaker.

"Did Ivy claim to have psychic abilities as well?"

"No. She was more like her mother. Sensitive. Which does lend itself to noticing things about others, don't you think?"

"Misty told me she and her sister haven't talked in years. Do you know why? Did it start back when Carla was charged with the murder of her abusive boyfriend? Misty said there was some sort of mix up, that she was charged as an accessory, but the charges were dropped or dismissed."

"A mix up?" Betty looked puzzled. "I'm not sure I would call it a mix up. Many people saw Misty as the instigator in the whole tragic event. Some even thought she was the one who stabbed Cash Irving to death, and those who didn't felt she was morally culpable."

THIRTY-FOUR

THE ICE IN our iced tea had melted. Drops of condensation now slid down the side of the glass, creating a watery coaster. Betty's face was flushed. I attributed it to the warmth of the room, as beads of sweat formed at the nape of my neck. I ran a hand across the back of my neck and wiped it along my thigh, under the table.

"When the girls were about twelve, their grandmother died. Doreen slid deeper and deeper into depression after her husband's death and the doctors started to think there might be something else going on. Doreen wasn't a strong woman, and, in many respects, Ivy had her mother's constitution. This time it was Misty who suffered. Having been as close as she was to her grandmother, it's not surprising that she didn't take her death well. Although always somewhat boisterous, Misty became…well, unruly.

"All three girls were good friends back then, at least until high school. Ivy had her sights set on university. She was the more reserved, bookish one and she wanted to study English literature. Misty didn't like school, neither did Carla. They decided to complete their high school by correspondence. Looking back, I can say that the lack of some much-needed parental guidance and discipline probably played a big role in the way things turned out."

"They lived alone, without an adult?"

"Doreen still lived there with the girls, at least technically. I'm not sure she was up to looking after the girls."

I had to remind myself, this was small-town living. Not much different from where I grew up. The parents were busy, if not working, then fighting off boredom by throwing themselves into some sort of church or town project. Or alcohol. The kids were often left to fend for themselves. There was an overwhelming sense that nothing bad could happen. After all, everyone knew everyone.

"Carla was about fifteen when she started dating the Irving boy. I shouldn't say boy, he was four or five years older than Carla."

"Carla's mother didn't object?"

"Most days, Carla's mother woke up hungover and was passed out again by evening. Carla had been the responsible one in the family for years, seeing to it that her mother had something to eat, fixing her own food, looking after her little brother."

"I gather Carla's dad wasn't in the picture."

"Not in that sense, no. A lot of people thought Carla was Norton Irving's daughter."

"Norton Irving?"

"Yes, Cash's daddy."

"That's interesting. That would make Carla and her boyfriend, Cash, half-siblings. If that were true, you'd think old man Norton would have discouraged his son's relationship with Carla."

"Norton Irving wasn't the kind of man who would admit to anything that would put him in a bad light. But the Irvings made it clear they didn't care for Carla."

"Misty told me the Irving family was wealthy, well thought of by the island residents."

"Well, some of that was true. Then again, there's the public view versus the private view of what people thought. I think some people were scared to say anything against the Irvings. They ran most of the businesses on the island, and people need jobs."

"I see. Do you remember much of what happened? Were you at the trial?"

"Yes. I remember. I can't say I know what actually happened, but I can tell you what came out at the trial."

"That's all I can ask for."

"The day Cash Irving was killed, Carla, Misty and Ivy spent the afternoon at the beach. Several witnesses say Carla and Misty were drinking, became unruly. The lifeguard ordered them off the beach, but they just laughed at him."

"All three were at the beach?"

"Yes—people saw them there. They were there until late afternoon."

"Carla was drinking. Wasn't she pregnant?"

"She was. She claimed she'd been careful in the first two trimesters but now that the baby was almost due, an occasional drink wouldn't hurt." Betty clucked her tongue in disapproval. "The girls were seen drinking out of a vodka bottle. At the trial, Carla insisted it was mostly orange juice and there wasn't all that much vodka mixed in."

"But people said she was unruly."

"That is what people said. Both Carla and Misty claimed they were just fooling around, exaggerating things, putting on a show, because they knew everyone was watching."

"Do you think it's possible?"

"Perhaps, but after what came out at the trial, I thought it less likely. Apparently, Misty and Carla got into an argument at the beach. Misty started taunting Carla. The fight turned ugly. People heard Carla scream that she was going to 'kill that son of a bitch.' Carla was clearly distraught…she was crying. If it was supposed to be an act, she either deserved an Oscar or it backfired on them."

"What were they arguing about?"

"Seems Misty told Carla that Cash was going to leave her. That he had been cheating on her. She claimed she even knew who he was cheating with. Carla called her on it that afternoon. Said she didn't know what she was talking about. She started yelling, screaming she was tired of all her visions and premonitions. That she was a liar, her claim of psychic gifts bogus."

"A liar? Interesting. This came out at the trial?"

"Yes. Apparently, they were loud, rowdy. When they started in on each other, at least a dozen people witnessed the whole thing."

This wasn't tracking with the story Misty had told me, at all. "Misty never told me about Carla and her fighting."

"I'm sure she'd like to forget the argument and everything that happened after it. Carla kept asking Misty why she was doing this to her. They were supposed to be friends. According to one witness, Misty shouted that if she really wanted the truth, she'd give it to her. She tells Carla she knows Cash is going to leave her right after the baby is born. She says she knows because Cash told her so. That Cash was planning to leave Carla for her. That she and Cash were in love and had been sleeping together for months."

"Holy Hanna. What a mess."

"It was. Carla ran off crying. Misty stormed off shortly afterwards. Then a little while later Cash showed up. He'd been drinking as well. Apparently, several of his friends had heard the fight between Carla and Misty and told Cash about it. He was heard to be yelling 'I'll kill the bitch,' although no one was quite sure which girl he was referring to."

"Based on what I'm hearing, my guess would be Misty."

"That's what the prosecutor proposed. But no one remembered him actually saying her name."

"What about Ivy? Wasn't she there too?"

"She was. She stayed out of it until Cash arrived and started throwing around threats about killing someone. She tried to calm him down. No one heard what was said but a few witnesses saw him push Ivy to the ground. He could be heard screaming, 'It's not my baby,' as he jumped in his truck and drove off. Ivy left and she and Misty both claimed Cash showed up at their place shortly after."

I nodded. That part of the story matched what Misty had said. Except she never mentioned that she and Carla had a fight, staged or otherwise.

"Misty told the court that Cash showed up at their place angry, borderline violent. He started pushing her around. She finally convinced him to leave. Misty said she ran down the wood path to Carla's house to warn her. It was about a half kilometre shorter than going by road."

Misty had told me that Ivy had been the one who ran to Carla's house to warn Carla. That they later decided Misty would be the one to say she had run to Carla's place to warn her. But Betty wouldn't know that, she was telling me what she heard at the trial.

"Misty said she was afraid for Carla, afraid of what Cash might do. She ran to Carla's to warn her. The prosecution cut that to shreds. He reminded her that they had just had this huge fight. He claimed Misty ran down there not to protect Carla but to protect Cash, stop him from doing something stupid. Maybe try to convince him that since now everyone knew, he didn't have to wait for the baby to be born to leave Carla."

"I can see how Misty's motive might be in question, especially after her and Carla's argument on the beach. I see your point. If the argument down on the beach was just a big show, some sort of prank or juvenile lark, it didn't serve Misty well. Misty told me a witness claimed to have seen her on the path behind Carla's house."

"Yes, a neighbour did, but later claimed he wasn't positive which Lane sister he saw. The man was well into his seventies, had poor eyesight. Even in his own testimony he confused the girls, calling Carla *Misty* more than once. He finally admitted he wasn't positive who he had seen but that it must have been one of the Lane girls. There were other problems. Like the timing. The prosecutor questioned how long it would have taken Misty to run to Carla's, find Carla unconscious and Cash bleeding on the floor, and then run back to the house. The neighbour who thought he saw her on the path claimed he saw her running back home at 6:10 p.m. But the call to 911 wasn't made until 7:05 p.m. If the neighbour was right about the time, Misty should have reached home long before that."

I thought about the story Misty told me. The time gap must have come about because it took a while for Ivy to tell Misty what she saw. Time the girls needed to plan their story. I still couldn't fathom why Ivy hadn't simply told the truth. But then, Misty hadn't either.

"A lot of people heard Misty and Carla arguing on the beach that day. Most people knew Misty couldn't stand Cash. She never hid the fact that she wished Carla would leave him. The prosecutor put the question to the jury. Would Misty really have slept with a man she clearly despised? He put forward the idea that it was more likely that the two of them planned the whole thing. Everyone knew Cash had a temper and drank, and that he had a history of fighting with Carla, accusing her of cheating on him and other things that weren't true. The prosecutor argued that Misty helped Carla get rid of Cash, that with him dead and the baby on the way the Irving family would step in to make sure Carla and their grandchild were well looked after."

"That might be a naïve assumption."

"In many respects, they were naïve. You have to remember they weren't even eighteen when this happened."

"But Cash did attack Carla that day, didn't he? Didn't she stab him in self-defence?"

"Yes. Well, at first, she claimed Cash hit her, knocked her down, that she passed out and didn't remember what happened. But later, Carla admitted to stabbing him. Her lawyer claimed it was a clear case of self-defence. She had the cuts and bruises to prove it. However, as the trial went on, the prosecution brought in several experts who testified otherwise. Although Carla had defence bruises on her arms, and several lacerations to her head and face, none of them seemed serious enough to have warranted her response. The prosecution even tried to suggest that Misty was the one who hit Carla with a rounded, blunt object, like a broom handle, to make it look like she was attacked. None of the blows were considered life threatening and none of the injuries would have hurt the baby."

I sat there horrified. "You've got to be kidding. That's why they didn't believe Carla's story about self-defence? What about his history of abuse?"

"He did have a history of verbal abuse and although Carla claimed he had pushed her around and hit her on occasion, they couldn't find anyone who could back up the story, except for Misty, of course, which in a way did them both no good."

"Seriously?"

"There's more. Cash was stabbed nine times, four stab wounds—the ones the coroner determined to be the fatal blows— were to his back. Based on Cash's blood alcohol level, one expert claimed Cash would have been hardly able to stand up. That Carla should have easily been able to get away from him and that the level of violence she exhibited wasn't warranted by the situation."

"So that's why they didn't buy the claim of self-defence."

Some of this made sense. Some of it didn't line up with what Misty told me, but the overarching details did.

"There was only one person to collaborate Carla's story of physical abuse, the same person who later admitted to making up a story about her torrid love affair with the victim and claiming that he was planning to leave Carla."

"I can see how badly this went. The jury would have a hard time knowing when Misty was telling the truth and when she was lying. I'm not sure it would have had the same outcome today as it did back then."

"Cash was an Irving. The Irvings were well known, they owned half the property on the island. Cash's father was the former mayor. His brother headed up the local police force. With the rumours about Cash's daddy having an affair with Carla's mother still floating around, he wasn't keen on any more attacks on the Irving family reputation."

"Wow. That's rather messy."

"Isn't it."

"What about Carla? What did she say?"

"She sided with Misty. Said they had made up the whole argument on the beach, as a lark. She never thought Cash would take it seriously. That he arrived home that day drunk and in a rage. He attacked her and she grabbed the knife in self-defence. She said she blanked out, had no idea how many times she stabbed him. She was a mess. Couldn't believe that she killed her baby's father. It didn't help when it came to light that the knife she used was one from the Lane household."

"Wow. What a mess. Are you saying Misty brought the knife with her?"

"Misty claimed no. Her lawyer argued it proved nothing. The girls were good friends, and were always going back and forth, eating at each other's houses, staying over sometimes."

"So, Misty got off and the jury laid full blame at Carla's feet."

"Pretty much, although a lot of people thought Misty was equally to blame. Whether it was just a lark, or a well-thought-out plan to kill Cash, Carla didn't deny stabbing Cash. I think most people believed the latter."

"Why is that?"

"Well, as the prosecution pointed out, if the story had been true, and Cash was cheating on Carla with Misty, her best friend, would Carla have been that forgiving? That quickly? Claiming Misty had nothing to do with it, that it was a lark gone bad, and that she and she alone fought with Cash and ended up killing him."

"So, you're saying she thought it was in her best interest to claim it was a lark gone bad rather than admit to a planned, premeditated murder."

"Either her or her lawyer."

"I looked for the trial records, but they were sealed."

"Yes, there was a publication ban on everything beyond the first few news articles about Cash Irving's death and Carla Princeton's arrest. Technically, since she and some of the witnesses were under the legal age at the time of the crime, the case records were treated much like they would be for juveniles even though she was tried in an adult court."

"She must have changed her name, shortened it to Prince, after she got out of prison."

"Can't really blame her."

"All things considered, she got off with a fairly light sentence." Even though Carla was barely eighteen when she killed Cash and was tried as an adult due to the serious nature of her crime, the judge went easy on her during sentencing.

"She was given ten years with no chance of parole for seven.

She left prison with lots of time to make something of her life. Too bad someone took that away from her."

A jangling phone brought both of us out of our silent contemplation. Betty excused herself for a minute. Either Misty had lied to me about Ivy being the one who had run down to Carla's that day, or she had perjured herself to protect her sister. That's the one piece I still didn't get. Why had it been so important to keep that little detail a secret?

THIRTY-FIVE

I COULD HEAR BETTY in the next room, agreeing to meet someone the next morning. She returned a minute later with a fresh jug of iced tea.

"My goodness, it's warm in here. This old house doesn't have central air and it's prohibitively expensive to retro-fit it in. I've brought us more iced tea, light on the tea, heavy on the ice." She picked up my glass, tilted and shook the pitcher until the ice cubes separated and rattled into the glass. "Sorry for the interruption. This is my week to do the gardening work at the church, along with Mary Jane. Now, where were we?"

"Was Ivy ever called as a witness in Carla's trial?"

"She was. I felt sorry for her, she was so shaken. They had to stop questioning her a few times, give her a chance to pull herself together."

"What was her testimony about?"

"The usual things—her relationship with Carla, her recall of events that day at the beach, and later when Cash showed up at their house. How she and Misty called the police after Misty came back from Carla's in a panic, saying she thought that Cash might have killed Carla."

"Misty says she and Ivy haven't spoken in years. Do you know why, or what happened to Ivy after the trial or where she is today?"

"Shortly after all this happened, Ivy left for college. Misty stayed home to look after her mother and deal with all the island gossip. Doreen was hospitalized the following year. The trial was held eighteen months after Cash's death but by then pending charges against Misty had been dropped. Misty left right after the trial ended."

"Why was Doreen hospitalized?"

"She had always struggled with health issues. Unfortunately, she turned to pills and alcohol. She tried killing herself several times. The last time she tried, she almost succeeded. That's when she was hospitalized and eventually diagnosed with schizophrenia."

"But Ivy came back for the trial. Did she not return later to visit her mother?"

"I only saw Ivy a few times after she left the island. She came back for Christmas the first winter Doreen was in hospital. I ran into her here in Powell River, shopping for Christmas gifts. She told me she was in college, studying English literature. Then the second time I saw her was at the trial. I haven't seen her since."

"How was she doing?"

"She was struggling with her own health issues. I remember hoping she wouldn't end up like her mother. After university she moved somewhere inland. Nelson, I think. She started writing."

"Good for her." I still couldn't see a reason for the sisterly discord. Did Ivy resent her sister for her growing fame? Her good health?

"Do you know where she is now?"

Betty leaned forward, her eyes glistening with excitement. "Want to know what I think?"

"Yes, of course."

"I think she's Janice Stone."

"Janice Stone? Who's that?"

"She writes mysteries, thrillers. Janice Stone is not her real name though, it's a pen name."

"And you figure it's Ivy?"

"I do," she chortled, gleefully. "I've been telling my book club that she's Janice Stone for ages—but no one wants to believe me." She laughed.

"What has you convinced?"

"After Ivy finished university, she published a few short stories, mostly in magazines, then in one or two anthologies. I took an interest in her career since I always encouraged her to write. But then she stopped writing and it was almost like she fell off the face of the earth. I worried her health might have become an issue." She slid forward until she was barely on the edge of her chair, eyes sparkling. "A few years later, I came across this new Canadian author, Janice Stone. The book jacket said she grew up on the west coast. No one knows who Janice Stone is. There's a lot of speculation and, of course, everyone is trying to figure out who is behind the pen name. It's a bit of mystery itself, and a very good marketing ploy."

"A brilliant strategy. This Janice Stone must be a bit of a recluse or you'd think she would slip up somehow. But there must be more. You can't have drawn the conclusion that she is Ivy simply on an unsubstantiated report that Janice Stone grew up on the west coast."

"No, no, there's more. Janice Stone first wrote a trilogy, the Blackbird Files. They didn't do very well. The writing was stilted, the plot convoluted, the characters flat. Perhaps too aggressive an attempt for a new author. Then she started writing the Niki Dillon murder mysteries, starring homicide detective Nicola Dillon. In the first book, a woman, and her best friend, who has psychic abilities, plan and kill the woman's husband."

"What?"

Betty nodded knowingly. "You see? In the book, you're led to believe that the two women only set things up to mess with the husband, give him a scare. They lure him to what is reputed to be a haunted house by taunting him, daring him. But things go horribly wrong, and instead of just scaring him, he ends up dead. Spoiler alert, as the kids say. The reader is led to believe this is all an accident, that the women were just having fun with him and didn't mean him any harm. But a bizarre twist at the end reveals that the woman psychic planned to kill him all along, because unbeknownst to anyone but her, he raped her little sister. She sets things up, so it looks like her friend plotted his death and killed him, and the friend ends up taking the blame."

"No way!"

"I thought you might see the similarities. I mean, some of the details are a little different, fictionalized, but I couldn't help noticing how similar the story plot was to the tragedy that unfolded, right here…on the west coast."

"Could it have been written by someone other than Ivy, someone who was at Carla's trial or knows enough of the trial details to craft an intriguing story?"

"Possibly. I must admit, as tempted as I was at that point to declare that I knew who Janice Stone is, I still had doubts. I could hardly wait for book two to come out. And not just for this reason. Readers loved the first book, as did I. Suddenly this Janice Stone has come into her own, found her voice, not to mention given us a hair-clutching thriller that's so windy and twisty it leaves you dizzy for more."

"Okay, you've hooked me. What happens in book two?"

"In book two, Detective Dillon is called out when a young girl is kidnapped from her parents' home. The parents engage a psychic's help to find their daughter. Detective Dillon is the detective who investigated the murder that took place in book one and is familiar with the psychic in question."

I sat up. *Shit.*

"Two murders occur in the three days following the kidnapping. The investigating homicide detectives find that the killer has left a clue with each victim leading to the next. Detective Dillon is brought in when the murder scene for the second victim holds a clue to the whereabouts of the missing girl. Dillon follows the clue, but it ends up being a wild goose chase.

"Meantime, the psychic is hot on the kidnapper's trail and following clues from her visions. She leads police to a remote rural spot where the girl is found alive. Although everyone is ecstatic with the outcome, Dillon suspects they have a serial killer on their hands and that the serial killer may have had something to do with the young girl's abduction. Or maybe it was a ruse to throw Detective Dillon off track. Regardless, the killer has left two dead bodies behind, and managed to stay one step ahead of the law."

"Wow. I take it you read about Misty's involvement in the recovery of the little girl in the Hasting kidnapping two years ago."

"Yes. I mean, I've always kept an eye and ear open for news on Misty and Ivy, having known the girls since they were little, and later so I could reassure Doreen they were fine, when she asked. But I'll admit, after I read about the Hasting case, I pretty much started looking for news on Misty, her events, what she's doing. Gosh, does that mean I'm stalking her?"

"I can see why it's hard to believe these stories are just coincidental. If the author isn't Ivy, it must be someone who is following Misty's career, knows about her involvement in these cases. Is there a book three?"

"Yes. Serious spoiler alert. You really want to hear this?"

"Yes, of course." I was still in shock over book two.

"In book three, the psychic's reputation continues to grow.

She helps the police on several occasions even when they don't ask her for it. She proves her worth when she helps police solve a double murder, committed by a bank robber on the run. Detective Dillon senses things are just a little too coincidental. How did the killer stay one step ahead of them? The psychic also made predictions, albeit in vague terms, which led to clues that only the killer and police should have known. The psychic, of course, claims she knows these details because—well, she's psychic. At the end of the book, the psychic predicts the serial killer from book two, who is still out there, will kill a woman on the eve of the summer solstice. The media attention this garners shoots the psychic's reputation into the stratosphere. But Detective Dillon is not impressed. She starts to believe that the psychic might be the serial killer they are looking for."

Goose bumps erupted down my arms and I shivered.

"Good, right?" Betty said gleefully. "Hope I haven't spoiled the series for you."

My mind was doing mental gymnastics. Could Betty be right about Janice Stone being Ivy? The stories were fictionalized, of course, but each used a kernel of Misty's public accountings of her involvement in solving crimes at their core. Or were they merely a kernel?

"Is there another book?"

"Yes. It came out early this year. That book erased any doubt in my mind. When I heard about Carla's death, I just about fell off my chair. I wrote Misty about Carla's death, but part of me thinks she already knew."

"What do you mean?"

"In book four, we see Detective Dillon going back to visit the woman who went to prison for killing her husband, the murder she and the psychic were rumoured to have conspired on in book one. Dillon wants to know more about the psychic, maybe get the real story. But the woman is afraid, won't talk, seems to feel doing her time is well worth it to have the psychic leave her alone. In the meantime, another woman is murdered."

"She's murdered on the eve of summer solstice—just like predicted in book three."

"Bingo. In the dead woman's hand, the investigators find a note for Detective Dillon. The note is a series of numbers."

My mouth went dry. The iced tea was gone. I picked up my glass and emptied the last few drops. Betty hurried on, oblivious to my reaction.

"Detective Dillon has been growing more convinced that the psychic is responsible for these deaths but is unable to pin anything concrete on her. She starts questioning herself. After all, there haven't been many female serial killers. She digs deeper, and discovers the psychic had some sort of run-in with the murdered woman just days before she was killed. A seemingly innocent encounter, where harsh words were exchanged. She suspects the psychic may be suffering from a mental illness, out to destroy anyone who has slighted her, real or perceived."

"This is incredible. And the woman in prison?"

Betty nodded; her lips pressed together in a grimace. "Yes. She's murdered, just weeks after being granted day parole. Found dead in the woods, several weeks later, her body eventually dug up by animals."

Carla Prince was dead, killed by someone unknown. Other than the timing and manner of death, the overarching story was too similar to ignore.

"Now you see why I've come to the conclusion I have?"

"I do. When did this book come out? Book four, I mean?"

"It came out last year. Just in time for Christmas."

"So roughly four months before Carla Prince is murdered."

We sat silently contemplating the implications. Finally,

Betty blurted, "Maybe whoever killed Carla is obsessed with the Detective Dillon mysteries and is carrying out the story in real life."

"That's certainly a possibility. It wouldn't be the first time a killer was inspired by a work of fiction." My head was reeling. "You have no idea where this Janice Stone is or Ivy Lane?"

"No, none."

"Any idea when her next book is out?"

"Book five is due out this September. Rumour has it that the hunt for the serial killer may end here. Or at least Detective Dillon will have a run-in with the serial killer. The trailer for the book should be out any day now."

I sat a minute longer. This couldn't be happening. The room tilted slightly. I realized I was holding my breath and let it out slowly.

"Well, Betty, if I was in your book club, I'd believe you."

"Wait until I tell the girls," Betty said, beaming. "A real-life detective believes my theory."

"How would the nursing home get a hold of Ivy if something happened to Doreen, or if she passed away?"

"Oh, I see where you're going with this. I'm not sure. I suspect they have an address or phone number on file. Maybe Misty knows and has been sworn to secrecy. If Janice Stone really is Ivy, keeping her identity a secret to maintain all the buzz around who she is, is worth untold thousands. It's hard to buy that kind of publicity."

My head was still reeling when I said my goodbyes to Betty Kennedy. She had presented me with a good case for thinking Janice Stone was Misty's sister. It shouldn't have come as a surprise—everyone knows librarians are good at conducting research.

Maybe Misty's reluctance to talk about her sister was just her fear about inadvertently giving away information that might lead to Janice Stone. And if the books she wrote were based on something that happened to Misty years ago, I could live with it. Authors often based the premise of their fictional stories on something in real life. Truth was, indeed, often stranger than fiction. But what really bothered me is that book four came out *before* Carla's murder. And in that book the psychic was playing mind games with the detective.

THIRTY-SIX

THEY WERE ANNOUNCING final boarding call when I arrived at the gate. I had driven down the sunshine coast like a Formula-1 driver on crack. But then, so had everyone else. It was a relief to be leaving. Today the ocean was grey and bleak, the road along the coastline boxed in claustrophobically by water and trees. My head started aching before I left Powell River. The mad rush down the winding coast added nausea to the mix. I checked in and rushed down the ramp to join the last few passengers boarding the plane.

Stuffing my carry-on in the overhead bin, I slid into the aisle seat next to a young girl who rested her head against the glass window and looked to be asleep. My frantic rush through the airport left a thin layer of moisture on my skin, which now solidified and sucked the warmth from me under gale-force winds created by the cabin's air conditioning. I pulled my phone out and stashed my handbag under the seat in front of me. I checked my messages. There was one text message from Tara sent about two hours ago. I opened it and read as the flight attendants headed down the aisle, shutting the overhead bins and doing their head count. Her message was brief; *They've arrested Lori Watson's killer. So relieved.*

I checked my voice message while the flight attendants

delivered their safety review and ended by asking passengers to turn off their electronic devices. Tara's text message didn't offer up any information about Misty and she hadn't left a voice message. Did *so relieved* mean that Misty had shown up and was okay? Odd that Tara didn't say. I quickly scrolled through my newsfeed to see if there were more details. The flight attendant was now looking directly at me. Nothing on my news app. I shut off my phone and put it away.

Who had been arrested? Someone obsessed with Lori Watson. Someone who mistakenly killed Watson, thinking it was Misty? The lack of details was frustrating.

I lay back and closed my eyes. My brain began to churn through everything Betty had told me. Was Carla's death just an unfortunate, untimely occurrence? Not untimely for whoever was writing the Detective Dillon books. Not many people would be familiar with Carla Princeton's story, the murder trial, her incarceration, the fact that she had been released from prison. But what parts in Janice Stone's books were fictionalized and what was real? In book one—someone rapes the psychic's little sister. Could Cash have raped Ivy? Could Misty have killed Cash or orchestrated the outcome as revenge?

Unreasonable thoughts had pounded through my brain during my mad dash down from Powell River. Betty Kennedy's theory that Ivy was writing a thrilling crime series loosely based on her own story was highly believable. If Ivy was Janice Stone, then she was also using what she knew about her sister's psychic abilities to create a realistic psychic serial killer. Could that be what drove the wedge between the two sisters? Was Misty aware of the series and although it was fiction, maybe it cut just a little too close to home for comfort. How close? And how had she come up with events in book four that would later prove to mirror real life? The possible answer to that question gave me the chills.

Might not hurt to give Corporal Reed a call and let her know the similarities between Janice Stone's book four and Carla Princeton's life and now death. Then what? Did I really think the RCMP would hunt down this Janice Stone and accuse her of murder? Based on a fictional story? *Crap.* I needed to let this go. According to Tara, the police had arrested someone in connection with Lori Watson's murder. Case solved.

As the plane waited to taxi out to its spot on the runway, I reached down and pulled out the book I had stopped to buy in the airport kiosk. *Death of Innocence* was the first book in the Detective Dillon series. I checked the back for a bio. It was brief, mirrored what Betty had told me, and didn't include a headshot or photo of the author. I looked at the front pages. The book was published by Stone-Broke Press. Cute. An indie press—probably Stone's.

We were delayed an hour and by the time we landed in Calgary I was almost halfway through the book. If Janice Stone wasn't Ivy Lane, she was certainly familiar with Carla Prince's case. Of course, there could be a dozen or more people, or ways for someone to get enough of the details to make it seem so. Disturbing was the character named Kayleigh Ginnel. In the book, Kayleigh, a psychic, is slowly going mad. She believes the townspeople are turning against her but is having trouble separating the voices in her head, real from fictitious. She's jealous of her best friend, Larissa, a kind, beautiful girl with blond hair, an easy disposition. She feels abandoned when Larissa starts spending all her time with the new love of her life, the son of a well-to-do family. Kayleigh feels alone, distanced. She starts acting out, withdrawn one minute, angry the next. Kayleigh is plagued by nightmares, dreams about rape, demons, violent death. I was at the part in the story when Kayleigh starts noticing disturbing little things in her real life, things she thought were only in her dreams, when I was jolted back to the present as the wheels touched down at YYC. The plane bounced slightly and roared down the runway to a full stop.

The events in Janice Stone's book were not based solely on Carla Prince's life twenty years ago. The author was weaving in current events with the past. Unless Janice Stone had psychic abilities herself and could predict the future, it was more likely that someone was playing out Janice Stone's books in real life.

I gathered up my belongings and filed out of the plane behind the others. It was already dark, the air cool by the time I stepped outside. I called Misty's cell on the way to my car, but there was no answer. I sent Tara a text asking her to call me.

Betty's quick review of each book made me quite certain that the author was following Misty's career and using Misty's real-life experiences to fuel her muse. Was Janice Stone Ivy or someone obsessed with Misty?

I wondered what Misty would think of the series. Who wants their life fictionized in someone else's book? And being made to look like a serial killer, who may be suffering a mental illness. That would be beyond irritating.

More troubling, I had to consider that the author might be injecting themselves into Misty's current life, threatening her, watching her, jerking Misty around like a puppet on a string. Then another thought stopped me cold. Was I just another puppet in the author's phantasmic world?

THIRTY-SEVEN

THE NEXT MORNING, I woke late. Justified, I told myself, for having stayed up until three a.m. reading the rest of Janice Stone's first book. The story was clearly inspired by the Carla Prince case, although the author did not acknowledge it. In the book, the psychic is the puppet master, orchestrating the death of Larissa's boyfriend without lifting a weapon. In the story, the psychic finds her sister's journal, reads about her crush on Larissa's boyfriend. As her sister's obvious infatuations grows, the psychic notices things about Larissa's boyfriend that confirms he is callous, evil. He plays with people's emotions. Then she reads the pages in her sister's diary about the rape. Something shifts in the psychic. Up until now, she's used her power for good but now she sees she can serve a higher good by eradicating all who are evil.

The book was well written, the plot kept me reading and now that book one was finished it left me craving to read book two. Whoever Janice Stone was, she knew how to write.

I had a quick shower, pulled on jeans and a navy cotton V-neck sweater. I left my towel-dried hair uncombed, hoping it would dry with a few waves to break up its poker-straight nature. Flicking on the TV, I walked through the living area to the kitchen and poured myself a bowl of cheerios. I checked the fridge. No milk. I eyed the expired orange juice. Not that desperate. I took my bowl of cheerios with me, sat on the couch, and opened my laptop.

I called Tara. Why wasn't she answering my calls? Her message had said someone had been arrested. How did he fit into the picture? I checked the TV channels. Since I missed the morning news, I opened my browser and found the news clip I was looking for. A man was being interviewed by a reporter in front of the downtown courthouse. I turned up the volume and hit the play button.

"My son is innocent. There is no way he did this. He's never harmed a living thing. He'd never hurt anybody."

"A witness apparently saw your son leaving the building in a grey Impala, where Lori Watson's body was found just minutes later."

"We aren't denying he was at the building. My son had dinner with me that night. I live in the building. It's entirely reasonable to expect someone saw him there. This is a nightmare. My son is terrified. Petrified."

"What is happening now?"

"Our lawyer is still trying to find out what's going on. My son didn't see anybody when he left that night, he didn't notice the woman in question or see anyone who might have killed her."

The reporter turned back to face the camera. "I'm here in front of the courthouse with Mr. Jackson, whose son was arrested yesterday in connection with the death of Lori Watson. A nightmare for any family, made even more tragic as his son, Tomas, has struggled his entire life to deal with his cognitive disability." The news clip ended with what looked like a school photo of Tomas Jackson.

I wondered who witnessed him leaving the condo. Surely not Misty. She claimed she didn't get a good look at the man. I glanced at my watch and called Tara again. I called the other number listed on her business website and got a recorded message stating the shop's hours and then voice mail. I hoped nothing happened to her. I gathered up my stuff and decided to go pay her a visit.

On the drive to Kensington, I mulled over the possibility that this Tomas Jackson had killed Lori Watson. The cops had to have something on him. They aren't known for picking up and charging perfectly innocent people. On the other hand, the reporter said he had been arrested, not charged. Could he also be the one who was targeting Misty? It's possible he had seen Misty in the building on the occasions he visited his father, became obsessed with her for some reason. But if he had developed some sort of infatuation with her, why the hateful nature of the messages? 'Die bitch die' and 'liar' didn't make sense.

On the other hand, it if it were someone living in, or with access to the building, it would have been relatively easy to vandalize Misty's car, leave a message scrawled on her condo door. Misty said she felt someone watching her. But what about the decapitated bird on the back step of her store and the bag of sand dropped off the top of the Legion? Tomas Jackson wasn't one of the five people we flagged who attended readings where Misty felt a dark presence. And if he were infatuated with Misty, why would he have killed Lori Watson? Or was that a mistake?

Tara called me just as I was parking, several car-lengths from her office door.

"Hey, Tara. I'm just parking down the street from your office."

"Do you want to stop in for a quick update? I have a customer coming in fifteen minutes, but I'm all yours until then."

By the time I walked into her office, she had two coffees poured and waiting on the table.

"Hi, Jorja. I just poured us a coffee. You take yours black, right?"

"Yes. Thank you. I can really use a shot of caffeine this morning. Have you heard from Misty?"

"No. I take it you haven't either."

"No. What about the police?"

"No. I got a call yesterday from a Detective Brighton. He's the one looking into Lori Watson's death. Oh, but you know that."

"What did he have to say?"

"Not much. He asked me a bunch of questions—you know, did I know where Misty could be, had she ever just closed up shop and taken off, that sort of thing. I told him she had several important interviews coming up. Interviews I worked hard to arrange. No way she'd just blow those off." She shook her head. "He did acknowledge that we have good reason for concern, especially after her building went up in flames in addition to her being missing."

"Well thank goodness for that. I asked Gregg Watson to give me a call if he hears from her."

"It's not like Misty to just disappear like that, especially since she committed to help the Watson family find Lori's killer. I thought maybe after the news about the man they arrested in connection with the murder came out, she would show up, or at least call. I'm really afraid something has happened to her."

"I share your fears. I flew to Vancouver Island yesterday. That letter you told me about—the one where Misty learned a childhood friend of hers died? Yeah, well, I followed up. The woman was murdered, strangled like Lori Watson. She also had dark hair. I don't know if there is any connection to Lori Watson, but it struck me as something worth looking into, because Misty's premonitions started right around that time."

Tara brought her hand to her lips. "Murdered. That's two women. Do you think it's a serial killer?"

"God, I hope not. I'm going to let Detective Brighton know

what I found. I'm really starting to feel out of my depth here." I got up and walked my empty coffee cup over to the sink and turned. "Tara, has Misty ever mentioned anyone named Janice Stone?"

A frown creased Tara's forehead. "The name sounds slightly familiar. Why, who is she?"

"A writer. She may have gone to school with Misty, way back when."

Tara shook her head. "She meets so many people. Her newsletter has several thousand subscribers."

"Can you do something for me? Can you check all the names you have on file for Misty, her fans, newsletter subscribers, any personal or business contacts and see if there is anyone named Stone? J. Stone or Janice Stone."

"Sure, I can do that."

I walked to the door. "Thanks for the coffee, Tara. Let me know if you hear anything. I'll do the same."

"Be careful, Jorja. The way Misty looked the last time I saw her…" Tara shuddered. "There's pure evil at work."

Tara's words stuck in my head as I returned to my car. With my client missing, I couldn't just go home and ignore the situation. *Evil.* I was hearing that word a lot these days. Time to go talk to an expert.

THIRTY-EIGHT

I FOUND THE PREACHER behind the Second Avenue church. He wasn't preaching today. At first, I thought he was sleeping. But as I got closer, I noticed his eyes, open, glazed over. The church wall was holding him up as he sat, legs splayed out on the concrete sidewalk.

"Hey, preacher."

He shifted his head but didn't reply. I wondered if I should call for medical help.

"Are you okay? Can I get you anything?"

He struggled to sit up. "Is it the Sabbath?"

"No, it's not." I noticed his forehead was still smudged in black, but any semblance of the cross was gone. "I don't know if you remember me. My name is Jorja. I'm looking for the psychic, Misty. She worked in the building that burned down."

He nodded, his chin barely lifting an inch off his chest.

"You told me you witnessed Satan. His cloak of evil. That he has made his presence known. How has he made his presence known?"

"Satan and his whore," he mumbled. "They were told not to hurt the grass of the earth, or any green thing, but only those who do not have the seal of God on their foreheads." He lifted his head, his eyes met mine. "Revelation. Chapter nine verse four." He gathered up what strength he had, pointed a shaking finger in my face and declared, "Look for he who defies the word of the Lord. Revelation 9:7: On their head they wore something like crowns of gold, their faces looked human."

His head rolled to the side; the effort of the delivery had depleted what little energy he had. I left, drove to Giovanni's deli, and picked up two coffees, a couple of paninis and a bottle of water. I returned to the church and walked to where the preacher sat. He didn't stir as I bent and set the water, a coffee and one of the paninis by his side. I watched for a minute, relieved to see his chest moving with each breath.

I felt like his belief in a higher power was the only thing keeping him on the side of the living. I had stopped practising my religion a very long time ago, but I couldn't help but whisper, "May your God have mercy on you."

Detective Brighton had shed his jacket, damp circles visible under each arm. It had taken several hours at the police station to get the story out in some sort of logical sequence. A more logical sequence than the twisted scenarios my mind continuously fabricated.

"Okay, let me see if I got this straight. After Lori Watson is killed, your client still feels threatened. You and Misty believe that the killer may have mistaken Lori Watson for Misty and killed her by mistake. She gets an anonymous call from someone claiming he killed someone."

"That's weird, right? Why call Misty? Why not the police or a news reporter?"

"Struck me as weird, too. It's like the killer was taunting her. Daring her to find him. You both thought if you could find Lori

Watson's killer then you'd also have the person who was threatening Misty or vice versa."

"Correct. Misty focused on what her premonitions were telling her, I took a more traditional approach and delved into who in Misty's life might have a motive for killing her."

"Got it." Detective Brighton tapped his pen on the notepad in front of him. "You learned a friend of Misty's died roughly the same time as Misty started to get threatening messages. You dug deeper and discovered the friend who died, Carla Prince, was the focus of a homicide investigation on Vancouver Island. That she had been strangled."

"Yes. Carla Prince, or Princeton as she was once known, grew up with Misty and her sister. Carla was incarcerated for the death of her husband, Cash Irving. Although Misty was originally thought to have helped Carla plan and kill her husband, no evidence could be found to substantiate this theory and charges against Misty were dismissed."

"Carla admits she stabbed her husband to death, goes to prison. Gives up a baby in the process. Rumours were floating in the community. Some said the child wasn't Irving's."

"Correct. What everybody did seem to agree on was that Irving was the spoiled son of a rich family, a bully, and a mean, violent drunk. I couldn't get access to the trial records, but I talked to a woman who knew the Lane family and attended the trial. Mrs. Betty Kennedy."

"So, because of the timing of these two murders, and the fact that both women had dark hair and died of asphyxiation, you think they were killed by the same person."

I sighed. "I do and I don't. I know. It's somewhat lame. But now Misty is missing, and someone burned down her shop. I can't help thinking it has something to do with her past. With all the accusations flying around during and after the Carla Prince trial, makes me wonder if someone thinks they have a score to settle."

I swallowed and debated if I should continue. I had nothing more than pure conjecture.

"The woman I talked to, Betty Kennedy, told me about a mystery series she's been reading. There are now four books in the Detective Dillon series. The author is Janice Stone, but it's a pen name. The books are fiction, of course, but I couldn't help but notice the similarity of the cases this fictional detective pursues to the police cases Misty has been involved with. The first book in the series reads pretty much like the Carla Prince case Betty Kennedy described."

"Seriously? You think this author—what? Killed Watson and now has Misty locked up somewhere."

I wiped away a bead of sweat making its way down the side of my face. It was hot, we were both tired, one of us was losing his temper.

"Look, I'm not saying it's the author. In book four, however, a woman is strangled—the same woman from book one who went to prison for killing her boyfriend. Just like Carla went to prison for killing her husband. The similarities between real-life events in Misty's life and the books are freakish. If it's not the author, then it could be someone with a fixation with Misty. Someone who tracks her in the media, follows her real-life stories, maybe is aware of the Detective Dillon books and decides to enact them."

Detective Brighton rubbed his face with both hands, maybe to wipe away the thin sheen of sweat or rub away the frustration.

"It's an interesting thought, maybe one worth pursuing. Let me think on it. Damn, it's hot in here. You'd think they would have turned on the AC for summer by now."

I smiled in sympathy. "I heard there were budget cuts."

He looked at me, then laughed. "Let's get this finished and out of here before we both melt."

"Sounds good to me."

I was halfway home when it hit me. Revelation 9:4, Revelation 9:7. Something on their heads that looked like crowns of gold. I heard Misty's voice in my head. Nines and sevens. This is how we will find him. What the hell was I supposed to do with that?

THIRTY-NINE

I PULLED UP TO Mike's place and climbed out of the car, purse in one hand, a bottle of scotch and wine in the other. Mrs. Niedswiki stood in her front yard, a thick plaid scarf wrapped over her head and knotted under her chin. Her flowered cardigan was buttoned up to her neck and thick nude-coloured stockings poked out from beneath a black dress and ended in a pair of brown, rubber-soled shoes. I wanted to check the cardigan to see if it was missing a button.

"Good evening, Mrs. Niedswiki," I called out as I headed up the short sidewalk to Mike's front steps. She gave me a small smile and continued to wave the end of the hose and its fine spray of water over her flowerbeds, her stubby squared-off front teeth barely visible through thin tight lips.

Yeah and up yours too.

I knocked on the front door, turned the handle and stepped inside.

"Hi, Mike," I called out. "It's me."

Mike poked his head out from the kitchen. "Jorja, come on in. Good to see you."

My nose led me into the kitchen. "I come bearing gifts." I set the bottles on the counter. "What is that? It smells delicious."

"Chicken parmigiana. Almost done. You didn't need to bring wine…or hey, scotch. You must have really missed me."

I snorted. "Yeah? Well, maybe you haven't noticed that I almost drained your scotch, not to mention that I probably traumatized Wess permanently. Where is he, by the way?"

"He's pissed at me. Hiding in the spare bedroom."

"Oh dear. Hey, Smitty." I reached down and gave him a little face rub as he wound himself around my legs. "Is your brother ever going to forgive me?" I stood up and pulled plates and cutlery from Mike's cupboards and set them on the table. "How's Julie?"

"She's doing much better. They let her out Monday morning."

"That's awesome. Talk about scary."

"Thank goodness for modern medicine."

Mike and I sat down to his delicious Chicken Parmigiana, creamy alfredo pasta and broccolini. We got caught up over dinner and a glass of wine.

"My god, that was good. Your ex-wives were crazy to let you go."

"Flattery will get you everywhere. What do you need?"

"Am I that transparent…is there no mystery between us anymore?"

Mike shook his head and laughed. "Don't worry. I'll never figure women out. Especially ones who are gorgeous, smart and independent."

"Oh, I do declare, Mr. Saunders," I drawled in my best imitation of a southern belle from bygone days and laid a hand on my chest.

Mike shook his head. "More wine?"

"I'd better not. I'm driving. Have you ever heard of Lehman Group?"

"You'd better be hanging on to your pearls if you're dealing with that bunch."

"Why? What can you tell me?"

"Benjamin Lehman is in front of the courts on a regular basis. He's been charged with fraud, racketeering and a litany of other offences. His current lawyer, Charles Valenti, originally practised law in some small-town law firm in Wyoming. He got lucky one day and ended up defending some high-ranking government types who purchased a mountain chalet that they used for their weekend debauchery, which unfortunately, involved some underage girls—illegal immigrants to boot. One of the girls leaked some rather incriminating photos to the newspapers. Valenti made the whole thing go away by getting his clients to throw a lot of money at the situation. After that he hightailed it up to Canada. Suddenly he's buying up property here, like it was penny candy. That's how he met Lehman. Last year Lehman Group was investigated when a property they were bidding on went up in flames. A guy was killed, trapped in a third-floor apartment. He jumped before the fire department could get there."

"Let me guess, arson."

"You got it. There have been other incidents. You know those four houses the city expropriated last year to widen Centre Street? Lehman just happened to have purchased them a year earlier."

"All four?"

"All four. He made good money on that little exchange."

I sat contemplating what Mike told me. "So, if Lehman wants a building or the land it's on, he's going to be aggressive about it."

"No. He's going to get it. One way or another."

"Interesting."

"Tell me you're not tangling with Lehman?"

"No, at least not yet. They purchased the building where my client has her shop. They offered to buy her out, but she didn't want to sell. There's been some vandalism, graffiti, phone calls with no caller on the other end. A few days ago, a fire destroyed the building."

Mike let out a low whistle. "The McLaren? Saw that on TV."

"It gets better. My client is missing."

"I don't like the sound of that. Watch yourself, Jorja. Some of the subcontractors Lehman does business with are thugs. Ex-militia from Croatia, Chechnya. These guys would take out their own mothers if there was money in it."

"Great. So why are they still in business?"

"You can bet Special Crimes has their eye on them. But they need to get something solid on these guys before they charge them with anything. Otherwise, they'll be out on the street and meaner than ever once their lawyer gets the charges dismissed. Maybe even file a few lawsuits against the city to even things up."

I scooped up the last forkful of alfredo sauce and savoured it with my eyes closed. "This sauce is so yummy."

"You don't want to know how much heavy cream and butter is in there."

I laughed. "I should have known."

It was already dark when I left Mike's. I was halfway to my car when I saw it. Something on my windshield. I took a few steps forward and peered through the dark. Then a few steps more. *Crap.* I turned and made my way back up Mike's sidewalk. Mike was still at the door watching me. He opened the door.

"Forget something?"

"No. Do you have a plastic bag or something? There's a dead bird on my windshield."

Mike returned a minute later, flicked on the outdoor light and slipped into his shoes. He walked out to the car with me.

"Must have really been cruising. Low altitude as well. And the chokecherries aren't even in season."

We stopped at the car and Mike shone his cell phone flashlight at the windshield. A large black bird lay against the glass.

"I've never seen a crow get drunk on chokecherries." Come the fall, the songbirds gorged on fermented chokecherry berries and swooped around like drunken kamikaze pilots, many to their deaths. Crows are omnivorous, they fed on small insects, seeds, weeds, frogs, earthworms, and carrion. But in the city the steady supply of garbage, roadkill or other waste seemed to satiate their desire for food, without them having to resort to eating berries. Besides the trees had barely leafed out, let alone produced berries.

"Do you think it might have just knocked itself out? Maybe it will come around."

Mike put his hand in the plastic bag and turned the bird over. "Nope. Not this guy. Its head is missing."

"No way."

"Way." Mike turned his wrist, pulling the bird into the bag, folded the top over and tied it closed. He looked over at me. "Anything you want to tell me about?"

"Someone left a decapitated bird on my client's doorstep."

Mike turned and surveyed the street.

"I don't like this, Mike. The fence fire. Maybe it wasn't set by vandals. One night I found the closet in your spare room open, when I was positive I closed it before stepping outside to look for Wess. Another night I found a black button, right in the middle of the living room. I convinced myself I was imagining things, thought maybe Smitty found the button under a dresser or something and shot it into the living room. When you told me Mrs. Niedswiki had come over to take Wess to her place, I thought it might have been hers. Now I'm not so sure."

FORTY

MISTY'S FACE WAS all over the news this morning. Police were seeking the public's help in locating her. Tara must be fielding hundreds of calls from people seeking more information or taking calls from well-wishers.

I decided the best thing for me to do right now was to go for a slow jog along the Glenmore Reservoir. Twenty minutes later, I hit the trail. A steady stream of bicyclists, joggers and walkers enjoying the sunshine filled the pathway. I breathed in the air, still cool and fresh, the ice just having recently receded from the reservoir. Halfway through my run I realized I was no longer seeing anything around me. One thought kept repeating in my head. *One of these is not like the other.*

I turned and headed back, forcing myself to focus on the scenery, the people on the pathway, not the questions hammering at my brain. Every few minutes I found myself back in my head. Finally, I gave in and sat down on one of the benches lining the pathway.

I should have never taken this case. I had let my curiosity get the better of me. The red flags were there from the get-go. Here was this woman who could only provide vague answers and spoke in symbols and feelings, insisted no one meant her any harm and yet hired a private investigator on an open contract. Of course, I really couldn't assume I was still being paid. And I certainly wouldn't be paid if Misty was dead, but that was hardly reason to feel irked. What did irk me, was the growing certainty that I was being used somehow. That I was a pawn in some sort of game. The decapitated bird on my windshield had cemented that thought. I shook my head. It's never a good thing when you start mistrusting your own client. *Prudent though.*

On several occasions I had seen Misty afraid, terrified. It proved nothing, except that maybe she was a good actress. Even her disappearance could be staged. There had been more than one occasion when I questioned whether Misty was using Lori Watson's murder to gain publicity. For all I knew, she could have written *liar* and *die bitch die* on her car and condo door herself. Sure, someone dropped a bag of sand off the legion roof as we were leaving. She could have paid someone to do it. Is this why she refused to share information with Detective Brighton? Information like the call from the supposed killer? Was she afraid if the police really dug into these things, they'd discover she was behind it?

I snorted in disgust. An older couple glanced over their shoulder at me and frowned. It barely registered with me. Now that I had given my imagination free rein, my brain spewed out possibility after possibility, none making Misty out to be the victim.

What was with the sevens and nines? Misty had been quite intense in her insistence that I remember the numbers, that they were key. To what? Was I supposed to find her now that she was missing then tell the whole world that it wasn't really my doing— that Misty actually deserved the credit because she had given me the keys to finding her *before* she was even abducted?

Revelation 9:7, Revelation 9:4. The reference numbers hadn't been lost on me. On occasion Misty had brought the preacher food and coffee. Had she paid him to quote certain chapters and verses of the Bible to me? Is that where he got the money for the drugs that laid him out cold?

Misty had seemed pleased with my strategy that we separate the past from the present. She would focus on the spiritual, otherworldly messages and I on the here and now. Except there was a linkage between the past and the present. And to Janice Stone.

Another idea popped into my head. What if Ivy wasn't just using Misty's life to fuel her Detective Dillon stories? Misty could be voluntarily giving her sister information on cases and events in her life. What if the Lane sisters where once again working together, muddling things, covering each other's backs? The animosity between them, their estrangement, could just be a cover story to help keep curiosity seekers at bay. They could even be orchestrating events so they could each bolster their careers.

So, what are you going to do?

I stood up and joined the foot traffic going south and contemplated my options. By the time I reached my condo I had eliminated one option—do nothing. If there was even the slightest possibility that Misty was on the up and up, that she hired me to help prevent her murder, I had to jump back into the game.

The various scenarios and all their permutations continued to churn in my head. It felt like I was being asked to reconstruct a failed brake system from a bad accident, but someone had taken away several key pieces and thrown in a piece from a space station, and I was trying to make it all work.

After showering and eating, I paced until the four walls of my condo closed in on me. I spent the next two hours just driving around. I drove to all the places Misty had been in or went to since

I first met her, hoping I'd remember something, see something that would provide the missing piece of the puzzle. Or maybe I was just waiting for divine inspiration.

I found myself at Misty's condo. I wondered if Misty's car was missing too. I climbed out of my car and made my way to the entrance of the underground parking garage. I tailgated the first car in. Once in the parking garage, I systematically strode through each row but there was no sign of Misty's Subaru Forester. It hadn't been parked behind her shop either. So, she could have driven herself off somewhere.

I followed a couple into the elevator and got out with them in the lobby. I swung by Misty's unit but got no answer when I knocked. I presumed the police would have gotten the condo manager to give them access to her unit.

I walked back to the condo lobby just as a man stepped out of the elevator. He rushed across the lobby toward the door. I recognized him from the news clip I watched earlier. He pushed open the door, turned and paused to hold it open for me.

I rushed forward. "Mr. Jackson?"

He held up a hand, shielding his face. "I'm not talking to any more reporters. Please leave me alone."

"I'm not a reporter. I'm a private detective."

He let go of the door and rushed down the sidewalk, calling over his shoulder, "Well, unless you're here to tell me you have some information to clear my son's name, I don't want to talk to you."

"I'm sorry, Mr. Jackson, I don't have anything concrete. Yet." I rushed to catch up to him. "I believe that your son might be innocent. I've been following the Lori Watson case, and there are a lot of pieces that don't seem to fit."

"Yeah. Well, when you have something concrete, give me a call. You know where I live." He gave me a final look, mouth set grimly, the anger clear in his eyes. He pulled open the door of a black Lexus parked at the curb and climbed in. He fired one last glance at me, shaking his head and pulled away from the curb. Point taken. I didn't have anything concrete.

I stared at the taillights, until the Lexus turned the corner. From all the conflicting images and thoughts swirling around in my brain, one had started to repeat itself. It was like taking a Rorschach test. Once you notice the first image, even if you can later see another image there, your brain keeps flipping back to the first one you noticed. I had to pursue it, see if it would lead me to Misty. But first, I needed Sal.

FORTY-ONE

IT WAS STILL early, but Giovanni's was hopping. We had to wait ten minutes to snag a table. "So whatcha got for me," Sal growled around a mouthful of Giovanni's spicy breakfast scramble. Various lengths of hair stuck out from underneath a mustard-yellow felt hat. Sal was too cheap to pay for a haircut, but her DIY job looked like she had used dull garden shears.

"I need you to take a little trip for me. Sunshine coast."

"Australia?"

"Sorry. BC."

"Not complainin'. What do you need?"

"I need an address or contact information for an Ivy Lane. Her mother, Doreen Lane, is a resident at the Sunset Terrace nursing home in Powell River. The daughter rarely visits but they must have some way to contact her if anything should happen to Doreen. I'm hoping the contact info is in her file."

"The old lady can't give it to you?"

"No. Dementia. Maybe schizophrenia. Seemed pretty much out of it, at least the one time I saw her. Now, how do I say this. I think this assignment is going to require some creative ingenuity."

"Angelina Jolie doesn't work for peanuts."

"I don't need you to make me a movie, I just need an address."

"Just sayin'. When am I leaving?"

"Today. If you can swing it."

"I can swing it. What are you payin'?"

"Standard rate, maybe a bonus for efficiency."

"And you just want the contact info?"

"Let me know when you have it. If it doesn't require a full-blown expedition down under, I might get you to go check it out."

"Gotcha."

"A ticket will be waiting for you at the West Jet counter. You get a smart phone yet, Sal?"

"Nope. You offerin' to buy me one?"

"With all the work I'm sending your way, I thought you'd have a shiny new iPhone by now. And a laptop to boot. Never mind. I'll send you an email later with the details, flight times, name and address of the nursing home and related details. You still have email, don't you?"

"I might not have the latest cutting-edge technology but I'm no luddite. You're not eating your toast." She nodded at my plate.

I pushed it over. "Help yourself." I pulled out a preloaded credit card and passed it across the table. "There's a thousand on there for expenses. Legit expenses. I need receipts."

She snatched up the card and tucked it into a shirt pocket. A man's shirt.

"When have I let you down, doll?"

"Never, Sal. Never. Don't break your winning streak."

I called for the bill, while Sal loaded up on little packets of sugar and jam. Maybe she was saving her dough for a hip replacement. I held the door open for her as she hobbled out behind me, today minus the cane. "You need a ride anywhere, Sal?"

"Thanks, but the walk will do me good. Gotta keep movin' or the joints stiffen up," I heard her muttering as she walked away.

I climbed into my car and laid my head back and snapped it

forward. Damn. The lack of headrest wasn't the car's only issue. This one was missing a passenger seat too. Plenty of room in the back if I ever needed to give someone a lift. I rubbed my neck. Other than the near whiplash, the car was pretty good as far as the JumpIn Jalopies fleet went. Most of their vehicles were mechanically reliable. All their vehicles had malfunctioning or missing features normally found in a car—features that didn't impact the overall driveability but were too expensive to replace. That's why JumpIn Jalopies rental rates were the best in town.

I turned over the engine and the car rumbled to life. The few hours of sleep I had was starting to feel like ages ago. I jumped as my cell phone pinged from the dashboard. Mike's number was on the screen. Just seeing his number come up made me smile.

"Hey, Mike. How are you doing?"

"You okay?"

"Yeah, I'm okay. What's wrong?"

"Someone wrote the word 'die' and your initials on the front of my house."

"What?" My voice rose several notches. My muscles tensed.

"Yeah. In blood."

I arrived at Mike's in time to see a black-and-white leave. Mike stood on his front steps. The word DIE and my initials filled the space below his front room window and the foundation. Capital letters, just like the messages left for Misty. I got out of the car and made my way up the sidewalk.

"God, that's creepy," I said, pressing my lips into a grimace.

"Glad you think so. It took a fair bit of blood."

"You sure it's blood?"

"Positive. Why? Would you be less concerned if it were red paint?"

"No. Sorry. I'm still trying to process." Mike sounded peeved. I got it; I was a walking disaster magnet. "I'll help you get it off. I'll run around back and get the hose."

"No need. I got a crew coming in the morning with a power washer."

"I really am sorry, Mike. I'll pay for it."

"I…look, I know it's not your fault. Professional hazard." He ran a hand down his mouth and chin, rubbing the day-old growth already visible there. "You do know you have a real knack for attracting psychos? Thirty years on the force, no one firebombed my fence or painted death threats on my personal property." I was glad to hear his teasing tone had retuned.

"Yeah, it's a talent all right."

"Got time for a coffee?"

"Thanks, Mike, but I think I'll head home. I still have a ton to do, and I didn't sleep well last night and I'm feeling kind of bagged."

Mike came down the steps and walked with me back to the car. He held the door for me as I slid in, then bent down. "I don't have to say it, do I?"

"No. I'll be careful. Double careful."

He grunted and straightened up, closing my door with a soft thud.

I started the car and glanced at my rearview mirror. Mike stood watching me pull away. An emotion I had never felt punched me in the gut. For one brief second, I saw all the grief and angst he had experienced during his time on the force, written on his face. One brief second and it was gone. I couldn't imagine my life without him. I couldn't keep dragging him into my shit. And this was clearly my shit. Whoever was leaving Misty messages and threats, must have followed me to Mike's when I was cat sitting, thinking the place was mine. I knew Mike could take care of himself, but worry sucked the moisture from my mouth anyway, and filled my eyes with tears.

I ran some errands and arrived back at my condo mid-day. I stumbled into my condo, almost too weary to think. I locked the door, set my alarm and staggered to the bedroom, checking messages on the way. Nothing from Sal. Then again, I didn't expect to hear from her unless there was a problem. I checked my watch. Her plane should be leaving any minute now.

After a quick change into an old T-shirt and way-past-expiry-date yoga pants, I called Betty Kennedy. I was about to hang up when Betty answered on the ninth ring.

"Betty, it's Jorja Knight. I hope I haven't caught you at a bad time."

"No. I just brought in the last of my groceries. The steps up to the house seem to get steeper each year." She laughed.

"Then I won't keep you. First of all, I want to thank you for the other day. I enjoyed our visit and I learned so much about Carla Prince and Misty. I don't know if you've heard, but Misty is missing. Don't know if you will see the news out there about Misty, but all the local newsfeeds are carrying the story."

"Oh, no. That's very troubling. Especially after hearing what happened to Carla."

"We're all very concerned."

"I don't know what I'm going to say to Doreen the next time I see her."

"She might not understand the gravity of the situation. Hopefully when you do see her next it will be with good news. You know, Betty, the more I learn of Misty's and Carla's past, the more I'm beginning to think that someone from their past is, rightly or wrongly, seeking revenge or retribution."

"But it all happened so long ago. The Irvings are retired—they'd be in their seventies by now. Who would want revenge?"

"Did Cash have any brothers or sisters or someone close to him who could have been gutted by his death?"

"Cash was an only child. A cousin or friend, I suppose, but not anyone I know."

"What about Carla's son? You said Carla gave him up for adoption. He'd be in his mid-twenties by now."

"Oh. You can't think…oh, I mean, I don't know anything about him. At one point I thought the Irvings might take him in. It would have been the right thing to do."

"Do you know anyone who might know more, might have some idea what happened to him? Even if it's just to say which province he ended up in. Anything would be helpful."

"Let me think. Hmm…there was a nurse who worked on the island. She knew everybody out there. Now what was her name? Anna. That's it. Anna Grange."

"Does she still live out there?"

"No…no. I'm fairly sure she moved to Lethbridge after she retired. She had a son out that way, a police officer, I believe. Peter. She wanted to be closer to him and the grandkids. I don't have an address though."

"That's okay. You've been an enormous help."

After saying our goodbyes, I pulled open my laptop and started searching. It didn't take me long to find a Peter Grange. Two phone calls later I had a meeting time set up with Anna Grange. I must have crawled into bed after that, but strangely had no recall until I woke to sunlight.

FORTY-TWO

ANNA GRANGE AGREED to meet with me at her favourite café. A tiny spot with six tables and an extensive menu, in a strip mall in Deer Ridge. She was sitting at a table for two in the far corner, drinking hot water with lemon when I arrived.

"Mrs. Grange? I'm Jorja Knight."

"Please have a seat. And it's Anna, not Mrs. Grange."

I pulled out the metal chair across from her. "What are you making?"

She held up a soft-mint-green mass of wool suspended between two purple knitting needles. "A sweater for my niece's little girl. See?" She turned it over and held it up. It had a cozy hood topped with little cat ears.

"Aww, too cute," I gushed not able to contain myself.

Anna settled back in her chair and rearranged the wool, a pleased smile on her face.

"Thanks for meeting with me. As I said on the phone, my client is missing and I'm looking into a possible connection between her disappearance and the recent death of her childhood friend."

"You said your client is one of the Lane sisters."

"That's right. Misty Lane. Someone has been harassing her,

threatening her, and now she's missing. I'm afraid she may be in trouble."

"Oh my. I do hope she is okay. How can I help you, dear?"

"Five or six weeks ago, a woman was found murdered on Vancouver Island, near Sooke. A hiker found her body on a beach. The police investigation is ongoing. The woman they found is Carla Princeton. She shortened her name somewhere along the way to Prince."

"Oh my." Anna's eyes widened. "I hadn't heard. That poor girl. I always wondered what happened to her."

"I went out to the coast to try and find out more, and while I was out there, I met with Betty Kennedy. She told me a bit about my client's and Carla's history and that Carla went to jail for killing her husband. It's sad to think she fought to save her child's life and paid for it by having to give him up and then spent all those years in prison. Do you remember the case?"

"Of course. It was all people talked about for a while. So tragic, all these young lives, ruined or thrown into turmoil. It wasn't a clear-cut case. Everyone had a different opinion on what happened. It divided the community." She sighed deeply. "What was clear was that young woman's drive to protect her baby at any cost. There's nothing stronger than maternal instinct."

I let the myth live. Not all mothers had that drive.

"I've been told the baby was adopted. I talked to a good friend of Carla's who told me the baby was a boy. She said Carla contacted child adoption services a few years ago to say she'd be open to re-establishing contact with her son, but as far as she knew no one had reached out to her."

Anna *tsk-ed* a few times.

"Betty Kennedy thought you might have some information. Do you know anything about the adoption or where the baby might have gone?"

"I do remember she gave birth while she was awaiting trial. They brought her to the hospital handcuffed. I was furious." Her forehead wrinkled in consternation. "Did they really expect a woman about to give birth to bolt and run off?"

"She was in jail at the time?"

"Stillwater Corrections Centre for Women. It's closed now. I heard they've refurbished the building into some sort of sporting centre."

"This hospital was in Powell River?"

"Yes."

"So, you knew Carla Princeton and the Lane Family."

"Oh yes. I spent my whole career in Powell River and worked part time at the clinic on Texada Island. It's not that big of a place. I don't know everyone, of course, but I do remember Carla."

"Any thoughts on where the baby ended up?"

She shrugged. "I always wondered if it was Marta and her husband that ended up with him."

"A local couple?"

"They lived up the coast, near Lund. An older couple. They always wanted children."

"What makes you think it might have been them?"

"I got to know Marta because she came to the clinic in Powell River a few times, wanted to know what was wrong with her, why she couldn't get pregnant. I remember her because she didn't want her husband to know she had come to see me. They were quite religious. He believed children were sent by god. Mortals were not to question divine decisions. I was pleased to let her know everything looked fine on her end."

"You think they adopted him?"

She shrugged. "It could have been them. Two people from social services came and took Carla's baby away the very day he was born. I do know that babies put up for adoption were usually placed within the province. In this case, social services would have tried to avoid placing the baby where people could figure out who he was, especially with Carla's trial looming. Marta and her husband moved away rather suddenly right around that time."

"They weren't planning to?"

"Not to my knowledge. But then again, they kept to themselves."

"They left before the trial?"

"Oh yes. Even before the preliminary trial. Tommy Cardago was the one who told me. He was married to my cousin, Mildred, at the time. He was a realtor back then, and eventually sold their place. They just took their clothes and a few dishes, left most of the furniture behind. Took Tommy two years to get the place sold."

"I see what you mean by a rather sudden departure."

"It might just be hearsay. But people like to talk. I wasn't the only one who thought they might have adopted a baby. One of my friends told me Marta came into her consignment store right around then and bought up a bunch of baby clothes. Could have been for a relative or friend, I suppose."

"Do you remember Marta's last name?"

"Now, let me see. I remember she was Marta, not Martha." She stared up at the ceiling. "His name was something biblical. Sorry, it escapes me. Now what was their last name?" She brought her eyes back down to mine. I marvelled at how her fingers continued to wind and twist the pale-green yarn from needle to needle without a glance. "Richards or Richlough…no that's not it. Yes. Rieckhoff. That's it! I'm surprised I remembered after all these years."

The hairs on my neck stood on end. A Daniel Rieckhoff attended three of Misty's readings.

"Are you sure?"

"I'm sure that was Marta's last name. Now, if you're asking me if I'm sure she and her husband adopted the baby, then I have to be honest and say I really don't know."

⚬

The trip back from Lethbridge took an agonizingly long time. The thoughts in my head picked up pace until I realized I was driving thirty kilometres over the speed limit. I needed to talk to Daniel Rieckhoff, or his mother. Or both. No one had contacted Carla when she filed her request to connect with her adopted son. Surely, Daniel Rieckhoff's mother would have told him he was adopted by now. He'd be a grown man. Was he Carla's son? Why had he attended so many of Misty's readings in the last few months? Was he aware of Misty's connection to Carla? Then why hadn't he contacted her? The blood in my veins turned cold, chilling me to the bone. Maybe he had contacted her.

But I didn't get a chance to ask Daniel Rieckhoff or his mother any questions. The last thing I remember is walking up to the front door of the little house in Bankview, at the address Sal had found for me. Then everything went black.

FORTY-THREE

MY EYELIDS WERE stuck shut. I raised a hand to rub them but couldn't. The panic tore my left eyelid open, leaving my eye watering, burning. I turned my head slowly, a scream rising up my throat, muffled once in my mouth. My left eye watered while my brain coached my right eye open. I blinked several times but the hazy film refused to clear. I listened, fought hard to stop the muffled sounds coming up my throat. The blackness returned.

Something was wrong.

I tried wriggling my fingers. I couldn't feel them. Were my fingers gone?

I jolted upright, but something held me down. The cold seeped through my jeans, fear tightened around my heart. I couldn't breathe.

Slowly, I pried open one eye then the other. The left one burned. It was dark, cold. I wiggled my fingers again. Pins and needles slowly replaced the numbness.

I peered through the darkness. The walls were rough, dark grey. The floor on which my metal chair sat made of concrete. My eyes searched from side to side. *Where am I?* I peered through the dim light. Stairs, not a ladder. *Not Mike's basement.* My heart pounded. The whimpering noise got louder.

I couldn't breathe. My chest heaved with the effort. My mouth was filled with something, dry, suffocating. I tried spitting it out but couldn't. My eyes spun around the room. I was alone. A brief flash of memory. Me walking up the sidewalk to a small bungalow. Mike's? No. Rieckhoff's.

I had been looking for the Rieckhoffs. The people who might have adopted Carla Prince's son. I forced myself to take a slow breath through my nose. Now another, this one longer. I could breathe. I stopped fighting and breathed.

My eyes circled the room, this time slower. A furnace and a water heater stood silently in the centre of the space. Neither made any noise. My arms and legs shook with the cold. Two pencil-thin streaks of grey light framed what was probably a boarded-up window. Below it stood a table. Various tools lay on top, more hung on the wall above. My eyes widened in fear.

I fought against the bindings holding me down. Useless. I glanced over my shoulder. An ancient freezer stood against the far wall. The blue-lit dot on the door told me the power was still on. I glanced down. Each of my feet were tied to the front legs of the chair, my hands behind my back. I rubbed my face against my shoulder, hoping to dislodge the cloth tied across my mouth. I judged the distance to the table. Ten—twelve feet, maybe. I began my slow progress toward it.

I pressed my toes to the floor, lifted my weight up ever so slightly and moved an inch forward. *Slow and steady.* I couldn't risk falling over. I paused; the table was so far away. My mind tried to trick me into giving up. The little voice in my head warned me of my impending death, then conjured up images of all manner of torture.

The preacher's words repeated in my head. *"They were not*

allowed to kill them but only to torture them…they will long to die, but death will elude them."

Where's Misty? Was she being held upstairs? Was she dead? Was I next? I inched forward. Where were the Rieckhoffs? Was I still at the Rieckhoff house?

The pencils of light were almost gone. *You can rest all you want when you're dead.* I crept forward. The table was almost within reach. I fought the urge to quicken my pace. *Slow, slow.*

Exhausted, I bent my head, my forehead touched the rough plywood tabletop. I inched forward. I turned my head and scraped my cheek along the table's edge. It hurt and felt good at the same time. The cloth slipped. I rubbed my cheek against my shoulder and used my tongue to push the dry rough material out of my mouth.

I gasped as the cool air hit my lips, my mouth gulping huge fistfuls of it and stuffing it down my chest. *Slow down, slower.* My tongue was thick, my lips dry.

It was pitch black by the time I got myself turned around, the rope around my wrists firmly pressed against one corner of the metal-clad wooden table legs. I pressed as hard as I could and began to saw my way through. I felt the rope give a little. My arms ached, and my shoulders burned. I sawed harder. *Hurry. He's coming.*

Finally, the rope gave. I fell forward, spent. I took a minute then gingerly brought my hands around to the front. Pain shot through my shoulders and back. I rubbed my hands, then reached down to undo the ropes at my ankles. My hands shook. I looked over my shoulder. I could no longer make out the small saw I had seen lying on the table earlier. It would take too long. I worked the knot at my ankle and sprung one ankle free.

I stood up, dragging the chair behind me as I turned, leaning on the table for support. Pins and needles shot through my foot. I reached out my hand and felt for the saw. I stopped, held my breath. Footsteps upstairs.

Here comes a candle to light you to bed. And here comes a chopper to chop off your head. Chop, chop, chop, chop, the last man's dead! The lines from Oranges and Lemons, a nursery rhyme my grandmother used to read to me in her scariest gramma voice, raced through my brain.

I felt the saw blade bite into my ankle. *Chop, chop, chop, chop, the last man's dead.* The footsteps stopped. I climbed up onto the table and froze as my knee bumped something solid. It was quiet upstairs. My fingers scrambled over the small square above. Cardboard, not wood. I found the edge and pulled. I startled at the ripping sound and almost fell over.

The footsteps started up again.

I pulled hard; the cardboard peeled away. My fingers shook, scraped around the edges of the small filth-covered window looking for a latch. There was none. *It's too small.*

The door at the top of the stairs opened. A single bulb hanging from the ceiling lit up, casting long shadows in the still dim room.

I picked up a hammer off the table, pulled the sleeve of my shirt down over my hand and swung at the glass.

I was halfway through when a hand clamped down on my ankle.

I twisted and kicked with my other foot. Digging fingers into the dirt, I pulled myself forward. My ankle slipped ever so slightly from his grasp.

I kicked my foot back, then yanked it free. My legs were numb. I crawled forward, then got to my knees. A weak cry escaped from my lips. *Scream. Run.* Why couldn't I scream? Where was I? All was dark.

I heard a door open. A dark shape loomed against the light inside. *The devil.*

I staggered to my feet and ran.

FORTY-FOUR

BLUE AND RED lights. I struggled to sit up, tearing at whatever covered my nose and mouth.

"Hey. It's okay, it's just oxygen, see. We'll leave it off for a minute."

I looked around. People milling everywhere, some in uniform, some not. I lifted my hand, a huge white club, and blinked stupidly.

"You're going to need stiches. We've stemmed the bleeding and given you a shot for the pain."

A different voice asked, "Can you tell me your name?" I turned to the voice. It came from a woman officer.

"In case I die?"

She smiled. "No. So we know who you are. We can't call you 'hey' forever."

"Jorja. Knight."

I closed my eyes. *I did it. I'm alive.* I started to cry, my shoulders heaving silently.

A woman officer rode in the ambulance with me. I remember giving her snippets of information about myself. She disappeared after they transferred me from the ambulance. I lay in a hallway for a while then someone whisked me away. Ceiling tiles flashed by. I felt the blanket beneath me shift and suddenly I was on another bed. One that didn't move. The walls were distorted, the ceiling curved like the entrance to a fun house. Voices swirled around me. My mind was a jumble of random thoughts. I closed my eyes against the bright lights.

I lost track of where I was, as they moved me in and out of rooms, first to get an X-ray, then to an operating room and back to a curtained-off cubicle somewhere. People floated in and out.

My throat was dry. I tried to swallow but I couldn't. I opened my left eye. Blackness. *I can't see.* Panic exploded in my chest. My right eye flew open.

A grey figure stood up, walked toward me. My lips stuck to my teeth. I couldn't swallow.

"Jojo. You're okay. Everything is fine now. You're in the hospital."

Mike's features came into view. I tried to say hi but emitted a croaking sound instead.

Mike helped me raise my head, then held a straw to my lips. I felt my lips slide away from my teeth as cool water flooded my mouth. A sharp pain filled my throat as I swallowed. I swallowed some more.

I lifted a hand to my eye, the one that couldn't see. A huge white blob filled my vision.

"You have a patch over your left eye. The cornea is scratched. You'll have to wear that for a few days until it heals."

I moved my hand away and looked at the gauzy blob.

"I'm guessing stitches."

I struggled to sit up. Mike plunked another pillow behind my back. I looked past Mike to the window. Dull grey skies filled the frame and let muted light into the room.

"How long have I been here?"

"They brought you in last night."

"How did you know I was here?"

"They found your purse. You listed Gab as your emergency contact. They called her number. Luckily, she answered. Given she's out of the country, she gave them my name. I got a call this morning."

"Thanks for coming. Just what you need with Julie having just been in the hospital."

"That's what makes me so good at this." Mike picked up the water off the small table and held the straw to my lips. This time I managed to get in several swallows without having the water dripple out of the corners of my mouth.

"God, Mike. What would I do without you here to pick up the pieces?"

"Stop already. You'd do the same for me."

I nodded as my eyes grew moist. The left one stung like a fire ant bite.

"Oh no. Gab."

"Already done. I called her an hour ago with a report of your survival. I told her either you or I would give her an update when we knew more."

I relaxed against the pillows as exhaustion took over. I must have dozed off. The next time I woke, Mike was speaking to someone in green scrubs.

Mike turned to me. "Awake again. I'm going to step out for a minute, let you talk to your doctor."

I nodded, not trusting myself to speak.

"Good morning. Or I guess it's already afternoon. I'm Doctor Walker."

I rubbed my right eye with my good hand. He looked fifteen.

He picked up my chart from the foot of the bed. "Everything looks good."

Oh good, he can read.

"You have a scratch on your cornea. Keep the patch over your eye for four or five days. Do you have a good ophthalmologist?"

I shook my head.

"We'll set up an appointment for you. I'll want them to check that eye, make sure there's no permanent damage. Otherwise— let's see, no broken bones—laceration to face, legs, torso. Lots of bruising. Forty-eight stitches in total."

"WHAT?"

"It sounds like a lot but it's not. Fourteen on your right hand and forearm, another seven on your upper arm and right shoulder, five on the back of your neck, ten on right thigh, five on left side of torso and seven on lower left leg. You've been given a hefty dose of antibiotics and a decent shot of painkillers. I'll write you a prescription for some painkillers and an antibiotic gel that I want you to apply to the stitches twice a day. Have you had a tetanus shot recently?"

"No, I don't think so."

He scribbled something on the chart. "We'll get that taken care of before you leave. The stitches should come out in about seven or eight days. You can have your own doctor remove them or at any walk-in clinic. Questions?"

How old are you? "So, I can leave today?"

"As soon as we get you that tetanus shot, you're free to go. Try to keep the wound areas clean. Change the gauze once you've applied the antibiotic gel and try not get the stiches wet—at least for a few days."

I nodded numbly. My brain was still doing mental gymnastics to try and match the stitch count to the body part.

"You don't have to try and remember everything. One of the nurses will give you care instructions."

Dr. Walker left and Mike returned.

"Well. Are you going to live?"

"Forty-eight stitches, Mike. Forty-eight. And maybe permanent eye damage. I have to wait and see. Ha ha—or wait and not see."

"At least your sense of humour isn't damaged. Could be worse. Besides, the stitches will make you look like a badass. A gorgeous badass."

"I just want to look normal."

"This might help." Mike dropped a bag on the bed. "I didn't know what you'd need or how long you'd be here, but you can't go home wearing the clothes they brought you in with. They had to cut most of them off. I stopped downstairs and bought you a clean T-shirt and sweatpants. Best I could do on short notice."

I could have wept. "Thanks, Mike. You are good at this. They're going to give me a tetanus shot and then I can go home. Shit—my car is somewhere in Bankview. I have no idea where my phone and purse are."

"Don't worry. We'll get it all straightened out. I think the police officers out in the hallway are waiting to talk to you."

"Right."

A nurse came in carrying a small tray with a hypodermic needle and a tiny bottle of what I presumed was the tetanus vaccine. Mike slipped outside while she helped me sit up. I slid an arm out of my gown and looked away while she stabbed me in the arm. "Your arm might be a bit sore for a few days," she cautioned. Considering the circumstances, I didn't think I'd be noticing.

After she left, I slowly eased myself out of bed, grabbed the clothes Mike brought and headed for the small, attached washroom.

I slipped out of my gown and stared at myself in the small mirror above the sink. My cheek was scraped, and several small nicks and gashes ran across my forehead. No wonder my face felt hot and tender. I turned to survey the damage and felt the pull of tape holding the gauze tight to the back of my neck and shoulder.

I pulled a corner free and lifted my hair. The stitches at the base of my hairline were caked in blood and looked like a grade-three sewing project. What did I expect from a fifteen-year-old doctor? Hopefully, it would heal to leave a much neater scar. Like the one that ran down the right side of my abdomen—compliments of Jason Marr—a fellow employee who lost his shit and killed two people and injured five more at my former place of business, Global Analytix.

I eased the T-shirt Mike brought me down over my head and bent to check out my leg. The skin around the sutures looked red. I couldn't tell if it was dried blood or inflamed. I grasped the edge of the sink as the room spun. My stomach felt queasy. I wet a paper towel and pressed it to my good eye. I pulled on the sweatpants, which were two inches too short, but remained grateful. Mike had also bought a toothbrush and comb. That man was an angel.

The nurse was in the room when I stepped out. "Glad to see your friend brought you a new shirt and pants. We weren't able to salvage much of what you were wearing. Some of your clothing was cut enroute to the hospital to assess the level of injuries."

"Yeah, he's the best. Not worried about the clothing, I'm thrilled to be alive. Was there a phone though, or a purse?"

"No, sorry. Your shoes are here in the nightstand. The police may have your purse." She went over some care instructions and handed me two prescriptions. A woman in uniform and a plainclothes officer arrived next. They introduced themselves as Constable Sommers and Detective Agawa.

After asking me some basic questions, like my name and occupation, they asked me how I came to find myself at the house they found me at.

"I'm still not sure. My client is missing. I went to this house, where I thought I might find someone who could lead me to her.

Next thing I know I'm gagged and tied to chair in the basement. I managed to escape out a basement window. I don't remember much else. Do you know if Misty Lane has been found?"

They exchanged glances.

"She's my client. Her publicist reported her missing."

Detective Agawa said, "We'd like you to come down to the station with us if you're up to it. I'm afraid it's rather complicated."

FORTY-FIVE

I TRIED NOT TO limp as we made our way past reception. I knew I looked a mess, but the dozen or so people in the reception area were too busy dealing with problems of their own to pay me any attention. Mike had taken my prescriptions to drop off at a pharmacy. Hopefully by the time I was finished at the police station they would be ready.

I prayed I wouldn't run into Inspector Azagora. Even though we were on a break from seeing each other, no woman wanted her lover, current or ex, to see her looking like a badly mended Raggedy Ann doll.

I reached the interview room and eased myself slowly into one of the chairs. Constable Sommers brought in a box of donuts and muffins and a large carafe of coffee. I felt tears well up and spill down my cheeks. I wiped them away and laughed.

"Bet you've never had a woman weep at the sight of coffee."

My hand shook so badly, Detective Agawa intervened to pour me a cup. I think I inhaled a muffin. One minute it was in front of me, the next it wasn't. I hope it hadn't been encased in paper.

"We'd like you to tell us what happened to you."

I took a shaky breath. "I'm not exactly sure I know. Some of what I remember is very vivid, some of it confusing."

"Take your time. Tell us what you remember leading up to last night. If you need a break, let us know."

"Do you know what happened to my purse? My house keys and wallet are in it. What about my phone?"

"We recovered some items at the scene. They'll be downstairs waiting for you."

"Okay." I took a deep breath and plunged in. "You already know that I'm a licenced private investigator. My current client is a woman named Misty Lane."

I told them that Misty had hired me several weeks earlier because she felt her life was in danger. I told them about the messages on her car, the dead bird, that Lori Watson had been found dead on her patio. That Detective Brighton was the investigator on the Watson case.

"After Watson was killed, Misty still felt in danger. She had strong premonitions about her own death, and she had been wearing clothing remarkably like that worn by Lori Watson the night she was killed. Misty and I both thought the killer might have made a mistake, that Misty might have been the intended victim."

My head was pounding. The nausea was back, and we had barely started. I really shouldn't be here. Might as well get it over with.

"I was pursuing several lines of thought. As time went on, I grew more convinced that whoever was harassing Misty, threatening her, might be related to her past. I dug in and learned that a childhood friend of Misty's, a woman going by the name of Carla Prince, had been murdered right around the time all these things started happening."

"Where was the Prince woman killed, here in Calgary?"

"No. She lived on Vancouver Island, in Sooke. She was strangled, as was Lori Watson. I'm not sure her death had anything to do with Watson. But there's a strong tie to Misty."

"What's the tie?"

"Carla Prince's original name was Carla Princeton. She and my client grew up together. Carla went to prison for killing her abusive husband. A man named Cash Irving. My client was charged as a co-conspirator in the crime, but charges against her were later dropped."

"This Carla Prince and Carla Princeton are the same person?"

"Yes. I'm sure the RCMP on Vancouver Island will be able to substantiate it for you."

"You talked to the RCMP out there?"

"I did. I talked to a Corporal Reed from the Sooke RCMP detachment. Of course, she couldn't tell me much, except that what originally looked like an accidental drowning or perhaps suicide is now being invested as a homicide. Carla Prince was strangled, her body thrown into the ocean and later found by a hiker when it washed up on shore."

"You think whoever killed Carla Prince wants to kill your client? And killed a woman named Lori Watson mistaking her for Ms. Lane?"

"Well, yes. That was one line of thought."

"Why?"

I took a moment. If I weren't careful, this would all come out sounding insane. The thoughts were already starting to jumble in my head. The problem was I didn't know why. Should I tell them about Ivy, that she might be Janice Stone? I felt my head starting to spin. I needed to focus. I poured myself another coffee. The painkillers they had given me at the hospital were starting to wear off. *Stay focused.* I had already blithered the whole Janice Stone – Ivy connection to Detective Brighton.

"Carla Princeton was pregnant at the time of her arrest. She gave birth to a baby boy. He was put up for adoption. The adoption records are sealed, but my sources led me to believe that an older couple, who lived on the west coast near where Misty and Carla grew up, adopted him. The woman's name was Marta Rieckhoff. I know this next bit might sound strange. My client is a psychic medium and a clairvoyant. She does private and group readings and has also worked with police to help solve a few crimes."

"A clairvoyant? You believe it?"

"Maybe. It's impressive to see her in action. She knows things about people that somewhat boggles the mind. Anyway, Misty claims she felt uneasy, felt a dark energy during several of her sessions. I started looking at the list of attendees at these sessions. I found Daniel Rieckhoff attended three of these sessions."

"The sessions where she felt a dark energy?" Detective Agawa asked.

I looked over at him, to make sure he wasn't mocking me. He had his poker face in place.

"Yes, that's correct."

"But other people attended these sessions as well."

"Yes, of course, but only five people attended two or more of the sessions where Misty felt this dark energy and one of those people was Daniel Rieckhoff. To be upfront, there were a few other sessions at which my client felt a dark presence and Rieckhoff's name wasn't on the attendee list. I discovered though, that walk-ins are allowed at some events, if there is room. Cash is paid at the door. I thought maybe he could have been there, using an assumed name."

"Okay. So, you're chasing a guy named Rieckhoff, who may or may not be the son of Carla Princeton…or Prince. You think this guy Rieckhoff might have killed his birth mother? That he's after your client because of…" He glanced down at the notes he had been jotting. "Your client's purported connection to the killing of Cash Irving."

Wow. The guy was sharp. Hearing it come back from him made it sound almost rational. But then he didn't have Ivy, Janice Stone, Peoria Benson and Lehman Group, the fire and Misty's disappearance rattling around in his head.

"Yes. I couldn't very well look up everyone who attended the readings where Misty felt afraid, felt this dark energy, but thought it might be worth it for her to meet the individuals we flagged in person, to see if what she had been sensing would repeat itself in their presence. We never got a chance to do that as Misty went missing. Then I found out that a couple named Rieckhoff may have adopted Carla's baby and I focused on finding them. I tracked an address down for Daniel Rieckhoff. I remember going there. It was an older house in Bankview with a little white picket fence."

"You have the address?"

"It will be in my phone. Isn't that where I was found?"

Detective Agawa nodded at Constable Sommers and she got up and left the room. The coffee was starting to kick in. Detective Agawa said he was with the homicide unit when he introduced himself. Why was I being interviewed by homicide? My heart pounded against my chest. Had someone been killed? I looked over at the door.

"I really don't feel well."

"Let's take a five-minute break. You're doing well. Just a few more questions. Corporal Sommers has gone to get your things. Do you want some water, or a rest room break?"

I nodded.

Detective Agawa walked me into the corridor. "Just down here to the exit sign and turn left. I'll have someone bring in some water."

I shuffled down the hall, holding my bandaged hand out close to the wall in case I needed to steady myself. *Was Misty dead?* In the washroom, I ran a paper towel under the cold water, squeezed it out and held it to my forehead. I looked at the mirror. Zig-zaggy lines filled the vision allowed me by my one good eye. I could barely see past the lines. *Had I killed someone?* I rushed to the toilet and threw up.

By the time I returned to the interview room, Corporal Sommers was there with my purse and phone. She poured me a water while I looked up the address Sal had given me for Rieckhoff.

"How did you find this address?" asked Agawa after I read it to him.

"Rieckhoff gave a PO box number as his address, when he signed up for one of Misty's events. A young man picked up mail from that PO box and returned with it to the address in Bankview."

"Can you confirm the man was Daniel Rieckhoff?"

"No, I can't."

"But you can ID the man who picked up the mail."

I felt my face grow warm. "No. I had an associate tail him to the house in Bankview. She can probably ID him."

"So actually, you don't know who really lives at that address?"

"No. I'd never been there, and I hadn't yet confirmed that the man my associate followed there was Rieckhoff. I was hoping to talk to him, see if I could get more information. I know it's not much, but believe me, I wasn't exactly given a lot of information by my client. She's scared. She had a premonition a woman was to be killed. Lori Watson was killed, right in front of her condo. The killer, or someone pretending to be the killer, called her, said she was next."

Detective Agawa scribbled something on the pad of paper in front of him.

"Why? What's wrong? Isn't that the house I was found at? I remember going up to the door and the next thing I remember is being tied up in a basement."

"Yes. Neighbours found you on their lawn and called police.

Did you see your attacker or anyone else at the location where you were held?"

I wiped at the sweat on my forehead. All I could focus on was the pain. An image flashed through my mind. A dark cloaked shape. *The devil.*

"Someone came down the basement stairs right before I got out." I took a deep breath. "I grabbed something…a hammer, I think…off a wooden table. I don't remember smashing the window but the next thing I remember was I was halfway out. Someone grabbed my ankle."

My right eye was stinging again. I realized I was crying.

"That's all." I wiped my face with the palm of my good hand. "I don't remember anything else until I saw the ambulance lights."

"Any idea if it was a man or a woman?"

I couldn't bring myself to say I thought it was an other-world presence, neither female nor male. "No. All I saw was a dark shape."

Detective Agawa looked over at Sommers and then back at me.

"What's going on? Why are you here? I mean, homicide. Have you found Misty? Is she dead?"

"I don't have any information on Ms. Lane at this time."

"What about whoever attacked me?"

"A neighbour heard you yelling and found you, lying half-hidden in their hedge. Whoever was at the house you were held at was gone by the time police arrived. We found a taser on the premises. We had our guys out all night door knocking, but no one heard or saw anything."

"But you know who lives in the house. The Rieckhoffs, right?"

Detective Agawa cleared his throat. "It's not exactly clear. The neighbours say a woman and her adult son lived there.

There's some difference in opinion as to how long or what their names are."

I stared down at my hand, now throbbing in its white cocoon. I needed this to end. "I didn't see who hit me, how I got into that basement. The last thing I remember was walking up the sidewalk to the front door. The house was dark, the curtains pulled, there were no lights on or signs of anyone. Next thing I know I'm gagged and tied to a chair in the basement. I wasn't even sure what basement."

"What did you see in the basement?"

"Nothing. I mean, there was a water tank and a furnace. I don't think the furnace was turned on. It was freezing."

"Anything else?"

"No. Just the work bench or table thing. It looked homemade. There were tools on the table. A small hack saw and a few other items, a hammer, some hooks and picks or screwdrivers." I shivered at the memory. "I noticed a small window above the table, but it was covered over. I didn't know with what at first. I'm glad it was covered by cardboard and not plywood and nailed shut."

"Is that it?"

"There was a freezer on the opposite wall from the worktable. A big old white freezer like my grandmother had. Can we wrap this up? I'm sorry, but all the pain medication is wearing off."

"Yes, of course. We'll get back to you if we have any more questions."

I picked up my phone. The low battery message was displayed on the screen. I opened my texts and breathed a sigh of relief. Mike was waiting for me downstairs. Constable Sommers walked me to the elevator.

"Thank god you're here, Mike. I really need to go home."

"Home or my place?"

"Thanks, Mike, but I just want to go home. Did you get my prescriptions filled?"

"They're in the car along with some water, gauze and tape so you can redo your bandages."

"Wow. You thought of everything. Thanks."

"Did you learn anything in there?"

"No. I mean, they kept asking me if I knew for certain that Daniel Rieckhoff lived in the house I had gone to. Then the usual stuff…did I see anyone or anything. Weird that Detective Agawa interviewed me. He's from homicide. I'm worried about Misty."

We reached Mike's car. "Here we are, let me get the door for you." Mike helped me in, then ran around to the driver's side and climbed in. "The meds are in the glove compartment."

My hands shook so badly Mike had to open the pill bottle and unscrew the water bottle. I swallowed two of the painkillers, praying they would kick in soon. Agawa's presence still bothered me.

"You haven't heard anything, have you? About Misty or whose house I was at?"

"The scuttlebutt is that they recovered a body at the house you were held in."

My vison grew blurry. Mike's voice faded then kicked back in.

I lay my head back against the headrest, thankful we weren't in my car. I cleared my throat. The grey blotches and pulsating lines messing with my vision were back. I didn't want to know the answer to my next question, but I had to ask.

"The body, Mike. Male or female?"

"My source wouldn't say."

FORTY-SIX

EACH TIME I woke I was drenched in sweat and afraid to close my eyes. Each time my eyes drifted shut, the nightmare returned. I enter a stairwell. The door locks behind me. I descend into a dark, decrepit space, tunnels splaying off the corridor, each one darker than the one before. Something evil is lurking in the tunnels. I'm lost, I can't find my way out. I descend another level. The walls are covered in strange formulas and mathematical equations. My heart races. I enter a room, an old laboratory, of sorts. I look at the strange instruments. My heart thunders. It's a torture chamber. I turn to run. A dark poltergeist swirls toward me.

Finally, daylight crept into my room, and I slept.

I woke up mid-morning, stiff, sore, and exhausted. I limped to the kitchen and made coffee, emptying the last bit of grounds into the coffee maker. I'd have to go out later, get some food. *Damn, my car.* I turned on the TV and headed to the bathroom for a quick shower. I cut up a plastic bag and taped it over the gauze on my leg, torso and shoulder. It took extra effort to wash my hair and face without dislodging the eyepatch or disturbing the various nicks and gashes which were starting to heal over. By the time I was finished showering, the coffee was ready and my morning dose of painkillers were kicking in.

I poured coffee, carried the mug into the living room and set it down on the coffee table. Picking up the towel still draped around my neck, I rubbed the ends of my hair and stood transfixed as a photo of Misty appeared on the screen.

Police are asking for the public's help in locating a local woman, missing since Sunday night. Misty Lane is five-seven and approximately one hundred and forty pounds with shoulder-length, dark-brown hair, green eyes. She was last heard from on Sunday night. If you or anyone you know has information as to her whereabouts, please call police or Crime Stoppers.

It wasn't easy to remain optimistic. Misty had been officially missing for over seventy-two hours, longer since either Tara or I had seen her. I sent Mike a text telling him I was okay, checked my watch and sent Gab a text saying I would try calling her this evening.

I walked into the bathroom and gingerly applied the antibiotic gel to my stitches. The cut on my left leg and the one on my arm was going to be noticeable for a while. I turned the tube of gel sideways and read. Supposedly, the concoction not only fought bacteria and promoted healing, it minimized scarring. I tossed the gel back into the drawer. At $5.49 a tube I had my doubts. Something on the TV caught my attention. I rushed back out.

Police were dispatched to the Bankview neighbourhood just before midnight on Thursday evening. A body was recovered at a house in the nineteen-hundred block of Thirtieth Avenue and one person taken to hospital with non-life-threatening injuries.

There is currently no information on the identity of the victim, but police are investigating the death as a homicide. The person taken to hospital has since been discharged. We'll have more news for you as it becomes available.

I had convinced myself that Daniel Rieckhoff was Carla Prince's son. Rieckhoff had attended at least three of Misty's group readings. Sal's description of the guy picking up mail at a PO box matched the description of the young man with the thick-rimmed glasses who had been at the group reading I attended at Misty's shop. A picture would have been better. I didn't see who attacked me. All I remembered was how strong the grip felt around my ankle. A man's grip, or someone training for the next national arm-wrestling competition.

Had Daniel discovered that Carla Prince was Carla Princeton? Found out that she was his birth mother? Carla had registered her name with the adoption agency, hoping to find and reconnect with her son. He might have found her that way. Then what? Killed her? Why? For abandoning him? Misty's explanation of her vision came back to me. *Junk or a junkyard could represent abandonment.* Could Daniel have discovered that Misty had been implicated in his father's death? The charges against Misty were dropped. Perhaps Daniel Rieckhoff was not as forgiving.

I pulled on a loose-fitting shirt and searched the closet for my fat jeans. The ones I wore in January, or after a particularly aggressive weekend of drinking. I gingerly pulled the jeans up over my legs, wincing at the pressure against my thigh.

Whose body had been found on the premises? The police were keeping things mum. It couldn't be Misty, if they were still issuing a missing person broadcast for her. Unless the body was so mutilated, they were having trouble identifying it. I shuddered as the image of the worktable came back to me, the tools…the hacksaw.

I was on the verge of remembering something or finishing something. The answer was there, waiting, just beyond my reach. The TV droned on in the living room. I peered out the patio doors. Low grey clouds, no rain, yet. I sat down on the edge of the bed. Where the hell was Misty? Her silence was disturbing. Surely, if she were able, she would have contacted me or Tara.

I picked up my phone and keyed in Sal's number. It went to voice mail.

"Sal, it's Jorja. Call me as soon as you get this. Sooner, if possible." It was the second message I had left her. She'd been gone two days now without a word. Then I sent Sal an email urging her to contact me. I didn't think she'd get it as I was sure she wouldn't have taken a laptop with her. I needed to talk to her. I cursed silently, convinced she was ignoring my calls on purpose. If she hit me up for a smart phone when I next saw her, I'd wring her neck.

I considered calling Mike for a ride, but he'd done enough for me. I looked up the city bus routes and found one that would get me close to Bankview and where I had left my car. I packed up my purse and walked to the door. My cell phone rang.

"Sal. Where the hell are you?"

"And a howdy doody to you too. What's wrong, doll, someone steal your lunch money?"

"Sorry. I've had a rough couple of days, long story. What have you got?"

"You sittin' down?"

"Yeah, shoot."

"Sunset Terrace is lax on its security. One of the inmates let me in. I hung around until the office admin went home, then had a look at the files. You know that little house in Bankview. The one I went to, following the kid who picked up mail from D. Rieckhoff's PO box?"

"Oh yeah—I know it."

"It's a rental."

"Interesting. What's that got to do with anything?"

"Just so happens it's the contact address for Doreen's daughter, Ivy."

"What? Are you sure?" My stomach muscles tightened.

"You heard me, doll. The address is the same as the address listed for Doreen's daughter—Ivy Lane."

"Whoa. That's interesting—real interesting. Let me get this straight. Are you saying Ivy owns the house and was renting it out to Rieckhoff?"

"Nope. Didn't say that at all. I said it's the address listed for Ivy Lane."

"Right. So, who owns the house?"

"Way ahead of you, doll. I did some digging. The house is managed by a company called Gunther Group. I gave Mr. Gunther a call."

"I'm all ears."

"They manage the building, look after paying the taxes, do major repairs, handle the renter agreement—"

"Property managers. So, they rented it out to Rieckhoff?"

"Not exactly. When they took over the management of the property, ten years ago, the agreement was already in place between the Rieckhoffs and the owner."

"I'm confused. You just said Ivy didn't rent the house out to the Rieckhoffs. Are you saying Ivy owned the property before the current owner and hasn't updated her address at the nursing home in all this time?"

"That's a possibility. But you know me, I'm curiouser than a Cheshire cat."

"So, you got the name of the current property owner?"

"You know I did, doll. But not from Mr. Gunther. Don't ask. The owner is listed as a J. Stone."

"No bloody way. Janice Stone?"

"You know her?"

"Not exactly. There's a writer by the name of Janice Stone. It's not her real name, it's a pen name. But someone who has read her books and knew Ivy swears they are one and the same." Which meant Ivy could own the Bankview bungalow.

"Couldn't find anything on this Stone. All roads ended at a law firm, Phelps and Bronson Law. You know lawyers, can't get past them even if you're greased up like a pig at the county fair."

"Was there a phone number for Ivy Lane on file at the nursing home?"

"Just so happens there was. Just so happens it's the phone number for Phelps and Bronson."

Bingo. "Good work, Sal. That's as close to conclusive as I could possibly hope for. You did good. So where are you now?"

"YVR. Thought I'd check in before I got on the big bird, see if you needed me to do anything else."

"I think that does it, Sal. Come on home."

FORTY-SEVEN

MY MIND RACED as I walked to the bus stop. Why were the Rieckhoffs living in a house owned by Janice Stone? And if Betty Kennedy's hunch that J. Stone was Ivy was right then she had to know Daniel was Carla's son, didn't she? The Rieckhoff connection wasn't a coincidence. It provided a definite connection between the present and the past.

I pulled out my phone and opened Janice Stone's website. I had visited her website before. Betty Kennedy said her next book was coming out in the fall and I was eager for news of its release. I sat up. There it was—up for pre-sale.

The cover showed a woman, dark hair reaching the collar of her red coat, entering a narrow, dark alley. The description below the cover read, "Smart, beautiful, Detective Dillon has one last chance to right old wrongs and stop a serial killer. But only if she can find missing psychic, Kayleigh Ginnel." Suddenly, I knew without a doubt whose murder I was meant to prevent.

The bus arrived at my stop and I shoved my phone into my purse and stood up. A woman ducked her head, embarrassed that I had caught her staring at me. My hand flew to my face. The eye patch was bad enough, but I should have taken time to cover up the scratches and scrapes with makeup. I got off the bus and what seemed like moments later, found myself standing in front of a small bungalow in Bankview.

The house looked tired and worn in the daylight and grossly out of place crammed in between the new two-storey infills on either side. Nothing looked familiar. Daniel Rieckhoff lived here. Had he attacked me? Was he the body they found?

Police tape sealed off the front door. I remember Sal mentioned a detached garage in back. I glanced around furtively and made my way up the sidewalk. The hair on the back of my neck stood on end. I rubber-necked my way around to the backyard. My knees felt weak. Shadows, sounds, and images from the night I was last here, played with my mind. I looked at the back of the house. Police tape fluttered against the back door. My eyes flew to the plywood now covering the basement window, bits of broken glass still lay between dead patches of grass. Bile bit at the back of my throat.

A six-foot cedar fence lined the left side of the yard. This must be the wall I vaguely remembered—an insurmountable barrier to my escape. But I had escaped. Something rustled to my right. I spun around. Nothing but the branches of a large spruce tree rubbing against the house. The yard was closed in, cut off from neighbours' eyes. I lost all interest in the garage and ran back to the street, my heart pounding. Besides, the forensic team would have poured through every square inch.

Tears blurred my vision as I searched up and down the street for my car. It had to be here. I rushed past a large dumpster parked in front of a house undergoing a reno and laughed with relief. My hands shook as I unlocked the car door and slid inside.

Back home, I put away groceries and took more painkillers. The whole exercise had left me exhausted, feeling antsy. I needed to do something but didn't know what. I wandered into the kitchen, flipped on the light and stared at the bottle of scotch.

The painkillers carried a warning to not to mix with alcohol. I poured myself a three-finger drink. Holding the glass against my chest, I circled the living room.

After gaining international attention and selling over a million books as an indie author, Janice Stone was a wealthy woman. Would she risk it all by killing someone or hiring someone to do it for her? Didn't sound like the quiet, withdrawn, frail Ivy of her childhood. Then again, schizophrenia didn't usually show itself until the sufferer was in their late teens or early adulthood.

I had mentioned my theory that J. Stone was Ivy to Detective Brighton, but I should have mentioned the connection to Detective Agawa. I could call him now. And say what? Oh, by the way, I noticed famous author Janice Stone's next book is about a physic who disappears. The detective in the book believes her to be a serial killer. Did I really think Misty was a serial killer? That she killed or had Lori Watson killed in front of her own condo just so she could solve the case and gain notoriety?

Tara said Misty had flown to the west coast to visit her mother. I needed to find out when she was out there. Could she have killed Carla? But why? Was it because Carla was the one person who knew that she had been the one who ran down to Carla's that day? Could Carla have known that Misty had been the one who stabbed Cash to death? That Ivy covered for her, not the other way around. And now Ivy was revealing the truth through her Detective Dillon novels. So why would Misty wait fifteen years after Carla's release from prison to kill her? This was crazy.

I lay back on the couch and closed my eyes. Misty had come to me proclaiming she or a dark-haired woman her age and build would be strangled. Two women who fit the bill had already been killed, and someone tried to kill me. Was I meant to be a third dark-haired woman, strangled to death? I sat up. Was Misty supposed to be the fourth? *One of these is not like the other.* The only one who had no connection to Misty was Lori Watson, or at least none I was aware of. The killer had made a mistake.

Something happened years ago that changed the course of several lives. Was someone trying to avenge Cash Irving's death? I thought about the version of the story Misty had told me. Misty lied for Ivy and said she had been the one to run down to Carla's place the day Cash was stabbed to death. She said she did it to protect her sister. That she felt guilty, responsible. For what? That she sent Ivy to warn Carla that Cash was drunk and raging with anger? Maybe Ivy killed Cash. But why would Carla take the blame? I rubbed a hand over my face, trying to remove the cobwebs that encased my brain.

I called Phelps and Bronson law firm and asked that an urgent message be delivered to their client J. Stone. The message said her sister was missing and asked that she contact me for more information.

I glanced down at my empty glass. I remember taking a sip but had no recall of draining it. I debated having a second drink. I glanced at my watch, poured myself a second drink, and turned on the TV. I must have fallen asleep as it was already dark when I woke up. The evening news was on.

First up was that the young man who had been arrested in connection with Lori Watson's murder had been released. Tomas Jackson's father had been right, his son was innocent. Either that or the police didn't have enough to charge him with Lori's murder.

A grisly discovery. The body found at the Bankview bungalow has been identified as Marta Rieckhoff. The police are now looking for the victim's son, Daniel Rieckhoff, in connection with the murder. I sat up. A picture came up on the screen of Daniel Rieckhoff. It looked like a head shot from a high school yearbook. Still, I had no trouble recognizing him as the man at the reading I had attended at Misty's shop. He was the same man I had chased at the scene of the building fire.

Police are not providing further details of the murder, only that the body had been there for some time. Anyone with information on the whereabouts of Daniel Rieckhoff is urged to contact police or remain anonymous by calling Crime Stoppers.

If I was going to save Misty, I had to move now.

FORTY-EIGHT

"HELLO, ANNA? THIS is Jorja Knight. I apologize for calling so late, but it's urgent."

"I just saw the evening news. Did you see it? They found Marta Rieckhoff's body. We were just talking about her the other day. She's been murdered!"

"That's why I'm calling. I need to find Daniel Rieckhoff. I think he abducted my client. Her life is in danger."

"What can I do?"

"Do you happen to remember when the Rieckhoffs moved from Lund? The month or time of year?"

"Oh my, that was such a long time ago. Let me think. I believe it was in the winter. Yes. I remember my friend Lorna saying she saw Marta buying baby clothes on Boxing Day. You know, when they have the big sales."

"You're sure it was January?"

"I think so, although I wouldn't want to stake my life on it. We usually had two or three adoptions a year, so I might have things mixed up. It was such a long time ago."

"Thanks, Anna. I'd like to talk to the realtor who sold the Rieckhoffs' place. You said he was married to your cousin?"

"Yes, my cousin Mildred. You think Tommy might know something?"

"I'm hoping he knows where the Rieckhoffs moved to after they left the coast."

"I'm not sure where Tommy is. He and Mildred divorced eons ago. I can call her if you'd like."

"I'd appreciate that, Anna. Anything you can find out will be helpful—a phone number would be great but even knowing where he might be living now would help. Please call me when you have anything, anything at all. Or you can have your cousin call me directly if you prefer."

The police were looking for Daniel Rieckhoff in connection with Marta's death. He couldn't go back to the house in Bankview. Maybe he had a secret place to go to. Is that why he maintained a post office box rather than having his mail delivered to the mailbox in his neighbourhood? Did he have a reason to keep certain correspondence out of prying eyes?

What had Misty said? *Remember the numbers nines and sevens. This is how we will find him. If anything happens to me, follow the numbers.* She had also mentioned the number one but said sevens and nines were key.

I pulled up a map view of the city. There were lots of streets, avenues and addresses that would include those numbers. Seventh Street, Ninth Street, Seventh Avenue, businesses and restaurants named nineteen seventy-nine, seventeen hundred. Assuming the numbers were even for a location in the city. I got up and paced. What could the numbers represent? A date or time? Digits on a licence plate? A phone number? Could the sevens and nines be repeated, like in seventy-seven? What order were the sevens and nines in? I sat down and scribbled on a pad of paper, trying out various combinations of the numbers Misty mentioned. After a while, I threw down my pen.

I turned to Google for help. The numerology sites said the number nine represented completion and fulfillment. The number one is a male number. One represents strength. One is also the number of the loner, someone who does not follow the crowd. Seven is the number of security safety and rest, something I now desperately needed.

I deepened my google search. Seven overlapping circles formed a symbol known as the seed of life. It in turn symbolized the six days of creation, the seventh circle in the centre the day of rest. There were lots of other interesting but pointless facts about the number seven. The seventh astrological sign in the Zodiac is Libra and seven was apparently a lucky number for Cancer and Pisces. Too bad I was neither. In Tarot, seven is the card of the Chariot. Googling further I learned that the Chariot is symbolic of the need to focus. *How ironic.* Reversed it signifies inabilities to see things through.

I regretted going down this hole, although the meaning behind the numbers was somewhat intriguing. But even I knew this was a very elementary way of looking at numbers. People with Misty's gifts knew numbers and symbols, like life itself, were much more complex.

I got up to pour myself another scotch. The room tilted, and I held out a hand to steady myself. I'd only had two drinks. The alcohol must be interacting with my meds.

I shook my head. Another rabbit hole. The scotch and pain-killers were taking over. I could barely keep my eyes open as I went through my bedtime routine. It took me a moment to realize my phone had pinged. I picked up my phone and saw that I had a new text. Anna had contacted her cousin who had given her Tommy's last known phone number which she was, in turn, sending to me.

I glanced at my watch and hesitated for a minute. Then I

reminded myself that killers don't care what time it is. I called the number.

Tommy was very accommodating after I explained the situation and waved off my apologies for calling him after midnight.

"Yup. I'm dead sure. The listing went live the first of March. They dropped the keys off with me the day before. I knew they were moving out, but when I went to check on the place, I was shocked by how much they left behind."

"I heard they didn't take much, just clothes and a few household items."

"I couldn't sell the place like that. It was hard enough to sell it as is, what with the place run down, needing repairs. I hired a couple of high school kids to come and help me haul most of the stuff to the dump. Took me almost two years to sell the place."

"Did the Rieckhoffs say why they were selling?"

"Nope. They weren't big talkers."

"Where did they move to? You must have had some way to contact them regarding the sale of the house."

"At first, all I had was a PO box in Calgary. Later Mr. Rieckhoff contacted me and provided a phone number. He was working at the meat packing plant and stockyards near Ogden, and they were living nearby in a rooming house. I believe the house was owned by the meatpacking company and rented out to some of their employees. The phone was shared by several families, but I could leave a message if need be."

"Sounds like they were in pretty dire straits."

"I figured it was the best they could do until they got the proceeds from the sale of their house."

"Hmm. Did they have children?"

"I never saw or heard any."

The information I got from Tommy was helpful but somewhat puzzling as well. Based on what Misty and Betty Kennedy told me, Cash Irving had been killed in the summer. July, to be precise. Betty said Carla had been drinking at the beach but claimed since it was her third trimester, drinking wouldn't harm the baby. I shook my head. If Carla had been in her third trimester, her baby would have been born in the fall, no later than the end of October. The Rieckhoffs didn't leave until end of February. Why would Social Services not have placed the baby with adoptive parents sooner? Maybe I had this all wrong.

I crawled into bed, removed my eye patch, scrunched the pillow below my head and closed my eyes. The events of the last few days plagued me as I tried to sleep. I woke several times, snippets of a previous dream under the surface. I was running, hiding to escape something or someone. I had Wess in my arms. No matter what I did, or how fast I ran, something was gaining on me. I had to find somewhere safe to hide. In desperation, I ran faster than ever before and felt my feet leave the ground. Airborne, I flew higher and higher and landed on Mrs. Niedswiki's roof. With Wess struggling to get out of my arms, I crawled into the attic. Wess stopped struggling. He was in familiar surroundings. He felt safe.

My eyes snapped open.

Daniel Rieckhoff would be hiding somewhere familiar to him, somewhere he felt safe.

FORTY-NINE

THE STREET WAS eerily empty under the soft glow of the streetlamps. A faint crescent-shaped streak to the east marked where the earth met the sky. I knew the house I was looking for. I had driven past it on more than one occasion. The building had been donated to Heritage Park and was to be refurbished, but the grant to restore the building had not come through and the project was in limbo. Hard to believe that it was worth saving. The windows were covered with plywood, the roof sagging, paint peeling.

An hour-long search through the online Glenbow Archives convinced me I had the right building. The house was originally built by a Canadian Pacific Railway executive in eighteen-ninety-six, and later sold to Calgary architect Theodore Hall, who disappeared after killing his wife and baby daughter in nineteen-thirty. The house stood empty throughout the great depression and was later bought by the Burns meatpacking company and turned into a rooming house for its employees. My heart had skipped a beat, when I noticed that the photo of the building in the Glenbow Archives was labelled CU 1949-779.

Over the years the building's various tenants reported strange sightings and occurrences on the third floor. Odd thumping, footsteps late at night, ghostly whispers, words appearing then disappearing on the stairwell wall. Even after the building was shuttered and the electricity disconnected, people still reported seeing the shadow of a woman holding a baby against the lit backdrop of the upstairs window.

I parked on the street, one of only three cars parked on the block. A few of the neighbouring warehouses had been converted to lofts, more than a few had already been torn down and replaced with high-rises. The old Burns rooming house stood alone on a large, gravelled lot, waiting to be moved to its final resting place in Heritage Park, and looked every bit the haunted house it was rumoured to be.

I pulled out my Walther BB gun, the closest thing I had to a real weapon, and loaded it. Mike had taken me to the gun range several times, showed me how to load a gun, how to store it safely, but I couldn't shift my mindset. If I carried a weapon, I had to be prepared to use it, didn't I? Finally, Mike bought me the Walther. I rarely took it with me, but this morning I had dug it out from my underwear drawer. It could do serious damage but was unlikely to kill someone. I inserted the magazine until it clicked, got out of the car, and slipped the gun into the waistband of my jeans. I looked both ways and crossed the street.

The house was creepier up close. Crisscrossed rusted-metal grills covered the basement windows. The front porch sagged, the exposed wood dark and rotted. The main and second floor windows were boarded up, the third-floor window cracked and covered with grime.

Gravel crunched under my feet as I circled the building. The air was still, the sky barely showing light. Two cinder blocks stood stacked below the gashed and nicked back door. I stepped up onto the blocks and reached for the tarnished brass knob. It jiggled in my hand but was locked.

I stepped down and continued around the building to the other side. Two wooden-hinged doors led to the cellar. A shiny new padlock held the doors in place. Maybe to keep squatters out. *Or to keep someone in.* I peered closer for any signs of recent use. A discarded needle lay next to the cellar entrance and a dirty, torn scrap of cloth. I nudged the cloth gently with the toe of my boot, it looked like it had been there awhile.

I continued around to the front and stood back. What was I even doing out here? The house had provided temporary refuge to many across the years, but it didn't feel like a happy place. Better than living on the streets for those, like the Rieckhoffs, who didn't have many choices open to them.

Had I really expected to find Misty here? I needed to get away from the building, find an all-night Timmy's and have a coffee, maybe go back to bed.

I turned to walk away, then stopped.

A dull muffled thump sounded. Then another.

I took a few steps back, held my breath and stared at the house. My eyes immediately rose to the upstairs windows. Nothing. I let out my breath.

Then another thump, this one weaker than before. I turned and scanned the streets. There were no road sweepers, no garbage trucks or large vehicles bumping their way down any of them. I turned back. The noises seemed to be coming from the left side of the house.

I walked past the front of the building, searching for loose boards, shutters or anything that could be making the noise. I rounded the corner, stopped, and leaned in, my ears inches from the side of the house. There it was again. The thumping noise was coming from deep inside.

I crouched near the gridded basement window. The next thump sounded louder here. *Probably old pipes.* The glass behind the metal grill was cracked and caked with dirt. I peered in but something covered the glass from the inside.

An involuntary shudder ran through me as I remembered my recent escape. My nostrils filled with the stuffy odour of stale air and damp cardboard. I stood up and spun around. The flat pitted ground surrounding the house remained empty, devoid of life. The odour of damp cardboard drifted away.

I spotted a fist-sized rock and picked it up. The weight of it comforting in my hand. I tapped it against the metal grill.

The responding thump sent waves of fear down my back. I tapped the grill harder.

A series of thumps returned.

I jumped back. The thumps stopped.

I needed to call Detective Brighton, or Agawa, or somebody. Tell them what? I hear noises in an old abandoned building, and I think it's Misty because a photo of the old building in the Glenbow Archives has sevens and nines in it. Then what? Would they need a warrant to gain entrance? Would they believe I heard thumps coming from within? I held my breath and listened. The only thumps I could hear came from my chest.

I put my ear up close to the window grill. My ears crackled with the silence. Was he down there with her? *The devil.* Had he heard the noises and silenced her? How could anyone be in there? The cellar door was padlocked from outside. But the back and front doors weren't padlocked. *What's it going to be, Jorja?*

I put my fingers through the grill and pulled. It held firm. Eight rusted screws held the grill in place. I moved down the side of the house to the next window. Someone had recently scratched the rust off several of the screws, the rust on the metal grill was chipped off in several places. I searched the ground until I found it. A bent nail. It wouldn't have provided much leverage even if the screw grooves were clear of rust. I picked up the nail and headed back to the first window.

I picked up the rock again and banged twice. Nothing. I pulled out my phone and sent Mike a text message telling him where I was. A precautionary measure. I walked around to the cellar door. A car rolled down the street and turned at the corner. If I was going to do this it was now or never.

The lock was exactly the type I used to demonstrate how to pick a lock in my 'So You Want To Be A PI' course. Two dollars and seventy-nine cents at the dollar store. I manoeuvred the nail into the opening and after a few minutes heard the rewarding click. I pulled the lock off and glanced over my shoulder. A dark figure emerged from the alley across the street and staggered away in the opposite direction. The hinges creaked as I pulled open the cellar doors.

I pulled my cell phone out from where I had safely tucked it into my bra and shone the cell phone flashlight into the gaping hole. I swallowed, my mouth dry, my tongue thick. My heart thundered in my ears.

A ladder leaned against the top of the wall. I knelt next to the opening and moved my flashlight around the hole. The stench caught my breath. I swallowed but the muscles in my throat seized. The walls were earthen, the unheated cellar once used to store raw and canned fruits and vegetables through the winter. The air was musty, dank. My head snapped back at a sound, but it was only a candy wrapper, rolling across the dirt in the gentle breeze.

I turned and placed one foot on the top rung and added my weight. I lowered my second foot until it touched the rung below. Two more steps down and my chest was at ground level. I turned, ducked my head and lowered myself to the next rung. The stench was overpowering now. I clung to the ladder and shone the light in an arc.

"Holy jeez." Something dangled halfway down the interior staircase. I gagged and swung the light back over the stairs. "Oh fuck."

Tentacles of fear closed in on me as I scrambled up the ladder. The vile, putrid odour filling my lungs exploded from my mouth.

FIFTY

I STAGGERED BACK FROM the cellar doors. My hands shook and my fingers fumbled to find the right numbers on my cell phone. *Fuck.*

"911. Please state your name and your emergency."

"God. I mean, Jorja Knight. I just found a dead body. A dead person. A dead person's body."

"Are you certain they're deceased? Can you check if they're breathing?"

I retched as my mind brought up the image. A body, the head and upper torso slumped over the lower limbs which dangled over the stairs. Something jutted out from the back.

"No. They're dead. Someone else might be in the building."

"Can you give me your location, ma'am?"

"I'm at an abandoned house just east of Blackfoot Trail on Sixteenth Street. Southeast, I guess." I thought back to the knocking sound. "The body is in the cellar. I think someone else might be down there."

After giving the 911 operator directions to my location, I crept to the cellar doors.

"Misty," I called down. "Misty are you down there?"

The sound of my own retching cut through the silence. I stepped back and spit as saliva filled my mouth.

A police cruiser barrelled down the street. I waved my arms and it pulled into the yard, raising a cloud of dust. The siren went silent as two officers got out. I met them halfway and explained my presence as we walked back to the house. I told them my client, Misty Lane, was missing. I followed a hunch that I might find her here, at the abandoned house. After hearing some faint banging coming from the basement, I had opened the cellar doors and started down the ladder. That's when I spotted the body.

I could now hear another emergency vehicle approaching.

"It looks like someone may have fallen through the interior staircase," I said.

"You say someone else might be down there?"

"I don't know. As soon as I saw the body I came back up and called 911."

"But you think someone else is down there?"

"Yes. I heard a kind of thumping noise. I banged on the window grate with a rock, the window around the corner there, and someone or something thumped back."

"Show me."

We went around the side of the house and I showed him the rock I had used to bang on the metal window grate. I took the rock and gave the grate a solid tap, then another.

"No sounds now."

"No." I shook my head. "The sounds I heard earlier were faint but definitely there."

Another police cruiser pulled into the yard, followed by an ambulance.

The other officer and EMS joined us. They conferred, while I stood by. No one was prepared to descend into the cellar without safety equipment. A call was sent out to the fire department. One of the officers handed me a form and clipboard and asked me to write down exactly what I did after I arrived here.

The first two officers who arrived returned from their circuit of the house. I called Mike and left another message, saying I was fine, to ignore my earlier message. A firetruck arrived. I waited while several members of the assembled team went around to the cellar door.

An unmarked car arrived. The blue light on the dash continued to flash as a man climbed out. He barely glanced in our direction as he strode around the corner of the house and out of sight.

I took a step forward.

"Please stay here, miss," one of the officers advised.

"What's happening?"

The officer shrugged. "They're still securing the premises."

The car radio crackled and the officer waiting with me reached in through the open door, picked up the mike and answered. A firefighter came running from around back and pulled an axe and several pieces of equipment from one of the trucks. I watched him rush back.

"Have they found her. Is it Misty? Is she in there?"

No one answered me. I paced back and forth, shaking a tingling feeling from the tips of my fingers.

Suddenly, the remaining few first responders standing by sprang into action. A wire basket was pulled off one of the emergency vehicles and run around to the back of the house. The medical examiner arrived. My heart sank. I was too late.

Voices floated toward us from the cellar side. Several first responders were gathered around the cellar doors. I took a step forward.

The officer waiting with me said, "Looks like they're bringing someone up."

The wireframed basket emerged. Hands reached out to steady it. I stretched up on my toes and craned my neck for a better look. Someone was strapped into the basket. A sheet covered most of the body. White gauze circled the head, mere inches of flesh exposed beneath.

"Is it her? Is it Misty?"

"Wait here." I watched the officer head toward the ambulance and meet the stretcher as it reached the ambulance. I broke into a run.

"Misty!" I called out.

Several faces turned toward me, blank. I realized they probably had no idea who I or Misty was. The plainclothes officer who arrived in the unmarked car stepped forward.

"Is it her? Is she going to be okay?"

"It doesn't look good." He stood next to me as we watched the paramedics load the stretcher into the back of the ambulance. Thirty seconds later the ambulance drove off.

A second wire basket was offloaded from the firetruck and carried around to the back of the house.

"Is there someone else?"

"Let these good folks do their work. We'll get an update later. If you don't mind, I'd like you to come down to the police station and tell us what you know."

I nodded.

On the way to the police station I wondered who Misty's emergency contact would be. Certainly not her mother. Probably Tara. *Hope like hell it's not her sister.*

FIFTY-ONE

SOMEONE WAS AT the door. Detective Brighton walked in. "How're we doing in here?" He turned to me and touched his face with his finger. "Ouch, I bet that smarts."

The scrape on my forehead had healed over and I had ditched the eyepatch but now I was sporting a long yellow-green bruise along my jaw line.

"Not as badly as getting stabbed multiple times, but close."

He raised an eyebrow and picked up the clipboard lying on the table. "Detective Agawa caught me up on what's been happening with you. Said you'd been tasered and held captive. Good job getting yourself out of there. How are the stitches, by the way?"

"Itchy as hell. I'm assuming it's a sign of healing."

Brighton ran his eye down the notes on the clipboard and flipped the page. "Last we chatted, your client, who was trying to find Lori Watson's killer, went missing. Next, I hear you've escaped your assailant at an empty house in Bankview, where a woman, named Marta Rieckhoff, was found murdered. Then I get a call that a body has been found at the old Burns rooming house. And surprise, surprise…there you are. Do you mind telling me what led you there?"

"It's a bit convoluted but I'll do my best. After Misty went missing, I turned my attention to finding her. Of course, I was certain that finding Misty and finding whoever had been threatening her were really one and the same thing. At that point in time, I was working to prove or disprove one of several premises I had, as to who might want to harm Misty.

One premise was that Peoria Benson, who owned the only other business, besides my client, in the McLaren building, might be behind the threats Misty was receiving. The initial vandalism occurred at Misty's shop. I wondered if it was an attempt to get Misty to sell her space to Lehman Group. Peoria Benson was quite clear about her intention to have the entire building to herself and was planning to expand her business. With Benjamin Lehman's help, of course."

"They've almost finished their investigation into the fire. It's looking more and more like arson. You might be right thinking someone wanted your client out of the building."

"Peoria Benson is much too vain to dirty her own hands, but I thought someone might have been commissioned to do the dirty work for her. Especially once I realized she was Benjamin Lehman's new love interest. Lehman seems to have a bit of a reputation for getting what he wants."

"You think he might be tied to this?"

"Maybe at first, not anymore."

"What made you change your mind?"

"When the building went up in flames, it made me wonder if I had it all wrong. I thought Peoria might be putting pressure on Lehman to leave his wife. Maybe she threatened to tell his wife about their affair, and he didn't like being threatened so he ended the relationship and took back the gift he was planning to give to her. But if any of that were true, why was Misty missing? It didn't make sense. They would have had no reason to torch the building and cause her to disappear."

"Okay." Detective Brighton sat back and folded his arms.

"Days before the fire, I saw a man watching Misty's shop. He took off in a big hurry when I spotted him. Misty had told me she too thought someone was watching her. The day of the building fire I saw him again. Watching the building burn."

"Think you can ID the guy?"

I nodded. "I believe it was Daniel Rieckhoff."

Detective Brighton let out a low whistle.

"Yeah, I know. I didn't know it was Rieckhoff at the time. I only connected the name to the face when the media released his photo to the public in connection with Marta Rieckhoff's murder."

"Interesting." Detective Brighton sat up.

"I thought so too. Especially as it fit my other premise that someone who knew Misty, someone who might have attended the events where she felt this dark energy, might be the one who wanted to harm her."

Detective Brighton made a rolling motion with his hand.

"Okay, okay. We found five names—people who attended two or more of the sessions where Misty claimed she felt a dark energy. One of the names was D. Rieckhoff."

"No shit."

"What complicated things for me was Misty's darn visions, although in the end her spirits came through for her. I already told you I thought Carla Prince's murder might have some connection to Misty's premonition."

"Yes. You thought her murder and Lori Watson's might be connected. We couldn't find any connection."

"Right. Well, I knew you'd look into it, so I mostly focused on Carla's connection to Misty."

"You mean you sent us off on a goose chase?"

"Not on purpose, I didn't. Remember the history Carla and Misty shared?" At his nod, I continued, "Carla was pregnant when she killed her husband. She gave her baby up for adoption. I located a nurse who was familiar with Carla and her situation. She told me she wasn't positive, but she always suspected that an older couple by the name of Rieckhoff adopted him."

"Now you've got my attention."

"That's why I went to that house in Bankview, where I was attacked. I had an associate run down this Daniel Rieckhoff and she found me the address in Bankview. With my Lehman premise lying in tatters, I started to think that if Daniel Rieckhoff was Carla's child, he might be seeking to avenge his birthfather's death. That he might be the one who killed Carla then went after Misty, who had also been at one time implicated in his father's death. I told all this to Detective Agawa after my attack. Don't you guys talk to one another?"

"Agawa put out an APB on Daniel Rieckhoff right after we found Marta Rieckhoff's body."

"The public plea helped. Once I saw his photo, I knew I was on the right track."

"What led you to the old Burns rooming house?"

"This is going to sound weird. Have you ever had something happen, but you're not aware of its importance until later—when some other circumstance or situation makes you realize the importance of what you saw or experienced earlier?"

Detective Brighton nodded. "I hate to say it, but I know exactly what you mean."

"I became even more convinced that I was on the right track after Daniel Rieckhoff disappeared. With the police looking for him, I knew they'd be watching airports, car rental agencies, that sort of thing, and he probably did too. A recent incident reminded me that when we, or most creatures, are afraid, they'll run to hide somewhere safe, somewhere familiar. Isn't that why the police go looking for suspects at their mother's house, or a former girl-friend's place?"

"True. But Rieckhoff's mother was found murdered and we were pretty sure her son killed her."

"Right. So, I started to think about when he might feel safe. Then I found out that when the Rieckhoff's first arrived in Alberta, Rieckhoff senior got a job working at the Burns meat processing plant and that the family lived in a nearby rooming house, owned by Burns. I wondered if his childhood might evoke happier times. I turned to the Glenbow Archives to see if I could locate the neighborhood where they had lived and found mention of a rooming house that came with its own mystery. It just happened that the number on the archived photo of the house was1949-779."

I took a huge breath. I had to get this right or he would think I was insane. "Misty had, at one point, insisted that if anything happened to her, the way to find her was through numbers, par-ticularly the numbers seven and nine."

"Numbers, huh?"

For one brief second, I wanted to tell him that I had also been entertaining the idea that Misty was leading me along in some sort of twisted publicity scheme. But that would take the conversation in a whole different direction.

"All last night I kept thinking about what those numbers could mean. I looked for dates, licence plate numbers, addresses, astrological signs. So, when I found the photo of the place where the Rieckhoffs had lived for a time, and the photo archive number had all these sevens and nines in it… well it seemed to fit."

"Seriously? That's what took you to that old abandoned house at five in the morning?"

"I admit, a long shot, but what did I have to lose? I was out of leads. Misty had been missing for over five days. Her publicist hadn't heard from her, nor had anyone else we knew. I knew if she wasn't found soon, she'd be found dead, if she wasn't already Her mother is in a home and doesn't even remember she has a daughter let alone two. I tried locating Misty's sister, Ivy, hoping she might have heard from her, but couldn't find her. The police were looking for Daniel Rieckhoff, in connection with his mother's death, and he was in hiding. Nines and sevens. It was all I had."

He rolled his eyes and shook his head. "Okay. I wouldn't have gone down that path, but I can understand why you did."

"Good, cause that's what happened, like it or not." I cringed inwardly. Part of me was as skeptical as Brighton.

"It's a wrap then. Thanks for coming down and giving us your statement."

"So, what's next?"

"We're still investigating, so I really can't say."

"Oh, come on. At least tell me if it was Misty in the basement of that house." Detective Brighton had been called out of the interview room several times during the last few hours. I'm sure Misty's status would have been part of the conversation at least one of those times. "You know I can phone all the hospitals, right? Why not save me the trouble?"

"Yes, we found Misty chained to some rusted pipes in the old boiler room. She's severely dehydrated, confused, has the usual cuts and bruises, some cracked ribs, a broken arm. She's in rough shape. We haven't been able to get her side of the story yet."

I swallowed hard. "God, I hope she makes it." We both sat for a minute, lost in our own thoughts.

"There was a second body down there. The one on the staircase. It was Rieckhoff, wasn't it?"

Detective Brighton's eyes met mine. "We did recover a second body. A male. We're working on getting an ID. Keep that under your hat for a bit."

"Will do."

Before I had a chance to exit the police station, my phone had rung three times. I looked at the screen. I didn't recognize the number. The phone buzzed in my hand. I was about to let it go to voice mail when I suddenly realized someone might be urgently trying to reach me.

"Hello?"

"Jorja Knight? Hi. This is Shaun Allen."

"Hi, Shaun. Hey, look, I'm expecting another call, I really can't talk now."

"You name the time, then."

"Sorry, Shaun, I really don't have the time."

"One question then. Has Misty Lane been found? Did she find Lori Watson's killer?"

"Sorry, Shaun, that's two questions." I hung up. Not that I wanted to be rude to him, I just had no bloody idea who killed Lori Watson.

FIFTY-TWO

"HEY, MISTY. HOW are you doing?" Her face was pale, the hand lying on top of her coverlet thin, frail. Her head was bandaged, her arm secured in a sling. The other arm was hooked up to an IV.

It had been five days since she was brought in. She looked rough, but she was going to make it.

"You found me."

"I did. Nines and sevens."

She smiled weakly.

"Have the police been able to talk to you?"

"Detective Brighton came by yesterday."

"The police have confirmed the body…person they found in the cellar of that god-awful house was Daniel Rieckhoff. It's been on all the news. They believe he killed his mother. I don't know if you heard but they're looking into the possibility that he killed Carla Prince and Lori Watson too."

"He tried to kill you. He tried to kill me. I guess it's why my premonition didn't go away after Lori Watson was killed. In fact, everything got worse. I was bombarded with messages; I couldn't tell what was real anymore."

"And now?"

She looked up at me, a half smile on her lips. "I'm no longer besieged with warning signs and messages, if that's what you mean."

"I was starting to lose hope that we'd ever find you. What happened? How did you end up in that cellar?"

"I got a phone call. A man said he was part of the reno crew working on the building. He said it looked like my back door wasn't secured properly. He didn't know if my shop had been broken into or that it simply wasn't closed properly. Detective Brighton said they are checking Daniel Rieckhoff's phone records to see if it was him "

I nodded. They would be able to check if he made other calls to Misty as well. "You went down to check it out."

"Yes. I mean, I heard earlier that they had arrested someone in connection with Lori's death. A young man with cognitive issues. Remember how I said I thought the man I saw driving off the night Lori was killed looked somewhat familiar? Well, the man they arrested often visited his father, who lives in my condo complex. I felt relieved, thinking Lori's killer had been found."

"A lot of people thought the same thing."

"I drove down to my shop. I noticed a dark-green car parked in back. I had seen it parked there before. Two guys with the construction crew often ate their lunches in the car, while listening to the radio. I thought perhaps one of them called me. I parked and went up to the back door. I could see it wasn't fully closed. I pushed on it and it opened."

"It didn't look jimmied?"

"Not to my eyes. Everything looked normal. I hadn't been at the shop for several days and the last time I was there, I was in so much turmoil, I convinced myself that maybe I hadn't locked it properly."

"So, you went in."

"I didn't get far. A few steps in something exploded and I went down like a ton of bricks."

She swallowed and ran her tongue over her dry, cracked lips.

"Water?" I jumped off my chair, lifted a glass of water off the side table and helped manoeuvre the straw to her lips. She took a sip and let her head fall back against the pillow. Memories of my own recent ordeal came flooding back—the fear, the hopelessness, the anger. I waited. I knew her mind would be replaying the images relentlessly in her head.

"When I came to, it was pitch black. I couldn't see my own hand in front of my face. I knew my arm must be broken. I couldn't move it and the pain in my shoulder was severe. I don't know how long I lay there, the room spinning. I was so nauseated. I threw up several times until there was nothing left. My feet were tied behind me, my ankles drawn up, the rope knotted around my neck." She started to cry.

"I'm so sorry this happened to you, Misty." I wanted to pat her hand, her arm, but was afraid I would aggravate an injury.

She waved the hand with the IV toward the Kleenex box sitting next to the water pitcher. I handed her a tissue. She wiped her eyes and blew her nose.

"The important thing is I'm alive. You're alive. We're both alive." She gave a shaky laugh.

I knew she was thinking of Lori and Carla. I was thinking of them too, and Marta Rieckhoff.

"I had no idea how long I was down there before he arrived. A man. He took the rope from my neck. For one brief second, I hoped I'd be able to reason with him. He sat on my chest and put his hands around my neck and started choking me. I don't know if I passed out from the lack of air or the pain shooting through my arm and chest. When I came to, he was gone."

"Did he…?"

She shook her head. "I wasn't raped. They confirmed it when I got here, because there were great chunks of time I couldn't account for. All I knew was that I was down there a long time. I couldn't hear anyone or anything. I remember calling out, yelling, but my throat got so sore, I lost my voice."

"I can hear how sore it still is. You're a brave woman, Misty."

"After an awfully long time the man came back. He wanted to know why I abandoned him, why, if I knew where he lived, hadn't I come to get him like I said I would."

"But that doesn't make sense. Was he insane?" Then I remembered that this was Daniel Rieckhoff we were talking about. I looked at Misty's downcast face. "You know, at one point I was almost convinced your sister Ivy was behind this. Betty Kennedy told me that she thinks your sister is Janice Stone, the mystery writer. I read Stone's first book, and the description of the other books in the series. Her novels sound like she's fictionalizing events in your life."

"When you told me Carla had been murdered, I worried Ivy might be responsible."

"I remember." A sudden flare of excitement made my skin tingle. "You said it changed everything but didn't elaborate."

"I wasn't holding back. But after hearing that Carla was murdered, I couldn't help but think her death had something to do with our past."

"So, you do know that Janice Stone is your sister, Ivy."

Misty chewed on her bottom lip.

"Come on, Misty. Give me something that will make me feel better about the forty-eight stiches I'm wearing." I watched Misty shrink into herself and instantly regretted my comment. She finally looked up; her chin trembled ever so slightly.

"I'm so sorry, Jorja. This is my fault. I brought you into this. I never meant for you to get hurt. I do owe you an explanation.

You have to give me your word that you won't tell a soul what I'm about to tell you."

"O…kay." I didn't like making promises without knowing what was at stake.

She breathed a sigh of relief. "Yes. Ivy writes under the pen name of Janice Stone. She'd been writing for decades, without much success. Then she decided to fictionalize what happened to us and she wrote the first of her Detective Dillon novels. It was an instant hit. She sold over 100,000 copies in just three months."

"They do say truth is stranger than fiction. I get the sense you weren't happy with your sister's decision to base the story on real-life events."

"The book makes little attempt to fictionalize it. I mean, the Lane sisters became the Ginnel sisters in her book." She shook her head. "Some of it is fictionalized, of course, but she used the book to reveal some truths we had agreed would remain hidden."

The novel's plot raced through my head. "You mean you ran down to Carla's that day and killed Cash because he raped your sister."

"No. What I told you was the truth. Ivy ran down to warn Carla that day, I covered for her, I lied and said I was the one the neighbour saw running down the path from Carla's."

"Why did you have to cover for her?"

Misty stared at her hands. "Ivy came back distraught. She had blood all over her shirt…my shirt." She looked up, her eyes heavy with pain. "More blood than you would expect from finding someone bleeding on the floor."

"Your sister killed Cash? And let Carla take the blame?"

"I don't know. I suspect she did…I never asked her outright. I felt horrible…what happened to Cash, to Carla, was largely my fault."

"How could it be your fault?" Now something was fluttering in my chest. I resisted the urge to press my hand over it.

"When Carla told me on the beach that day, that she was seriously considering leaving Cash, I saw my chance to help push her in that direction. I never liked Cash, he was a bully and a pig. When Carla told me that their fights had escalated from verbal to physical, I told her that she had to leave him. There were rumours that Cash was cheating on her. Carla had heard them too. I told her the rumours were true. Even worse, I told her Cash raped Ivy but she had sworn me to secrecy."

I couldn't help myself and gasped out loud. "That's what Janice Stone—I mean, Ivy—says in her book. So, it's true?"

"Not exactly. It was obvious to everyone that Ivy was infatuated with Cash, just like Carla had been at her age. Ivy was withdrawn, awkward. She didn't date. I was afraid she'd end up like our mother. When Cash was around, she doted on every word, laughed at his stupid, sexist comments. Carla was furious when I told her Cash raped her."

"So that's what started the fight."

"Yes. When he came to the house that day, I thought he was going to kill me or Ivy. He called me a bitch, ranted and raved; said Ivy was going to pay. Ivy didn't really know what was going on at that point, but clearly she knew word had gotten out that she and Cash slept together. I told her to go, warn Carla, tell her to get out of the house. I tried to calm Cash down, keep him at the house at bit longer so Ivy could get to Carla and warn her, but obviously wasn't able to keep him long enough."

"Slept together? You said he raped her."

"I told Carla that he raped her. I lied."

"I don't understand."

"About a week before this all happened, I found Ivy's diary. She was always taking my stuff without asking so I read it. In it she talked about wanting to be like all the other girls. She hated being a virgin. Cash knew she was obsessed with him. He'd flirt with her. The diary laid it all out. How she approached him one night when he was drunk. Told him she wanted him to take her virginity, no strings attached. Apparently, he obliged."

"Oh, no. I feel so sorry for her."

"That's not all. Instead of having sex with Cash and moving on, she grew more obsessed with him. She started the rumours that he was cheating on Carla. The last entry I read blew me away. She was pregnant."

"Oh my god. Did you ever confront her, admit that you read her diary?"

"I did—after she came back from Carla's that day. Her being pregnant with Cash's child gave her the motive that could have put her behind bars. All I could think of was that I had done this, I had to protect her."

"I remember Mrs. Kennedy saying Ivy left the island shortly after Carla was killed, while you stayed behind to look after your mother."

"Ivy had to leave, or everyone would know about the pregnancy. She planned on having an abortion. She moved to Vancouver Island."

"After I read Stone's first Detective Dillon novel, I was ninety-five percent sure Stone was Ivy but I was stunned when I learned that Daniel Rieckhoff and his mother were living in a house that belonged to Janice Stone. Now I get it. She must have felt guilty over what she did to Daniel's birth father and mother."

"Well, she did feel guilty, but that's not why the Rieckhoffs were living in a house paid for by Ivy. Daniel is Ivy's son."

FIFTY-THREE

SLOWLY, STEADILY, MISTY'S strength returned. The rest of the story came out in dribs and drabs, some of it from Misty, some of it through the news. The body recovered from the old rooming house was indeed Daniel Rieckhoff's. His death was ruled an accident, but police found evidence linking him to the death and dismemberment of Marta Rieckhoff. Marta had been killed a year earlier; her body cut in pieces and stored in a freezer in the basement of the Bankview house.

Today, Misty looked better—some colour had returned to her face. She was sitting in a chair by the window.

"Jorja. So glad to see you, come join me. I can't wait to get to out of this place."

"Have they said when they're springing you free?"

"Tomorrow, I hope."

I noticed a bouquet of miniature roses on her bedside table. "Has your sister been by to see you?"

"Ivy? No. You know, I've had a lot of time for contemplation these last few days. I have to let go of the idea that I owe her something." She picked at a hangnail, then looked up, her eyes moist. "I can't help her anymore. I now realize that I probably did her more harm than good."

"What do you mean?"

"She's unstable, she always was. But I never imagined she would go the lengths she did."

"Why, what's happened?"

"You promise. You won't say anything?"

What more could there be? I nodded, but just barely.

"You've read the descriptions of Janice Stone's books, right?"

"Yes, and Mrs. Kennedy gave me a pretty good summary of each of them."

"Then you know Ivy fashioned her antagonist after me. A psychic who helps police solve crimes. Detective Dillon suspects the psychic is a serial killer and is getting perverse pleasure from 'helping' the police."

"The psychic in her books is definitely a dark character and getter darker with each new installment." I didn't tell her that I had considered the possibility that she might have killed Lori Watson or at least had been volunteering her own experiences to help her sister write her novels.

"I started to worry that Ivy was losing touch with reality. She would take things that happened to me, cases I worked on with the police, but then add a level of depravity to her stories that I found disturbing. Then in book four she kills the character modelled after Carla. Imagine how I felt when you told me Carla had been murdered, strangled like Lori Watson."

"Yeah. That was a little disturbing. Especially since book four came out about four months before Carla was murdered." My eyes widened. "Are you saying what I think you're saying?"

"While Daniel had me tied up in that house, he told me a lot of things. Some I believed; some I still don't know what to make of."

My heart rate shot up. Did I want to hear something I'd regret promising to keep quiet about?

"Daniel told me he hated Marta. She was deeply religious, controlling. One day, Ivy contacted Daniel. She knew where he lived. She bought the house after his father Isaac died. She let Marta and Daniel live there for free. He was her son, after all."

"Did Daniel know Ivy was his birth mother?"

"Not at that point."

"So, Marta never told him he was adopted."

"*I* didn't even know Ivy had a son. I was shocked when he told me. Ivy always said she'd had an abortion. Apparently, she didn't. Everyone knew the Rieckhoffs didn't have children but always wanted one, so she approached them to see if they wanted her child. It was a private adoption and meant to be an open adoption, but Marta didn't like Ivy coming around, refused to give her access to Daniel. Apparently, Ivy sent letters, gifts at Christmas, the occasional cheque. Marta didn't pass the letters on to Daniel. He found them hidden away in the attic after Ivy contacted him and told him that she was his birth mother and that Marta had prevented her from seeing him all these years."

"When was this?"

"About a year ago. Daniel told me he had no idea who she was when she approached him. He was livid that Marta hadn't told him anything. He was shocked when he found out he was adopted and furious that Marta had kept it a secret."

"That might explain why he killed Marta."

"I can't believe she kept it a secret all these years."

"Why do you think Ivy contacted him now, and not earlier?"

Misty hugged herself, rubbing one arm with the other. "I don't really know. Maybe because she was finally rich and could have what she wanted. Or maybe she just wanted someone in her life. Whatever the reason, Ivy saw it as an opportunity to spin her version of reality." Misty bit her bottom lip and shook her head. "Ivy told him she and Cash were in love, that Carla wouldn't give

Cash a divorce, without making things ugly for him. That Carla and I conspired to kill his father, believing that the Irvings would take care of Carla and her baby for life, even though the baby wasn't Cash's. She told Daniel that Carla and I set things up and killed Cash, making it look like he attacked Carla and was killed in self-defence."

"Whoa. This is crazy."

"Yeah. I guess I deserve it. I mean, yes, Ivy had a lot to do with what happened, but I was the one who blew the whole thing sky high by telling Carla that Cash raped her. I should have never told that lie, but I was still shocked, angry that Ivy had thrown herself at Cash and got herself pregnant. Even though I disliked Cash, I felt that Ivy had somehow betrayed me, betrayed Carla."

Tears sprung up in Misty's eyes. I suddenly realized how alone she had been in all of this.

"After Ivy told Daniel her warped version of what happened that night, I guess Daniel sought his own revenge, believing that Carla and I were the catalysts for the horrid life he had growing up with an overbearing, controlling mother."

"He must have confronted Marta. That must be when he killed her. Do you think he killed Carla too?"

"He admitted killing Carla and said he was going to kill me too. I was terrified. Sometimes when he came, he'd bring food and water and let me relieve myself. Then he'd sit there and talk, rant, scream questions at me or hit and choke me until I passed out. I never knew what version of him would show up. But that was less terrifying than knowing what my sister had done, was doing."

Ivy had apparently found out that Carla was living in Sooke and told Daniel where he could find her.

"She wanted him to find and kill her." Tears finally poured from Misty's eyes. "She knew he was going to kill Carla. She even wrote it into her last book, months before it even happened."

I handed Misty another Kleenex and waited for her quiet sobs to subside. I know I had promised to keep whatever she told me a secret…but this was too much.

"Misty. He admitted it to you. Ivy must know he killed these women."

"Clearly Daniel had his own mental health issues." Misty dabbed at her eyes. "But Ivy is sick, she's lost track of what's real and what's fiction. She planted ideas in Daniel's head, fed him a pack of lies. She got him to toy with me, threaten me. He then went after me but killed Lori by mistake. When you came into the picture, you became a threat to him, and he went after you too."

"Ivy was using you—us, like guinea pigs, to see what we would do, how we would act. Fresh fodder for her books." I reached out and grasped her hand, which lay shaking in her lap. "I'm so sorry, Misty. That's so sick. Did you tell Detective Brighton all of this?"

She took a huge breath. "I said Daniel told me he killed Carla, intended to kill me and killed Lori by mistake. He said he wouldn't be making a mistake this time."

I gave Misty's hand a squeeze and let it go. Was that why Lori's body had been positioned into a cross? A sign of contrition when Daniel realized he killed the wrong woman?

"Did you tell Detective Brighton what you've told me about Ivy? That she was his birth mother, that she was feeding Daniel all these lies, fuelling his hatred."

Misty looked out the window for a few minutes then turned back to me. "I told Detective Brighton that Daniel told me Ivy was his birth mother. I also told Detective Brighton that I thought my sister was pregnant at one point, but she told me she had an abortion. Is any of it true? I don't know. I'm sure he'll be trying to find evidence of this private adoption to the Rieckhoffs. He's asked me to provide DNA—they'll be able to tell if Daniel and I are…were related."

"What a mess" So this was how she was going to play it. She was still protecting her sister, who might very well be an accessory to murder. At least the DNA results would confirm or negate part of Daniel's story.

"Detective Brighton said they're trying to find direct evidence that might link Carla and Lori's murders to Daniel."

"But he confessed to you."

"With Daniel dead, whatever he told me is hearsay unless something concrete can be found. However, given that they know he murdered Marta, it's likely he was telling the truth."

"Speaking of Daniel, they're calling his death an accident. Do you know what happened?"

"Oh god, Jorja, it was awful. Like I said, Daniel would leave me for what seemed like days then show up from time to time. I don't know which was worse. One time, I heard footsteps coming down the stairs. There was this sharp crack and an unearthly scream. I don't think I'll ever get that sound out of my head."

"How awful." The image of a body floating, hovering on the staircase flitted through my mind. "He fell through the staircase?"

"Detective Brighton said it looked like the stair gave way and he fell against the rail, which splintered, and impaled him. It was awful." She took a shaky breath. "It took him hours to die."

"Oh god." The thought made me feel weak in the knees.

"When it finally stopped, I realized no one had come to help, no one heard him. So, I knew I was being kept somewhere where no one would hear me. They figure I was down there for three days after he died—chained to a pipe running up the wall. I remember I found a piece of wood. I just banged on the pipe with it whenever I could. I asked spirit to summon you, to bring you to me, to rescue me. But when you didn't come, I knew I was going to die." Her shoulder shook as sobs wracked her body.

I got up and wrapped an arm around her shoulder. I knew

that feeling, the moment everything stops, when you believe your life is over. "It'll be okay, Misty; it will be okay. The spirits did look after you and me too."

FIFTY-FOUR

MIKE AND I were heading to Spruce Meadows to take in the National—which featured some of the best show jumping horses and athletes from around the word. I glanced out the window, grateful that my eye had healed nicely with no damage. The sky was blue, the trees in full leaf, the city planters filled with flowers. My best friend, Gab was back, my stitches had been removed and the marks they left had faded from angry red to pink. Mrs. Niedswiki smiled at me today and I had a new client. Although it had only been several weeks, everything that happened now seemed so long ago.

Misty had given her story to Shaun Allen, who wrote up a three-part exposé about her abduction and Daniel's admission to killing Carla Prince and Lori Watson but hadn't shared that Daniel might be her sister's child, or any of the story she had shared with me about what happened the day Cash Irving was killed. Misty credited me for preventing her death by following the numbers nine and seven, but I refused a follow-up interview with Shaun Allen. I still didn't know what to make of all that had transpired. And Misty's continued protection of her sister had once again raised the thought that the two might in some fashion, be working together.

The police had poured hundreds of manhours into finding evidence that would prove Daniel Rieckhoff's admissions to Misty that he had killed both Carla Prince and Lori Watson were true. Airport security cameras showed him arriving in Victoria four days before Carla was killed. His name was not on any passenger list, which meant he flew there using a false name, which further fuelled speculation that he might have indeed had something to do with Carla's death. There was no record of a return flight.

Street cameras also confirmed my assertion that Daniel Rieckhoff had been in the vicinity of the McLaren building the day it went up in flames, although nothing linked him with the arson itself. I had occasionally wondered if the preacher were to blame, but he had moved on.

The burnt-out shell of Misty's Subaru Forester was found near the turnoff to Moose Mountain a week after Misty was found. A traffic camera on Highway 8 showed Daniel behind the wheel. The latest statement from police said their review of forensic evidence would be completed in a few weeks and once an update was provided to the families, the information would be released to the public. Police also said that it might prove difficult to determine a motive for the killings because the suspect was dead, although if DNA could establish that he was related to Misty, the police would likely go back into the Cash Irving murder and all that led from it.

I last saw Misty two weeks ago. She invited me out for dinner, a formal thank-you for saving her life. I finally got a chance to give her the painting Carla's friend had asked me to give her. The watercolour Carla had painted of Texada Island, where she and Misty had grown up. It had moved her to tears. I'll even admit that her reaction caused me to get a bit emotional as well.

I had pre-ordered Janice Stone's next book, the one where the psychic, Kayleigh Ginnel goes missing. I was curious as to how closely it would mirror Misty's own disappearance. Some fans were already speculating that it might be the end of the series while others thought she might give Detective Dillon the slip and go underground, either forever or to reappear later in the series. I had asked Misty if she knew where her sister was, what had happened to her.

"I don't know," she had answered. "I know it's hard to comprehend but I really don't know."

"Aren't you worried, Misty? What if she has lost touch with reality? What if what Daniel told you is true. What if she is capable of orchestrating another murder?"

Her hesitation told me everything, but she had replied, "She's my sister. She's all I have left."

For a brief time, I wondered if all the publicity around Carla's death would draw out her son. I could only hope he ended up with better adoptive parents than the Rieckhoffs. Would knowing his tragic history help him or would it just mess with his mind, the way my past did with mine? Besides, Carla was dead, and it was doubtful that the Irving family would welcome him after all these years. What would he gain by coming forward?

"You warm enough?" Mike's voice broke through my thoughts as he leaned forward to adjust the fan on the AC in his truck.

"Oh my god. That's the third time you asked me. I'm fine. I'm not some delicate orchid."

"But you're every bit as beautiful." He looked over and winked at me. "So have you given it any more thought?"

"Okay, okay, I'll think about it." Mike was thinking of retiring a second time, but he wasn't done working. He had approached me with the idea that we could set up shop together and hunt down cold cases, like his friend Howard was doing. I liked Mike, but I liked being my own boss.

"We'd make a good team," he continued. "Like Sherlock

Holmes and John Watson…or Batman and Robin, Bert and Ernie, Mario and Luigi."

"You realize those are all fictional characters, right?" I laughed. Suddenly I noticed how good-looking Mike was. How solid. How trustworthy. How blue his eyes were, how close his arm was to mine. I felt the blood pumping in my neck. I brushed a strand of hair off my shoulder and crossed my legs. The conversation was making me nervous.

"Hey, did I tell you I pulled the World Tarot card when I had lunch with Misty?"

Mike looked at me. I saw something flit across his face and then it was gone. "Am I going to regret asking you what it means?"

"Probably. The World Tarot card shows that I've endured hardships and learned my lessons and that now I'll reap the rewards. The universe is smiling on me and luck is on my side. Money will come my way and opportunities to further my business will abound."

"Really?" He raised an eyebrow and glanced over at me. "So, you're paying the entrance fee today, right?"

"Gladly." Mike was joking but I thought about all I had gone through the last two years, how far I had come. It hadn't been easy, but I had done it—set up my own little business, was making money and getting some much-welcomed recognition—at least in some circles. I understood myself better and felt at peace with my place in the world.

"You could just come work for me."

"Work for you?" Mike rubbed his hand over his chin. "What are you paying?"

"Going rates. I could maybe throw in a bonus…you know… if you go above and beyond."

"Oh yeah. Like what?"

I laughed as a flutter rippled across my belly. "Oh you know, keep the wooden stakes sharp and a good supply of garlic and holy water on hand."

Mike laughed.

My world has certainly turned.

YOUR FREE BOOK IS WAITING

She wants to prove her worth as a new PI…but first she has to survive.

Find out how it all began. Knight Shift is the prequel novella to the Jorja Knight Mystery Series.

Your free copy is waiting for you *at: www.alicebienia.com*

ACKNOWLEDGEMENTS

When I began thinking about the premise for Knight Vision, I recalled a recent discussion I had with author and podcaster, Joanna VanderVlugt. During the podcast, Joanna mentioned a scene from my first novel, Knight Blind, where one of the characters in the story mentions that whenever she sees a butterfly, she's certain it is the manifested spirit of her departed mother. Our conversation made me realize how many of us, even if we don't truly believe in spirits and an afterlife, have on occasion, marvelled at the synchronicity of certain events, thoughts, people, or objects appearing in our lives at the most opportune moment and wondered…what if?

Those initial musings led to the idea for Knight Vision. What if I paired Jorja Knight, my logical, smart, protagonist, who believes in science—that which is measurable, observable, with a psychic clairvoyant client? This somewhat unconventional pairing took the story in directions I never imagined!

Writing these stories is largely a solitary endeavor, creating a book and getting it out there, requires a team. My team is small but huge in terms of skill, wisdom, and enthusiasm. First, I would like to thank my fabulous editor, Taija Morgan. A good editor is a gift, and I'm so lucky to be working with Taija. Not only does she inspire me to be a better writer, her combined talent for editing, her sense of humor and warm friendship make her an awesome gift indeed.

A big thank you to fellow author, and podcaster, Joanna VanderVlugt. I've been a guest on her JCVArtStudio from the Dressing Room podcast a few times now, and we always have so much fun. I appreciate the time she takes away from her own writing to promote fellow authors to her listening audience.

Thank you to Brian Richmond, Blue Devil Books, for showcasing my novels to his UK audience and the rest of the world. So exciting to see I now have readers in the UK, Europe, Australia, and New Zealand.

I'd also like to acknowledge the support and friendships offered to me by the many talented members of the Calgary Crime Writers, Sisters in Crime – Canada West, and Crime Writers of Canada. No matter how small or inane a question I may have, I can always rely on this group of talented writers for help and advice, always given willingly and often with great humour.

I'm blessed to have the most amazing family and friends. Thank you to Kevin, Sean, Katherine, Leanne, Tyler, Malcolm, and Paige, for your constant love and support.

Thank you to Brenda Domeij, Brenda Lissel and Sue Matsalla, for keeping me sane through what has been a difficult year for all of us as we maneuvered through yet another year of the pandemic. We've been friends for decades and I'm sure we'll still be laughing and exchanging stories when we're ensconced in our respective retirement homes.

And last but not least, a huge thank you to you, my readers. Thank you for reaching out to me on social media, joining my Readers Bulletin newsletter, and for all the messages you send me, telling me you love my books and are eagerly awaiting more. I hope you enjoyed reading *Knight Vision* as much as I enjoyed writing it!

Thanks for Reading

I hope you enjoyed reading *Knight Vision*! Authors largely rely on word of mouth to gain exposure. Please let other readers know how much you enjoyed *Knight Vision* by leaving a review on Amazon, Goodreads or at your favourite online bookstore.

Read on for an excerpt from the next
Jorja Knight Mystery

KNIGHT IN THE MUSEUM

Available Fall 2022

CHAPTER ONE

I NOTICED HIM RIGHT away. The guy was twitchy, like he'd just done something stupid or was about to. You didn't have to be a cop or a private investigator to figure out he was up to something, although being the latter made me predisposed to noticing such things. I pulled my sunglasses down over my eyes, shook back my shoulder-length bob, and stepped out of the Starbucks into the sunshine.

Keeping a firm hand on my pocketbook, I strode past several patrons lingering on the sidewalk in front of the coffee shop. The man with the shifting feet and buggy eyes stepped closer to the cluster of people, trying to make it look like he was one of them, and doing a poor job of it. His eyes never focused on any one thing; his head swivelled from side to side as he scanned for who knows what. I gave him a wide berth and gazed across the parking lot. The sun gleamed off the rows of cars. Everyone moved at a leisurely pace.

The maples and ash trees were already showing their autumn colours, their red and golden leaves a sharp contrast against the pale-blue sky. Soon they'd be carpeting the ground. It would happen quite suddenly; a gust of wind would strip the branches, sending down a cascade of leaves from their lofty heights. Nature's reminder that life marched on, and nothing we could do would change it. I shook off a twinge of melancholy and crossed the lane to where my car was parked.

Resting my coffee momentarily on the car roof, I noticed the barista had spelled my name Georga not Jorja. I had equal luck with the correct spelling of my last name, Knight. I unlocked the door and slid in. Resettling my coffee in the cup holder, I pulled down the sun visor, applied lip gloss, and tucked a strand of my newly cut, dark-brown hair behind my ear.

A noise startled me. I turned as the passenger door opened. The man I'd noticed in front of the Starbucks jumped into the seat next to me.

"Drive! Drive!" His blue-grey eyes bulged as they darted from side to side. His head whipped around to the rear window and back to me.

My hands tightened on the steering wheel, my nails digging into my palms. Blood pounded in my ears. He was beyond twitchy now. I could smell his frenzied panic.

"Go, dammit. Go."

He glanced over his shoulder and swore. He turned to me, his eyes jumping wildly, his forehead beaded with sweat.

The noise of the outdoor mall faded. Everything around me slowed, each second stretched to ten.

His face was thin and pockmarked. One of his front teeth was angled to the rest. His thin lips moved. He was shouting again, but the words didn't register. A speck of spittle left his lips and arched toward me. My eyes locked with his, my breath caught in my throat. A drop of sweat rolled down his face and dangled at his jawline.

This can't be happening.

A burst of adrenaline shot through me.

I turned. My hands clawed at the door handle; my shoulder

rammed the door. My foot shot out onto the pavement. I felt the car shift.

I scrambled out, wasting a precious second to glance back.

The passenger door stood open. The man was gone. My knees were already rubbery from the adrenaline spike.

Leaning one hand on the car roof, my eyes swept the parking lot. Customers sauntered down the aisles; the sun glistened off the cars around me. All the familiar noises of the outdoor mall returned.

Someone shouted.

I turned in time to see my unwanted passenger push a man aside, leap over a black lab that was tied to a lamppost and disappear around the corner of the Starbucks. Several people stared after him.

I blew out the breath I'd been holding. The world was churning out more and more crazies. The stress was going to kill us all.

I shook my head and slid back into the car.

My hand trembled as I pulled off my sunglasses and stared into the visor mirror. Hazel eyes speckled with yellow flecks looked remarkably unperturbed despite the loops and gyrations my organs performed inside. I slid my glasses back down, picked up my coffee and took a sip. Cradling the hot cup against my chest, I tried to process what just happened while the rest of me caught up. An attempted carjacking. Should I report it? He was long gone now. Maybe the guy was on drugs or having a psychotic episode. I scanned the parking lot, but all was calm, everything back to normal.

I turned the key, still dangling from the ignition, and the engine sputtered to life. A light on the dashboard told me one of the doors was still open. I glanced at the passenger door. It had swung closed but wasn't quite shut. I set my coffee down, leaned over the passenger seat, tugged the door handle, and it clicked shut. That's when I noticed it.

A small white triangle poked up from between the door and the passenger seat, barely visible. Sprawling across the seat, my fingers teased the white triangle upward until I could get a grip. Pulling it free, I saw it was a business envelope, folded over in half. It wasn't mine. My heart rate started to climb.

I unfolded the envelope. There was nothing written on either side. I lifted the flap and peered inside. Puzzled, I pulled out several pieces of newsprint, each folded over several times. A headline came into view as I unfolded the first newspaper clipping. "Massive Winnipeg drug bust collapses. Defence claims police accessed lawyers' communications."

I scanned the article. Apparently, the largest drug bust in the region's history collapsed before it reached trial. The prosecution's case crumbled after defence lawyers attacked police conduct in the investigation, claiming they violated solicitor-client communication privileges. Charges were stayed.

I flipped through several more clippings until another headline caught my eye. "Ancient curse drives businessman to take his own life." My eyebrow rose.

I spread open the article and skimmed the story. Guy Palermo, a well-known businessman in the energy service sector, had thrown himself off a forty-two-storey high-rise, here in Calgary. An avid collector of Mesoamerican and pre-Columbian artifacts, Palermo had blamed a string of bad luck, including a house fire, the death of his wife, and failure to win an expensive lawsuit, on an ancient jade statue he had recently acquired. The article went on to talk about the power of myths and referenced the Guennol lioness, which was said to bring great power to whoever owned it.

I checked the dates of the articles. The first one was three years old. The one about Palermo was written a few weeks ago.

I refolded the articles, slipped them back into the envelope, and threw the envelope onto the passenger seat. I didn't know much about ancient civilizations, but I did know that since the earliest of times, humans have attributed events, both good and bad, to creatures, gods, entities not of this world. It was easier to believe that the universe was ordered, that the chaos around us wasn't random, that someone or something was in charge.

The man's face came back to mind as I exited the parking lot, my hands still shaky from our brief encounter. It brought back memories of my assailant, Jason Marr, the man who became the impetus for my decision to leave my job as a forensic lab analyst to become a private investigator, but I had never seen anyone's eyes look as terrified as the stranger who tried to hijack my car. If anyone feared for his life, it was him.

ABOUT THE AUTHOR

Alice Bienia is a Canadian Crime Writer and author of the Jorja Knight mystery series.

With a Bachelor of Science degree in geology, Alice spent her early career conducting field exploration programs in remote regions of Canada, where she honed her passion for reading, storytelling, coffee, and adventure. After riding the energy industry rollercoaster for thirty years, Alice has found a way to put her inherent introversion to use and now writes full time.

When not plotting a murder, Alice amuses herself watching foreign flicks and exploring Calgary's urban parks and pathways. Visit her at *www.alicebienia.com*

www.ingramcontent.com/pod-product-compliance
Lightning Source LLC
Chambersburg PA
CBHW032148190726
48290CB00005BB/1463